The Starter Marriage

Also by Kate Harrison

Old School Ties

The Starter Marriage

KATE HARRISON

ORION

First published in Great Britain in 2005 by Orion,
an imprint of the Orion Publishing Group Ltd

Copyright © Kate Harrison 2005

A CIP catalogue record for this book
is available from the British Library.

ISBN 0 75286 881 0 (hardback)
0 75286 882 9 (trade paperback)

Typeset by Deltatype Ltd, Birkenhead, Merseyside

Set in Adobe Garamond

Printed in Great Britain by Clays Ltd, St Ives Plc

The Orion Publishing Group Ltd
Orion House
5 Upper Saint Martin's Lane
London
WC2H 9EA

www.orionbooks.co.uk

Acknowledgements

The best thing about finishing a book (apart from typing The End) is being able to thank the people who've put up with me while I've been writing it, so . . .

Thank you:

. . . to my brilliant colleagues in the day job for hearing me witter on about the novel – especially Emma, Kate, Linda, Louise, Lucy, Mandy, Mark, Peter, Rob, Rosy and Susie.

. . . to all on the Board, especially Chris Manby, for so much knowledge and encouragement. To Stephanie Zia, for incisive read-throughs and hysterical emails, and to the Girly Writers: Jacqui H, Jacqui L, Linda and Louise. Also to Crysse Morrison; to Hilary Johnson and all in the RNA, especially Anne and her family.

. . . to James Williams, for a brilliant website.

. . . to Gareth Moss of the Thames Young Mariners for putting me right on the difference between a canoe and a kayak!

Special thanks to my agent, Barbara for the wisdom, guidance and support – it makes all the difference.

Three cheers to all at Orion, especially my lovely editor Kate Mills. I'm having a ball . . . Thanks also to Lucie Stericker for all the work on the gorgeous cover.

Love and thanks to Pat and Pete, and to all the girls: Adele, Alison, Andrea, Betsan, Carrie, Fiona, Lisa, Liz, Lynn, Mary, Sarah, Trudi and especially Geri and Jenny.

Lots and lots of love to Toni, mum and dad. And to two Carters: my much-missed grandfather, William. And to Rich, without whom Tess and her Survivors' Course would never have existed.

Lastly, thanks so much to you for picking up the book. I really hope you enjoy reading it as much as I loved writing it . . . let me know what you think via my website, www.kate-harrison.com

starter marriage: *noun*. A first marriage that lasts only a short time, does not produce children and ends in a clean divorce (*see also* STARTER HOME).

Chapter One

When Barney came into the kitchen on Boxing Day and told me he was leaving me for his secretary, I didn't cry. I didn't cling on to his ankles, begging him to stay. I didn't attack him with the Le Creuset pan I was drying at the time (the thought did occur to me but it was part of a set of five my parents bought us as a wedding present and a gap in the display rack would have added insult to injury).

All I said was, 'Let's try to make sure things don't get messy.'

He laughed, a dry, coughing sound that made me wince. 'No, of course not. There'd be nothing worse for Tip Top Tess than to make a mess, would there?' And he left the room and the house and our marriage. I finished drying the pan and hung it up before I burst into tears.

Tip Top Tess. It's not a sexy nickname, but it is accurate and if wanting things to be neat and tidy is my only fault, I don't think I'm doing too badly. I give to charity, I'm kind to animals and small children and I remember all my friends' birthdays. Since when has tidiness been a crime?

So when I spent the first New Year's Eve of my life alone, my resolution was to avoid nastiness, to stay as civilised and proper as I would in any other situation, to keep things shipshape. Ready for when Barney came back.

And, as far as my nearests and dearests are concerned, I've been pulling it off. Somehow I've managed to maintain the status quo, or at least the illusion of the status quo, for five months. Only I know how far I've slipped.

Until tonight: the doorbell rings and it all falls apart.

I tiptoe into the hall and peer through the spyhole. Mel's face looms up at me, distorted by the fisheye lens so she looks all eyes and nose ... exactly the features I don't want scrutinising my current living arrangements.

I wonder if she's seen me through the glass panel. I'm trapped now, unable to escape upstairs in case she catches a glimpse of movement and realises I'm here. Maybe if I crouch down behind the door and wait, there's a chance she might leave. No harm done.

The reproduction Edwardian bell rings again and I feel the reverberation through the wooden frame. Of all my friends, Mel is the least likely to give up easily. After fifteen years as a reporter, she's used to hanging about on doorsteps, playing cat-and-mouse with the criminals or adulterers inside. They always break before she does.

She sticks her hand through the letterbox, so I try to manoeuvre my body out of range. This means crouching down even further so that my head is on my knees and I get a close-up view of the carpet. It's worse than I thought: there are grey clusters of dust gathered like storm clouds at the edges of the skirting board and a pair of worn tights under the console table. She definitely can't come in.

But my faint hope that she might get bored and settle for leaving a note is dashed when she screams, 'Honey! I know you're in there! You forgot to turn the telly off.'

Oh God. The duh-duh-duh of the *EastEnders* theme tune booms from the living room, reinforcing my basic error. I feel like a character in a French farce, playing hide-and-seek with my best friend, only I don't feel any urge to laugh. Crying seems the more appropriate response, but my biggest fear is that if I start, I will never stop.

'Come *on*, Tess!' she shouts. 'I'm not going anywhere so you might as well open the door.'

My legs are aching now: I might have had a chance of sitting, or rather crouching it out before Christmas, when I was going to step classes three times a week and had thighs of steel. But then again, before Christmas I had no need to avoid Mel or anyone else.

On my hands and knees I reverse away from the door as far back as the stairs, stand up and then pound loudly on the bottom step as if I'm walking down. I put the security chain in place, take a deep breath and finally open the door a few inches.

'About bloody time! What the hell have you been up to in there?'

'Um ... sorry, I was in the bath.'

She stares at me through the gap in the door. I'm still wearing my work clothes, there are biro marks all over my hands and my hair hasn't been washed in a week. 'Really?' she says. 'Well, now you're *out of the bath*, don't keep me standing here like a door-to-door salesman. I've brought a bottle of wine.' She waves an Oddbins bag at me.

'It's not a good time.'

'Don't be daft, honey. I'm fed up with you not returning my calls so I thought it was time to take affirmative action.'

'Honestly, Mel, I'm not in the mood ... I appreciate the gesture, but why don't we arrange to go out next week instead?'

'What, so you can cancel on me again?' Her face takes on the same determined expression she used to adopt on anti-apartheid demonstrations when we were students. She was always getting arrested, unlike me: a bolshie, busty black woman is bound to attract more attention from the cops than a tidy, skinny white one. 'No way. I am going to stay here until you let me in.'

'Give me a second,' I say, pushing the door to, while I consider my options. They're not exactly promising. If I let her in, she'll see the shocking state of my house and, by implication, the even more shocking state of my mind. But if I leave her outside, it'll give the neighbours something extra to gossip about. I'm sure it's only a matter of days before they present me with a petition about the height of the weeds in my tiny front garden. Victoria Terrace is that kind of street. I can't afford to give the Residents' Association any more reasons to complain.

'OK, you win.' I fiddle around with the chain before opening the door. The sunlight illuminates a million dust particles in the hall: I dread to think what it's doing to my poor, tired face. As Mel steps into the hall, I brace myself. 'Don't say I didn't warn you.'

'About what?' she says, then stops short, looking around in

confusion, as though she's walked into someone else's house. 'What the hell's happened to Tip Top Tess?'

I've been wondering the same myself. My latest theory is that my alter ego slipped away with Barney – since he walked out with his suitcases, simply existing has taken all my energy. There hasn't been any left for the housework.

But there's a difference between a dim awareness that I might have let things go, and seeing the reality through someone else's eyes. Which is why I've let nobody across the threshold for five months.

'Mel, it's not as bad as it looks; I haven't had much time lately to do the housework, but—'

'I had no idea things were as bad as this . . .'

'Yeah, it's a bit depressing, I grant you. But, look, as you've come over, why don't we go out, grab a pizza?'

'Not till I've had a proper look,' she says, stepping cautiously over the piles of project work and free newspapers I've allowed to build up in the hall. To my worn-out mind, it's a logical place – handy for me to grab what I need before heading to school, and close to the recycling box I keep by the porch. Except I haven't got round to recycling since . . . well, since Christmas. 'At least now I can see why you haven't invited me round to supper for a while.'

I dash ahead of her to close the door to the kitchen; the mess in there makes the hallway look like Buckingham Palace. 'I haven't really been up to a six-course dinner party.'

The living room presents the next logistical problem. Every surface is covered in *stuff*. These days I tend to slump onto a floor cushion as soon as I get home, but it wouldn't be polite to expect a guest to do the same. I calculate instantly that the armchair will take the least time to clear. It's only holding a few dozen Sunday supplements and an empty pizza box. At least, I hope it's empty. The sofa is a different story, the tan leather barely visible under crisp packets and clothes and exercise books and unopened post. And as for the coffee table . . .

Mel pulls the tissue-wrapped bottle of wine out of the bag. 'I think it's time we had a little chat.'

My heart beats faster. Will I be able to track down two clean glasses anywhere in the house? Perhaps the tooth mug will do for me, the one Barney and I brought back from Corfu in 1994 because its cobalt blue sheen reminded us of the painted houses. It might look a bit less decrepit than the chipped black enamel camping beaker I've been using for all forms of liquid refreshment, from morning coffee to evening whisky nightcap.

Who am I kidding?

I scrunch the blue tissue paper into a loose ball, and bounce it towards the gap under the sofa. Now I've given in to slob-dom, I must confess there is the occasional frisson of pleasure to be had from adding to the chaos.

'Nice wine,' I say, reading the label. I retrieve the corkscrew from under an upturned foil box that once held chop suey. I've developed a kind of radar which means I can always locate my Waiter's Friend. The same applies to my other lifeline, the TV remote. I use it now to mute the ever-whingeing cast of *EastEnders* and pass Mel the corkscrew. 'Back in a sec.'

It does pong a bit in the kitchen. I never quite got round to taking the rubbish out last week and this is the hottest room in the house. It's still only May but the slight whiff of sweet decay propels me back to the summers of my childhood, when the days were long, the tar melted beneath our feet, and the binmen went on strike.

There's bird shit splashed all over the window, just below the Perspex feeder that's attached to the glass with suckers. The few remaining seeds in the tray have sprouted spindly yellow shoots, like an experiment I'd do with the kids on photosynthesis. No wonder my feathered friends have taken out their frustration in a dirty protest on the decking. Judging from the kaleidoscope of different coloured droppings – black, green, mulberry-red – spring has been and gone.

Some people wouldn't bat an eyelid at this level of mess, but for me it's damning evidence of my failure. I can't manage to keep my house tidy, never mind hang on to my husband. And worse still, I can't ever imagine having enough energy to clear up again.

I deserve a stroke of luck, and at last I get one: there's a clean glass right under my nose, the one I got as a free gift for buying six bottles of Grolsch in the supermarket last weekend. The beers are long gone – the empty bottles glint in the sunlight as they wait to make the perilous journey to the recycling basket all of six metres away in the hall – but I hadn't needed the glass because I'd drunk the contents straight from the chunky bottle necks.

I shut the door behind me again. Mel will never have to see the kitchen if I'm careful. If we need more booze, all the spirits are in the dining room, in what Barney used to call the drunks' cabinet. Food? I've got a collection of takeaway menus, which have the spooky ability always to rise to the top of the clutter in the living room, the same way scum always rises to the surface of a pond. The grease-marked photographs of pizza and curry tempt me night after lonely night, and my skin is suffering – pimples on top of my freckles – but what difference does it make? If anyone but me has noticed the state of my complexion, they haven't mentioned it. Perhaps they're just being kind.

By the time I return from my sortie to the upstairs bathroom to collect my tooth mug, Mel has opened the Chianti. I hold out the mug, hoping she won't notice the minty scum that a quick splash under the hot tap has failed to shift. 'Like being a student again, eh, Mel?'

'You were never like this as a student.'

The main problem with my best friend is that she's always right. The compulsion to keep mess under control started early for me: my plastic work tray in infant school was always beautifully neat, the pencils sharpened to the same length, felt-tip pens arranged in the order of the colours of the rainbow. *Tess is the most methodical child in her class*, my teacher wrote in my first ever report.

Now I have a classroom of my own and it is the tidiest in the school. I'm not obsessive about it. A group of twenty-three ten-year-olds will always cause a certain amount of disarray and it doesn't faze me when a field trip or an art session degenerates into an all-round dirt or paint fest. But I love the feeling when we restore order, the transformation of a squirming minibus full of energy and mud into a semi-circle of calm and concentration, gathering round me on the floor to listen to a story. They might be nearly ready to move to secondary school, they might be more used to the instant gratification of Playstations and X-boxes at home, but this is my gift to them – the ability to be quiet *and* enjoy it. A life skill, if you like, and one their parents thank me for. Self-control is an asset as far as I'm concerned.

'Well, maybe it was about time I let go a little; you're always telling me to chill out.'

'This isn't chilling out, it's giving up the ghost. I mean, this is no worse than my place – you know I'd live in a pigsty quite happily. But not you, honey. You should have said something, asked me for help.'

But when you're the kind of person who only ever *gives* help, asking for it feels like an admission of failure. The only time I considered it was when I had that letter from Barney's solicitor and realised that I would need to engage one of my own. The first thing we could never share. The obvious solution was to call our university chum Sara for advice: she's always telling us that she's the best family lawyer in Birmingham. But asking one of our oldest friends to play piggy in the middle seemed more likely to increase the mess and that was the last thing I wanted. All the same, I was hurt that she never called me to offer.

The lawyer I picked from the Yellow Pages had a box of tissues on her desk, and tried to encourage me to 'let it all out'. She didn't seem to understand that spilling my guts in her burgundy leather-lined office would, for me, be as humiliating as appearing naked in assembly. Not to mention the fact that she'd be charging £150 an hour plus VAT for the privilege of listening. She suggested mediation, but that sounded even messier. So now Barney and I are in legal limbo, neither of us making the first move. And while part of me hopes that's a good sign, the organised side of me thinks it might be easier when everything's done and dusted. Especially dusted.

'I didn't think I needed any help.'

'What, you hadn't realised that you've turned into a candidate for those two battleaxes on *How Clean is your House?*'

'It's a gradual thing,' I say. 'An untidy house is the least of my worries and anyway, how could I ask for help when there's nothing anyone can do?'

'The hoovering would be a start.' She smiles at me, and I try to smile back. The muscles in my face feel brittle, as if they might snap from this unfamiliar movement. Mostly these days I don't change my expression at all; it's too much effort. Why pay for Botox when splitting up can paralyse your forehead for free? Only it hasn't made me look youthful. Instead, everything is slumped, like a stroke victim with the dubious good luck of finding that both sides have been rendered equally droopy.

I suppose that's the difference between a broken heart at fifteen and a broken heart at thirty-five: the elasticity has gone. Maybe my ability to bounce back has gone, too.

We sit there for a while in silence. I don't do silence any more. The radio or TV always has to be on, voices in every room. Aural clutter, glorified white noise to stop me thinking about anything more meaningful than a soap-opera storyline.

I go over to the stereo and open the CD tray to see what's in there. Something mournful by Annie Lennox. I swap it for the new Coldplay album that Barney overlooked when he separated our music collections. That must have been a hard task. We'd been together so long that it'd never occurred to me whose musical taste was whose. It was a joint thing, a shared consciousness. Only the techno stuff was obviously his, the most recent arrivals and the first manifestation of the fact that he was changing. I should have noticed that, too.

I never, ever thought of myself as smug, but looking back, I was insufferable. We both were. Joined at the hip from the unnaturally early age of nineteen. Mel called us the Siamese twins, which we pretended to find irritating but would laugh about in bed when we got home from the pub, before falling asleep lying like the brand-new blue-handled spoons in our cutlery drawer.

'You shouldn't have cut yourself off from everyone, Tess. So many people care about you, but you have to open up, show us you need us.'

'I know.'

It's not that I don't feel as deeply as other people, it's just that baring your soul doesn't get you very far with ten-year-olds. Barney was the big kid in our relationship, his gorgeous round face as full of enthusiasm as any of my pupils'. If someone called him immature, he'd take it as a compliment. He was always talking me into doing childish things: flying his kite in the Botanical Gardens, trying to teach the mynah bird swear words, dragging me into the rhododendrons for a kiss. I was the practical one, doing mental arithmetic with the entry charges to work out how much we could save by buying a Couples membership to the bloody place. How middle class. How middle aged. We were only twenty-one.

Perhaps that's why Barney's mid-life crisis came about ten years sooner than it should have done. On paper we were born into Generation X, but our role models were Terry and June. Maybe I bored him into adultery.

The stage was set the day we bought our first place together, leaving behind the sowing of wild oats in place of the laying of laminate. We even threw a party to celebrate our new floor. Wipe-clean. As the first of our posse with our own place, we had parties at the slightest provocation. We claimed we were taking the piss out of our domesticity, but there was pride too in how we'd spent three full weekends tearing out every trace of the faded granny-chintz carpet and laying those photographed pieces of wood. Clean, new, fresh. Very 1991. We made cocktails, blasted out club tunes on the still-cutting-edge CD player. Everyone knew we'd be the first to tie the knot, which we dutifully did five years later, and we also seemed the only ones of our set likely to stay the course. Mr and Mrs Leonard and their perfect life, to be followed in the perfect period of time by two perfect children.

Except of course, without us noticing, our friends began to overtake us. While they were pushing out offspring in maternity wards, we were laying newer floors, real oak in place of the laminate, hand-crafted Tuscan tiles in place of the lino, though we'd decided to keep the living room floor the same, as a memento.

And now? I've hung onto the house for the time being, but I don't know if the pain is worth it. Having to live with an endless set of reminders, from the IKEA loo-roll holder to the brushed chrome door furniture, means there's no escape. Barney's probably got less floor-space in the Curved One's teeny, trendy loft apartment in St Paul's Square, but he's also got more thinking room.

The Curved One – I can't bring myself to use her name these days – is the biggest fake I have ever come across. The first time I met her was two years ago, at the annual Christmas house party Barney and I have hosted since the year dot. She arrived with the rest of the dull-as-ditchwater contingent from Barney's depart-ment at Cole, Murray, Tilbrook. But she couldn't help standing out, squeezed into a red sequinned dress that Pamela Anderson would have dismissed as too revealing. It matched her sparkly make-up and emphasised her artificially inflated cleavage, which in turn matched the false little giggle and flick of the wavy fringe that was her automatic response to anything any of the lawyers said.

I avoided her, because she made me feel unfeminine. Usually I'm grateful for the practical benefits of my boyish shape, having seen the agonies that Mel's gone through trying to be taken seriously with a chest that can stop traffic. It's only at parties that I miss having an hourglass figure with curves that are crying out to be contained in crushed velvet, or swathed in sheer black numbers, like a parcel waiting to be unwrapped.

But Mel, with her hundred-per-cent natural and hundred-per-cent astonishing breasts, was not so easily cowed by the cow. She put her best features forward and soon had the lawyers gawping like brickies and the Curved One pouting like a small girl denied an ice lolly. When she rejoined me by the mulled wine, Mel whispered in my ear, 'Chicken fillets, I'm sure of it. Imagine how some poor bloke feels when he gets her home, gets her kit off and finds she's filled out her bra with the high-tech equivalent of a pair of socks.'

We laughed at her, confident that as safely partnered grown-ups, we had no need to resort to underhand tactics in our underwires. It never occurred to me that she might have been competition. We just thought she was a silly little girl who needed to be taught a feminist lesson.

But Dawn had the last laugh.

Oh, shit. Her name makes me feel so sick.

'Tess . . . ?' Mel nudges me back into reality. It's quite shocking how little it takes to send me off into another world. Too much time on my own lately. My tooth mug is empty already and I hold it out for a refill of wine.

She hesitates, then pours it and says: 'I thought . . . well, we all thought you'd turned a corner. I mean, you'd stopped crying every time we went out.' She stops for a minute. We haven't been out since March; I don't have the energy any more. 'I thought, with it being . . . what, getting on for five months . . . well, you might have started to feel a bit brighter.'

I stare into my red wine as the bloke from Coldplay sings mournfully that nobody said it was easy.

'I never expected you to get better overnight,' Mel mumbles. She seems embarrassed at her shortcomings as my best mate, but I don't have the energy to be angry.

'I can't imagine ever getting better. I can't get him out of my head. He's been there for nearly half my life. How can I get rid of all that history, all those memories, without getting rid of what makes me me? There's no way . . .' I spot that the bottle of wine is nearly empty, and although it's only a couple of minutes since my last refill, I hold it up again, greedy for the last drop. 'Except for this way, of course . . . and booze only gives temporary relief.'

'The thing is, Tess . . .' Mel hesitates, then takes a breath. 'Well, I was in the library doing some research for an article and I found a leaflet. I kind of wondered . . . look, just think about it, OK?' She rummages in her handbag, draws out a piece of pink paper, and hands it over.

I unfold it and have to read it a couple of times before it sinks in. 'Divorce Survivors at St Gabriel's?'

'I know it sounds a bit naff, but anything's worth a try.'

'A "sympathetic, supportive environment to explore our past experiences and move on towards a better future"? Tell me you're joking, Mel.'

'No, look, maybe it's the wrong time for you. But maybe later . . . ?' She tails off.

I feel anger spreading through my body from the pit of my stomach, like a wave of nausea. 'Of course! You're right, this is bloody perfect. I can't imagine anything I'd like more than "a meaningful yet non-religious exploration of what you'd like to keep and what you'd like to change as you begin a new life". Fantastic. Just what I need to bloody well cheer me up. A bunch of God-botherers picking my sores once a week.'

She shrugs, defensive. 'It says they're *not* religious. I thought it might help. I didn't realise things were still as bad as—'

'Oh, right. So that's it. I'm such a boring loser that you thought you'd palm me off on some therapy group. Well, cheers. That's what friends are for, eh?'

Mel is staring at the floor. The celebrated floor. That bloody holy grail of coupledom. 'Tess, I'll listen for as long as you need me to. But I just thought you might get something out of talking to people who know what it's like. I'm sorry for misjudging the situation so badly.'

It is exactly the right thing to say. And exactly the wrong thing, because it triggers a drunken waterfall of tears that I've been damming for weeks. I try to get her to go, but she shakes her head and holds me until I give in. Not only won't she leave, but she then insists on trying to tackle the pile of washing up while I sit at the breakfast bar, surrounded by an avalanche of tissues.

She manages most of the crockery before giving up on the pans. 'I'll call James, let him know I'm staying here with you tonight.'

'What about Leo?'

'I kissed him goodnight. He won't even know I'm not there. No arguments, honey.' Then she takes me to bed with two big tumblers of tequila.

'If only *we'd* had kids,' I say, in the midst of a growing fuzziness. 'He'd have made a great dad.'

He probably still will make a great dad. Just not with me.

I wake up at four a.m. My drunken mind has been playing tricks on me, sensing the presence of another human being and concluding that Barney is back in his rightful place, by my side. I roll over to embrace him, but realise my mistake just before I throw a dead arm across his shoulders.

My sleeping partner isn't snoring.

Slowly, so as not to wake Mel, I edge my woozy body towards the opposite side of my marital bed.

Chapter Two

It takes three more days of staring at my collected debris before I decide I've got to do something, anything. Well, anything except don the Marigolds and fill a whole roll of bin bags with the festering excesses of my new single life.

Instead, it's the pink piece of paper that tempts me out of my torpor. The leaflet seems to follow me around, taunting me. It flutters shyly as I walk into the living room laden with Class Six's imaginary diaries of Second World War evacuees. It somehow tucks itself into the takeaway menu when my hunger for Barney is temporarily overtaken by my hunger for pizza. Its preachy pinkness stands out against the beige and sand shades of my tastefully designed home. It was always going to win. On Friday night I admit defeat.

I dial the number twenty times before I finally allow it to ring, like a teenage boy plucking up the courage to ask someone out. Five rings, just enough for me to start hoping there'll be no reply and I'll be off the hook, it wasn't meant to be—

'Hello?' A man's voice, calm, low, a hint of a Black Country accent.

'Hi, is this the right number for . . . the group?' The group? I'm making it sound like a cult. Maybe it is.

'The group?' He sounds amused. 'Yes, I run the survivors' course. I prefer to think of it that way. Group suggests something you're locked into, a kind of purgatory. Course is more transitory: you learn the skills you need, and then you move on.'

Neither of us, I notice, has used the word divorce. I search his voice for clues to help me work out his age, his background, but

I come up with nothing. Ideal for a therapist, which I suppose is what he must be.

'Is it for yourself, or someone else?' I think he already knows, but then perhaps some people who call him are so nervous they pretend they're calling for a friend, like those letters to problem pages about rubber fetishes or genital warts.

'For me.'

'Right. Well, I'll get the technical stuff out of the way first. Come along for the first session. If you don't think it's for you, then there's no obligation, no hassle, walk away. But if you sign on the dotted line after that – mentally, that is; there's not really a contract – then I would expect you to keep coming for the full eight weeks, for everyone else's sake as much as your own. It's about trust.'

'How much does it cost?'

'An optional donation at the end of the course. And three pounds a week for coffee, tea, orange squash, photocopying and the electricity in the hall. Though we can even waive that if it's a real struggle.'

'No, that won't be necessary.'

'Great. Now, some people like to think about it for a while after they've made the call, but if you're sure – and you sound like someone who knows what she wants – you're in luck, because the next course begins on Tuesday. Otherwise you'll be waiting till September.' He leaves it hanging in the air.

Behind the touchy-feely language, I detect the killer instinct of a double-glazing salesman. But what is he trying to sell? If money isn't his objective, why is he so keen on touting for business to ensure full attendance? The word cult comes back into my brain, but I cast it away. Surely no one would be allowed to leave flyers for a cult in Birmingham Central Library.

'No ... no sense in hanging about,' I find myself agreeing with him, despite my reservations. Perhaps he has sent telepathic hypnotic signals down the phone line. Or maybe I've run out of other options.

'That's excellent news. What's your name?'

'Tess. Tess Leonard.' Still hanging on to my married name,

just as I haven't stopped wearing my wedding ring. I don't know how I will go back to being a Marshall. The messiness of changing so much paperwork makes me weary just thinking about it.

'Fantastic, Tess. I'm William. Anything else you want to ask me?'

'Um. Is there any kind of regulation? I mean, are you approved by anyone?'

'I've got my cycling proficiency. Only kidding. I've been running courses for six years and the curriculum is based on an American scheme that's been going two decades, with very good customer feedback. Ninety-two per cent say they'd strongly recommend it to friends going through a divorce.'

'Right.' I've always been a sucker for statistics.

'If there's anything else, it might be better to ask face to face at the first session.'

'Yes. Yes, of course.'

'Excellent. Well, I'll look forward to seeing you next Tuesday at St Gabriel's church hall, behind the station. Kick-off at seven, so to speak.' I hear him chuckle before I put down the phone.

I wake up at five a.m. on Saturday, relieved to be out of a horrible recurring dream about drowning, but distraught to be back into the horrible recurring nightmare that is The Weekend.

Weekdays are bearable – just – but Saturday and Sunday are the pits. Before Barney left, I'd never taken stock of our lives or thought about how every spare day was booked months in advance. From April to October: weddings, christenings, barbecues, house parties, city breaks, boat parties. From November to March: bonfires, Christmas house parties, endless jollies paid for by the law firm, more city breaks, birthday dos. And all year round, of course, the equally weighted and carefully scheduled trips to his folks and mine, to his brother and his kids and to my sister and hers.

I tried to see the positive side when we first broke up – at least I'd never have to see his ghastly niece and nephew again – but right now I'd almost welcome an afternoon with the Loathsome Little Leonards.

If I was being really vindictive, I could blame Shaun and Wendy (named, without a hint of irony, after that bloody Wallace and Gromit cartoon) for the fact that Barney and I hadn't quite got round to having kids, and maybe for the fact I may now *never* have them.

It's hard to know where to start explaining what makes them so loathsome. I'm professionally inclined to like most children – including three with Attention Deficit Disorder in my class alone, and the legendary Charlotte Mullins, a violin-wielding despot whose only talent was for extortion – but I still find it impossible to think of a single redeeming feature about those two.

I rarely judge anyone on looks alone, but from babyhood, their dumpling little faces have been corrupted by expressions that reveal their true characters, like angels wearing Halloween masks. Wendy's mouth is turned downwards as though someone has just fed her pureed lemon. Shaun's eyes are always scrunched up, while his chubby cheeks are permanently scarlet and marked with snail tracks of dried tears, because he grizzles at the slightest provocation, even though he's now coming up for five.

The thing about the Loathsome Leonards is that they don't do things that are unremittingly awful. There's no tying firecrackers to kittens' tails (Shaun is too scared of loud noises, and his sister is so lazy that she'd expect someone else to do the dirty work). They don't deliberately throw bowls of jelly onto the carpet (they don't eat jelly anyway because of my sister-in-law's endless worrying about E-numbers, but they do have additive-free gelatin-free fruit desserts, and I have seen one thrown across the kitchen in a fit of rage). No, entering Casa Leonard is more like walking into a force field, where all your energy and enthusiasm are sucked out of you, leaving you a husk. They are to childhood what Mavis Riley was to *Coronation Street*. And they sucked the desire to have children out of Barney.

My sister Suzy's two are an altogether better advert for the joys of childbearing, but by the time Kim arrived, only a couple of years after Wendy, the damage was done. If it'd been the other way around, if Suzy's children had been born first, perhaps

I'd have two of my own by now. Would that have stopped Barney going, or would it simply mean I'd be facing single motherhood as well as divorce?

I spend so much time going round in circles, speculating about what might have been, because apart from my regular Saturday phone call to Suzy, there's nothing else to punctuate my long, long weekend.

'Southampton Super Sail, Suzy speaking, good morning.'

Oh, it's good to hear her voice. I have to ration myself to one call a week because she's got enough on her plate without counselling me, what with the girls, a monosyllabic husband who works all hours and a thankless job as chief receptionist/course booker/dogsbody for the sailing company they run. But I look forward to these brief conversations more than anything else these days. 'Hi, sis. How's it going?'

'Hello, gorgeous,' she says, switching seamlessly out of call-centre mode and into supportive big sister mode. 'How's the best teacher in Birmingham?'

'Glad it's the weekend,' I lie. It's too embarrassing to admit that I prefer the long, tiring days at work to the yawning gulf of two days off with nothing to do but mope. 'And how's the south coast's top female entrepreneur?'

'Knackered. Patrick's running a beginners' dinghy course all weekend and Kim's got a cold so Rosie'll have one by tomorrow. But apart from that, I'm good. I'll be better when I've seen you, though. How about it, Tip Top?'

Every week she asks me the same question and I am running out of excuses. 'Yeah, soon . . . I'm just not great company at the moment.'

'All the more reason— Rosie, no! Hang on a second, Tess . . .' The phone thumps as she lays it down and in the background I hear a smash, a slap, then a moment's silence before a whimper from my youngest niece. 'Come here, sit on Mummy's lap . . . right, I'm back. Another mug bites the dust. So we were talking about when we can come to see you.'

It's precisely because my sister is a twenty-first-century superwoman that I am so reluctant to let her know how badly I'm doing. She'd sort me out, that's for sure, but I'm not sure my pride would ever recover. And pride is the one thing the Marshall family have always had in abundance. Just ask my mother. 'And I was saying that I'm really busy at the moment. Honestly.'

'Hmm. If you say so. Mum and Dad are worried, Tip Top.'

'They needn't be. I'm still here. I'm surviving.'

'You don't have to pretend everything's OK, Tess. Not to me, anyway.'

But she's wrong. I do have to pretend. Like I pretended for a whole week after Barney left that he'd just gone off in a bit of a huff. Even when I called home on the second of January to say that he'd left, I insisted it was a 'trial separation'. I didn't mention the D word until April.

The moment I stop pretending, I start hurting. Look what happened when Mel came round the other night. 'I'm coping, really I am. Oh, and I'm not on my own; you'll laugh at this – I've only signed up for some sort of support group for advice on how to get divorced as painlessly as possible.'

'I didn't know there were groups for that kind of thing,' she says, dubiously. 'It's not a Moonie thing, is it? They target vulnerable people, you know.'

I smile to myself. We don't really look alike – voluptuous would be the polite description of her body shape – but we think alike. 'It's fine. I'm going to try one session and then see.'

'And have you heard from Barney?'

'Not since that solicitor's letter.' Suzy is the only person I'd admit *that* to.

'Oh, Tess. Of all the people this had to happen to, it shouldn't be you . . .' She tails off, and when she speaks again, her voice is artificially cheery. 'So what have you got planned for the weekend? Something more exciting than mine, I hope. The most thrilling moment will be the trip round Asda with two snotty-nosed kids.'

'I've got to check with the girls, see what they're up to. Dinner and a movie, I think.' I'm not exactly fibbing: I'm planning a video and a Chinese takeaway later. It's just that I'll be enjoying them on my own.

'Great. You know who your friends are at times like this.'

'Yeah. Listen, I'd better go, sis. Give the girls a kiss for me, will you?'

'Yep. And let's talk next week about meeting up, or they'll have forgotten who their auntie Tess is, eh? Ring me if you need to, gorgeous.'

And that's it. The only thing on my 'to do' list for the weekend ticked off. I'd go to bed if it wasn't still eleven o'clock in the morning.

I boil the kettle for another instant coffee, my fourth since the drowning nightmare woke me up, but the few remaining grains in the jar are black and smell musty. Normally I'd sneak to the mini-mart on the corner, but my sister's exciting planned trip to the hypermarket makes me think. Perhaps I should go on a Big Shop too. At least it'll get me out of my horrid house.

The weather's irritatingly typical of May, hot and cold depending on the positions of the clouds, but I shiver even when the sun struggles through. I drive to the budget supermarket on the outskirts of Selly Oak, because I can't face seeing anyone I might know, and no one I know shops at Aldi. I load my basket with sliced bread (for the freezer), a huge tub of margarine, and a big bag of apples, which I already suspect will go the same way as all the others; hot-housed in a plastic polybag, a time bomb of apple skin that looks fine until – convincing myself I need something more nutritious than my usual diet of buttered toast – I pick one out and it collapses in my hand.

At the last minute, I remember my domestic hygiene crisis and embark on a bulimic raid on the household aisle. J-cloths, air fresheners, bathroom cleaners, kitchen sprays, carpet deodoriser and extra-strong bin bags join my pathetic groceries in the single-person's trolley. I drive home even faster than usual, with a new conviction that I can start to make inroads into my chaotic environment.

But when I get back, the cloying smell of rubbish saps my strength. I can't even find the energy to clear a space in the cupboard for all the detergents. Instead, I rummage around in the bag for the bread, then leave everything else on the kitchen floor as I return to my bed with a bottle of red wine and four slices of toast. At least Barney didn't take the Dualit toaster.

Lesson One

How the Hell Did We End Up Here?

William Campbell surveyed the seven people sitting in front of him with the tenderness of a nursery teacher about to begin the process of civilising yet another class of semi-continent infants. Though there was also a hint of the hunger of the wolf weighing up the snacking potential of Red Riding Hood.

'Hello and welcome aboard. I won't tell you to relax because it would be like asking an elephant to tap dance. Right now – and I know this from what other groups have told me – relaxation would be an impossibility.'

Big Hair Woman, he noticed, was the only one to smile. He couldn't read their name badges so nicknames would have to do for now. Big Hair was easily the oldest person there – either an exhausted late-fortysomething or a well-preserved fiftysomething. Her cherry-red curls were the first thing to attract his attention. Below them, her round, open face was punctuated by two thinly drawn eyebrows, two unblended stripes of rouge and two scarlet-coated pouty lips which retracted to reveal two rows of tiny teeth.

Women didn't age well, unlike William, who liked to think he was entering his Harrison Ford stage. Granted, Harrison Ford had kept most of the hair on his head, had a lover twenty-two years his junior and probably didn't need to go to the lavatory eight times a night, but otherwise the two men shared a dignified approach to growing old.

'The next eight weeks will be a journey through uncharted waters. At times you'll find it uncomfortable, claustrophobic. It might make you feel sick. But this is *your* rescue boat. If we all pull together, I promise you we'll make it to safety and the voyage will have been worthwhile.'

Big Hair smiled again. William knew that sometimes he went over the top with his analogies, but surely it was better than being bland. That had been the trouble with the Californians: their course materials were brilliantly structured, but they'd allowed no room for manoeuvre or deviation from the lesson plans. For a creative man like William, it had been like working in a straitjacket. So gradually he'd introduced his own ideas: British comparisons to make the point of a lesson clearer, ice-breaking exercises to help them relax.

The Yanks weren't happy, of course. The training manual might have preached emotional honesty, but it didn't help three years ago when the powers-that-be were deciding whether to expel him from their approved register. They'd labelled him a Rogue Leader, a maverick, in that very straight-faced, sincere American way, as though they were handing down a death sentence. What they didn't appreciate was that the label was strangely appealing to William. He strove to be an original, and being a rogue *anything* at the age of fifty-nine was a bit of a bonus. He had been slightly worried that the removal of approved status might affect the turnout, but he'd hung on to his faith. And still the casualties of divorce flocked to him, giving up two hours a week in return for an unconventional form of absolution. After all, they had nowhere else to go.

'My previous students have told me that the worst thing about coming here for the first time is the fear of the unknown. Well, let me try to reassure you by telling you what we *won't* be doing.'

He moved away from the virgin whiteboard, towards the window. A branch burdened with cherry blossom brushed against the glass, leaving a faint powder of pollen behind. Something else to clean. It never stopped. Maintaining the church hall was like painting the bloody Forth Bridge, though at least the Forth Bridge had architectural merit. St Gabriel's Hall was one step up from a mobile classroom. But all seven people in front of him wanted it to be a place of transformation, the halfway house to a new life, a new love, a new outlook, or at least a temporary sanctuary from pain, timetabled every Tuesday evening.

'We won't be doing trust exercises that involve falling back into someone else's arms. Well, not unless you choose to do that after hours. Most of the homework is better done on your own.'

Big Hair smiled again, and this time she was joined by Waif, the skinny, freckled girl sitting at the very end of the semi-circle of eight chairs. One seat was still empty, a no-show. But Waif's smile didn't look genuine; it was more of a polite reflex response to a joke. It lasted a fraction of a second before her pale face sagged again, like an old woman's.

'We won't *necessarily* be baring our souls and we definitely won't be baring our bodies unless, again, you want to do it in your own time. It has been known.'

The seven exchanged sly looks of appraisal. Peter Stringfellow the Second was the most blatantly lecherous. How many of them would be hoping for a bit of rebound romance to set them on the road to recovery? The Yanks had frowned on it, denounced intra-group relations as indisputably A Bad Thing, but in William's view there was no point trying to resist the inevitable. And sometimes it could be a useful learning experience. Though poor Stringfellow, whose hanging curtain of a hairstyle must have been modelled on the legendary London nightclub owner, or maybe an Afghan hound, was probably the least likely to benefit.

'We won't be practising flirting techniques or swapping tips on how to get revenge, although the old "stuffing the ex's hollow curtain poles with sardines" trick does remain the all-time winner in my book. Tuna works well too, so I'm told.'

This time it was the Pretty Blonde who smiled. It made William feel slightly dizzy: whatever her personal heartache, she hadn't lost the glow that beautiful women have. He liked to look after the pretty ones – not that he would ever take advantage of his position, but it was usual for one of the group to get a crush on him, so why not stack the odds in favour of adoration from the most attractive female there? Especially when she appreciated his jokes.

'You also have my word that there won't be any religion, and that applies to all religions. So Buddhist chanting is also out.'

Only the Ageing Hippy looked disappointed. He was a far

better bet for the women present than Stringfellow. Haggard, definitely, and that scruffy blond hair could do with a good cut, but there was a defiance in his eyes and a suggestion of danger in his posture, his long, denim-covered thighs stretched out ahead of him. He didn't fit the profile of the downtrodden men who normally came to the group. Perhaps Ageing Hippy had encountered a wife even more dangerous than himself, and needed to reassure himself that he could still pull. It didn't bode well for the establishment of a healthy, supportive environment, but William enjoyed a challenge. The Hippy might liven things up.

'There are also some things I'd love to do, but can't. Sometimes people come here thinking that they're going to get off the hook, that because they are the one who has chosen to come here, they will automatically win victim status. One woman expected me to act as a witness in her divorce.'

He looked at each person in turn and, as expected, most couldn't hold his gaze. They almost always expected this exemption from responsibility, but it would take more than turning up once a week to take away the culpability.

Only one of his audience members returned his look. Asian Babe was probably in her mid-forties, but it was hard to judge because her brown skin appeared completely unlined. Her hard eyes were at odds with the softness in her face and her well-cushioned body. Perhaps she was one of those women who blamed men for everything. She wouldn't be the first.

'I also don't have a magic wand; I can't take away the guilt. I really wish I could because I don't believe in it – pretty much the most useless emotion known to man, or, more often, known to woman.'

Most of them were smiling by now. Only Supermarket Guy – dishevelled and so out of it that he'd forgotten to remove a badge from his uniform that proclaimed he was 'Assistant Manager, Happy to Help' – seemed unamused. William diagnosed unresolved anger towards women, with a side-order of single fatherhood. That wasn't an amazing sixth sense on William's part; it was the bumper-sized tins of SMA poking out of the carrier bag at the man's feet.

'But I can give you the tools to help reduce the guilt and to move on. I see my role as giving you a lifejacket and enough first aid to make it to dry land, and then you can choose whether you need further treatment, in which case I can point you in the right direction. Most people at least start making a recovery while they're here. They even occasionally admit to having fun.

'And in return? Well, I'm not expecting the earth. All you need to do—'

As he moved towards the climax of his speech, probably the last chance he'd have to talk uninterrupted in the whole of the next two months, the back door squeaked open. He wasn't sure what irritated him more: the disturbance to his dramatic moment, or the need to add oiling the hinges to his list of things to do.

A groomed woman with a highlighted ponytail swished through the door and moved towards the others with not nearly as much urgency as William felt she ought to show, given that she was a full nine minutes late.

'Sorry,' she said, sounding the opposite. Oh, Ponytail believed she was a cut above the rest. Everything from her mascara-framed baby blues – this woman had no intention of bursting into tears – to her immaculate trainers screamed *I am in control*. Well, William thought, we'll see about that.

He smiled at her as warmly as he could. 'As I was saying, all you need to do for me and for each other is to promise total confidentiality, and if you decide to attend after today, to commit to attending every session, however much work or children or your own discomfort try to sabotage you.'

He breathed deeply, savouring the silence in the hall. Soon there would be nothing but anguished noise.

'Well, if none of you have already decided it's not for you . . . ?' This moment always reminded William of the moment in the wedding service when the priest would invite lawful impediments as to why people could not be joined in holy matrimony. It had never happened in all the hundreds of wedding services William had witnessed as caretaker and member of the congregation. In his own black period, when he was totally disillusioned with marriage, he'd really wished that someone would object, because at least it'd mean there'd be less confetti to clear up. Confetti was a complete bugger to remove but the priest had refused the very sensible suggestion to ban it entirely. He'd accused William of being a spoilsport.

Everyone waited.

'Good, good. Then we'll make a start. Take one of these questionnaires to fill in before the end of the night to tell me a bit more about your situation, so I know what to concentrate on – all confidential of course.' He handed a pile to Big Hair woman, then when they'd each got one, he smiled.

'Each of our sessions has a subtitle, to give you a focus for the week. And today's introductory topic is . . . How the hell did I end up here?'

At least the late arrival of Ponytail made the pairing up easier, William thought as he crossed the hall to press play on his classical music compilation tape. Odd numbers were a nightmare because in therapy, as in sex, threesomes never quite worked for all parties. There was always someone feeling left out or sidelined from the real action.

The first session was the biggest leap of faith. In their pairs, he would instruct them to take fifteen minutes each to explain the critical moment that had brought them to the Survivors' Course. Every time he made it clear: 'There's no need to bare your souls. All I want you to talk about is where you were when you saw the ad, or maybe when it was you decided you needed some help. On the bus, in the bath. Call it your eureka moment.'

But then every time, that human compulsion to spill out all the horrible details of their loss overcame the natural reserve of the broken-hearted, exactly as the Californian therapists had predicted it would. It took a little longer with buttoned-up Brits than it did with the emotionally aware Americans. It wasn't the only deviation William had made from the US curriculum: the choice of relaxing background music was another. Whale song proved a damp squib in Birmingham, but Mozart seemed to do the trick.

The students would start tentatively, grasping for ways to explain how they'd reached rock bottom and when they'd decided they were desperate enough to seek help. That's how the classical music helped, filling in the gaps between the most painfully articulated words until something caught fire in each speaker. Injustice, hurt, anger: the triggers were different, but the motive was the same: unburdening and understanding.

He went to the kitchenette at the end of the hall on the pretext of preparing tea and coffee for the break, but really because the slightly raised floor offered him the best observation post. For the first session he allowed them to work with whoever happened to be closest. The alchemy came later. William would try to mix and match people according to their ailments. Introvert with extrovert, guilty with angry. There were so many combinations but some would be more effective than others. Like a chemist, he would experiment with unstable elements to achieve the most dramatic reactions in eight short weeks, though he had to acknowledge that even without his intervention, something about this human laboratory – eight suffering people forced together, scrutinising each other's souls – always produced a healing effect.

The couples were scattered around the room, pairs of cells under William's microscope. In one corner, Ponytail and Supermarket Guy sat stiffly in their own personal spaces. His unkempt appearance was hardly likely to impress her: she looked like the kind of woman who wouldn't consider answering the door without full make-up. He was talking and she was nodding with the weary boredom of someone who wanted to be somewhere else. Then, suddenly, Supermarket Guy stood up. For a moment it looked like he was leaving and William prepared to march over for some damage limitation – he couldn't let his nice even-numbered group descend into oddness so soon.

But then Supermarket Guy reached into a back pocket, removed his wallet and, as he sat down, produced a crumpled photograph. From a distance, William could make out two small figures on a beach. A moment later, Ponytail reached into her posh handbag and pulled out a photo of a small baby.

They swapped the pictures, and when Supermarket Guy resumed his story, Ponytail's response was different. She smiled encouragingly, frowned when he frowned and reached out a tentative hand when he fell silent.

Stringfellow and Ageing Hippy looked even less promising together. Despite William's strict instructions – 'the point of the exercise is learning how to listen by concentrating on the other person's story' – the two men were interrupting each other so much that it was impossible to tell which one was meant to be telling and which listening.

William shrugged. Some things never changed and man's compulsion to compete for space, time or breathing room with other men was one of them.

In contrast, Asian Babe and Pretty Blonde had taken to it instantly. William stepped down from the kitchenette to try to eavesdrop. Babe was sitting with her knees just inches from Blonde, her head to one side, chin resting on chubby hand. Her hastily scribbled name badge showed her real name was Rani, while Blonde's was Jo. Rani managed to convey sympathy and warmth without simpering, an expression William had failed to master despite years of practice adopting different facial arrangements in front of the bathroom mirror. Instead of sincerity, he always saw amusement staring back. He tried to shape his forehead into concerned lines, but the jaunty angle of his eyebrows spoiled the effect: they seemed to say 'are you *serious*?' As for his smile . . . it seemed to mock, not empathise.

He'd given up in the end and had trained himself to maintain a 'one size fits all' neutral expression, whatever the revelation.

'. . . so of course I had to come back up here; she needed me. But then I realised that though I missed London life, I didn't miss my husband. And there were complications . . .' Jo paused, sensing the eavesdropping and shooting William a warning stare. When she resumed, her voice – as silky smooth as her hair – was too quiet to be intelligible.

He moved towards the remaining couple. Big Hair was holding forth as Waif listened. William stood in her eyeline and waved a wary hand. 'I wondered . . . please do tell me if you'd rather I didn't, but it's very useful at this stage to listen in, to see if everyone's understanding the objective.'

Big Hair turned to the other woman. 'Is it OK with you,

Tess?' she asked, before motioning to William to sit down. 'I'm Carol-Ann, by the way.' Then she patted her name badge and giggled. 'But I guess you can see that. I was just explaining that I shouldn't really be here at all.' Her voice was softer than he'd expected, her accent more Mancunian than Brummie. 'I could already teach you more about being a survivor than Scott of the Antarctic or whatever that guy was called. Especially as he never made it back. And I'm still here.' She giggled again at her own joke.

William said, 'We're probably all somewhere between base camp and the Pole. Denial is a pretty common feeling, if that helps. But it's best to think of yourself as being in the same boat as everyone else, or maybe on board the same life raft. You'll only reach shore if you work together and that's not going to happen unless you paddle in the same direction.'

She blushed through her make-up. 'God. Sorry. You know, I didn't mean to suggest that anybody here is . . . inferior . . .' She looked over her shoulder at the others, as if she was seeing the damaged people around her as human for the first time. 'I'm here because of my daughter. I mean, I might think I'm well over my ex-husband, but she reckons I'm a cynical dried-up old prune who needs to get off the bloody shelf and start looking again. It's been three years now and she doesn't seem to realise that I might be happier on my own. She's got this theory that until I sort out why it all went wrong with her dad – apart from him being a philandering liar – I won't be able to find *true happiness.*'

The sourness in the last two words told William that she needed his help every bit as much as the people who'd be fighting back tears during every session. 'And what's made you decide to come now?'

Carol-Ann grimaced, revealing more of her tiny kitten teeth. 'Ah. Well, believe it or not, I've agreed to come as part of my wedding present to her. My little baby has decided to ignore my advice and is getting married soon. She's only nineteen. And with her dad gone, guess who gets to give her away? Muggins here.'

'Right. I suppose that could be tricky.'

'I'm quite happy to be bitter and twisted. It feels right to be like that at my age. Laugh at life, but be realistic; that way you'll never be disappointed. But Georgie's got this strange romantic view of the world. It's like a huge blind spot that stops her seeing the truth about love, marriage and her bloody father. And she wants me to pretend I go along with it.'

William nodded. It made a change to have someone as upfront and open as Carol-Ann on the course and he really wanted to listen some more. 'I'm not meant to ask outright, but what exactly were the circumstances?'

She smiled back. 'Oh, don't worry. You want the potted history? Alan swept me off my feet in a disco when I'd given up hope of meeting the bloke of my dreams. I was a home economics teacher and you don't exactly come across a whole heap of studs when you spend your working life showing teenage girls how to make apple crumble, do you? I was that desperate I moved from Manchester to bloody Birmingham with him.'

Tess frowned. 'You must have been pretty keen on him.'

'Yeah. The fact he'd knocked me up had something to do with it as well, if I'm honest. All the time I was pregnant, Alan was on the road during the week, selling his stuff. "I love Spaghetti Junction," he used to say to me. "It's like being at the centre of the universe, all the possibilities, all those roads as far as you can see into the distance. So many cities, so many markets for beverage vending machines." Of course, as it turned out, he was offering more than instant coffee to selected office managers. But I didn't realise that then.'

'He was having affairs?' Tess asked.

'Oh yes. Affairs, flings, one-night stands. His sales patch was like one big playground. No wonder he was always too knackered to play with Georgie when he got home.'

'How did you find out?'

'I didn't find out exactly. I just sensed . . . you know . . . that he wasn't really with us, even when he was there in the flesh. And then one day – Georgie was three, and I was starting to think about going back to work, which he was resisting like crazy – I asked him straight out. "Is there anyone else?" When he hesitated, I tried flattery. "A man like you, there must be so many temptations on the road." And that was it. He admitted that, as he put it, "Sometimes it is more than a red-blooded male can take. But it doesn't mean anything. I would never leave Georgie and you. My little family."'

Carol-Ann paused. Despite her flippancy, her expression had changed while she recalled that moment. Fifteen years on, the hurt was still visible.

William said, 'That must have been very tough going.'

She grinned. William recognised this as her first line of defence against acknowledging pain. 'Yes. Having an extrovert three-year-old who wanted to be friends with everyone left me no time to think during the day. But in the evenings it *was* bloody tough, as you say, but so am I. It made up my mind about not having another kid, and I decided I would go back to work. I couldn't stand the idea of teaching again, but I still loved food. So I set up my own catering company. Weddings, birthdays, christenings. I started locally, leaving Georgie with a neighbour, while I laid on these fantastic feasts. It was such a treat to get out and about again, and Georgie loved the leftovers. Other kids with working mums were stuffing their faces on fish fingers and Smash, but we'd sit down to sausage rolls and melon boats and Swedish open sandwiches. She must have been the only child in the infants with vol-au-vents in her lunchbox.'

William laughed at the joke, though he noticed Tess had gone white.

Carol-Ann was into her stride. 'I decided that what was sauce for Alan was sauce for me, so when the chances presented themselves to have the odd liaison myself, I took them. Didn't enjoy them that much; a grope in the kitchen between canapés is never going to be Mills and Boon, is it? But it made *me* feel better, like a person in my own right again.'

William checked the clock on the wall. Fifteen minutes had passed while he listened to Carol-Ann and it was time for the changeover. But he couldn't bear to cut her off before the end of her story. 'We'll break for coffee in a moment, but if you want to finish off . . .' Please.

'OK, edited highlights, then. I was bored. So was he, probably. But it wasn't a bad life and what you don't know for sure won't hurt you. It was the days before you could catch people out by dialling 1471. The devil of adultery is in the detail and so long as there were no details, no names, no pack drill, it was bearable. One minute Georgie was going to Tumbletots, the next thing doing her GCSEs. I'd left catering by then: all that washing up for sod-all money. So I got a job in the Nightingale brewery instead.'

'You work there? They brew the best IPA in the Midlands.' William suddenly recognised a faint familiar perfume coming from Carol-Ann – the comforting aroma of yeast and hops and home.

She smiled. 'Oh, just you wait. When I set up my own micro-brewery, mine'll be better. I had to fight to get into the brewhouse; they reckoned a woman's place was in the office. But I was buggered if I'd given up my business to be a secretary, so I just nagged and nagged until they let me in.

'I was a natural. By the time Georgie was doing her mocks, I was deputy head brewer. Pissed all the blokes off, of course. Including my husband.'

William said, 'I can imagine.' Tess was still staring into space.

'But I didn't care what Alan thought. We hardly saw each other. Then the day after Georgie's last exam – fourteenth of June, 2000 – he buggered off. No warning, nothing. I came home and his clothes had gone from the wardrobe, his passport and driving licence taken from the document file – I hadn't even realised he knew where I kept them; he could barely find his socks most mornings. He'd even cleared the loose change from the Corby trouser press. He loved that thing, bought it second hand in a hotel clearance. He'd probably have taken that press too if he'd been able to fit it in the bloody Cavalier.'

She sighed. 'Alan was a man who should never have settled down. He belonged on the open road, a Ginster's pasty in one hand and a mobile in the other.'

William felt slightly sick. He'd built up a professional resistance to most of the stories he heard, but now and again one broke through his defences and reminded him of his own past, the one he'd fought so hard to forget. 'Even so, it must still have been a shock.'

'Yeah. Georgie had been out that night, celebrating the end of her exams. She found me in the garden, stone-cold with a big glass of brandy. We sat and cried till dawn. But at least her tears were for her dad. Mine were for myself. Why couldn't he have left years before? I could have had a life . . .'

For the first time, Carol-Ann was quiet, the energy that had propelled her story seemed to have disappeared.

'And then . . . ?' William prompted her gently, aware that the classical music tape had finished and his other students were fidgeting, waiting for instructions about what to do next.

'Oh . . . he'd cleared the bank account as well as the trouser press. Bastard. I didn't report him missing in case the police found him and brought him back. All I had to do was wait two years, then Citizens Advice said I could divorce him for desertion.'

Tess was still very quiet, shaking her head slightly. 'Are you OK, Tess?' William asked, knowing all too well how someone else's story could trigger unsettling emotions.

'I feel a bit . . .' She looked embarrassed. 'I'm fine. Honestly. Sorry.'

William said, 'Well, if you need a bit of air, feel free to step outside for a few minutes at any time.' He turned back to Carol-Ann. 'We ought to finish now, but about your daughter . . . I know it's hard, but have you thought about trying to track him down, let him know she's getting married? Maybe he'd send her a card or something.'

'Huh. It'd be a miracle if he did. Last April the police came. Alan's dead – a heart attack. He was sitting in the pub with his wife. Or the woman who thought she was his wife. He was living in Manchester, a mile from where I grew up.'

Tess put her hands to her mouth in shock. 'Oh, Carol-Ann! Poor you.'

She smiled back. 'It's OK. Being married to him was worse. At least it's all over. So you see, I'm here under false pretences, really. I'm a widow, not a divorcee. Maybe you'll have to drum me out of the Brownies.'

She looked at William, daring him to throw her out. He checked the clock: they were running way behind. 'There's no entry qualification for coming here, Carol-Ann. If you think it'll help – never mind what your daughter thinks – then you'll continue to be very welcome.' He felt an urge to hold her, reassure her, because it was clear to him that there was enough emotional baggage behind the shiny painted façade to sink a cruise liner. Instead he said, 'Thank you for sharing the story. Now I think you deserve a cup of finest instant coffee. And, Tess, you're having two sugars.'

Chapter Three

The hall is closing in on me. It was all going fine until Carol-Ann mentioned vol-au-vents. One chance reference to a filled pastry canapé and I'm back in the worst week of my life.

The last time I spoke to the Curved One, I was offering her a 1970s-style chicken vol-au-vent at the final Christmas house party I guess Barney and I will ever host. I was circulating with a tray of snacks and when I came to her, she said, 'No thanks, Tess, must watch my waistline.'

And all the time she must have been thinking, 'I don't want your bloody vol-au-vents, you stupid Stepford wife, because I've got my teeth into your husband.'

The vol-au-vents, like everything else about our party, were meant to be ironic. We'd started having a Christmas bash in our third year at university, taking recipes from a high-camp guide to gourmet entertaining that my mum handed me on the day I left home. Quite what gave her the impression that I'd be knocking up Duck Breasts with Double Cream and Calvados or Crepes Suzette in the halls of residence, I've no idea, but as soon as Barney and I moved into our first flat together, we raided Robert Carrier's recipes for inspiration.

For fifteen years, the Christmas party menu was the same: mulled wine, pina colada, chicken supreme vol-au-vents, asparagus rolls, angels and devils on horseback, caramelised nuts, mince pies with home-made brandy butter, and Irish coffee to round things off. Fiddly, fussy food but everyone loved it – we'd tried to shelve the event a couple of times over the years, but our friends protested as strongly as they used to against the Poll Tax. So we carried on the tradition, though there was no longer anything ironic about playing at being grown-ups. We *were* grown-ups. It was exactly the kind of party you'd expect a couple in their mid-thirties to host.

But last year, something *was* different. Barney. I've relived it a million times, seeing the clues I failed to notice at the time. The first one came as soon as I arrived back with the last of the shopping. He was in the kitchen, wearing his stockings-and-suspenders plastic pinny and stirring three curly pieces of whole orange peel into the pan of boiling red wine.

'Oh, shit, Barney, you can't do it like that.'

He shrugged. 'I don't see why not; I'll fish them out before everyone arrives. It's less fiddly than your method, all that sieving to try to get rid of the grated bits of zest. And you never get them all and we always end up with them stuck between our teeth.'

'It's not *my* method, it's Robert Carrier's,' I said, nudging him out of the way.

Barney stood sulkily next to me as I removed the orange peel and began stripping tiny pieces of zest into the pan with the tool I'd bought specifically for the purpose from the Lakeland Plastics kitchenware catalogue.

'You always do this,' he said.

I put down the zester and slid my arm around him, feeling sweat through his shirt. It was hot in the kitchen. Condensation gathered on every surface: our beech kitchen units, our sash windows, our foreheads. 'Don't be daft, it's easier for me. Cavemen never learned to make mulled wine, Rubble.' Barney got his nickname from the Flintstones.

But he didn't smile. 'You always take over. You always act like I'm incapable of anything, like one of your bloody pupils.'

I tightened my grip on his waist: 'Don't be silly, Rubble. It's just easier if I do it. Listen, why don't you have a shower, get changed and then get wrapping the presents? It'd be lovely to have them all laid out under the tree when everyone arrives.' I knew if he did it, he'd use twice as much paper and Sellotape as me, but sometimes you had to make little sacrifices for the sake of domestic harmony.

He gave me a dirty look, but disentangled himself and headed upstairs as I'd suggested. I heard the boom of the boiler and imagined him stepping into the shower, standing under the pounding water for a few seconds as he always did, then doing a funny little jig as the pleasure lifted his mood. Barney's boyish qualities had always been the ones that attracted me to him, and even aged thirty-six, with love handles, a £45K package and company car, he was still that overgrown schoolkid.

In all my analysis of that fateful night, this moment stands out. Just for a second I considered going to join him. We hadn't showered together for ... I couldn't remember how long. But there was so much to do before everyone started arriving and instead I added a note to my mental to-do list to suggest a shower together in the next week. There'd be plenty of time over the Christmas holidays.

Or so I thought.

My last missed clue came during the party. Barney was at the saucepan, ladling out mulled wine, missing the glasses and covering the work surfaces with sticky pink stains as usual. But he was also knocking back neat whisky. Not usual.

'Are you OK, Rubble?'

'Yeah.' He sounded defensive.

'It's not like you to hit the hard stuff this early. What's up?'

He shook his head. 'Don't you ever get fed up with all this pretending?'

'What do you mean? It's just a giggle.'

'Who are we doing it for, though, Tess?'

I was torn between attending to the needs of our guests in the living room and dealing with Barney's weirdness. I'd never seen him like this. I walked past him to the oven, pulled out a tray of just-cooked vol-au-vents, then turned towards him again with a bright smile on my face. 'For our friends, Rubble. You know that. But ... maybe we need to take a break next year. They'll cope.'

He stared at the floor. He was usually so transparent and I felt uncomfortable that I couldn't work out what was the matter with him. Then he looked back up at me. 'Yes, you're probably right.' But he sounded like he meant the complete opposite.

'I'm always right,' I said, before leaning forward to kiss him on the nose.

'Always.' He smiled ruefully.

The doorbell rang. 'I'll go,' he said and downed the last of the whisky. 'Once more into the breach . . .'

Unto the breach, I whispered under my breath.

'. . . *All I had to do was wait two years, then Citizens Advice said I could divorce him for desertion . . .*'

It takes me a moment to remember who Carol-Ann is and why I'm supposed to be listening to her.

'Are you OK, Tess?' The guy in charge, William, is peering into my face. Too close.

'I feel a bit . . . I'm fine. Honestly. Sorry.'

'Well, if you need a bit of air, feel free to step outside for a few minutes at any time.'

It's all very well him saying that, but I can't seem to catch my breath enough to reply, and when I try to stand up (a pretty essential precursor to my next plan, which is to get the hell out of St Gabriel's church hall as fast as my skinny white legs can carry me), my lower body has gone on strike. So all I can do is listen as this person I've never met before tells me and William the most intimate details of her life.

Even when the session is over, and a few people are hanging back and mumbling vaguely about going down to the pub without daring to risk rejection by asking directly, I feel so sick I can't work out how I'll ever make it to my car.

I try giving myself a talking to. Pull yourself together, you're a responsible thirty-five-year-old primary-school teacher with a car, a house and a soon-to-be ex-husband. Eventually, while the young trendy guy with long hair is distracted trying to chat up the blonde and the woman with the swishy ponytail (he seems to be hedging his bets), I push myself up from the chair with my hands, like one of those 'tone your upper arms' exercises from a women's magazine, and scuttle out into the street where my car is parked.

The feeling of relief when I hear the sigh of the central locking is immense but it takes five minutes' concentrated heavy breathing to make my heart stop thumping. As soon as I can speak, I dial Mel.

She picks up on the second ring. 'Hey, how was it?' The first time she did that I thought she was psychic, but then she showed me how she'd typed my name into her mobile. She did the same on my phone, but when it came to Barney's number, she keyed in 'Shitface: DON'T ANSWER'.

I start to describe my horrible symptoms. 'I just don't know what came over me, Mel, but it's obviously a sign I shouldn't go back.'

'Bollocks, girl. It was just a panic attack. No big deal.'

I've never had a panic attack before. Don't really believe in them, if I'm honest, though I wouldn't dream of saying that to Laura, our reception class teacher. She is always having panic attacks, caused by everything from houseflies to the film that forms on top of the canteen custard.

'A panic attack?'

'Yeah, classic symptoms. Heavy breathing, weird thoughts, loss of control. You're nobody until you've had one. It's up there with wheat intolerance and Seasonal Affective Disorder – pretty trendy.'

'So do you get them?'

She laughs. 'Nah, don't be daft. I just researched them for an article I was doing on twenty-first-century illnesses. But, you know, I bet Geri's had them. And Posh.'

'And that's meant to make me feel better? The fact that I've now got the symptoms of imaginary medical conditions that only pop stars can usually afford to suffer from?' I start the engine, determined to prove to Mel and myself that I haven't turned into some dippy hypochondriac.

'You're very judgemental sometimes, Tess.'

'That's a real case of the pot calling the kettle black,' I grunt, reversing viciously out of the parking space.

'Yeah, but I'm a journalist. Cynicism's in my job description. You're a teacher; you're meant to be nurturing and sympathetic.'

Maybe that's why Barney left me. I didn't meet the criteria for wife because I am not squidgy enough. The Curved One is bound to be ten times squidgier than me; you can tell just by looking at her. If you're looking for a shoulder to cry on, you'd always choose a well-upholstered version – it's like the choice between resting your head on a pink satin cushion, or the sharp corner of a wooden table.

'Tess? Are you still there?'

'Yeah, sorry. I don't think I'll be going back, anyhow. Too touchy feely for me.'

Mel says nothing as I weave my way through the streets round the back of New Street and head for the dual carriageway. Speed limits are for pensioners: being behind the wheel always makes me feel in control. Usually I like driving through the city centre at night when the roads are empty, but tonight it's like being the last person left in the world after some kind of catastrophe. I couldn't feel any lonelier.

'What alternative have you got, though, honey? I mean, you're not coping, are you?'

I veer into the filter lane towards the top end of Broad Street. People begin to appear again: teenagers leaning against the expensive sculpture that looks like a jelly mould, a snogging couple waiting for the lights to change opposite the Walkabout Australian bar, a few brave souls sitting around bistro tables outside the Repertory theatre . . . I still don't feel any less alone.

'I don't know.'

Mel goes quiet again as I roar across Fiveways roundabout, but in my phone earpiece I can hear the tinny symphony of domestic bliss. Something smooth and soulful on the stereo – Café del Mar, at a guess – the ring of glasses knocking together and then the sound of pouring, and as the music gets louder, I picture her walking back through to the living room, the handset in the crook of her neck, passing James one of the two glasses of New World wine she's just poured, putting her index finger to her lips to stop him talking to her. Mouthing 'Tess' at him, and shrugging her shoulders in response to his raised eyebrows. James is a long-standing fixture by Mel standards; he appeared four years ago and he is as near to permanent as anyone has ever been. She refused to marry him when she got pregnant with Leo, but despite her protestations of independence, they're more bonded than any married couple I know.

Before, I felt irritated by her stubborn refusal to tie the knot.

It seemed like she was mocking those of us who had. Now I am just jealous of her happiness.

'So, what did they do in the group that made you freak out? Primal scream therapy?'

'No, nothing like that. I don't know ... it was hard going.' I can't think how to explain it. The bloke running it seemed sound, though he did laugh too loudly at his own jokes. But that's standard male behaviour. The rest of the people were ordinary, the sort you'd see in a queue at Tesco, going about their everyday lives without a care in the world.

Which just goes to show how wrong you can be. If every one of them has a story as horrible as Carol-Ann's, then you begin to wonder if anyone is truly happy.

Even the exercises in themselves weren't *that* frightening, in theory at least. I was relieved that we ran out of time in the first half: my own experience seemed so ordinary compared to Carol-Ann's. But now I wonder how it might feel to be listened to *properly* myself, without the other person trying to make me feel better. Or make themselves feel better.

'So you're definitely not going to bother next week?'

I turn off the High Street, then right twice into our road. For once there's a space outside the house. I open the front door and the musty smell hits me. God knows how I could have ignored it for so long. I suppose it crept up on me, the way Barney's unhappiness must have crept up on him. 'I dunno, Mel. Maybe I could give it one more go ... oh, I've got a message, is that from you?' The answerphone is blinking, red flashes illuminating the darkened hall, on-off, on-off.

'No, I knew you were out.'

'My mum, then, I bet you.' I couldn't face calling home over the weekend, so she'll be checking up on me. 'I think maybe I might try going again, you know. I hate to admit you're right, but at least I'm kind of ... doing something.' I press the answerphone playback button. 'And we've been set homework to do – quite fun really, we've got to—'

'*Tess, hi ...*'

'Shit. It's Barney.'

'What?'

'Barney's left a message, listen.' I angle my mobile towards the speaker so Mel can hear.

'*It's me . . . um . . . listen . . . I need . . . I mean, we should get together. To talk.*' His voice makes my legs feel strange. He sounds nervous. '*I wondered if we could meet – on Thursday. In town, maybe?*'

Oh, God. This is it. He is coming back. He's got tired of the Curved One and wants to be back with me. Where he belongs.

'*Give me a call . . . no, no, actually, it's easier if you email, we can sort it out that way . . . no, hang on. Text me. Yeah, text me. It's tricky for me. You understand? OK? Hope you're free. It's been such a long time . . .*' There is a long pause, the whooshing sound of wind blowing into his mobile the only indication he hasn't hung up. '*Um, bye then.*' A click, then nothing.

I let my legs buckle underneath me and slump against the wall, kicking over a pile of old *Times Educational Supplement*s. 'Did you hear that, Mel?'

'Yes.'

'What do you think?' I know what I think and suddenly it makes sense. I feel silly that I ever imagined we could separate properly, still less divorce. Throw seventeen years down the drain in favour of some floozy? Some giggling girl who thinks Wham! is retro, and the miners' strike ancient history.

'How long has it been since he got in touch?'

When was the last time I spoke to him? I let myself down on Valentine's Day, sending a card to his work, and he called me then to tell me how embarrassed he'd been because *she* had seen it. But that can't have been the last time, can it? I certainly can't remember anything more recent, but I'm not about to admit it to Mel. 'Not sure. A month or so, maybe?'

'Well, why do *you* think he's got in touch now?'

'I suppose . . . well, why would he unless there was something he needed to tell me personally? I mean, we've got solicitors for all the negotiations, so there's no reason for him to call unless . . .' I let it hang. I can't say what I most want in all the world.

'Unless he wanted you back?' Mel's voice is unusually flat, like she's trying not to say what she really feels.

'Yes. Oh God, Mel, why else would he call? You heard him,

how nervous he sounded. Of course he'd be nervous; he must be thinking that I might say no, that I might have found someone else.' It's so obvious now, I feel angry and irritated at myself for spending so much time agonising over the last five months, when all I had to do was wait . . .

'I hope you're right, Tess, I really do. I just think you need to wait and see what he has to say before you get your hopes up. I mean, if he *does* want a reconciliation, why would he be so worried about letting the cat out of the bag to Dawn?'

Hearing her name feels like a punch in the belly. 'He probably wants to sort it out with me first. To be sure.'

'What, hedge his bets, you mean?' Mel's profession has made her so sceptical about human nature.

'No . . . look, I know I mustn't get too excited.' But I can't help myself. We'll try again. He'll work at it, and although it won't be easy, I know we can make it work this time. What marriage doesn't go through problems over the years? The secret is love, and a determination to get through it. Now that we both have that, we'll make it better.

'I know you think I'm a cynical old hag, Tess, but I just don't want you to be hurt again, that's all.'

'Fair enough.' I know I sound dismissive, but I don't like her tone. I force myself up from the floor and flick the light switch, gasping at the mess. I want to get off the phone and start clearing up. OK, he wants to meet on neutral territory but by the end of Thursday night, he could be back in our bed.

'Look, I understand why you don't want to hear anything bad, honey. But . . . I don't know, just don't make any rash decisions about anything. The course, whatever.'

'No, I won't,' I say, already feeling a huge sense of relief that I'll never have to go back to that draughty old church hall and the misery that hangs in the air like cheap room freshener. 'Tell you what, I'll even do the homework, how about that?'

'Great, great. Listen, Tess, I am really pleased. Truly. I really am. I can't think of anything that'd make me happier than to see the two of you back together.'

'Sure. Yeah, thanks, Mel. Not just for now, for the whole

time. I couldn't have got through it without you ... night, night.'

I switch off my mobile and thrust the kitchen door open. It's ten p.m. and I've got some clearing up to do.

Chapter Four

I've been singing more or less non-stop for thirty-six hours.
Even the kids have noticed.

'Miss,' Sanjay shouted tonight as he left the classroom at
hometime. 'You really shouldn't sing, you know, miss. It sounds
horrible.'

'Thanks, Sanjay. Lucky I don't intend to enter *Pop Idol* then,
really, isn't it?'

He's got a point – singing isn't my forte, but I am in such a
good mood I don't see why I shouldn't let everyone know. It's
partly William's fault. Our homework for the next session was
to think of three songs: one to represent our married lives, one
for our lives as they are now, and one for the future we want for
ourselves when all the shit is over. Except the shit is already
over, and although I won't be going back to the group, singing
seems the best way to express how I'm feeling.

I sang while I cleaned the house all Tuesday night after the
class and Barney's message. Or I would have sung all night if the
neighbours hadn't come round to point out that hoovering and
singing past two a.m. was probably against the law, or at the
very least, a good reason for manslaughter on the grounds of
diminished responsibility. The songs were pure Doris Day. 'Que
sera sera', followed by a joyful stab at 'Teacher's Pet', rounding
off with a top-of-my-voice rendition of 'Secret Love'. A strange
one to sing about my husband, maybe, but then for five months
I'd felt ashamed of still loving him. It was so humiliating, the fact
that I couldn't manage to fall out of love with him, even though
he'd fallen out of love with me. One phone message had
transformed me into Calamity Jane, and I wanted to shout it
from the highest hills:

I LOVE YOU, BARNEY LEONARD.

I was almost tempted to text that to him, but despite my excitement I sensed it might be a slightly disproportionate response to what he'd said on the answerphone. Instead, I spent most of Wednesday at school in a daydream, ignoring the kids as they chattered about boy bands and flicked bits of spit-soggy paper balls around the classroom. I was too preoccupied composing the perfect message. I wanted it to convey so much: forgiveness, acceptance, openness, a willingness to change, desire and, of course, love.

I finally sent it on Wednesday night:

I AM FREE TOMORROW. BRINDLEY PLACE SOME-WHERE? TESS XX

The kisses were about as far as I dared to go without scaring him off. He had to tell me how he felt in his own time. Declaring my endless love – much as I wanted to – could be counter-productive, might make him feel cornered. I've never played games before but the Curved One wasn't so scrupulous and look where it got her. For five months I've been nursing my war wounds. Now it's time to plan my campaign, gather my reserves. Let battle commence.

My mobile buzzed with a response reassuringly quickly. I savoured the moment, picturing him making some excuse to get out of her flat and wandering round St Paul's Square, maybe sitting in the churchyard, wondering how much he dared read into the kisses. I opened the message:

9PM, PITCHER AND PIANO?

It had all the poetry of the Haynes Manual for the VW Polo. But it was a date. I left the kisses off this time, and sent back a simple SEE U THERE.

I felt quite flat, but forced myself to resume my mission with the bin bags. I'd managed to fill ten of them in the kitchen alone on Tuesday night, but it was so hard to know what to prioritise next. The kitchen had always been top of the list, because the smell was polluting every other room, but now I needed to work out what I could do elsewhere in the limited time I had left. I plotted Barney's most likely route through the house: hall, bathroom . . . bedroom? I hoped that after all this time, his first instinct was hardly going to be to go into the lounge to watch a DVD.

It was time to transform the Technicolor decay around me into gleaming modernist monochrome. The bathroom was the easiest. I sang watery songs – 'Ocean Drive' and 'Sailing' – as I sprayed and scrubbed and rinsed. It all had to go. Rust-orange mould on the shower screen. Turquoise algae around the bath taps. Charcoal-grey finger marks on the door we'd painted pure brilliant white when we moved in. We never got round to replacing the cheap doors in the house with those reclaimed pine ones we coveted. Maybe that should be our first act when he moves back in: a trip to the reclamation yard, to invest in our future.

Mopping the bathroom floor would have taken too long, so I improvised: splashing Pine Fresh Gel everywhere, and using bits of loo roll as dusters to pick up the worst bits of hair and dirt. I just hoped he wouldn't look too closely. I did consider removing one of the light bulbs so he wouldn't see the ingrained muck in the grout of our lovely chessboard tiled floor, but I thought that would just make me look like I couldn't even change a lightbulb on my own.

The bedroom wasn't as cluttered as the other rooms – only three bin bags for the magazines and newspapers spread across the duvet and the floor, which lay unread because I'd lost my powers of concentration for anything except work. But there was a musty, charity-shop smell. I changed the bedding for the first time since he left; it had been such an exhausting prospect on my own, and I'd hung onto the comfort offered by the faint smell of him on the sheets and the creases his face had left on the pillowcase – the reassurance that he had existed and wasn't just a figment of my imagination. Now I'd hopefully have the real thing back in my bed by tomorrow night.

But I didn't wash his old T-shirt. Just in case.

In my boudoir, I became Aretha Franklin, belting out 'I Say a Little Prayer' and 'Respect', as I opened the windows, which creaked in surprise. In the en-suite, I found an aromatherapy gift set Barney had given me as a Christmas present last year. Another missed clue: normally his gifts were thoughtful, playful, touching: hand-tied bouquets bought 'just because you're you' or hot-air balloon flights together over the Lickey Hills. This was a department store stand-by you'd give to a maiden aunt, or a secretary. I suppose the Curved One got the thoughtful present instead.

I couldn't find any tealights to use in the burner, though I knew there was a huge bagful from IKEA somewhere in the house. There was no time to waste trying to locate them, so I dribbled different oils onto cotton wool balls, and placed them in strategic places around the room. Rose underneath my pillow, jasmine in my underwear drawer, patchouli (isn't that the stuff that made hippies get stuck into free love?) tucked under some books next to the lamp. Hopefully the heady perfume would distract him from the carrier bags of stuff I'd stashed under the bed. There wasn't time to sort through it all.

The only thing I needed to hide properly was the shoebox of unsent letters to Barney. This was my guiltiest secret, proof of my weakness: more than forty envelopes full of reasons he should come back. December's were full of optimism, describing the moments we'd shared that I knew he'd find impossible to forget. January's were more desperate, telling him how I was suffering, how I would be someone else, anyone, if he'd consider having me back. February and March were the worst: pages and pages of furious scrawl, calling him and the Curved One every name under the sun. But by April I was back into reasonable mode, trying to strike a deal with him, with myself, with God, desperate to find a way we could resolve the stalemate.

I never sent a single letter. Maybe I always knew he'd come back of his own accord. I taped down the lid and put the box inside an old suitcase at the back of the wardrobe.

Satisfied by the overall effect of my hard work, I felt anything was possible. So I called home.

'Mum, it's me.'

'Oh, hello my darling.' She spoke the sentence like a musical scale, moving down the notes from high to low in sympathy. 'How *are* you?'

It's the sympathy that has stopped me ringing her more often since Barney left. It'd be different if I could talk to Dad, because he knows me so much better, but the chances of him answering the phone are nil because Mum always beats him to it.

We're not the closest of families, but we're not a dysfunctional disaster either. Mum always says running a home is like running a business, and if the Waltons are Microsoft, and the Addams Family are Enron, then we'd be Marks and Spencer: solid, dependable but not exactly high-flying.

My mother certainly had FTSE-100-level ambitions for us, but in the end, she had to settle for cottage-industry-level achievements. Suzy was due to marry Prince Andrew, but obviously no one told him, so she settled for Patrick and his dinghy sailing empire. And I was meant to discover a cure for cancer, until Mum realised that my preference for history over biochemistry would make scientific breakthroughs less likely. Being deputy head teacher is never going to win me the Nobel prize but she always made a deliberate effort to be brave in the face of such disappointing daughters.

But Barney leaving was beyond the pale. A failed marriage was something that happened to other people's children. Whenever I hear her muted, funeral-director voice, I wonder if she's trying to comfort me, or herself. Now, at last, I have something to say she might welcome.

'I'm well, thanks. I thought you'd like to know Barney's asked to see me tomorrow.'

'My goodness. Well, that is good news.' She never did really like Barney – something to do with his Staffordshire roots – but a Northern husband who is still on the scene is preferable to one shacked up with his secretary. 'They generally do come back, Tess.'

'I hope so.' Suddenly, telling my mum made me feel less certain about Barney's intentions. Beyond the plain fact that he wants to meet up, there is no indication that he wants us to try again. I tried to dismiss the thought while she droned on, more talkative than I've known her since I first announced my engagement, full of Dolly Parton wisdom about standing by your man.

When I eventually got her off the phone, I felt ready to tackle my biggest challenge: the hall.

Ain't no mountain high enough...

It had become the dumping ground, not just for recycling and kids' coursework, but for everything I didn't have the energy to carry through the house. Somehow I had to sort the wheat from the chaff, and each item seemed to bring a whole new set of tasks: bills I'd opened and abandoned unpaid on the console table; shoe sprays and hair sprays and deodorants stored there because now I only seemed to remember to use them if they were right under my nose; and discarded layers of clothing I'd shed as soon as I got in at night. When I crawled behind the table and the coat rack, I counted numerous unmatched socks, plus pairs of tights in diminishing deniers, reflecting the change from winter to spring since Barney left.

Even when I'd put everything washable in the washing machine and stowed everything else in drawers or corners or cupboards so random I'd be surprised if I could ever find them again, the hall felt seedy. But I was too exhausted to do any more and I knew I'd have my work cut out when it came to making *myself* presentable. But I had four hours for that on Thursday, so I took myself to bed, and tossed and turned without sleeping in air thick with aromatherapy oils.

And now it's here. The day that feels like Christmas, my birthday and the afternoon I finished my O-levels all rolled into one. The kids haven't wasted an opportunity to take advantage of my mood. My continued karaoke performances have alerted the little buggers to the fact that my mind's still elsewhere, and they've played up from registration till quarter to four. But it's not their behaviour that's made the day such hard work. It's the butterflies I obviously swallowed in the playground while I was singing my hopeful heart out. They've made it as far as my stomach, found it unexpectedly hospitable and decided to set up home and start families there. I don't really mind, such is my feeling of generosity towards all creatures great and small. But it means I couldn't eat any lunch, for fear of suffocating the growing colony of insect life.

I've decided to skip the staff meeting, and although I don't think Roz, the head, believed for a millisecond that I have a man coming round about the damp-proof course (the first excuse that popped into my head), she didn't challenge me.

The sunlight streaming into the hall shows up a dust-storm as I step through the door, but I'm more worried about making myself look tidy. Attractive would be a bonus, but tidy is the absolute minimum.

My life has been punctuated by hair crises, but I suppose the compensation for my thin, dry, mousy locks has been not having to devote much time to drying and depilation. However, I've never left my body hair untouched for a full five months before, and in the shower I see the full effects: long strands of tawny brown stretching two or three centimetres along my legs plus an overgrown patch under my arms I can only describe as resembling a rusty scouring pad. But as I inspect my body with growing disgust, there's worse to come.

Peering down at my belly, wondering whether the Curved One has hipbones as prominent as mine, I spot a strand of white cotton in my pubic hair. I reach down to pull it away.

'Ouch.'

Oh my God, a white pubic hair.

I didn't know you could get them. I look again, closer than I've ever looked at that mysterious clump of hair, and realise there's more than one. I count to ten before giving up. They're all in the same central area, like the stripe down the centre of a badger's head.

I try to stay calm, rinsing away the shower gel and deep-conditioning treatment (the latter from my scalp, though maybe I've been going wrong all these years and should have been applying a weekly dollop down below), and then towel myself off before going into the bedroom to look more closely.

Under the bedside light, I realise it's definitely not an optical illusion. My pubes are going grey. It sneaks up on you like that, age, and until the arrival of the Curved One, I wasn't nearly as bothered about it as most of my friends. But now I wonder why the hairs around my genitals are showing the signs of stress sooner than the ones on my head. It doesn't bear thinking about.

There is nothing I can do, not this evening anyhow. I suppose there might be some kind of Grecian 2000 for the bikini line, probably on one of those shelves in Boots that you don't realise is there unless you stumble across it looking for Vaseline: the same shelf that holds the haemorrhoid cream and the gluey stuff that allows you to eat apples while wearing dentures. I could nip round to our tiny local branch where I know all the girls behind the counter, but the risks involved in applying dye to your groin area before going on a hot date with your husband seem to outweigh the potential benefits. Soft lighting later on is the key.

The shock does make me more determined to wear the girliest clothes in my wardrobe. I have to out-flounce the Curved One. I find a floaty turquoise skirt I bought for a christening a couple of years ago, and team it up with a little cream chiffon top and matching cardigan. Ambitious for May, perhaps, but about the only truly feminine outfit I own apart from my wedding dress. I step into my sole pair of kitten heels and order a cab: I intend to get there first and down a drink or three to calm my nerves. In the time it takes for the taxi to arrive, I spray on Beautiful – the perfume he bought me for our Big Day seven years back – and try not to chew my nails.

I find a table in the Pitcher and Piano, overlooking the canal. Two leather sofas facing each other – we can start on either side of the table, as he searches his soul and tells me how he's missed me, and then I'll gesture towards the empty space next to me, and he'll move round to join me, the first of a thousand tiny steps that will hopefully take us back to where we were before the Curved One sashayed into our lives.

I buy a Sea Breeze and sit down. I love the colour of cranberry juice, plus I have this hunch there'll be some sex on the cards tonight, and it'd be just my luck to end up with cystitis. Hurrah! My famous practical approach to life is showing the faintest sign of re-establishing itself.

My phone vibrates. A text from Mel: GOOD LUCK, HONEY. AND DON'T FORGET YOU CAN CALL ANY TIME.

I giggle. She's obviously desperate to get the full blow-by-blow account of the big reconciliation. I do love her to pieces, but I'm not about to interrupt our emotional reunion to give her a bulletin. She'll have to wait till tomorrow morning.

It's colder than I expected on the balcony, and I'm realising that the downside of girly flimsy clothes is their very flimsiness. I was trying to look like a delicate waif but I probably resemble those desperate Brits who insist on wearing a bikini on Blackpool Beach, with a fixed grin to stop their teeth chattering in the icy wind.

But apart from my goosebumps, this is the perfect location. The city has changed so much, tarted itself up and managed to put together a convincing case for truly being Britain's second city. I believe it, anyhow, maybe because I'm trying to do the same kind of thing. I've been resting on my laurels, and it's time to reinvent myself, like an old-fashioned company that tries to rebrand itself with a new logo and a funky name. Maybe I could try a new name. Trouble is, you're a bit stuck with Tess. I could play with the initials, like those ultra-cool rappers the kids at school love – Ice T? T Bag? Cuppa T?

'Tess.'

He looks the same, of course, but it's still a hell of a shock. Barney has always been a barrel of a man, even aged nineteen, and now he's finally growing into that body, it suits him better aged thirty-six than it did as a teenager. Skinny men age far worse than the rugby-playing kind, and despite the expansion of his waistline and the slackening of his jawline, Barney looks more handsome than ever. The shirt helps – it's black and fitted and new. And it shows off his tan.

Tan?

'You look well.' What should you talk about to your husband when you haven't seen him since the night he picked up his belongings, three months ago? 'Been away?'

I follow his eyes as he looks down at his two-tone shoes. Very trendy. Very Italian. Very mid-life crisis.

'Yeah, you know. Spring break, kind of thing.' He points at my drink. 'Can I get you another one?'

'OK, yes. A Sea Breeze please.'

'Oh, get you!' He grins at me, joking the way he always did, but then his face falls. 'I won't be a minute.'

I'm glad to have a moment to try to make sense of it all. I don't like his tan. It hasn't been a brilliant spring so far, certainly not sunny enough to produce a tan that makes the green in his eyes stand out so much. I only remember him ever being that brown after our honeymoon in Sri Lanka. In all the photos from our second week, his eyes draw you in, as though all the other colours in the picture are unreal, pale imitations of that moss green. Even the deep blue of the Indian ocean looks insipid in comparison.

I'm getting distracted. Why can't I concentrate on the matter in hand? What is he doing here? Where the hell did he go on holiday?

Somehow I found it easier to cope with Barney no longer living at 107 Victoria Terrace when I was also convincing myself that his everyday life was otherwise exactly the same. The same cheese and pickle sandwiches and carton of Ribena Toothkind in his lunchbox, the same arguments with the newsagent round the corner from work about the merits of West Brom over Villa.

In my own mind, I'd managed to turn his absence into an extended business trip. But the tan and the new shirt are irrefutable proof that his life without me is different. Now I feel sick as well as cold.

'There you go.' He passes me my glass and puts his down on the other side of the table. Clear, fizzy, slice of lemon. Not a mineral water, surely? Things are going from bad to worse.

'Where did you go, then?' I try to sound casual.

'Uh, the bar.' He gestures behind him as if I'm an idiot, then shakes his head slightly, and looks pained. 'You mean, on holiday?'

I nod.

'Look, Tess, what's the point in . . . ?' He tails off.

I feel sicker. He is not following the script I had been rehearsing so hard in my head, but I plough on with hairdresser's questions. 'Where did you go? Honestly, I'm interested. Might fancy a trip myself soon.' How ridiculous am I being? But once I start, I'm not giving in. 'Not like it's a state secret, is it?'

He shrugs in defeat. 'Italy.'

Oh, silly, silly Tess. You thought it couldn't get any worse for you? Try those images for size: Barney and the Curved One walking hand in hand along the Bridge of Sighs; the golden couple rubbing each other with sun-tan lotion on a Neapolitan beach; my husband and his lover making love on a rickety Italian bed in a topsy-turvy Venice pensione, like the one where we spent our first Valentine's Day as husband and wife . . . but he wouldn't, would he?

'Lovely. Whereabouts?' Stop there, Tess. While you're at it, stop talking to yourself. A split personality is rarely attractive in a woman.

'Tess, I don't see what this is achieving.'

'No, well, neither do I. What are you doing here, Barney?' Oh, nice touch, Tess. If he was feeling unsure about coming back to you before, that openly aggressive approach is bound to be a real come-on.

But however hard I try to maintain the illusion, something tells me he is not coming back to me. That nothing I can do – from belly-dancing to brandishing a jackpot-winning lottery ticket – will make the slightest bit of difference.

He says, 'I . . . I need to talk to you.'

'Great. What about? We've been getting along just fine since there've been five of us in the marriage. The addition of a mistress and a couple of lawyers is always a great way to spice up a flagging relationship, don't you find?'

'I know I've hurt your feelings, but this isn't getting us anywhere, is it?'

'Hurt my feelings? You hurt someone's feelings when you buy the wrong thing on your wife's birthday or accuse her of looking a bit porky. Not when you leave her for the office slag.'

I've really burned my bridges now, I can see it in his face, and feel it in my own as my cheeks catch fire. Tip Top Tess has deserted me again, at the worst possible moment.

He doesn't even give me the satisfaction of shouting back. We both look down at a party barge sailing along the canal, the sounds of giggling and music taunting us until it disappears from sight.

'Tess. That . . . *slag* is having my kid.'

Chapter Five

It was Dad who gave me my nickname, after Mum shouted at me for polishing her dressing table with butter. I was only four, and after noticing how butter made my fingers shiny, I thought it'd be the perfect polish.

'COL-IN!' she'd shrieked from upstairs. My dad, my sister and I all answered the call and I was horrified to see her expression as we surveyed the admittedly unevenly polished wood. Surely she should have been delighted? I'd spent ages trying to smooth out the circles with my fingers, and it looked an awful lot better than it had when I first smeared the butter on.

'What were you thinking, Tess?' I knew not to answer. My mum expected the full attention of the floor in situations like this, and to attempt to explain yourself would just draw out the drama still more. 'You're an impossible girl.' She turned to my father. 'She's an impossible girl, Colin.'

My father knelt down alongside me. 'Why did you do it, Tess? You know how precious your mum's dressing table is.'

'Thought it was kind . . . a good deed.' I had an obsession with the Brownies and was practising, although I had another three years to wait before I'd be old enough to join.

My father sighed, but Mum was quite unmoved by my touching explanation. 'Why are they always creating more work for me? It's non-stop. Why don't you just *think* before you act, Tess?'

'Because she's a child, Dorothy.' He only ever called her Dorothy when he was annoyed. 'Tess, I know you want to help out, but next time ask Mummy first, all right?'

I nodded, biting my lip to stop the tears. Even at that age, I wasn't upset by my mother's anger, but frustrated at the injustice of her reaction.

Dad noticed, and put out his big hairy hand to take my buttery one. 'Don't be upset, Tess. I think it's very sweet that you're so clean and tidy. You just like everything to be . . . tip top!' He smiled to himself. 'Tip Top Tess. That's what you are. I can't think of a better thing for a little girl to be.'

I wonder what might have happened if he'd chosen 'Tearaway Tess' or 'Tess the Terrible'. As it was, I was permanently tainted with a nickname that proclaimed to the world that my most interesting quality was a premature urge to become a housewife.

If I was Tearaway Tess, maybe I'd empty the Sea Breeze over Barney's head. Tess the Terrible would go one better and push him off the balcony into the canal.

But Tip Top Tess doesn't believe in acting impulsively or making people feel awkward. So when he passes on the glad tidings, I simply nod, then ask him when the baby is due.

There is a pause – you might call it a pregnant one – and when I dare to look at him again, he is blushing. 'Well, um, I never have been terribly good at remembering dates.'

That's not entirely true. It's only in the last couple of years that he's forgotten our anniversary. I try again. 'Roughly?'

'Well. Roughly, kind of the end of August.'

I do the sums. Oh God.

TTT wavers momentarily, a hundred swear words on the tip of her tidy tongue, then her good manners reassert themselves. I pick up my drink, swirl the ice around in the glass, take a little sip to clear the bitter taste from my mouth. 'Right. Well, that makes a few things clearer.' Like why he left and why he really isn't coming back.

'I know how this must look, but . . . it wasn't planned.'

'Huurgh,' is all I manage in response to that. Wasn't planned? I should bloody hope not. How many married men sit down and plan to have a baby with their mistress?

'Are you OK?'

Oh yes, Barney. Fantastic. Never been better. 'I think I'll get a taxi.' Before TTT deserts me entirely, leaving someone far scarier in her place.

'Can I get you one?' He won't look me in the eye.

'Honestly, I'd rather just go now. There should be loads of cabs on Broad Street at this time of night.' I stand up, and see Barney clocking my outfit properly. He sighs and I hate myself for being so transparent. A T-shirt reading 'Take me, I'm yours' would have been subtler.

Once I leave Brindley Place with its patio gas heaters and neon lights, it feels even colder. I count six taxis going past but I can't be bothered to stick my hand out, in case they ignore me. I've had enough rejection for one night. And the bus feels too exposed, too bright. I can hide in the dark.

I walk the four miles home very slowly. The blisters start forming before I make it to the top of Broad Street. The pain in my feet is all I can feel, and then eventually they go numb like the rest of me. I stop to sit down at bus shelters and on benches. As I hobble along the Hagley Road, through Edgbaston towards Harborne, I observe life around me like a primatologist watching gorillas in the wild: the primitive need of men in red cars to cut people up at traffic lights; the first queues outside Liberty's nightclub, where the women are already identifying the targets for the strange courtship rituals they plan later in the night; the lemming tendencies of young lads on pizza-delivery bikes.

I have never felt so removed from other members of the human race.

It takes me an hour and a half to get back to Victoria Terrace, and by the time I walk into the house, my feet are bleeding. It's not until I've finished washing off the dried blood and the dirt that I allow myself to cry. Again, it isn't the hurt of what he's done to me, but the injustice. Just as it had been with Mum and her dressing table.

I tried so hard. All I want is to make other people happy. The smell of rose, of jasmine, of patchouli fills the bedroom, and I choke myself to sleep.

I wake up to the news headlines on the clock radio. Four dead in a bomb explosion in Israel. A report that Britain is the fattest nation in Europe. A city lawyer suing her company for sexual harassment.

And an unexpected pregnancy in the West Midlands. Hardly the stuff of front pages, I tell myself, trying to find the will to move. It might be another minor tragedy for me, but as far as the statisticians are concerned, it's a welcome blip in the falling birth-rate, another citizen to help pay the pensions of an ageing population.

I have never had a day off sick in my career, and it's only an instinctive determination not to blot my copybook that finally forces me up from my bed.

'Ouch.' I'd forgotten about the state of my feet. Once I am up and about, I have to talk myself into everything – into the shower, into my clothes, definitely into my shoes. Then I realise I'm half an hour ahead of my usual timetable, and once I sit down on the sofa with a cup of tea – all I can manage – it is so much harder to make myself move again. 'It's Friday, Tess. One day. That's all you need to get through. Then it's half term.'

I drive to work carefully, with the painstakingly choreographed movements of a drunk trying to avoid being stopped by the police. Thank God there's no test for being emotionally over the limit – on the surface, you'd never know I'm anything other than a calm, responsible teacher looking forward to a week's well-deserved break. The only thing holding me together is my iron self-control, and even that has slipped since last night. I can't afford another lapse, or everything might fall to pieces.

I'm still early into work, the opposite of what I'd planned. I try to sneak past Roz's office, but she has superhuman hearing. 'Tess?'

I force my face into a smile and pop my head round the door. Roz is the best boss I've ever had, but even after eight years, we don't see each other outside work. Weird, really. She's ultra-professional at all times, and I've never seen the mask slip. I think she knows things 'aren't brilliant at home' but she's never quizzed me – another thing I respect her for. 'Thank God it's Friday, eh?'

'You look tired,' she says. Her clothes are ominously smart, despite her trademark low-cut top. What has she dressed up for? I hope we don't have any governors' tours or Local Education Authority officials coming down. I can cope with the kids for one more day but I'm not sure I can perform for demanding adults with clipboards as well.

'Yeah, you know. It's been quite a tiring term so far, don't you think?'

Roz nods. 'Perhaps. I'll be glad of the break, that's for sure. We're taking the girls to Herefordshire. What are you up to?'

The girls are Roz's red setters, and Herefordshire means her country cottage. I don't think she needs to work – her husband owns a chain of estate agents – but she's from that bra-burning generation of women who would see it as defeat to give up work just because they can afford to.

'Oh, you know. This and that. Pottering, mainly.'

She looks at me evenly and I wonder if she's going to ask me straight out. Instead she says: 'Tess, I would never pry into anything that isn't school business, but I hope you know that if there's anything I can do . . . if you want to talk anything through . . . I would be happy to help.'

I can't bear kindness when I am already upset; it always threatens to tip me right over the edge. I gulp. 'Yes, I know. Everything's fine, though.'

'Right. Well, if you change your mind . . .' She seems hurt and looks down at the pile of admin in front of her on the desk. I turn to go, and she says, 'Oh, Tess. I hope this is OK with you, but as you weren't in the staff meeting, I put you down for your usual role in the festivities. We ran through it all last night, but it's no different from last year.'

'Festivities?'

'Oh dearie me, you really aren't yourself at the moment, are you? What do we always do on the last day before summer half term? Like we have done every year since we arrived?'

Oh shit. Bugger. Bollocks. I open my mouth to speak but nothing comes out.

Roz looks at me curiously. 'After all, we'd never have thought of the Mock Wedding if it hadn't been for you.'

Summer term 1996 and I was gearing up for My Big Day, as the dinner ladies insisted on calling it. Being a C of E school, everyone glossed over the fact that I'd been living with Barney for eight years. As, in fact, had the appointments board when they interviewed me nine months earlier. They hadn't exactly been spoiled for choice with candidates for the job, after Old Oak primary school was named and shamed as one of the worst in the Midlands. The governors had made the headlines for all the wrong reasons, being singled out for special mention as the most meddlesome yet least effective the inspectors had ever encountered. Of course, the final report hadn't used those words exactly, but the meaning was crystal clear to anyone considering answering the ads for new teachers. I'd only applied after a call from Roz, who had been a mentor of mine during teacher training, and had been pressured by the county council to take over as head teacher. For me, the chance to be her deputy aged twenty-seven was too good to miss.

Roz and I arrived in the September and there was no doubt who was ruling the roost: Charlotte Mullins, aged ten, and her cronies. Maybe you'd expect the kids to take control in an inner-city comp, but this was rural Worcestershire. The village even had a thatched pub and was exactly the kind of chocolate-box commuter destination that parents dream of moving to. The job I'd done before was in a hardcore Birmingham primary, but those first months at Old Oak were a hundred times tougher. Our pupils were divided, with spoiled ex-city brats on one side, and rough, chip-on-their-shoulder country cousins on the other. Every breaktime was a battle.

But we worked at it, rallied the remaining demotivated teachers who'd been left to fend for themselves by the old head (he was always too busy drinking the thatched pub dry to take an interest in what was happening in the classroom) and used the kind of 'tough love' discipline that would have *Guardian* readers writing to their MPs. There was no physical violence, though I often had to shout so loud I was worried that the kids' eardrums might burst.

By the spring, though, we were winning. And somehow my wedding became the event of the century, something to look forward to. They all seemed far more excited than I was. Unlike most little girls, I'd never fantasised about bouquets and chiffon. With my tomboy figure and mousy hair I knew that the sole characteristic I'd have in common with the archetypal blushing bride would be the blushing. I hated the idea of everyone looking at me in some meringue frock. No, unlike most brides-to-be, I was looking forward to the bit afterwards: the marriage. A partnership. I was old-fashioned like that.

'Oooh, tell us the latest!' Every Monday morning I'd have the same question. With four out of seven staff female *and* unmarried, I was regarded with reverence. I'd done it, overcome the odds against a single female primary-school teacher ever tying the knot. Perhaps it gave them hope, too. I didn't have the heart to tell them I'd met Barney at university.

As soon as any arrangement was made – the car, the honeymoon, the knicker-and-bra set I'd chosen in the intimidating lingerie department of Rackhams department store – it would be discussed and debated by the staff with the kind of passion most people only showed for rises in interest rates or their favourite football team.

It was the same in the playground, though the subjects of the conversations varied according to the age of the gossipers. The little girls by the sandpit were talking about princesses wearing dresses made of lace and white satin. The final-year boys – still pissed off at being usurped as the most powerful people in the school since Roz and I arrived – hung out by the swings and discussed in Anglo-Saxon precisely what happens on a wedding night when a man and a lady decide that they love each other very much.

Roz called me in. 'Your bloody wedding has driven the school bonkers. I can't get any sense out of anyone, and we've got another eight weeks to go before the end of term, never mind the Big Day itself.'

'I know. Sorry,' I said, not meaning it.

'Yes, well, it's very inconsiderate of you to do the nuptial thing when we're at such a crucial stage in turning this place around.'

It took me a couple of seconds to realise she was joking, but I had to admit that behind the teasing, she had a point. We'd achieved a lot in two terms, but it wouldn't take much for the place to descend into chaos once again.

'I'm not sure what to suggest. I mean, short of inviting every one of the little buggers to the ceremony . . .' It was an amusing thought.

'That'd just make it worse. It's the build-up, like waiting for Christmas.'

'Unless . . .' I had a thought. 'Unless we hold the wedding here.'

'Well, Tess, much as I appreciate your dedication to this place, I can't see your husband-to-be being too chuffed at that idea.'

'No, what I mean is, we could have a ceremony here, like a wedding. I remember an RE module when I was training, where a school somewhere in Staffordshire did it. We dress all the kids up, choose a bride and groom, get the rev in to mock it up, have a party afterwards. They'd love it.'

Roz sat forward in her chair, revealing a bit too much of that crepey cleavage for my liking. 'A mock wedding? Yes, yes, I can see it now. Fits our new Christian ethos like a glove, plus we can get the local rag in, a bit of positive publicity for a change. Tess, that's genius. I knew I appointed you for a reason!'

And so it came to pass that the mock wedding of Miss Charlotte Mullins to Master Wayne Brown took place ten weeks before mine.

Roz was, as always, right about the publicity, and the governors decided that the nuptials should become a regular event. Most of all, the kids loved every moment. Someone told me the other day that Charlotte, who recently abandoned violin practice in favour of underage drinking, was overheard telling her pals down the King's Head that the mock wedding still counts as her best ever day at school.

But that's little consolation now, as I sit in the staffroom wondering whether I can get through the day, and knowing I only have myself to blame.

If we're trying so hard to prepare the kids for reality, I wonder if the governors would consider a mock divorce.

Chapter Six

We did our best to tame Charlotte, Wayne and their cronies when we arrived at Old Oak, but there's a limit to how much damage you can undo and we knew they'd probably stay decidedly feral. No, our guinea pigs were the babies, the kids who started as infants in the year or two after Roz and I arrived. We would judge our success or failure by how they turned out.

And, sitting at the far end of the front row of the congregation for the 'marriage' of Chloe Smith and Thomas Watson, I feel a sense of near-maternal pride. They've turned out pretty bloody well – not just those two, but the other Chloe, the two other Thomases, Laura, Stuart, the two Sams, Caroline, Ramon, Amy, Gemma, Emma, Bethany, Brendan, Hope, Florence, Whitney, Cameron, George, James and Joe.

Maureen, our dinner-lady-in-chief and the *real* powerhouse behind the school, is sitting to my right, as self-satisfied as any mother of the bride. She's left two of her staff to put the finishing touches to the wedding breakfast, while she takes what she sees as her rightful place in the hall.

'They grow up so quickly, so they do.' Sometimes I think Maureen plays up her Irish roots quite deliberately. Her accent is pure Brummie, her family moved to England two generations ago, but she uses the phrasing of *Father Ted*.

Years ago, when she took the job, Maureen had insisted on getting special dispensation from her parish priest to make sure God would be OK with her working in a heathen school. Now she runs the place from command control in the kitchen, supported by a mafia of women from her church. They all work part-time at her insistence, so they don't get ideas above their station or plot to take her throne.

'It doesn't seem like yesterday that my Roisin was a baby and now there she is with babies of her own,' she carries on the conversation, without worrying that I haven't responded.

Roisin is Maureen's only daughter, which makes me wonder whether for all of her piety, she practised what the Pope preaches when it comes to contraception. I'd never dream of asking her. Knowing people's business is her speciality, but it's a one-way street – Maureen guards her own privacy jealously, deflecting any questions with ever juicier bits of gossip. Every day I walk into school convinced that she'll come up to me in the canteen, place a plump, pink hand on my poor scandal-tainted shoulder and tell me how well I am coping, in a loud enough voice to make sure everyone knows. And her tone will make it pretty clear that she expected no more of me, because I not only lived 'over the brush' with Barney but am also not signed up to any religion, not even the Church of England.

Or else if it's not Maureen who gives the game away, it will be the slimy chairman of governors, who seems to have forgotten he was ever named and shamed as the worst in the country. He'll smile a patronising smile and tell me that 'It's alright, Tess. I know you might be worried about how the break-up will reflect on the school, but I can assure you that we don't think any the less of you for it, and we'll all do our best to avoid letting anyone know.'

So far, though, there's been nothing. Roz suspects something's up, but she's no idea what. I wonder how much longer I can keep up the pretence.

I look behind me at the rows of 'guests'. The Year Six kids who aren't in the procession as bridesmaids or best men have the prime view. They look so different in their party clothes; their mums have gone to town as they always do. It's the perfect excuse to force their offspring into something more appealing than their school uniform of maroon sweatshirt and grey trousers, and their home uniform of sportswear and trainers. The mothers can dress them one last time in children's clothes: frilly shirts and frilly frocks, sugar pinks and sickly peaches and baby blues. But it's too late, really. Maureen's right about children growing up faster: they look awkward, overgrown, especially the girls. Some are already wearing bras and their breasts are squashed under the tight satin bridesmaids' bodices which allow no room for manoeuvre.

Our token male teacher, Kevin Williams, as fresh-faced as they come, goes over to the groom and to his mate, Brendan, and nudges them towards the 'altar' where our vicar is waiting. The rev, as he is universally known, is at the trendier end of the C of E spectrum, much to Maureen's disgust, but he knows when to make a meal of tradition. He nods gravely at the boys: marriage, as he told the whole school a few minutes ago, is not to be taken lightly.

I feel someone tug at my sleeve, and I know before turning round who it is. Craig. His smell is unique to him: a top note of sweat, a base note of damp clothes and a lingering scent of institutional soap. Craig is nine, but he's already wearing clothes for thirteen- to fourteen-year-olds. He's fat but he's definitely not jolly; every attempt he's ever made to reach out to the kids in the class has been rejected. The smell doesn't help and he comes in early every morning to try to wash it away. It breaks my heart to know how hard he tries to seem normal. Every now and again he'll nearly succeed, almost break through the cruel indifference of the other kids, but there's always something separating them. I try really hard to encourage them to include him, but Craig's problems are more fundamental than his weight.

I have a real dilemma with Craig. I can't see how me making friends with him will help him in the long term. Being teacher's pet is hardly going to endear him to his classmates. But I think he senses my weakness, so he'll try over and over to attract my attention, and I will fight the urge to sit him on my knee, talk to him, try to make things better. Apart from anything else, I'd do my back in. Old Oak is his fifth school in as many years and I have to keep my distance, if only to protect him when his mother decides to move him yet again because 'he really isn't thriving'.

But today I can't turn him away. This will be his first mock wedding, and he needs someone. Maybe I do too.

'You'll have to keep very still,' I whisper, gesturing towards the empty space to my left. He grins at his rare stroke of luck, and nestles next to my knees, though there's barely enough room and he can't be comfortable. The hair on his head is greasy brown, arranged in clumps on either side of a dog's leg parting. He makes me want to cry.

Maureen leans over. 'Working mother,' she spits. We've all met Craig's mum and she hasn't done much to win herself friends. Her opening gambit – 'I would have sued Craig's last school if I'd thought they had the money in the budget to make it worth my while' – was ill-judged to say the least. The relief the other staff felt when they realised he was nine and so belonged in *my* class was a clear sign that we'd all registered trouble on our radars. I made my assessment immediately: Craig's mother, who is pretty high up as some kind of manager in local government, is good at blaming other people, without ever seeing the need to look at her own behaviour. She is large and bullying and poor Craig has inherited her weight without her forceful personality. It is clear that to get involved with him would be extremely unwise.

I look up to see Roz at the piano, peering over her shoulder through the glass doors into the hall to check the bride is poised for her grand entrance. I love the way Roz combines all the traditional skills of a primary head – piano-playing, poster-painting and folk-dancing – with an accountant's head for figures, a terrorist's determination, and diplomatic abilities worthy of Kofi Annan. Not to mention Pamela Anderson's cleavage.

Her tanned fingers hover just above the keyboard and she catches my eye. She smiles as she plays the first notes of the wedding march and I have to gulp back tears. I peer down and Craig's oily scalp fills my field of vision. That makes me choke more, and I try to clear my throat.

Maureen pats my knee. 'Just you wait until it's one of your own.'

The music fills the hall and the doors creak open. Everyone but me turns round to look at the procession. I don't dare make any sudden moves because it would upset the balance of water in my eyes, and just keep staring ahead, willing the tears to be reabsorbed into my body or to evaporate in the warmth of the room. If the kids were from my class, maybe people would be fooled into thinking I'm crying over the 'wedding', though even that is doubtful. In all my years at Old Oak, I've never cried about anything, even when one of Charlotte's cronies thrust a sharpened pencil into my eye.

As I sense a white, gauzy blur drawing alongside our row, I move my head as slowly as I can towards the aisle. Bugger. A teardrop slips from the outside edge of my left eye.

Chloe's mum has done her proud. Her sandy hair bounces in ringlets against her shoulders, which are covered in net-curtain lace. It must scratch like crazy but it looks effective. She's not the kind of girl who's already fighting to wear make-up, which makes the addition of a little dab of frosted pink lipstick more striking. With the exception of the first year, when Charlotte was chosen to keep the peace, we always pick the bride from the group of girls who could do with a bit of a boost. It's not like Florence or Hope need any encouragement to be the centre of attention, whereas Chloe's ordinariness means she's had precious few 'moments' during her school career. It's tough for kids like her when they go to secondary school – they can be swallowed up whole in the system – but at least she'll have a great memory of the day she was special.

The procession stops at the 'altar'. Chloe blushes, sensing the unusual level of attention she's getting, but Thomas is staring straight ahead. There is never a fight for the role of groom, but he is a sweet boy, and we know he won't spoil the ceremony by making jokes or blowing raspberries at the crucial moment.

Roz stops playing and it takes a few seconds for the reverb from the piano to fade away. The rev looks thoughtfully at his congregation. 'Dearly beloved,' he begins, his plodding delivery enhanced by the acoustics of the hall, 'we are gathered here today . . .'

Barney and I had the time of our lives on our wedding day, though for the strangest of reasons. It seemed so formal and so unlike us, and when I took my place next to him in the church, it was all we could do not to laugh. The more I tried not to look at him, the worse it got, like those moments in the back of the classroom when you're thirteen and the teacher has said something unintentionally rude, and you feel like you're going to burst if you don't giggle. It was only when the vicar – a man I'd only met once before, at the rehearsal – got to the part about 'till death us do part' that we managed to bring our hysteria under control. I remember feeling so calm, then, hearing those words. The certainty and the eternity felt totally right for the two of us. Despite everything our friends thought we'd given up – the flirting, the thrill of the chase, the one-night stands – we both knew there was no sense jumping through sexual hoops with other people to prove what we knew: that we were meant to be together.

'I . . . Thomas, take you, Chloe, to be my wife,' says Thomas, so quietly that only the front row can hear him without straining. Which, I suppose, is exactly what he intends. Perhaps it's always this way with boys. They'll go along for the ride, but it's not of their choosing. Except for Barney: he had seemed keener than me to acquire a spouse.

The rev leads Thomas through the vows, before switching his attentions to Chloe. She is much less hesitant as she repeats his words, loudly and with frightening sincerity. Like so many women before her, Chloe is in love with the idea of marriage. The other half of the partnership is scarcely relevant to her Big Day.

'Chloe and Thomas. If this were really your wedding, then at this point I'd be pronouncing you man and wife, and inviting you, Thomas, to kiss your bride.'

'Uuuugh.' Thomas suddenly finds his voice and Chloe flushes again, though she must realise it's nothing personal. Yep, we've done a good job with our babies; they are still prepared to be childish and immature, to be repulsed by rather than attracted to the opposite sex.

'Don't worry, Thomas, kissing isn't compulsory. But it is in marriage. And I'll tell you something even more important than kissing. Can you guess what? It's love.'

Oh God. Happy-clappy wisdom from the rev is all I need. I wish I'd let my hair grow, because I might be able to put my fingers in my ears without anyone else noticing.

'Now most of you children are too young to remember the

song. And so, probably, are your parents. But the Beatles were talking an awful lot of sense when they said that money can't buy you love. That's why all the finery and all the dresses and the cakes and the bridesmaids that you might think are the most important thing at a wedding are nothing of the sort. They're just a red herring.'

Craig turns his head to look up at me. 'Red herring?' he whispers. 'Why's he talking about fish?' It would be fair to say that our lovely rev is not as up-to-date as he might be when it comes to communicating with the Younger Generation.

'Money alone won't bring you happiness, or make a marriage work. It's hard if you're poor, of course, but a couple who want to be together can survive being broke for a while. What they won't survive is a marriage without love.'

Craig is still looking at me, as if I can interpret the meaning for him. I suspect his home life is somewhat lacking in love. Or maybe it's just that he's spotted the tears I can feel building up again in my eyes, and is intrigued to see what happens next.

'That's another thing people forget,' says the rev, and I can tell he is really getting into his stride. 'They think about the wedding, plan every minute of the day but they forget that what they should really be planning for is the rest of it. If the wedding is the party, then the marriage is the hangover . . .'

Despite myself, I feel a chuckle in my throat, but as it rises up through my nose, it turns into something else. The tears I've been trying to gulp back gush out dramatically with the release of pressure, and one drop falls onto Craig's confused face. The genie is out of the bottle, and as the rev's words disappear under the buzzy ringing that fills my head, I start to whimper.

Poor Craig. Of all the adults in his funny, dirty little world, seeing me break down must be the most shocking thing that could happen. I can't imagine his mother ever cries; her well-made-up skin is thicker than most. But after an initial look of confusion, Craig reaches out a fat, grubby hand and tentatively places it on mine. I hold it, gripping quite tightly, unsure if I am comforting him, or he is comforting me.

Around me the scene shifts as everyone stands up to sing, the squeaking of metal chair legs against parquet floors finally cutting through the white noise in my head. Roz's assertive piano-playing rises above the tumult, and I stand too, my head bent over in the vain hope that no one will see the tears that are now running freely down my cheeks. I let them go, and can feel them soaking through my blouse, but I'm scared that wiping them away will draw more attention to myself.

All things bright and beautiful, all creatures great and small . . .

All things wise and wonderful, the Lord God made them all.

When Maureen takes my elbow and leads me out, Craig still clinging to my hand, I feel like a child again. The singing falters as eighty pairs of eyes follow us leaving the hall. Poor Chloe. Even today she's got competition for her role as the centre of attention.

Craig, Maureen and I enter Roz's office, the strangest trinity. I slump onto the sofa, which is covered with soft toys, for those moments when small children need comforting after a fall in the playground or a wasp sting.

'Shall I get rid of the boy?' she whispers, raising her eyebrows at our untidy sidekick. I shake my head. A tray of tea and biscuits arrives, courtesy of one of the canteen ladies. Maureen pours me a cup, adding four teaspoons of sugar. I can hear dull piano chords and reed-thin children's voices vibrating through the door.

He made their glowing colours, he made their tiny wings . . .

'It's your other half, isn't it?' Maureen tuts, wipes her brow. 'They will become bored so quickly. That's why Rome is right not to hold with divorce. I know it seems old-fashioned, but the rules are there for a reason: you need a father and a mother in a family, and if there's no reason for them to stay married, then men will stray. It's what they do . . .' She looks at Craig, and seems to be struggling with the idea of him ever becoming somebody's husband. 'Even this one. He'll be no different if he thinks he can get away with it some day.'

If I felt in control of my speech, I might tell her that Craig is proof that the opposite can apply, that mothers can be as inept and disloyal as fathers, that blaming one gender is too easy. But there is something comforting about her 'all men are bastards' worldview. To try to make up for the slights on his sex, I grip Craig's hand a little harder. He stares into my eyes, and it reminds me of the way my computer at home takes so long to do anything, the faint green light on the hard drive flickering and blinking as it tries to raise the brainpower to understand what it's been asked to do.

'I've known you long enough, Tess – um,' she shoots Craig a nervous look, aware that he should never, ever know a teacher's first name or the whole order of the school risks a rapid descent into anarchy, 'Mrs Leonard, to know that you don't give up easily. I think that however hard it might be, however much you might hate whatever floozy has been after your husband, that you should be fighting for him. You will only regret it if you don't. A marriage is worth fighting for, whatever you believe in.' She sits back and takes a sip of her own tea, pleased with her sermon.

I hate to shatter her illusions – after all, twenty-four hours ago, I was as hopeful as she is. But I know there's no point in trying to keep the secret any more. And if I tell her now, the news will spread faster than if I'd taken out an ad in the *Birmingham Post*. 'Even if the floozy is pregnant?'

'Ooo.' She makes a noise like she's been punched, then glances quickly at Craig. I half expect her to cover his ears, but my words don't seem to have registered with him.

Outside, the party is breaking up. Through Roz's window, I can see the children gathering in the playground. The dinner ladies are about to distribute the wedding cake – normally it's my job to make sure everyone gets a piece – and all the Year Six girls are dancing and twirling around, unused to wearing long skirts.

Maureen's shoulders slump in defeat. 'I don't suppose you'd consider taking the baby as your own?'

There is something charming about the naivety of her suggestion, but I shake my head.

'No, no, I don't think to tell the truth that I could do that either.' She takes another sip of tea, mulling something over. 'Craig, child, we're about to run out of milk; would you go to fetch some more from Mrs Fitzpatrick in the kitchen?'

We still have a full jug of milk, of course, but despite his obtuseness, Craig knows when to make himself scarce. He gives my hand an extra squeeze, then sidles away like a crab. A very fat crab.

Maureen closes the door behind him. 'I don't hold with divorce, as you know, Tess, but in your situation, I can't see what other course of action you have. I don't believe it's always a sin.'

I smile weakly, as I can see that she does mean this to be reassuring.

'You're still young and . . . well, you know. You're a catch for an older man who doesn't mind too much about the whole scandal thing, who's maybe looking for a professional woman with her own life.' She frowns, searching for convincing evidence of something she clearly doesn't believe for one minute. 'Perhaps a nice divorcee with some children of his own. They do exist; one of my second cousins found one who had been treated shamefully by his wife, and now he's a perfect gentleman to Diane, honestly. And very sprightly, considering the age difference.'

I don't know whether to laugh or cry. The prospect of scouring the playgrounds or singles clubs for some past-it Baron von Trapp looking for a free nanny is, if Maureen's to be believed, about the best I can hope for.

'And I'd take your man for everything you can get. Leave enough for the child, of course, but apart from that, he deserves what he gets. Make sure—'

Craig reappears through the door, to my relief and Maureen's irritation. She stands up. 'It's early days, Mrs Leonard. But you must come and see me any time you'd like some advice. I've seen it all in my time.'

She moves towards me as if she's going to kiss me, but then thinks better of it. I wonder if that's why Barney left me. I am the most self-contained person I know, someone whose personal space might as well be staked out with barbed wire.

She closes the door behind her, and I pat the sofa, urging Craig to join me. He sits quietly next to me, his bottom taking up as much space as an adult's.

'I bet you think grown-ups are funny sometimes, Craig,' I say.

He doesn't reply, but takes my hand again and starts to circle around the centre with his oily finger. I can't imagine any other child I've taught doing this, but sometimes he seems quite fearless, because he doesn't see things the way the rest of us do.

I find it strangely soothing. The careful little circles remind me of two things: of that game, round and round the garden. And of the time after I met Barney when we would spend hours on end playing with each other's hands, as though they were the most fascinating things in the whole world. We could waste entire evenings on each other's hands . . .

The crowds in the playground thin out, then there is no one there at all. Roz comes in.

'How are you two getting along?'

Her wallclock says four o'clock. I realise I've stopped crying. 'I'm all right, but what about Craig?'

'I'll call his mum.'

Another half hour passes before a pale, chunky woman arrives, carrying a jumbo bag of crisps. Craig's mum's cleaner has been despatched to pick him up, because Craig's mum has to stay later than usual in the office. I wish I felt some kind of sympathy – isn't she doing her bit for feminism? But instead I just look at him and wonder if I could adopt him. And put him on a diet.

After he's gone, Roz takes his place on the sofa, though she's much smaller. 'I feel quite bad that I haven't tried harder to help, Tess.'

I'm surrounded by people feeling guilty. 'It's OK. I've always been able to manage things on my own.'

'Maybe you should realise that there's no shame in asking for help.'

So everyone keeps telling me. 'Did you say anything to the kids?'

She smiles. 'They forgot about it once the wedding cake appeared. And they'll not be able to remember a thing by the time they come back after half term.'

Half term. Nine days stretch in front of me like a life sentence. Roz reads my mind. 'Tess, I know the thought of coming to stay with us and the dogs is probably not the most tempting offer you've had in a while. But if you want to get away, there's all the countryside you need, the dogs are good listeners and they know where the pub is . . .'

Yet again, I feel the acid of tears rise through my throat, and try to think of unemotional things. The working of a four-stroke petrol engine. The declension of French verbs. Anything to stop myself crying.

'Thanks, Roz. I will think about it. I reckon what I really need is more sleep.'

I submit to her hug for the shortest period I can get away with, then manage to drive a mile and a half to the end of a cul-de-sac before I break down. I cry until the snot covers my face – there are no tissues in the car, so I use my hands instead and the tears loosen my wedding ring.

I take it off. The only possible benefit of humiliating myself in front of the entire school is that now I can leave it off for good. I don't have to pretend to be happy – or married – any more.

Lesson Two

The Stocktake

William hummed as he set up the ghetto-blaster in the corner of the hall.

You make me feel like a natural woman . . .

The electrical socket wiggled in the wall as he plugged in the ancient Toshiba. Even calling it a ghetto-blaster probably dated him. And like him, it had seen better days.

He always looked forward to the second session. Time to get down to business, to start revealing the secrets that made it all worthwhile. Sure, the process itself was rewarding, seeing these damaged people begin to heal and make the first steps towards their new lives, but what he really loved were the stories: life's rich pattern, like a tapestry unravelling in front of him. Or a jumper. It was more like a big Fair Isle sweater attacked by a litter of kittens. Or tigers. A solid thing pulled apart to reveal a long thread. Maybe the class was the knitting needles to help people pull themselves back together again, a little more dishevelled but more interesting this time around. Or maybe he, William, was the pattern . . .

Knit one, purl one. Cast off the old life, cast on with the new . . .

He was off again. Sometimes his homespun wisdom or wild analogies confused people, but a few unusual metaphors were never going to do anyone any harm. That's why he still thought the Yanks were wrong to dump him as an Emotions Recovery Inc. affiliate. But by then he'd reaped the benefits from their supervision, not just learning how to help, but also helping himself. It had given him a purpose, after so many years without one. William the course leader was a very different man from the one who'd wasted a decade or more seeking revenge on the entire female population for a betrayal by just one of their number.

And the difference had come from applying those trite American rules to his own life. Life is a journey. Ride through the potholes. Enjoy the view. Share it with your fellow passengers, realise they may get off at different stations and remember in the end only you can choose your destination. And William's own particular favourite homily: loss is more.

A mousy head peered through the door. The Waif. What was her name? He had to use memory tricks these days, ones he'd read in a book he'd ordered from a Sunday newspaper, *101 ways to improve your recall*. But the trouble with suffering was it always looked so similar, course after course. How could he possibly remember all their names? The questionnaire they all filled in helped a bit, gave him facts to focus on, but every time he started running a new course, it got harder.

His favourite method usually involved inventing strange rhymes that associated the person's name with a truly memorable mental picture. He stared at her, trying to summon up the image he'd created, then closed his eyes as it became clearer. Her delicate frame became swamped in a mass of rubbish, and in William's mind, her hair became tangled and her cheeks smudged like a street urchin.

Untidy . . . grimy . . . what the hell was the word?

She looked paler than she had last week and being the first to arrive was a sure sign, in William's experience, that she was in dire need of help. That things were going to get worse before they got better for her.

'Hello, my dear.' It was one of the few consolations of age, being able to get away with terms of endearment that just a couple of years before would have suggested to the recipient that William was a dirty old man.

'Hi.' She peered around the hall, registered that there was no one else there and instinctively looked back to the entrance.

Just as he'd given up hope, it came to him. Mess! That was it: mess rhymes with Tess! Better late than never. Instant recall was, after all, too much to expect at fifty-nine.

'Why don't you help yourself to a sneaky coffee, Tess? I won't charge you extra.'

She smiled so briefly he wasn't sure if he'd imagined it. Her shoulders were slumped and she shuffled towards the kitchenette area with less energy than most of the over-eighties who came for the weekly tea dance.

Something had happened to her since that last session, William knew that much. He had to bite his lip to stop himself asking. Sometimes he thought that his almost overwhelming desire to know people's secrets would find a physical manifestation, perhaps in a John Cleese-style funny walk. It was like that syndrome that made people swear in supermarkets, Tourette's. In William's case, the tic was wanting to fire off questions: 'How do you feel? What made you feel that way? Why do you think it affected you so badly?'

The door squeaked again and in bounced Carol-Ann. He had no trouble remembering her name. This time her lips were more cerise than scarlet and he realised she'd done it to match her outfit.

'Hi there, rev,' she shouted. He wasn't going to correct her. People filled in the gaps for themselves. They were coming to a church hall, so many made the most obvious assumption – that he *should* be a man of God. Well, he did believe, up to a point; it was one of the reasons he'd been given the job as caretaker at St Gabriel's. As well as the fact that he was ridiculously over-qualified, of course. The church interview panel hadn't liked to ask why a successful builder wanted to leave his home and his business and move thirty miles to look after a decrepit hall. Clearly, he was a gift from God and, like the Foreign Legion, the Church didn't need to pry into a man's reasons for joining up.

'Oh, call me William,' he said. 'Lovely to see you again.' He already knew she was going to create havoc with his routines, but he thought there was no harm keeping friendly with a woman who planned one day to open her own brewery. And she was the kind of person you couldn't help liking, the kind of person Tess would benefit from talking to right now. 'The kettle's on, I think.' He nodded in the direction of the kettle.

She walked confidently to the other end of the hall, and he

watched her approach Tess, exchange a few words, and then open her arms for an all-encompassing hug. Tess seemed to surrender reluctantly at first, but then she stopped fighting it and stayed very still as Carol-Ann stroked her shoulder.

The rest of the group were piling in now, even that snotty Ponytail woman who'd been late last time. He tried to summon up the image that would remind him of her name. In place of the ponytail, he conjured up a plait as thick as rope. Plait. What rhymed with plait ... Hat, maybe, for Harriet? No, she definitely wasn't a Harriet. Bat ... Mat ... Nat? Natalie. That was it. She looked a little more subdued this week, though still immaculately turned out in her pastel tracksuit thing.

Ah, this was easier. The Hippy. William instantly remembered the image of this hippy with two AA batteries in his ears. AA-ron. Aaron had made an effort too, with a slightly tidier pair of jeans and a dark bruise-blue shirt that was fresh from the packet, judging from the creases. It looked wrong on him, like a red tartan pet jacket on a fox. William felt more certain than ever that his presence was going to liven things up. Women were always the mainstay of the courses, but the men dictated the tone. A kind, victimised man would restore the faith of the others in the opposite sex; a man full of anger and resentment at the entire female population cemented the friendships of the women into a wall of solidarity.

William couldn't predict the effect Aaron would have – it all depended whether any of the women decided to sleep with him. Aaron was hovering at the side of the hall now, pretending to text on his phone, but he kept sneaking looks around the space. He was casing the joint, not for what he could steal, but for who he could pull. William didn't blame him. Any man who'd been betrayed – and he'd never known a man come to the sessions if he was the betrayer – had an instinctive need to get his leg over again as soon as possible. What was intriguing about Aaron was that he was easily good-looking enough to find any number of one-night stands in the bars on Broad Street. There was no need to prey on vulnerable women when there'd be a queue of pretty but gullible ones quite happy to boost his ego. Or suck his dick.

Natalie had taken her seat and was rubbing her ring finger

absently. There was something about the movement, and the occasional guilty look back over her shoulder, that suddenly convinced William she was still very much married. Her rings were probably hidden away in that expensive handbag of hers. Even the handbag irritated him – it was one of the ones by the French designer who makes suitcases, brown and beige with lots of strange symbols printed on it. You could buy them down the market for a fiver, but glossy gleaming Ponytail would have the real McCoy, he was certain.

'Right, let's get going!' William clapped his hands and the sound echoed in the hall. Carol-Ann and Tess returned from the kitchenette, walking close together and in time, having bonded in that amazingly fast way only women can. They sat side by side and Aaron quickly moved to take the seat to Tess's left. Now that was a surprise development . . . time to have some fun, William thought.

'Welcome back. It's always a relief to see I haven't put anyone off. Before we go any further, has everyone done their homework?'

Tess and Aaron looked down. 'And I'm not having any excuses like "the dog ate it" because frankly all I was looking for was three song titles. So if you didn't write them down, I'm sure you can remember them. What I'd like you to do is work in pairs and just tell each other about those songs, why you've chosen them, and in particular what the song for your future life represents for you. And to make it easier for anyone who's been lazy, you can always let the other person go first, while you make some up on the spur of the moment. Actually, sometimes it works better that way. The first thing that comes into your head is often the most revealing.'

He paused, and just as everyone started looking round for their partners from the previous week, he clapped his hands again. 'Oh, sorry, I forgot to say. You have to change round. Don't work with the same person as last week: we mustn't get cliquey. Right. You've got ten minutes each, and then we'll come back together for a bit of a feedback session.'

Tess stared at her lap as though she was about to cry and William almost felt guilty, but he knew it was for her own good.

Carol-Ann patted her hand sympathetically, then pointed towards Aaron. Tess nodded, stood up and allowed him to take her chair and move it to the corner of the room. She followed him and raised a listless eyebrow when he bowed with a little flourish, offering her the chair. Even when Aaron carried his own chair over, he walked jauntily, for the benefit of Tess and every other woman who might be watching.

William had to admit that the guy had class. Maybe his relentless flirting would do Waif some good.

Around the room, the conversations began, tentative at first, as the four couples got to know each other. Carol-Ann with Tim the Supermarket Guy – would he survive the conversation unscathed? Natalie had teamed up with Rani, and Stringfellow Malcolm was talking *at* the Pretty Blonde. What the hell was her name? William cursed himself for forgetting the name of the most attractive woman there.

Malcolm spoke loudly, and even from the other side of the hall, William caught phrases like 'women today expect too much' and 'she'll be back when she realises what she's done'. He waved his fists around, invading the Pretty Blonde's space without seeming to realise, like a frustrated two-year-old. She nodded politely, as if she was used to aggressive men haranguing her for things that weren't her fault. Perhaps she worked for the Child Support Agency. But she obviously needed some help.

'How are we getting on?' William squatted alongside Pretty Blonde and was stunned by a frightening wave of halitosis from Malcolm's open mouth. He felt new admiration for this woman, calm and unflinching in the face of such unpleasantness. 'I hope he isn't taking over, my dear.' He wished he could remember her name.

'No, no,' she said. 'Malcolm's going first, and because he's only chosen one song for the past, present and future, he was telling me a bit more about himself.'

She really was exceptionally pretty and the evening sunlight was streaming through the windows, highlighting the downy hair that softened the wonderful angle of her cheekbones. She could be a model. William had to fight the instinct to reach out and stroke her. Instead, he reluctantly turned back towards

Malcolm and his poison breath. 'One song, old boy? That's cheating.'

'I would have thought the point of the exercise is to assist us in identifying our objectives? So mine are the same as they've always been.' He spoke in a deadpan tone, like a voice synthesiser.

'Hmm, well, I suppose that's fair enough. So what's the song?'

'"The Way We Were". Barbra Streisand.' Malcolm folded his arms. 'We were very happy, my wife and I. Traditional, perhaps old-fashioned, but there is nothing wrong with that in my view. You choose your life partner to fit your expectations and ours were the same. It was her that changed.'

Poor Malcolm's wife, thought William. No wonder her expectations changed, if the alternative was living with halitosis and attitudes that belonged in the last century but one. And he couldn't even come up with an original song – 'The Way We Were' cropped up at least once in every group. 'I think it's very natural to want to return to a time when things seemed to be going well. That's what's so wistful about that song. Everyone loves nostalgia, but there comes a time when you need to move on. That's why many people come to the course. Does that make sense to you?'

Malcolm stuck out his bottom lip. 'Not really. I mean, I'm not very happy with the way things are now, so it seems practical to do something about it. That's why I'm here. But she changed, not me.'

Softly, softly, William thought. 'That's the hardest part of accepting something's over – accepting that the other person can do something you really don't want. As I explained last week, there are five recognised stages of grieving, and denial is the first of those. I think that's where you are now, Malcolm, and I'm afraid there's no way of avoiding the other steps before you finally reach acceptance—'

'I have no intention of accepting it, because it isn't over. She may think it is but she's not seriously going to divorce me. Not after twenty years. This is just her way of getting whatever it is out of her system. And the reason I'm here is frankly not for your mumbo-jumbo pop psychology, but because I thought you might know some of the legal ins and outs, and it's cheaper than a bloody solicitor.'

'Right. OK.' It wasn't the first outburst William had been subjected to, and it wouldn't be the last. He found it refreshing when people said what they really thought and he could see from the crinkling around Pretty Blonde's eyes – a rather beautiful pale-blue pair – that she was trying not to laugh. He winked conspiratorially, and then turned back to Malcolm. 'I try not to make any kind of judgement about anyone's motivations, old boy. I hope you might be surprised by what you gain from the mumbo-jumbo, if you give it half a chance, because my legal knowledge is certainly not going to impress you. But then again, you might get some good advice from the others here who've been through their divorces. All I'd ask is that you try not to let your scepticism affect everyone else.'

Malcolm was pouting again. 'Fine.'

William turned to Pretty Blonde and gave her his most self-deprecating smile. 'So . . . are you immune to my mumbo-jumbo as well, my dear?'

'No, but I'm probably resistant to your charms.' Her eyes were still laughing. 'You can't remember my name, can you?'

William shrugged. Shrewd as well as attractive. He could probably forgive the cynicism in the light of her other qualities. 'No. You're right. I'm a hopeless case. If I can guess one of your songs, would you tell me? Three guesses, for an old man.'

'Go ahead and try.'

He had an unfair advantage, in some ways. With a dozen of these courses under his belt now, he had a thorough knowledge of the songs the broken-hearted used to lift their spirits or to accompany a drowning of sorrows. He'd thought more than once that he could sell his expertise to Telstar or another one of those compilation labels, so they could make *Now That's What I Call Divorce – the Album* or perhaps *Love Don't Live Here Any More – Twenty Songs to Slash Your Wrists To*.

'OK, let me try to think.' He looked at her, pretending to mind-read, but actually enjoying the view. She would like to think of herself as subtle, smarter than average, which ought to rule out the most obvious tunes. Yet there was always the trend for irony; young people liked to embrace the cheesy and the retro. '"I Will Survive"?'

She giggled. 'What makes you think I'd ever choose something so obvious? That's one life lost.'

William laughed back. So she didn't do irony. 'Right . . . then you're not going to be doing Phil Collins either, really, are you? It's a shame; I'd had you down as the sort to go for "If Leaving Me is Easy" or even "Separate Lives".'

'That ought to be your guesses gone. Stop fishing.'

'You're tough, you are. If I don't get it next time, I'd like a clue. But let's see . . . "Nothing Compares to U"?'

She shook her head and her short blonde hair swished. William thought he could hear it, like silk rubbing together. 'It's a decent song, but it's not how I feel. This is like candy from a baby. You want a clue? OK. A woman singer, not as straightforward as she seemed.'

Dusty. It had to be. William had to admit that La Springfield had cropped up before, but working out which song it might be was not easy. 'I Just Don't Know What to Do With Myself' . . . he couldn't see Pretty One ever feeling unsure. 'You Don't Have to Say You Love Me'? He reckoned most of those submissive, walk-all-over-me tunes would be anathema to her.

'I've got it. It's your past life song, and it's "The Look of Love". Dusty at her most powerful.'

He'd got her. She looked surprised, annoyed, uncertain. 'Well done. You're frighteningly good at this. I'm Jo.' She held out her hand, and returned his handshake firmly.

'And your other songs?'

'Can I guess now?' asked Malcolm. William had forgotten he was there.

'I don't think you've got a hope of guessing,' Jo said. 'Right now I'm mid-Morrissey stage with "Heaven Knows I'm Miserable Now".' She grinned. 'Well, at least I'm honest. And as for the future, what else would it be but "Get Happy"?'

'I like your style,' said William. The truth was, he'd have liked it just as much if she'd chosen songs by Ken Dodd and Chas 'n' Dave. 'Maybe you'd like to explain why you've selected those when we come together again.'

He stood up and surveyed the rest of the hall. Natalie and Rani were chatting animatedly, mirroring each other's movements and interrupting each other, the way people do when they've known each other for years. Carol-Ann had taken Tim's hand and was stroking it maternally as he talked. Even Tess looked a little less defeated as Aaron mimed playing the guitar, his legs wide open, his long fringe falling into his dark eyes. It was incredible how such a diverse group of people could bond over shared experiences: music, solicitors, divorce.

'OK, guys. A few more minutes of chat, then we'll come back together and *then* we'll get going on the real business of the evening. The stocktake.'

Pens, paper, clipboards. As he handed out the tools of the self-help trade, William saw the expressions change from relaxed smiles to irritated frowns. Which was as it should be. They were starting to get too comfortable, imagining they were here for a glorified gossip. But there was work to be done.

'Imagine running a shop. A supermarket, say . . . you run a supermarket, don't you . . . um?' William grappled for the name, frustrated that he'd forgotten it again so quickly. 'Go on, introduce yourself to anyone you haven't met.'

Supermarket Guy stood up hesitantly. He was wearing a suit, shiny with age, that clung to his skinny frame. This time at least he'd remembered to take off his name badge. 'Yes, hi. I'm Tim.' He gave a pathetic little wave.

'Tim. What are the key things about running a supermarket?'

Tim's face froze and a little sweat appeared instantly on his temples, even though the hall was on the cold side tonight. 'Um . . . customer focus. Good service – our mother-and-baby parking spaces are always well-used and thanks to our team in the car park, it's also policed pretty well, unlike other stores I could mention. And I'm a stickler for well-maintained trolleys; you don't want somebody turning up at the customer desk with laddered tights because they've ripped them on a jagged bit of metal—'

William held up his hand. 'Quite, Tim. But I suppose I'm thinking of something more fundamental. Like . . . stock?'

Tim's eyes opened wide, like a schoolboy given the answer to a maths problem he'd been struggling with. Then his face fell. This was a man used to disappointment. 'Stock. Yes. Sorry. Obvious really – why would anyone come to a supermarket without stock?' Tim was tall but seemed ashamed of his height, so his posture was stooped. William could imagine the checkout girls running rings around him.

'Exactly, Tim. Equally you don't want so much stock that your storage areas are packed out and your fresh produce goes rotten, do you?' Tim shook his head. 'And you also need to be ready for the unexpected. For excellent weather, say, so you can sell gallons of ice-cream. It's OK, you can sit down now. You see, as Tim's just explained, running a shop is a balancing act. And the way you can manage that balancing act is through the stocktake.'

He saw Jo smiling a superior smile. He had to admit it wasn't the best of his metaphors, but he liked to relate what they were doing to real-life situations. He pressed on. 'It's the same for all of you. Separation has come unexpectedly for most, so like the canny store manager, you need to decide what your needs are likely to be in future. Where reserves are running low. Can anyone suggest anything that might be running low?'

He looked around. No one said a thing. Then a raised hand. 'Yes, Jo?' At least he could remember her name, though he was unsure what she was going to say.

'Sun-tan lotion?' She looked deadly serious, except for her eyes, which challenged him to laugh. 'After that excellent weather you were talking about.'

'I was thinking more of emotional stock. Self-confidence, for example. That tends to plummet when divorce rears its ugly head. Appetite – for life, for food, for pretty much everything that gives us pleasure, including sex. Faith tends to be in short supply as well – faith in God or in the future or in yourself.'

The words resonated around the hall and there were a few tentative nods of recognition, from Tess and Tim and Rani. 'Of course, it's not just losses. You're likely to have an oversupply of other feelings: guilt, hurt, anger, to name just a few. What I am saying is, it's all totally normal. Whatever you're feeling is OK, but it can be overwhelming. That's where the stocktake comes in.'

William reached into his briefcase for the pages he'd photo-copied at the library earlier that afternoon. The costs for the course mounted up but he couldn't bring himself to charge more to compensate. Who'd have thought he'd end up such a big softie?

He passed the small pile to Jo. 'Sometimes it seems impossible to see the wood for the trees, and it helps to write it down. You'll see the page is split in four, for emotional surpluses and deficits, but also for the practical ones. Cash is almost always in short supply when people break up. You might find, too, that there's too much space in your house, a spouse-shaped hole that makes you feel completely hollow. Write it all down. Talk to the person you're working with as you come up with new ideas. I promise – money-back guarantee, just like in Tim's supermarket – that it'll help. And if that doesn't convince you, then look at it this way: it's a record of where you are now, warts and all, and in six more weeks, you'll be amazed at how far you've travelled.'

Chapter Seven

First impressions can be so wrong. When Aaron walked into that first meeting, his hair and his stubble and his swagger told me three things about him. Number one, he was arrogant as hell. Number two, he probably smelled the way he looked – seedy. Number three, he was the total opposite of my type.

But then we happened to be sitting next to each other in tonight's session and things changed. It had been such a gargantuan effort to get myself to the course at all; I hadn't left the house since arriving home on Friday night and would have been quite happy never to go outdoors again. It was only Mel threatening to drag me to the Survivors' Course like a truant being delivered to school that made me get my act together.

Carol-Ann knew something was wrong as soon as she walked into the hall. She found me by the kettle, where I was stirring the same cup of coffee over and over again, looking at the pattern the movement of the spoon created. 'You look bloody rough, love, if you don't mind me saying so.' What a way with words she's got. I suppose if you've been through as much as she has then you're entitled to a colourful use of language. I'd be a gibbering wreck.

It was all I could do not to gibber anyway. I managed to say, 'My ex's girlfriend is pregnant,' before the lump in my throat threatened to cut off my air supply.

'Oh, love. What a bugger. You'd think the sod could have waited a decent interval before knocking her up. It won't last between them, I'll tell you that for nothing. Men who leave their wives get a taste for it – first hint of trouble or hassle and they think, blimey, this is a bit boring, I fancy a change again. Got away with it last time. And a baby makes things a hundred times harder.'

She was probably right, but it isn't much consolation. Nothing is much consolation. Finishing off Barney's finest aged Laphroaig whisky just added the pain of a monster hangover to the smarting of my broken heart. Smashing up the gravy boat from our wedding service with the only golf club he'd forgotten to take away hasn't helped, either, although Mel swore it would. I think she's even angrier with Barney than I am.

'I'd kind of wanted one for myself. A baby.'

'How long were you married?'

Were? The past tense stopped me in my tracks for a moment. We still are married, I wanted to say. Instead I said, 'Seven years.'

'Don't you think that if you'd *really* wanted one, you'd have got on with it. Unless—' She looked worried. 'I mean, sorry, maybe there were problems.'

'Oh, no. Nothing like that.'

'Well, be thankful for small mercies. A baby won't mend a bad relationship. All it does is give you another thing to fight over during the divorce.'

'Yeah. I know you're right. Doesn't make me feel any better, though.'

'Well, it won't. Not right away. But it'll get through sooner or later.' She took the coffee from my hands and put her arms around me. I could smell her perfume, something overwhelming that reminded me of the 1980s. Poison? Obsession? It caught the back of my throat and I longed to pull away.

She seemed to sense it and gave me a final pat on the shoulder before letting go. 'Tell you what: would you like to come over to mine one night? Maybe one or two of the other girls would fancy it too. You can't really get stuck into the tissues here, in front of him,' she jerked her thumb back towards William, 'and the rest of those daft sods. Complete bloody waste of space, most blokes. The sooner they develop a vibrator that can shoot sperm, the sooner all our troubles'll be over.'

William's ears must have been burning, because he clapped his hands to signal he wanted to get going. Carol-Ann's invitation was the first thing I'd felt half enthusiastic about in five exhausting days. Her determination to grab life by the bollocks was fun to witness, though I couldn't ever imagine feeling that way myself.

We sat together and I ignored Aaron as he took a seat on my left. A hint of aftershave – something spicy, quite unlike Barney's tasteful lemon-scented choice – wafted towards me. I ignored that too, as far as I could without holding my nose, which would have been plain rude. Even so, I resented the invasion of my nostril space.

I was quite looking forward to hearing all about Carol-Ann's songs. I guessed she'd be a fan of Motown-drenched soul classics, belted out by the kind of divas she resembled, in spirit if not in body. She was looking pretty diva-like, anyway, in her bright pink shirt with matching lipstick and beads.

Then William announced we had to team up with someone we hadn't worked with last time. I should have predicted it – I've been on enough training courses where they do exactly the same just to unsettle you – and there was bloody Aaron, virtually dragging me off to the corner of the hall. You'd have thought he fancied me if it wasn't for the fact that I am a clapped-out, washed-out primary teacher, and he is a good-looking Lothario with grey-blue eyes and beautifully manicured hands. I couldn't help noticing them: short nails on his left hand, longer on the right, as he carried both our chairs towards the radiator. It was the prime position in the hall, which was getting colder as darkness fell outside.

This was not what I wanted. I was in mourning for my marriage and despite Mel's theory that what I needed was in fact a rebound fling, what I actually needed was to lick my own wounds, not have someone else kiss them better.

Aaron didn't so much sit on the chair as morph into it, become part of the furniture. He moved his long limbs slowly and seductively, like the colours in a lava lamp. 'I'm glad you came back this week,' he said, his granite eyes meeting mine. 'I thought one or two people might drop out. Hoped it wouldn't be you, though. You looked so much more interesting than the others.'

His words drizzled over me like honey. I didn't quite believe them but they were soothing, gave me a glimpse of a world where I wasn't the rejected spouse, left behind for the life less ordinary. I felt myself blushing. 'It's quite surprising that we're all still here. He must have struck a chord.' I nodded towards William, who was stalking around the room pretending not to listen in on people.

'Well, it's tough finding anyone to talk to about it. My friends are all bored rigid with me now.'

I nodded. 'And even if they say they're not, you feel like you've said the same thing so many times that they could repeat it back to you, word for word.'

'Right!' He smiled in recognition. Two deep lines appeared to frame his full mouth and I found it was all I could look at. The words stopped making sense as I followed the movements of his lips.

'Tess?'

The spell was broken. 'Oh . . . sorry. I'm really tired. *Really* tired, haven't been sleeping too well. You must think I'm so rude.'

'No. Just honest. My wife would have pretended she had been listening. Then she'd bullshit me till she worked out what the hell I'd said.' Those eyes locked onto mine again. Fight it, Tess, fight it.

'I suppose we ought to do the task. What were your songs then?'

This time he blushed slightly. 'Promise you won't think I'm a bit of a wanker? In my defence, I used to work in the music industry. So my record collection is full of out-there kind of tracks.'

Bloody hell. What was he going to think if I told him my job? I can't sing a note and the only music I hear at school is 'The Wheels on the Bus Go Round and Round' when the infants are performing in assembly. I maintain an interest in Britney Spears or the Spice Girls or whichever artist is currently the 'in thing' among the under-tens, but I couldn't imagine that 'Hit Me Baby One More Time' was going to be one of Aaron's choices.

'Go on then,' I said, hoping I'd at least recognise some of the bands.

'OK. For the old days, it has to be "Suspicious Minds". The Flaming Lips cover version obviously.'

I was relieved. At least I'd heard of the track, if not the artist. 'But isn't the first song meant to represent when you were happy?'

'We always had ... quite a passionate relationship. Quite jealous, almost. It's complicated. Maybe I'll tell you all about it some day.'

So this was what divorced people did: compared notes on their exes then tried to talk you into a date with a promise of more traumatic tales. It wasn't the best offer so I ignored it. 'And what about your song for now?'

'I'm kind of partial to a bit of Coldplay. That one, "The Scientist", you know how it goes . . .' He started to hum, totally unselfconscious.

'Yes, it's a good one. And your future?'

'I'm a bit of an old romantic under the layabout exterior. It'd be Burt Bacharach. "She".'

'Which version?' I was pleased with myself for knowing there was more than one.

'Oh, Elvis Costello every time. Otherwise it's pure saccharine.'

'Quite a few old cover versions for a muso, aren't there? I thought you'd have chosen lots of things I'd never heard of.'

'What, like Blink 182? Or The Persian Gulf Potatoheads?'

'You just made them up. Didn't you?'

He smiled. I wished he wouldn't do that. 'The second one I did. The first one is real. I'll play it to you some time.'

Again I managed not to react to this hint of a future date. But I began picturing it. I imagined he lived in some kind of studio-cum-workspace in the city centre, all bare boards and exposed brickwork, with a gorgeous music system, maybe something made by Bang and Olufsen. Or then again, wasn't it trendier to have decks plus speakers the size of fridge freezers? Guitars, a couple maybe suspended from the wall and then one on the floor next to the futon, which was artfully unmade yet not sordid, like its owner, with a huge cotton-coated duvet . . .

Duvet? Get a grip, Tess.

'Tess? Are you OK?' I pulled my focus back from the middle distance. He looked concerned. 'Don't go all weird before you tell me yours.'

'My— Oh, my songs. Yes, my songs. Um. Right, well, for the way things were when we were together . . . well, bloody hell. How do you sum it up? I mean . . .'

Aaron raised his eyebrows, which were as well-groomed as his nails. He was very smart for a former rocker. 'Tut, tut, Tess. You haven't thought about it, have you?'

'I . . . I . . . no. You're right, I haven't.' I felt my mouth move in an unfamiliar way, then realised what it was. A smile. The real thing, a genuine one, the kind that starts somewhere at the corner of the eyes and moves its way down till it takes over your face. 'It's the first time ever. I've never failed to do my homework.'

'And how does it feel?'

'It feels . . .' How did it feel? Dangerous. Reckless. Exhilarating. Like doing a parachute jump without learning the safety drill. But I wasn't about to admit to Aaron that one small act of disobedience could have such an effect on my adrenalin levels. It didn't exactly paint an enthralling picture of the other aspects of my life. 'It feels . . . fine.'

'Well, I won't tell if you don't. On one condition.'

'What?'

'You have to agree in advance.'

'But you could ask me to do anything.' The direction my mind had been taking – towards his scrunched-up duvet – seemed suddenly to be embarrassingly obvious.

'You're not really in a very strong negotiating position. I mean, it's a bit dismissive of the rest of us. You couldn't be bothered to do your share. Seems like you're holding back.'

I couldn't tell if he was serious. 'I suppose you're right. OK then. Whatever it is.' Debauched images set in a warehouse apartment flashed in front of my eyes.

'I want you to help me rope this lot into going to the pub after the class. Tried last week and it was a dead loss. I'm sure the women just think I'm some sleazeball trying to chat them up. I thought maybe if I had you on my side, they'd be more likely to come.'

I nodded. I couldn't decide if I was relieved or disappointed that a couple of drinks before closing time was all he had in mind.

Chapter Eight

Only five of us have made it to the pub. Our group, it turns out, is divided down the middle between the haves and have-nots. Children, that is. And the haves have all headed home to relieve babysitters/mothers/next-door neighbours.

Which leaves me, Aaron, the scarily gorgeous Jo, horrid Malcolm plus Carol-Ann, whose daughter is more than old enough to fend for herself while her mum enjoys a pint of bitter or two.

'Surprised that Natalie's got an eight-month-old baby,' Carol-Ann says, as we settle down in a tartan-upholstered corner seat. 'Looking bloody good on it. Mind you, she told me over coffee that she runs her own gym so I suppose she was back on the running machine the day after the birth.'

I'm starting to realise that Carol-Ann could give MI5 a run for its money when it comes to finding out about people.

Aaron's suggested a true Brummie pub. No Firkin in the sign and no leather sofas or choice of wines: the kind of place Barney and Mel and I would never have dared enter as students in case we were beaten up. Student-bashing would have been one of their traditions; they probably had an inter-pub league. It's built under a concrete pedestrian bridge and should have listed building status as a prime example of Sixties progressive architecture. Inside, the floor is covered with swirled carpet to hide nightly spillages of beer, blood and vomit. The paintwork and wallpaper are as lurid as the flashing lights on the fruit machine.

'Too much make-up,' says Aaron. 'I mean, she's a pretty enough girl. But I always worry that a woman wearing that much slap is trying to cover something up.'

'Like the shadows under her eyes from trying to look after a baby single-handed?' Carol-Ann glares at him. 'You don't have children, do you?'

'No. I didn't mean—'

'Whatever.'

We sit saying nothing. Without William's carefully constructed activities, the situation suddenly feels awkward. During the sessions, we feel bonded by our experiences, but outside that tatty hall the intimacy vanishes. All we have in common is a legal definition: separated/divorced. And even that will ultimately apply to forty per cent of the married population. Hardly unique. We stare into our glasses as though we've never seen alcohol before.

Jo breaks the silence. 'So what do you think William gets out of all this? It's not untold riches, is it? Unless there's some kind of indoctrination process in session three and we all end up donating our life savings to St Gabriel's.'

It's a smart question, based around the only other thing we have in common. So she isn't just a pretty face.

'He's like a bloody emotional peeping Tom.' Carol-Ann looks at me and winks. 'I reckon he gets a kick from hearing our sagas. It must be pretty entertaining, if you're not the poor sad bugger that's going through it.'

I feel shocked. 'That's a bit sick.'

Jo nods. 'Yes, but then so are most of the population. It's like rubber-necking on the motorway. You know, when there's a crash, and the drivers on the other carriageway all turn round to look at the wreckage. It's voyeurism, that feeling of "it could be me and thank Christ it's not". Trouble is, when you turn round to gawp at other people, you're putting yourself at risk.'

'Sounds like you're speaking from experience,' Aaron says.

'Yeah. Yeah, enough experience to last me a lifetime.' She stares out of the window, as though she's weighing something up. 'We don't really know anything about each other, do we? It's weird, but quite exciting at the same time.'

Malcolm speaks for the first time. 'You know about me now.' And then he leers at her.

'Yes, but *we* don't,' Carol-Ann says. 'Why don't you give us the potted life history? Maybe we should all go round and do it. Break the ice. Why don't you go first, Malcolm?'

We'd only scratched the surface of the ice in the last session. I know more about the two people I worked with after the 'stocktake' exercise, but with the others, I have no more to go on than their taste in music. And knowing Malcolm likes Barbra, that Rani likes Toni Braxton or that poor downtrodden-looking Tim likes Peter Gabriel doesn't offer the insight that William obviously thinks it should.

Malcolm takes a sip of his beer, wiping his lips on the back of his hand afterwards. 'All right. I'm a principal development control officer. Fellow of the Royal Town Planning Institute. My main responsibilities concern enforcement and permissions for major domestic and commercial structures. It's a good job, good pension, reasonable working conditions, and I hope to—'

Carol-Ann holds up her hand. 'Malcolm, mate, we don't want your bloody CV. We want to know the juicy stuff. Did you leave her or did she leave you?'

He stares at her. 'We are separated until she realises that her options without me are limited.'

Carol-Ann frowns. 'So she left you, then? There's no shame in it, Malcolm; I'd bet most of us here are the dumped not the ones who did the dumping. Otherwise, you wouldn't be coming to a class to get over it. I was dumped and I don't mind admitting it. Though I should have done it to him years before. Anyone else willing to come out as a dumpee?'

I raise my hand tentatively. 'My husband left.'

Aaron shoots me a sympathetic look. 'I left my wife, but only because she was carrying on behind my back.' He was very cagey about it earlier so it's a relief to hear that we have adulterous spouses in common. That we've both been betrayed.

'I suppose that just leaves me,' says Jo. 'It was me that left Laurie, actually. Sorry. But I didn't only leave him; I left my job, left London, left it all really. So I reckon I still qualify for a bit of bonding.'

Carol-Ann is thinking it over. 'I suppose so ... providing you're as fucked up as the rest of us. Another drink, anyone? Then we can raise a toast to being damaged goods.'

We laugh obligingly and Malcolm heads over to join Carol-Ann at the bar. 'Thank God he's gone,' Jo says.

Aaron raises those coiffed eyebrows. 'Was he giving you a hard time? I bet he couldn't believe his luck. Twenty minutes to chat up a girl as pretty as you? Normally he'd get the brush-off straight away, no messing.'

The compliment irritates me but I try to ignore it. What right do I have to feel wound up? 'I can see him being really creepy. He doesn't seem very streetwise. Or experienced.'

Jo says, 'He wasn't really leching, not as badly as some people.' She gives Aaron a meaningful look, but I don't think he gets the hint. 'Malcolm's just boring. All he could talk about was how his wife would be back – he was guessing how long it'd be – and how he would make her realise her mistake when she did come back. Creepy stuff. It wasn't like he really noticed I was there.'

Aaron shakes his head. 'What a fool. He can't be much of a man.'

Bloody hell. I can't hack any more of him fawning over Jo. 'Ought to go to help Carol-Ann out, I think.' I bump into Malcolm coming back with the tray of drinks.

'He's such a flirt, that Aaron,' I say to Carol-Ann as she pays at the bar.

She laughs. 'And there was me thinking he'd got you under his spell. I think he's all right, really. Bit thoughtless, but not bloody pretending to be anything he's not, after all. That makes him a decent guy in my book. And he's better company than old Victor Meldrew there. How his wife stood it for twenty years, I have no idea. I'd have buggered off after twenty minutes.'

'I think he likes Jo.'

'What, Malcolm? I don't think he notices anyone except himself.'

'No, Aaron. He was just telling her how any man would fancy her.'

She smiles. 'Getting jealous, are we?' She turns slowly to look over her shoulder. 'You could do worse for a rebound bonk, though. Jo's not going to go for it; she's just flirting because it's the way she gets round people. Women as well as men, I'd say. Must be an essential requirement in her job!'

'Why, what does she do?'

'Don't you recognise her? Off the telly?'

I look at Jo again. 'What? Is she some kind of actress?' There *is* something familiar about her and she's almost too pretty to inhabit the same world as the likes of me or Malcolm.

'No. She does the news. Reporter, presenter, whatever you call it. She's the one in all the dangerous places. I almost didn't recognise her without her bullet-proof jacket, to be honest.'

'She's slumming it here, isn't she?'

'I overheard her saying she's staying with her mum in Solihull. Bit of a comedown, eh? Something going on there that she's not telling us.'

'Nothing gets past you, does it, Carol-Ann?'

'No . . . including the fact that the way is clear for *you* if you want Aaron.'

'Don't be daft! It's only four days since I found out my husband's having a baby. The last thing I need is to rush headlong into a relationship with someone else.' Though after cheating by not doing my homework, I am feeling more reckless than I have in years.

'Somehow I doubt Aaron would be up for anything heavy-weight.' She puts down her cigarette, takes a sip of beer, then her pink tongue darts out and licks away the froth from the top of her lip. It makes her look like a hungry viper. 'Ugh. Barrel needs changing. So, when was the last time you slept with anyone other than your husband?'

I stare at her, wondering for a second whether I've heard her right. She raises her eyebrows. I heard her right. 'Um . . . well, I suppose, not since me and Barney got together. Which is . . .' I feel foolish, naive saying it, 'December 1986.'

'Holy shit! Seventeen bloody years? You must have been a child bride.'

'Not a child *bride* exactly, but we did get together when we were in the first year at university. The second term.'

'Well, I bloody hope you made the most of the first term.'

I giggle, still embarrassed. The truth is, I was too fastidious to sleep around. Tip Top Tess didn't really like the idea of a cocktail of sperm swilling about inside her. I tried a single one-night stand in freshers' week. It seemed like the done thing, especially after me and my sixth-form boyfriend Ian had taken the mature decision to split up amicably, so he could sow his wild oats at Sussex while I did the same in the West Midlands.

But the reality was that after spending a sweaty, unsatisfying night in my room with Andrew Potter (a second-year Geology student with hardly any hair on his head, but fur like a teddy bear's from his collarbone to his feet), I felt sick. I'd been on the Pill with Ian, so pregnancy wasn't a fear, but as soon as Andrew swaggered out of my room, I became convinced that I'd contracted some horrible disease. I dressed and made my way to the university bookshop, and found an enormous feminist-gynaecology tome called *Our Bodies Ourselves*. I bought it hurriedly, trying to hide it under my duffel coat on the way home. It cost more than my weekly groceries budget and I sat down and read the details of all the bugs I could have picked up, from crabs to chlamydia. I kept the book stashed away under my bed and its nightmarish visions seemed to creep through the mattress into my subconscious, coming out in increasingly graphic dreams. After a fortnight of symptomless worrying, I took myself to the clinic advertised on the back of the doors in the union loos, and was given the all-clear. Two months of abstinence later, I met Barney.

'No. I wouldn't say I did really make the most of the opportunities.'

'You want to be making up for lost time, then, don't you, Tess?'

'Aren't we meant to wait until William gets to that bit in the curriculum? Isn't it week six, moving on, or something like that?'

Carol-Ann smiles at my joke. 'I can't wait. He'll have us putting condoms on bananas, I bet you.'

I stop midway through a sip of gin and tonic. 'Oh, bloody hell.'

'What's the matter now?'

'The only time I've ever even seen a condom in real life is

blown up on someone's head at a hen night. Oh bloody hell, Carol-Ann. How can I ever go to bed with someone ever again when I'm so naive?'

'I thought you guys were the safe-sex generation.'

I shrug. 'In theory, yes. But by the time they did the campaign with all the icebergs and the God-like voice about not dying of ignorance, Barney and I were a cast-iron item. So now – well, I haven't got a clue about the etiquette. Does he put it on? Do I put it on? I'm sure I read in *Cosmo* that you're meant to put it on with your mouth.'

'Calm down. By the time you get to that point, no bloke is going to care who puts it on.'

'But what if ... I dunno, I can't tell which end is which? Bloody hell, do you think I can find a convent that would have me, if I take some sort of born-again virgin vow of celibacy?'

'No need for that. Trust your auntie Carol-Ann. I'll tell you the key. You've got to make sure the first one you go for isn't a fumbler. You need the sort of guy who won't make it awkward. One who's had the practice.'

I giggle. 'Oh, that makes it all easy-peasy then, eh? How exactly do I go about spotting one of them?'

She winks at me, before looking over her shoulder again. I follow her gaze towards Aaron as she says, 'I spy, with my little eye, someone beginning with A.'

Chapter Nine

Aaron's flat wasn't the loft apartment I'd been expecting. Even to call it a flat would be an exaggeration. There was no exposed brickwork, no reclaimed oak doors, no guitar collection suspended from the ceiling.

I should have known as soon as he told the cab driver to head for Kings Heath, but my thought processes were already impaired by the gin. And the tequila and the vodka and that nasty pink teen drink, Aftershock, that tasted like cinnamon cough medicine. So I didn't really remember that Kings Heath is the place for terraces and semis, solid steady buildings with period fireplaces and ceiling roses. Not stainless steel kitchens and old railway sleepers for floorboards.

In fact, Aaron's flat had no features, period or otherwise. It was over a pound shop near the Moseley end of the High Street and as I followed him up the stairs, the smell of curry from the restaurant next door made my mouth water. I wondered about asking whether we could get a takeaway, but I guessed it might spoil the moment. Not that I was sure there was a moment to spoil.

Neither, apparently, was Aaron. As he reached the top of the steep staircase, the unshaded bulb went out and for a few moments as he fumbled for the time-switch his face was lit only by the blue neon filtering through the window above the front door. He looked like a spectre and I guessed I didn't look too great either because when the bulb came back on, he said: 'Tess, you know, I can get you another taxi if you . . . I mean, if you're not sure . . .'

But he couldn't come out and say what we knew we were both contemplating, because somehow we also knew that you can't mention *it*, not until you're down to your underwear, or maybe later than that. We were grown-ups acting like teenagers.

'It's OK, it's not a school night,' I said, giggling at my weak joke and then remembering that I'd been too embarrassed to confess to my uncool profession. But I felt rather touched that he should be so concerned for me. Gentlemanly. If they all behaved like this, perhaps I needn't be so worried about doing the dating thing again.

'Great!' He managed to turn the key in the lock. 'Just hang on a minute, will you? I'm just . . .' And he disappeared behind his front door as the light went off again.

I stood in the dark, trying to think back to the last time I'd been anywhere that had those awful communal time-switches. Somewhere the landlord was mean enough to begrudge more than twenty seconds of electricity. Even at university the switches gave us a good two minutes to clear the back stairs and the corridors. Barney and I had timed it once, seen if we could manage a quickie before darkness descended.

When had been the last time we'd fallen upon each other in that way, grabbing at clothes and hair, kissing and biting and groping for something only the other person could give? I couldn't remember. What's more, it hadn't occurred to me that I'd forgotten. No wonder he'd looked for passion with the Curved One, when he could no longer find it with me.

'Tess?' As Aaron opened the door the chink of light grew, dazzling me for a moment. 'Sorry about that. Flat's not exactly tidy, you know.'

I followed blindly, waiting for my eyes to adjust to the brightness. But even once they started sending pictures back to my brain, I couldn't quite believe what I was seeing. This wasn't the home of a thirty-eight-year-old man; it was the crash-pad of a nineteen-year-old on the minimum wage with a serious partying habit who didn't need anything more than a bed to sleep off hangovers and a Baby Belling to reheat the takeaway curries that were so readily available next door.

Maybe the alcohol had disorientated him, sent him into a timewarp so that he'd accidentally returned to his student digs with a key that miraculously still worked. Implausible, but still somehow more likely than this place being his home.

'Um, it's a bit of a temporary thing.' Aaron hurried to take my coat and then looked around to see where he could hang it. He pulled a bar stool out from the little melamine breakfast bar that divided the kitchenette from the rest of the room, and draped my coat across it. 'Sit down. I'll get you a drink.'

'Thank you.' I fell back on my manners while I tried to calculate how I could get out the door, down the squeaky stairs and back to my lovely Harborne terrace with minimal embarrassment. I decided on one quick drink and then I could justifiably start yawning, ask him to order a cab. I scanned the room for something to talk about and finally spotted a guitar case in the corner. 'So do you still work in the music business, then?'

'More of a hobby now. After all, gotta pay the mortgage. Or rather, my wife's mortgage.'

'So what do you do now?'

'Oh . . . this and that.' He wasn't exactly a master of the art of conversation, but maybe he was used to speaking through his music.

'And do you still play?'

'Haven't been in the mood lately.'

The sofa looked very new, but it was made of foam and it swallowed me up when I sat down. It's hard to stand on ceremony when your bottom is no more than twenty centimetres from the floor, but it did afford me a close-up view of the multicoloured rug that covered an unspeakable-looking brown carpet underneath. Aaron was rummaging through his drawers and cupboards, taking out his apparent frustration on the cabinets, which seemed unwise, because every time he slammed something, the whole kitchen quivered.

'Aha! I knew I had a packet somewhere,' he said and for a horrible moment I wondered if he'd found condoms. Surely he wouldn't be that blatant. We hadn't kissed yet. 'I've got six left.'

I turned round and to my relief he was clutching a packet of Price's nightlights. He lit them with his chrome cigarette lighter, then placed a couple on the work surface, one on the breakfast bar and three on the coffee table by my feet. He switched off the main ceiling light and the fluorescent bulb in the kitchen and almost skipped back towards me. 'That's better, isn't it?'

'Hmm.' It was all relative. There are few rooms that candlelight won't improve, but Aaron's studio was one of them. The fuzzy yellow flames gave it a haunted look, like Miss Havisham's dining room, and I imagined someone finding us both in a few months' time, coated in cobwebs, with the little tin nightlight shells long burned away.

Aaron opened the fridge and pulled out a wine box. 'It's white or white, I'm afraid.' He opened another cupboard and found a brand new pack of six glasses. He tore the cardboard to release two and put the rest away again. As he filled each glass, I suddenly realised I was the first visitor he'd had in his bachelor pad. He'd done such a good impression of a lustful Lothario that it was hard to believe he'd been too embarrassed to invite any woman back. But I could see why. Either he'd have to be very drunk, or the woman would. I'd thought *I* was very drunk, but this place was having a sobering effect.

He hovered for a moment with a glass in each hand, looking down at me on the sofa. It wasn't solid enough to allow for any subtle seductive moves; he would have collapsed into my lap as the foam gave way.

To give him his due, Aaron seemed to see the possible problems of an attempt to cuddle up, so he put both glasses down and opened a wardrobe next to the window, to remove a pillow. Except as he pulled it out, a duvet, a blanket and several shoes clattered out onto the floor. 'Oh, fuck.' He began trying to stuff his belongings back into the wardrobe, but every time he replaced a shoe, another few pairs fell out, a cascade of footwear. At one point I'm sure I saw a long leather boot and a peaked cap, but then other people's sex lives are none of my business.

'Honestly, don't worry on my account,' I mumbled. Poor sod. Imagine being his age and living here. Somewhere so small you didn't even have a bed to sleep on, only a foam sofa-bed . . .

Ugh. I suddenly thought of his long, lonely nights spent on the same man-made fibres that were enveloping me. At least it was too dark now for me to be able to spot any stains. 'How long have you been living here?'

He abandoned the pile of laundry and shoes with a sad backward glance before throwing the pillow onto the floor next to the sofa and sitting down. 'Six months. Yeah, I know. Not exactly a little palace, is it? I tried staying with friends for a bit but it didn't work out. Meanwhile my wife's still in our house. With her . . .' he hesitated, '. . . lover.'

'Oh dear.' It didn't seem an adequate response, but then I knew full well there was no such thing. Aaron and I were like mirror images of each other: the wronged husband and the wronged wife. An outsider would never have guessed that a man so cute and charismatic would end up in a seedy bedsit, yet here he was. It made me sad and strangely exhilarated at the same time. Maybe it wasn't my fault that Barney left. It really could happen to anyone.

'Shit happens.' Aaron hadn't told me much in the pub, but what he had said was enough to make me curious and sympathetic. Unlike Malcolm, he didn't seem to blame his wife for what had happened. 'Takes two to tango,' he'd said, so maybe Aaron hadn't always behaved himself. All he'd revealed was that his wife had nagged him into marriage in the first place and was unfaithful within five years. He'd tried to forgive her, but by the time he'd calmed down enough to want her back, she'd decided she preferred her lover anyway.

I raised my glass. 'A toast to shit, perhaps. Or to shits. Like your wife's bloke?'

He frowned at me, then we clinked. 'Yes. To shits. Of both sexes.'

'You mustn't judge us all by your wife's standards, you know. I'm trying very hard not to hate all men just because of Barney's behaviour. And like you said in the pub, it takes two to tango . . . the guy was just as much to blame.'

Again he frowned. The brooding look suited him so much better than smiling. 'It's never simple, Tess. That much I do know.'

We drank in silence. Or it seemed like silence until I tuned into the other sounds: the heavy hum of the fridge, the whine of the traffic and the whispering fans of the takeaway next door. They formed a soulful lament in my head. I grasped for something to say, just to drown it out. 'So there's no chance at all of a reconciliation?'

He mumbled something unintelligible – a swear word, perhaps – then said, 'No, no, I wouldn't say there's any chance of that.'

'William said it happens fairly often before the decree absolute is granted. He usually has about one per course. True love conquering all and everything.' When he'd said that in class, we'd all looked at each other, trying to work out which of us it might be. Tim and Rani had wistful expressions, while Carol-Ann looked smug. There was no danger of it being her, unless her odious husband could rise from the dead.

Aaron smiled at me pityingly. 'It's not going to happen, Tess. Trust me.' As if he thought I was asking for myself, sussing out the competition. 'How about you? Is there any possibility that you'd forgive and forget?'

I nearly told him. That this time last week I was convinced reconciliation was a certainty, not a possibility. And then a bundle of cells in my husband's lover's womb changed the course of my life as well as theirs. No argument. 'No, the situation's too complicated,' I said, with a sigh I hoped would be enough to stop him probing further.

He stared at the candles and I thought I saw tears in his eyes. Suddenly I understood the difference between our two situations: mine was hopeless, but Aaron could still win back the woman he loved. The alcohol made me brave and in the one-track way all drunks have, I wanted the man I was considering sleeping with to know that he should go back to his wife. 'But if you really love her, you should try again. Just once more.'

There was a flash of anger in his face, making him look more desirable, in that wild rock-star way. He slammed his glass down on the floor. 'You don't let go, do you? OK. You want to know what it would take for us to get back together?'

'Um . . .' I wasn't sure I did any more, but there was something very watchable about his anger.

'I'd have to turn into a woman. That's right, cut it all off. She doesn't like cocks. Or that's what she's decided now. My wife reckons she's a lesbian, so she's now living in lovely coupledom in our house with her dyke girlfriend. Sorry, but your touchy-feely words of wisdom don't exactly make me want to rush round there with a bunch of petrol-station carnations and a box of Milk Tray.'

I was just wondering how exactly to react when Aaron stared at me with an intensity that made me afraid he was about to hit me. Then he moved the glass onto the coffee table, leapt onto the spongy sofa and kissed me with the intensity of a frustrated teenager.

After all Aaron had been through, my drink-fuddled morality decided it would be unfair to resist. You can take a girl out of the Brownies, but the compulsion to do Good Deeds lasts a lifetime.

Chapter Ten

Another day, another taxi. It's the difference between being single and being married. When you're married you travel in tandem; you can always talk the other half into driving, or if you're weak, you always end up staying sober to drive *them* home instead. Love is never having to find a minicab number.

The Toyota is coloured shamrock-green but this clearly hasn't brought it or its driver much good luck over the years. Both are battered and dented but at least the car has been patched up with fibreglass filler and nearly-matching paint. The driver is not so lucky and he wears his knocks resignedly. He's fat and pockmarked and I wonder if he ever actually climbs out of the car. Probably only the seat cover – made up of dozens of wooden massage balls – stops him sticking to it permanently.

Despite the smell of musty fried food, garlic and sweat, the torn upholstery of his taxi is a refuge. And I won't be winning any prizes for good grooming myself this morning – my hair is matted and my chin is raw from stubble-burn. I pull out a handbag mirror and try to scrub away the dark-grey vestiges of my supposedly non-drip mascara, before I realise the shadows are wholly mine. I shut my eyes but as well as the strange hangover firework display that appears, there are fragments of the night before. I open my eyes again but the images are still there.

Oh, God.

Which is the worst picture? It's hard to tell. Maybe that first awkward kiss, when our noses collided in a violent crash, as if we were both incompetent virgins rather than worldly-wise thirtysomethings.

But hang on. That pales into insignificance compared to the

clumsiness of Aaron's groping. Just thinking his name makes me blush. It felt as though he had spades instead of hands and they dug and drove into my flesh in a horrible parody of a caress.

I moved my lips away from the vacuum he was creating with his mouth. 'Hey, slow down . . .'

He opened his eyes and they were a deep, dull black for a split second before his pupils shrank in response to the candlelight. 'I want you, Tess. I want to fuck you. Can I fuck you?'

Talking dirty has never been one of my things. I would defend anyone's right to freedom of speech in the comfort of their own bedroom, but Anglo-Saxon does nothing for me. Barney and I gave it a go once, but his soft tones couldn't convincingly capture the urgency of the language: he sounded like a schoolboy trying to impress his mates behind the bike sheds. And I couldn't use any of the four-letter words without feeling silly. We collapsed into giggles, finding it more romantic to do it without speech, punctuated by the odd groan (him) or whimper (me).

But that linguistic experiment came after two years together and a bit of a chat about it in advance. Aaron's words were sharp and unexpected. I felt panicked. Could you refuse a man who was talking like that? Was it naïve to find it objectionable? And what was I supposed to say in response?

I pulled away from the spade hands as gently as I could. I didn't want to antagonise him. 'Aaron . . .' I began, but he pulled my face back towards his. I resisted. 'Aaron . . . I . . . can we just . . . talk?' It sounded feeble, even to me.

'I've got condoms, if that's what you're worried about,' he said, and there was a note of impatience in his voice.

Oh God, condoms.

That has to be high up in my Top of the Pops of embarrassing moments from the previous nine hours. I blush again in the back of the cab and try to slink down in my seat so the driver can't see me in his mirror. He might think I'm about to throw up. He could be right.

'Not just that.' The truth was that though I'd gone back to the flat half-suspecting we might have sex, I'd been thinking of a kind of dreamy, cloudy, falling into each others' arms sex, rather than the rude, grown-up, latex-coated variety. 'I suppose . . . the thing is, I do find you attractive . . .' though that feeling was definitely fading rapidly, 'but, I haven't. I mean, it's the first time since—'

'Since your husband?' Aaron pulled further away, far enough for us to be able to focus on each other's faces. 'Would it make you feel any better if I tell you it'll be—' He stopped himself, trying to make it sound like he didn't see me as a dead cert. 'I mean, if you do decide to do it, it *would* be the first time since my wife.' He gazed sadly at the nightlights and I felt myself changing my mind again.

'Isn't that a reason to take it slowly?' But I had a suspicion that there was no 'it' beyond tonight, at least as far as he was concerned. Wasn't it better to get it out of the way, soon, with someone I didn't care about? A bit like those measles and chicken pox parties parents held when I was a kid, trying to get us all infected so we'd get the nasty diseases out of the way early on. The longer we left it, the more unpleasant it would be.

Aaron took a sip of his wine. 'Slowly? Marriage is about taking things slowly. Steadily. Thinking through the consequences, acting responsibly. We've done that, Tess. It didn't work. Don't we owe it to ourselves to live a bit?'

The argument was so much more persuasive than the four-letter words. I turned my head towards his and he took my answer from that tiny movement. This time he was gentler at first, the hands less invasive, less grabby, though I could still feel the energy behind them.

He pulled off my top and when he began to snog me again, I opened one eye to see where he'd thrown it. It looked sordid on his carpet, out of place. I shut my eyes again as I reached for his waistband.

'That's it, baby,' he murmured. Shit, he'd done it again. I couldn't think of a less erotic thing to say, but I pressed on, fumbling with his zip as he fumbled with my bra strap. We'd have been better off doing it for ourselves, but then that probably applied to the whole process: we had to somehow pretend that this was about pleasure and joy and a mutual experience, rather than a calculated act of self-preservation.

I reached his boxer shorts and hesitated. The thin piece of cotton between my hand and his penis was a rubicon to be crossed. No going back. I felt for the fly and reached inside.

It was only the fourth erection I'd ever held – a fact that would have shocked Mel to the core – and somehow I'd forgotten they came in any shape or size other than the Barney model. This one was thicker and stubbier and as I started to move my hand, I felt that panic begin again, a far stronger emotion than any lust I could still muster from Aaron's rather cursory tweaking of my left nipple. Was this the right way to do it? I felt sure that he was about to stop what he was doing and scream at me for giving the worst hand job he'd ever had. Meanwhile, he'd pulled down my knickers – I sneaked a quick look at them and was relieved to see they were my inoffensive black Knickerbox hip-huggers – and was rubbing away like Aladdin trying to summon up an oversleeping genie. I doubled my speed.

'Oh yeah, I want you now, baby. Yuh, want to be inside you . . . you . . . so hot . . . the best . . . yuh . . .'

This didn't reassure me. He sounded like he was working from a script, maybe the script of his favourite blue movie, one he'd memorised after repeated stop-starts, with remote control in one hand and that stubby penis in the other. But I felt it'd gone too far to pull away now. Sure, a woman has a right to say no at any time. I just didn't feel I could say no, yes or maybe with any conviction at the moment, so I hoped Aaron's enthusiasm would somehow carry both of us through the experience relatively unscathed.

'Babe . . . babe, are you ready?' Aaron whispered. As I'll ever be, I thought, and nodded, my eyes closed because I worried he might see the doubt if I kept them open. I liked to think he was enough of a gentleman to stop if he had the impression I wasn't sure and I wanted to save him the bother of being polite.

He pulled away and I tried to position myself in a dignified yet appealing position on his foamy sofa. I heard the loud whirring of an extractor fan and realised he was in the bathroom. Then I realised how part of the erotic tension I'd thought I was feeling was actually a full bladder – no wonder, when I'd consumed so much alcohol on an empty stomach – but I wasn't confident enough of my ability to stand up unaided to risk a trip to the loo.

The sound of smashing glass came from the same direction, followed by 'Fucking hell! Fuck . . .' This time I smiled at the language; it was so much less threatening. I rearranged my legs again, placed them side by side on the sofa, with my ankles just leaning over the side. I waited.

The noises continued. Muffled swearing and things dropping onto ceramic tiles. The echo of little packages – headache pills, perhaps, or razor blades – bouncing as they hit a bathtub.

What position was the most flattering? Missionary seemed the best bet, but would this be enough to satisfy Aaron? Something told me that a guy who likes to talk dirty before he's reached second base would be expecting more than a couple of thrusts with me lying passively below.

Oh God, and would he expect me to put the condom on for him? I remembered the conversation with Carol-Ann in the pub. She seemed to think it was enough just to open my legs, but the magazine article about sneaking one on during oral sex was surely more up-to-date on the etiquette of the dating scene than a fifty-something brewing manager. And did I want to give him oral sex anyway? The longer I waited, the more confused I became.

'At fucking last,' cried Aaron, sweeping into the room wearing his socks and a satisfied smile. And a horrific greeny-yellow thing on the end of his stubby erection.

He caught sight of my expression as I recoiled from the day-glo condom. The organ it contained seemed to wilt a little before he said defiantly, 'It was the only one I could find. It's not past its use-by date.'

I was transfixed. The thing hovered in the semi-darkness like Casper the Friendly Ghost after a night on the tiles. It was the least erotic thing I had ever seen in my life, and yet as it drew closer, like a heat-seeking missile, I knew it was too late to back out.

'Hey baby,' he said, towering over me with Casper bobbing about at my eye level. 'I want you so bad.' It was all I could do not to embark on a grammar lesson. Instead I smiled stoically. I just hoped he'd be as out of practice as I was and would therefore come quickly.

He grabbed my hands to pull me up from the sofa and I wondered if he was seriously going to try doing it standing up, an exercise Barney and I had never mastered after seventeen years together. It always seemed to me that sex standing up required a midget man and a very tall woman, both with considerable gymnastic prowess.

'Let's make things a bit more . . . comfortable,' said Aaron, as he pulled open the foam cushion to create something like a bed. I took my cue and lay down, even though the 'mattress' was so thin I was sure I could feel the ridges of the rag rug under my back.

He lay down beside me and reached down to remove his socks. A slight smell of ammonia wafted from his feet. His mouth on mine brought a little quiver of desire back into my body and I tried to allow the moment to overwhelm me.

'Oh Tess,' he said as he nuzzled my neck, 'Big Mr A wants to get to know you better . . . I want to get . . . right . . . inside . . . your soul.' He bared his teeth, the way a lion grimaces at its prey, and moved over me as though he was about to do a press-up. As he lowered himself back down, I prayed silently that it wouldn't be as bad as I feared.

'Tess, we're going in . . . Tess . . . we have lift off . . . Tess, we—'

'Whereabouts down here, love?' The taxi driver is the most welcome interruption I've ever had. I'm back in my road, so close to my bed. I pay him, let myself in and pick up the post. But before I can allow myself the luxury of sleep, I have a phone call to make.

'Mel? Mel, it's me. I need to see you. I've just committed adultery.'

Chapter Eleven

She's waiting for me when I arrive at Hudson's.

'You can't call it adultery when your husband's girlfriend is expecting his baby,' she declares, a little too loudly. Two woolly-hatted women at the table next to the piano reward her with open-mouthed gazes. Mel continues, a little quieter, 'Sorry, but you needn't add guilt to all the other bloody emotions you've got to deal with. A one-night stand doesn't count when Barney's shacked up with his secretary.'

I sit down. 'Who says it was a one-night stand?'

'Put it this way: I'd be very pissed off indeed if you'd been hiding a proper full-on love-of-your-life romance from me. I want all the details, though. After we've ordered our food.' And she disappears behind the leather-backed menu.

Hudson's is an institution that unites Birmingham's disparate shopping communities. Pensioners, students cadging a free lunch off their parents, trend-setters – they all make the journey to the top floor of the Plaza shopping centre for gourmet sarnies served by men dressed like butlers. Tiny tables are clustered together outside the café at the top of the escalator, or you can hope for one of the sofas or high-backed chairs in the back room, a Victorian parlour recreated in a 1980s glass and chrome building.

The menu is packed with tempting things, so usually it takes me a good ten minutes to choose between the scores of sandwiches which are a gastronomic world away from the greasy bacon rolls available from the stall on the street outside. Then there's the decision about what to drink, from teas and coffees whose names (Blue Mountain, Assam, Hawaiian Kona) summon up images of steamy plantations in faraway countries, to 'real' lemonades and ginger ales.

Today I have no appetite. I stare hopelessly at the yellowed playbills that hang on the wall, advertising music-hall artistes who must once have been as famous as Posh and Becks. Fame, fortune, love, they all fade in the end.

'Right,' says Mel, closing the menu in triumph. 'Sorted. What are you having?'

'I don't feel very hungry.'

She tuts. 'Bollocks, Tess. If you can't be bothered to order, I'll have to do it for you.' As ever, the waiter senses the right time to come over. 'Right. I'm having the smoked salmon and cream cheese bagel, plus a fresh apple and mango juice. And then she'll have . . .' Mel flicks the menu back open, 'a roast beef and English mustard on multigrain, with a proper hot chocolate. The one you can stand your spoon up in? Thanks.' She smiles at the waiter as he glides away like a mannequin on wheels.

'I feel sick. I'm never going to be able to eat that.'

'Oh, for fuck's sake, Tess. The beef'll put hairs on your chest, and the hot chocolate will put the lead back in your pencil. Or something like that. Anyway, we're not here to talk about the nutritional benefits of comfort food, are we?'

'No.' I know she isn't going to stop until she's found out all the details, but I don't feel very excited by the prospect.

'Well? He's obviously someone from your group thingy, isn't he? Unless you picked someone up randomly, in which case I will have to applaud you *and* tell you off in equal measure.'

'He is from the course.' I pause while the waiter puts cutlery and napkins down on our table, then I start again more quietly. 'His name is Aaron. He's thirty-eight, he's not divorced just yet, but it's pretty certain. His wife's decided she's a lesbian so I can't see them trying again.' As I say it, I wonder for the first time whether Aaron's technique had anything to do with her decision. It wasn't that he was a *bad* lover, but there was something very testosterone-fuelled about his style. I suspect he's more tender towards the fretwork of one of his beloved guitars than he was to me.

'Blimey.' She raises her eyebrows in that irritating way she has, knowing I will fill in the blanks sooner or later. 'That must have been a shock. Sounds like one of those stories you read in a trashy magazine in the dentist's waiting room. But I want to know more about what *you* got up to.'

'What? We went to the pub, we both got drunk and then the pub closed and I went back to his flat.' I'm not planning to tell her the full squalor of the place; she's going to think I'm mad enough as it is.

'You needn't think you're getting away with that, madam. You're making it sound like what you'd do any day of the week. When was the last time you went back to a man's flat on your own? It must be about 1990 or something.'

Give or take four years. I'm not going to give her more ammunition. 'Well, when was the last time I was ... single?' There, I've said the word. There is nothing comforting about any of the ways you can describe my current status. On my own? It conjures up the inner fear of every woman: a final exit in a bedsit full of cats and a sheepskin coat. Unattached? It's only a step away from unhinged. On the pull? That really means on the edge of desperation.

The waiter brings our drinks over. I have to admit that the cocoa vapours rising from my mug are making my mouth water unexpectedly. It's as thick as soup when I stir it. I raise it to my lips and when it hits my tongue, I can't help sighing.

Mel says, 'See? I told you so. Just what you need after a frenzied night of shagging, I always find. Or found ... hey, it's weird now, this role reversal thing, don't you think?'

'Tell me about it.'

'Sorry. I didn't mean to rub it in. I know it's the least of your worries, but it must be weird for you, too.'

'It's about the one thing I can say without a shadow of a doubt. Life at the moment is totally bloody strange.' The sugar hits my bloodstream and I feel a little burst of energy. 'I never thought I'd ever sleep with anyone else. Never. But that didn't scare me, Mel, you know. I wasn't worried about what I was missing. It seemed right with Barney.'

'I can't imagine sleeping with only one person for the rest of my life. I mean, I love James more than I've ever loved anyone, but still ... I know myself too well to marry him.'

'Poor bloke. But at least you're honest. How many people

really think through the "till death us do part" bit? Never mind talk about it. Well, we did talk about it. I even liked being bored, sometimes, just for the security of it all. The permanence.'

Mel reaches for my hand. 'It isn't fair, Tess. No one ever deserves to be dumped. Especially not you.'

We don't say anything for a while. I can see Mel watching me nervously, perhaps fearing I'm about to burst into tears before the sandwiches arrive, but the truth is I feel empty rather than emotional. My thighs ache and I remember why with a strange detachment. The snapshots – Aaron pulling my legs up over his shoulders, then pulling me on top of him, all the time with that odd intense expression men only ever have when they're having sex – no longer make me blush. It's taken me less than twenty-four hours to lose the shame. Or perhaps it's because while I was being pounded and manoeuvred, it didn't feel like it was happening to me. Even my orgasm, which crept up on me unawares, felt distant, like one in a dream. Now, sitting in Hudson's with Mel like a million times before, I'm not sure I haven't dreamt it all. Except for the ache.

The sandwiches arrive. We finish half the round before Mel puts her napkin down and eyes me carefully. 'I was just wondering whether you're too fragile to tell me all the gory details. After all, I've given you enough in the way of juicy gossip over the years. Payback time, don't you think?'

I grin. The roast beef is going down rather well. 'It was fine, you know. Not brilliant, not awful. Just sex.'

'Bloody hell, aren't you Mrs Super-cool? So does this mean you swapped mobile numbers?'

'We already had them – the leader bloke gave us a list of everyone's contacts during the session. And it's not like I'm not going to see him again in class, is it? Anyway, you've always told me that following up on a one-night stand is like eating leftover pizza: only to be done if there's nothing else to plug the gap.' I force out a laugh, but I don't feel as confident as I'm trying to sound. Aaron and I didn't talk at all this morning, beyond an 'All right?' swiftly followed by 'I'll call you a cab.' And though I hadn't expected a declaration of undying love, I found it unsettling that he hadn't mentioned meeting up.

She sees through me immediately. 'That's not what I asked. It's different for me. I'm a woman of the world, aren't I?'

'And I'm a suburban abandoned wife with a little teaching job?'

'You're just not, I dunno, experienced. Accustomed—'

'Well, unaccustomed as I am to short-term shagging, I think I went into it with my eyes as well as my legs open.'

Mel looks doubtful. 'If you say so . . . but I still think you need some diversionary tactics for the next few days. It's not as if you've got a class full of horrible brats to teach to take your mind off things. So what are you going to do now you've got your groove back?'

I play with the remaining half sandwich on my plate. My appetite's gone again. 'God knows. Maybe a bit of gardening . . .'

'Gardening? More like sitting next to the phone, wondering if he's going to invite you over for another session. You need some day trips. Cheltenham, Leamington or something.'

'I don't think so, Mel. What I should probably be doing is clearing junk from the house. I've been thinking about it. Barney's going to want me to sell up now the Curved One is pregnant.'

She snorts. 'He'll have me to deal with if he gets stroppy. And however much I support clearing out your clutter, going through old stuff is the last thing you need at the moment. Though the same couldn't be said for a bit of basic disinfecting. You're like those people who get evicted by the council for creating a health hazard. You haven't started collecting your piss in milk bottles yet, have you?'

'No! I don't know, Mel, it all feels like filling up time. Gardening, cleaning. Just a way of passing the time till I can go to bed. And retire. And die.'

She looks up from attacking the salad garnish. 'What about hiring a cottage or something? You know what they say about a change of scenery.'

'I don't think I've got the energy to take myself . . .' I tail off, remembering something Roz said to me on that last day. 'Hang on. You know Roz?'

'Saint Roz?' Mel doesn't like my boss. A lot of people don't. She makes them feel inadequate.

'Yes, well, she's got a place in the country—'

'She would!'

'She said I could go to stay. I'd forgotten, what with the horrors of that last Friday, but maybe it'd be what I need.'

Mel chews thoughtfully on the last mouthful of her bagel. 'Mmm ... great salmon. I'm not sure that Saint Roz is the obvious choice, but she's probably your only option right now. I'll let you go on one condition.'

'Which is?'

'You leave your mobile with me.'

Chapter Twelve

Barney's colleagues are knee-deep in country retreats, but Roz is the only one of *my* friends with a cottage, so I've no idea what to expect as I meander my way towards the Herefordshire village marked on my map. I'm lost but in no hurry. I have a suspicion that the signs round these parts haven't been touched since they were deliberately turned in the wrong direction to confuse the German invaders expected in 1941. I doubt this would have been one of their key targets for occupation, as sheep seem to outnumber people by about twenty to one.

I could have called ahead, if I'd had my mobile with me, but Mel was insistent. 'How can I be sure you won't bloody text the hippy from your rural idyll? You've just got to trust your auntie Mel. If he gets in touch, it won't do him any harm to be kept waiting for your reply. And if he doesn't, the worst thing you can do is call him.'

I hate the idea of playing hard to get, but then again I don't know if I want to be 'got' by Aaron. I'm not convinced I like him, yet there is something about him . . . or more accurately, his situation. It's like putting my own under a magnifying glass. I've been dumped by someone in favour of a younger model: he's been dumped in favour of a different gender. I am uncertain if I'll be able to stay in the home I built with Barney: Aaron is already out on his ear.

I drive past the same village school sign I've seen twice already on my circuitous journey. OK. There is at least one reason that I can claim extra misery points over Aaron. My ex is having a baby with his new, improved woman. In rejection trumps, that has to be a winning card.

Finally I take a right turn, and thirty minutes later, I am in Roz's kitchen. It's as brightly painted as a canal barge and reminds me of a scene from Alice in Wonderland, because everything in it seems to scream *eat me!* or *drink me!*

'So we can add domestic goddess to all your other skills now, Roz?' I say, sipping homemade elderflower and ginger infusion.

'It's my stress-relief safety net. I *never* bring work to the cottage; it's a rule I made as soon as we bought the place, and I ban Gerald from bringing paperwork too. Though he sometimes sneaks some in, hoping I won't notice. I can tell it a mile off when he does – after thirty years in teaching, he can't pull a fast one on me.'

'Where is he now?' The cottage seems resolutely feminine. Even the dogs are female. Jackie and Joan – named after the glamorous Collins sisters – sniffed around me when I first arrived but now they're snoozing happily on a rug by the Rayburn.

'He's gone to do some shopping – and as the nearest place is twenty miles away, he won't be back for *hours*.' She sounds so relieved that I wonder if their marriage also has its cracks. Perhaps that's why she's invited me here: to show me that perfection is an elusive state. Or to fill the gaps in their conversations.

My room is small and packed with hangings and knick-knacks from hippy holidays the world over. Roz and Gerald were flower children and most of their souvenirs from the sixties and seventies seem to be crammed into this box room. They must have seemed exotic, once, but now the turmeric and ochre colours have faded and the objects themselves have become clichés, a part of the travelling experience as hackneyed and humdrum as bringing back Eiffel Tower pens from Paris, or straw donkeys from the Costa del Sol.

They still got further than me or Barney. We managed a couple of summers inter-railing, one August on a Thai beach and that honeymoon in Sri Lanka. Hardly free spirits. I suppose now I have the option of travelling to my heart's content, but what's the point? Holiday resorts are full of couples fawning over each other in candlelit restaurants, pitying the odd single woman who's been brave enough to venture out with only a paperback for company. We used to do that ourselves, speculating on the broken romances or bitter divorces that had driven people to admit defeat and travel on their own. I suppose I'd been tempting fate.

It's different for men. I can imagine Aaron rejoining the hippy trail, a rucksack and a guitar strapped to his back, sampling the narcotic delights of successive Indian states, a henna tattoo on his ankle and a host of impressionable younger women on his arm. In fact, it's much easier to see him doing that than playing the devoted husband, hosting dinner parties and mowing the lawn. I still don't understand why he ever decided to settle down. And after what happened, I guess it's not a mistake he'll repeat.

I unpack in seconds, leaving my clothes in one small pile on the intricate iron rack and my few toiletries on the painted dressing table. There are benefits to my newfound slobbishness. In the old days I'd have tidied everything away, my underwear neatly divided from Barney's with a row of socks, our T-shirts for sleeping in under respective pillows and the numerous deodorants, shower gels, shaving foams, his 'n' hers moisturisers, contact lens solutions and massage oil all arranged according to function, in aesthetically pleasing groupings.

Downstairs Roz is applying cream cheese frosting to a wonderfully uneven slab of carrot cake. 'Would you like to lick the spoon afterwards? I always find it such a treat.'

I nod, sit down in the closest chair to the Rayburn and wonder how long it will take before Roz starts probing. It's natural, after all, for her to want to know more about the reason why her ever-capable, ever-efficient deputy has turned into a basket case. This is surely the deal I've accepted by taking up her offer of a break from the city?

But she doesn't say anything. She just smiles as she moves the palette knife up and down across the top of the cake. The frosting is all spread now, but she seems to be trying to make it as smooth as possible. 'Bugger,' she says, when a perfectly flat layer goes a bit wonky as she pulls the knife away. 'It always does that! Hardly something for a grown woman to get in a state about, is it? I just love it when I can get it flat and untouched, like snow. It's better with sugar icing, of course; that kind of naturally rights itself, like self-levelling concrete. Gives a lovely smooth surface, but it's not very suitable for carrot cake. Too sweet.'

'If you say so, Roz.' I grin at her. She has so many different identities, from trouble-shooting head teacher, to spiritual hippy chick, to glamorous property tycoon's wife, to country-bumpkin earth mother. Except, of course, she isn't a mother at all.

'Bloody hell, I do go on, don't I? I'm so used to it being just me and the girls. I think they find it soothing when I chatter away to them; I see their little ears twitching and then their paws moving a little bit, their tails swishing. And even if they don't find it soothing, I do . . .' She looks down at the cake. 'That's as good as it's going to get.'

She holds out the bowl for me and I take it. I wipe my finger along the knife, feeling the creamy-yellow frosting build up in a dense coating. I check if Roz is watching – it seems a naughty, childish thing to lick my finger, although she's given me permission. My mum always discouraged us from scoffing the leftovers, however delicious they were. 'Not good manners, girls.' But then again, while Roz was smoking dope in Goa, Mum would have been trying to persuade my father to move to a semi in preparation for the two children plus goldfish she'd decided they were going to have.

I take a deep breath. Then I lick.

'Hmmm,' I sigh. The rich, tangy thickness of the cream cheese is softened by a taste of honey that lingers on my tongue.

'Good, isn't it?' Roz turns round, obviously pleased at my reaction. 'I hope you'll polish off the lot. Otherwise the girls will get it, but I think it's wasted on them. It's one of my few regrets about not getting round to having kids. Dogs don't really appreciate top-quality cakes.'

The comment hangs in the air like the lingering smell of vanilla from the baking. She turns her back to wash up the non-stick tin and a row of coffee cups. But she still doesn't seem to feel the need to ask about Barney.

I work my way through the bowl, methodically scraping out little rows of frosting until all that's left is a network of tiny lines of white where I've missed a bit. Still no questions. I almost feel annoyed that my situation isn't interesting enough for her to want to pry.

I take the bowl to the big Belfast sink where she's nearly finished the washing up. 'Thank you. Feel a bit sick now, though, I must admit!'

She takes the bowl then looks at me, weighing something up. 'Tess . . .'

Here it comes, I think. She's bound to let her curiosity get the better of her sooner or later. 'Yes?'

'I want you to feel comfortable here. I won't ask, though I will listen if you want me to. But the most important thing for you to know while you're here is . . . well, you just don't have to pretend.'

The kitchen table swims before my eyes. I'm crying again.

Chapter Thirteen

Other people's relationships are like magic tricks. You can't see the join, unless someone decides to let you in on the secret. How the naked lady stays afloat in mid air below the silk cloth. Or how the woman in the coffin smiles manically while she seems to be sliced in two – or four, or six – by razor-sharp metal sheets. How she grins even when her partner moves half of the coffin across to the other side of the stage, her stilettoed feet wiggling 'hello' to her disembodied body.

It all seems incomprehensible until you see it close up, behind the smoke and mirrors. Even then, it takes the magician or his glamorous assistant to take you aside and explain the trade secrets before you realise that, exactly as you'd expected, their lives are as full of artifice and fantasy as your own. The perfection of their relationship was a figment of your imagination.

Roz and Gerald seem like the ultimate conjuring trick – or more like the ultimate con trick. He's an estate agent, therefore inevitably the slimiest of slime balls, while she's a primary head teacher: tough as old boots, but still Mother Theresa to his Robert Maxwell. They are childless, reduced to spending their weekends baking cookies for the ghosts of the grandchildren-who-should-have-been, and to calling their dogs 'the girls'.

Yet as I prepare to leave after two days with them, I have to admit that their illusion of happiness is starting to look like the genuine article. No wires, no sleight of hand, just plain old-fashioned contentment.

The first night, when I'd spent at least two hours (I lost track of time) crying into Roz's not inconsiderable cleavage, the sound of the four-wheel-drive along the gravel outside their cottage made me jump. Then I felt resentment at Gerald's arrival, although it was his house.

'Roz . . .' He came bursting through the back door, which was unlocked. Everything stays unlocked here, I realised soon enough. They even leave the keys in the Mitsubishi. If Roz did that at school – though we're hardly an inner city sinbin – the car would last eight minutes at the absolute outside. 'Oh, sorry,' he said, taking in the tableau: me, Roz, the girls; a monstrous regiment of females, surrounded by tissues.

'It's OK,' I sniffed. 'It's your home, isn't it?'

His left arm, which had been tucked behind his back, suddenly sprang forward, artificially extended by a huge bunch of pink gerberas. 'I got these for Roz but I think you're the one who needs cheering up.'

It's been years since anyone's given me flowers. Barney stopped somewhere around the millennium. I felt the tears welling up again and pinched myself hard to try to stop them. 'Thanks, Gerald.'

He walked straight to the fridge and pulled out a bottle of champagne. 'It's a pleasure. Roz told me what happened. Never liked your pompous husband, if I'm honest.' He put the bottle down with a thump, then took three flutes from the rustic limed Welsh dresser. 'Don't mind me being honest, I hope. I mean, I know I only met him a couple of times, but you can always tell—'

'*Gerald!*' Roz used the same tone she inflicts on children who talk in assembly. 'I'm sure Tess already realises what the problem is and she doesn't need to listen to your inane ramblings on the matter.' She put her arm round him. 'Champagne's not a bad idea, though.'

'Sorry, Tess. Don't mean to put my size ten in it. I missed out on the tact gene, I'm afraid. I've been doing it since I learned to speak. First word was "Daddy". Trouble was, I said it to my uncle in front of the whole bloody clan. There'd always been rumours about Uncle Ron and my mother but that was enough to cement them for life. Out of the mouths of babes, eh? Watch out, here she goes,' he said, as the champagne cork eased out of the neck of the bottle with a determined pop.

'He makes it all up, Tess. Loves to be the centre of attention and doesn't care whether what he's saying is true or false, so don't believe a word he says. Easier that way.'

'You see what I put up with from my beloved wife? A woman's duty is to respect her husband, isn't it? Ooh, sorry, don't mean to . . . here, have some champagne. I think I will shut up.'

'God alone knows how he ever manages to sell a house, Tess,' Roz said. 'How he doesn't just blurt out "as you'll see, a particular feature of this ramshackle property is extensive rising damp" I have no idea.'

'That's why I leave it to my staff, Roz old girl. I used to have a little bit of a reputation for honesty, it's true, but don't think it did too much harm. Supply and demand. There was demand for an estate agent who was as honest as the day was long, and I supplied it. Honest Gerald. Made a nice change, built up my reputation and then once I had the money I employed some sneaky fibbing bastards to do the job for me. But we've hung onto the reputation as the agents who always speak the truth. Ha ha.'

They are a supreme double act. Abusive to each other on the surface but there's no doubt that underneath they're in love. Gerald and Roz don't love each other in a simpering way. No, they express it when they giggle over secret jokes. He still makes a grab for her bottom when she passes him in the kitchen or the hallway. She still stares out of the window when he's unpacking the shopping, just watching the way he moves.

I'd seen them together three or four times before, at events the governors insisted on holding to mark the progress of Old Oak from sink school to 'the Midlands' most improved'. But I hadn't noticed any of it; I'd dismissed Gerald on the basis of his job and I suppose I ought to admit that I'd dismissed them as a couple on the basis of their childlessness. I'd assumed that their status must either have indicated their own unwillingness to grow up, or some sort of *problem* with her system, or his. Either of those options meant the kind of desperation I didn't want to see in close-up.

But actually, it would have been Barney and I who'd have

looked desperate. Superficially we were like Gerald and Roz, joking around, the perfect situation-comedy couple. But our jokes had developed to cover up our differences, to distract from the thinness of our real-life act. We didn't argue because our lives, our expectations, our world views were so estranged that there wasn't even enough common ground for a row.

'The girls could do with a W-A-L-K, if you've got time before you go?' Roz spells out the letters because they have the ability of all dogs to hear the word, however quietly it is spoken. I've done a lot of walking over the last couple of days, at my own suggestion and occasionally at Roz's or Gerald's. Sometimes it felt like code for 'we'd quite like to be alone for a while', the way younger friends of mine have a Sunday afternoon routine of setting the kids up with a Disney video and an instruction not to disturb Mummy and Daddy while they have a 'rest'. I wasn't sure if Roz and Gerald were using my dog-walking for sex or just to 'be' but it did make me appreciate what a big deal it had been for them to invite me to stay. They had a huge social circle at home, but this was their retreat.

'You don't have to take them,' Roz says, interpreting my delay in replying as unwillingness. 'I thought that you might like to take a last look. Not that it has to be the last time here, of course, but you've got a journey ahead of you, so stretching your legs might be a good thing.'

'Yes, you're right.' I pull the leads from the drawer where they're kept and before I open my mouth to call, 'Jackie, Joan,' they are scrabbling at my side, nought to walkies in two point three seconds.

The weather is hazy, not quite faultless, which will make it easier to head back to the city, to let go of the rural experience. My body is sluggish from the massive Sunday lunch we finished an hour ago but there's enough chill in the air to jump-start my system. It's not cold, exactly, but enough of a contrast with the comforting heat radiating from the Rayburn to make my face tingle.

The girls run ahead of me once we reach the footpath down towards the village. Their red coats seem to be on fire, even in the little sunshine that is reaching us through the haze. Their energy makes me feel inadequate.

The village is scarcely that, more of a hamlet, with a general store, a tiny chapel and a pub. Through the window I can see a few old guys and a barmaid who dresses with all the glamour of a farmhand. The Ring o'Bells has nothing to offer city-dwellers, no rocket salad or riverside garden. The Ploughman's Lunch is composed of cheese from Kwik Save, bread from the freezer and pickle from a catering-size jar. And the coffee is instant. So it remains a place for locals only. I haven't dared go inside, though Roz assured me they would be curious and nosy, rather than hostile. That's probably what put me off.

Mel was right about me needing to get away. It's not that it's stopped me thinking about Barney, the Curved One, or even Aaron. On the contrary, I've done little else. But the change of location has given me the freedom to think about them without distractions, like worrying about my mobile not ringing, or being reminded by every object in my home of what I've lost.

And being so far away has given me a sense of proportion about that loss – and made me face some uncomfortable home truths. The most shocking is the realisation that The End with Barney wasn't on Boxing Day night but months, maybe years earlier. That he hadn't been the only one responsible for the demise of our relationship, though he'd been the one to recognise the symptoms, to decide it was terminal and then to put it out of its misery.

It's taken spending time within the Magic Circle of Roz, Gerald and the girls to see what I've lost, but maybe also what I could have instead. How there might be someone out there *better* than Barney, or better for me at least. Even more surprising is the proof that life without kids can be as satisfying and as rewarding as life with them.

I kneel to poop-scoop Joan's and Jackie's shit into a couple of plastic carrier bags I've brought out with me. Gerald insists it doesn't really matter here in the countryside, but old habits die hard. Pleased with themselves, the girls turn tail, back towards the cottage.

The question that's gripped me since I admitted to myself that the future may not be as scary as I'd thought is whether Aaron might be a part of that future. The logical, Tip Top Tess side of my brain tells me that it's silly and girly to imagine that one rubber-insulated act of sex should give me any kind of part in his life.

But maybe being sensible has got me nowhere. Maybe Aaron, for all his flaws, is as needy as I am and that meeting of body parts could ultimately lead to a meeting of minds. Perhaps not for ever, but then I've tried marriage, and that isn't for ever either.

Aaron is wrong in so many ways: a forceful, slightly clumsy lover; a charming, chaotic boy-man; a wronged and bitter husband. And then there was that terrifying bondage-style uniform I saw falling out of his cupboard . . . But he's also in the same boat as me and right now that seems the most important factor. He might bring me a little comfort and joy. And I could do the same for him.

I call through the door as I arrive back at the cottage. 'Hello?' The girls go straight to their water bowls. In the empty kitchen, the lapping of their tongues sounds as loud as oars in a river. Then Roz appears, a little red in the face.

'That was quick,' she says.

I blush, thinking about what they might have been doing. 'Yes, they weren't for hanging around this afternoon. And neither am I. Got to be up and organised ready for work again tomorrow. After all, the head teacher I work for, she's a demon! Won't stand for any slacking . . .'

She smiles broadly. 'So I've heard. Come here, Tess.' She opens up her arms and holds me for a while. Tears gather again behind my eyelids but this time they don't feel like they're heralding a terrifying descent into emotions I can't control. They're thank-you tears.

I pull away a little. 'I can't begin to tell you how much you've helped me—'

'Then don't!' Roz snaps back into teacher mode. 'It's enough to see the difference in your face.'

'What, my puffy eyes from all the crying?'

'You'll see it yourself soon. I think things are turning the corner for you, Tess. It's not going to be plain sailing – nothing this difficult ever is – but things will get easier. I promise. And you know, I don't promise anything I'm not sure of . . .'

I hear Gerald clatter down the stairs. 'You off now? Back to the big bad city?'

'Yep. Thanks for letting me stay.'

'Oh, I just do what I'm told, you know. But it's been nice to have someone to relieve me of my dog-walking duties.'

Roz thrusts a carrier bag into my hands: eggs, bread, some leftover chocolate brownies wrapped in greaseproof paper. The kind of supplies a mother might give to her hard-up undergraduate daughter.

'Are you trying to fatten me up?' I say, to wish away some more tears. I put my stuff in the boot and start the car, reverse out of their gravelled driveway and watch them grow smaller in my mirror: Roz, Gerald, Joan and Jackie all waving or wagging until they're too tiny to be recognisable.

It's getting dark by the time I arrive home. The other houses in the street have switched on their lights but not drawn their curtains, and I see children, parents and blinking TVs as I try to find somewhere to park.

My house is in darkness and I realise I'm dreading the first ten minutes before the heating kicks in, the soullessness of a chilly, empty home. But as I unlock the front door, I can smell warmth and flowers. I switch on the hall light and follow my nose.

The living room is transformed. Where there were magazines and newspapers and pizza boxes, there are simply the clean lines of furniture and the first uninterrupted view I've had of my carpet in months. On the coffee table, there's a pile of letters and a huge vase of Stargazer lilies, sending the powerful perfume of jasmine into the air.

From Barney?

Even as I think it, I know they're not from him.

From Aaron?

He doesn't know where I live.

They must be from my fairy godmother. Then I see a note.

Tess, honey, hope you don't mind, I thought your place could do with a belated spring clean. Well, it was that or call in the environmental health. Hope you're feeling better. There's wine in the fridge plus I've replaced some

of the mouldy stuff with things you can actually eat
without contracting salmonella. Give me a shout to let
me know you're home safely. Mel xxx.
PS. You didn't think I'd done this myself, did you?
The Yellow Pages is the best book in the world.

I go into the kitchen. The rubbish sacks have gone, the wine rack is full again and when I look in the fridge, its shelves are like those you see in magazine articles about how celebrities eat, loaded with organic vegetables, dusky raspberries, marinated chicken breasts. Only the family-sized tiramisu stands out as an aberration: a welcome one.

Upstairs, the bathroom floor is white again. My bedroom smells of newly washed cotton sheets instead of aromatherapy air freshener.

I go back to the kitchen and pour myself a glass of wine. Then I remember the mobile. Will there be a message from Aaron? I find my phone under the pile of letters: bills, circulars and a thick cream vellum-envelope of the kind you only get from department stores and solicitors.

Solicitors.

I put my glass down and check the letter's postmark. Birmingham. The envelope tears with an expensive sound.

Dear Mrs Leonard,

As you know, I have been instructed by your husband to act for him in the divorce proceedings. Further to my letter of 27 January, I am writing to outline my client's suggested timetable for the sale of the marital home and the subsequent division of assets on completion of the divorce . . .

The rest of the letter goes unread as all the positive thoughts of the last two days seem to taunt me.

I run to the downstairs toilet – which reeks of bleach and Mr Muscle – and throw up into the bowl. I perch on the seat for ten minutes, twenty, maybe half an hour. Who will get the chrome towel rail? The bevelled 1920s mirror we'd picked up at the antiques fair in Stafford? The daisy-embroidered lilac hand towel and matching flannel from Rackhams?

I want to be in bed. I leave everything where it is – the lights on, the glass of wine untouched, the letter and envelope abandoned on the floor. I only have the energy to set the alarm for school in the morning, before climbing into bed with my underwear on. I reach under the pillow for Barney's T-shirt, the one I hadn't washed because he'd been wearing it to bed the week before he left, the one that still has a faint lingering smell of *himness*: whatever the chemicals or pheromones are that make him distinct from all the other men I could have loved and married. It's my comfort blanket when things are bad. It always triggers tears of longing and loss but sometimes that's what I need.

But it's not there. I jump out of bed, tear open the wardrobe, the drawers, a woman possessed.

In the end, I find it in the airing cupboard, pressed and folded into a neat square by this unknown cleaner who has sterilised my life in my absence. When I press it to my nose it smells of fabric conditioner and a hot iron. Barney has gone for good.

Lesson Three

Great Expectations

William was in a foul mood. No-shows always did that to him. Not the no-shows to the first session; that was fair enough. Cold feet went with the territory. He was a Christian man and if they called to apologise, he might even let the nervy ones join in his next course.

But once someone had given their commitment to attend every session at the end of the first evening, that was that. Death and childbirth were the only excuses William thought were justified, though the women in particular were often late, complaining about unreliable babysitters and problems getting their children to do their homework. He wasn't happy about it, but at least they always called to let him know. It was the least he and the others could expect.

'Tonight's session,' he began, fighting to keep the irritation out of his voice, 'is called Great Expectations.'

The group was unsettled by Aaron's absence, he could see that. The empty chair was as much of a presence as its occupant would have been, telling them things a real person might shy away from.

To the other two men, Aaron's chair was screaming, '*LOSER! Why are you hanging about with a bunch of women in therapy when you should be out getting your revenge on them?*' Supermarket Guy would be mentally rolling over to accept the humiliation, knowing that as his wife had said, he was a supreme wimp, while Malcolm would be squaring up to fight the chair, the anger he normally reserved for his missing spouse directed at Aaron for his lack of moral fibre or staying power.

To the women Aaron had barely engaged with – Rani, Natalie with the ponytail, Carol-Ann – Aaron's chair said, '*You are not worth my time. I can't be bothered to come back to get to know you.'* William sensed the only person who'd be immune to this insult was Jo, who was wearing the same wry smile she'd adopted for most of the last session.

But Aaron's chair seemed to be speaking the loudest to Tess, who was casting nervous glances at it every minute or so. She had, after all, spent the whole of the last session with him, sharing not just song titles but also emotional pain and intimacies. *'You were so dull,'* the chair sneered, *'that I couldn't face coming back to listen to any more of your self-indulgent banging on . . . No wonder your husband left you!'*

The first time there'd been a no-show at one of his sessions, William had gone against his training and made a point of discussing it, asking people to vent their anger and disappointment. He'd even suggested they shout abuse at the empty chair, to express and banish their anger, which made for an uncomfortable moment when the absentee turned up thirty minutes late, hands oily from changing a burst tyre.

Now he knew from experience that the group would survive the non-appearance of someone they'd met only twice. He resolved to make sure poor Tess got to team up with Carol-Ann this time, to offer a bit of support.

'The thing about expectations is that they often go unspoken. We don't think they need to be spoken, in fact. When we fall in love and decide to get married, we assume that this person who feels like our other half, our soulmate, will understand what we want, because they want the same things. Obviously. Just like we expect them to mind-read when we want sex, when we're in a bad mood, when we need space.

'So we choose the church or the reception venue, we pick the flowers and the dress, the bridesmaids, the best man, but we don't sit down and talk about what happens after the honeymoon's over. Take kids: this is one of the biggies, after all. Do we definitely want them? If so, when? Do we want them baptised? Who will take the lion's share of looking after them? Where do we stand on smacking, sweets, private schools?'

He looked at each person in turn. 'Maybe I'm wrong. Maybe you did talk through everything – not just kids but housework, money, in-laws, all the stuff that tends to drive people to the divorce courts. But if you'd kept talking, I don't think you'd be here now.'

William saw Jo wince, then glare at him. The gloves came off from now on. He knew the routine: two weeks to build trust, five weeks to challenge and threaten and cajole and drive them crazy. And the final week to give them the tools to head off into the world again. It was like a boot camp for the broken-hearted.

'Anyway, last week's homework was to come up with a book or a story that represents how you thought your marriage would be. It might, of course, have been *Great Expectations*. Or *Cinderella*. Or even *Catch-22*. Though if you think your marriage was meant to be like *Catch-22*, you kind of got what you deserved.'

He was rewarded with a smile from Jo. 'So I want you to write the title of your book at the top of the handout. I've got one of these for everyone. Then underneath I want you to write down a bit about your expectations of marriage according to each of the categories in the boxes on the left side – there's romance, religion, sex, fidelity, family, all the big ones. Keep the book in mind while you write it. And then in the columns on the opposite side of the page, I want you to write down how things changed or were different once you'd actually tied the knot. Then I want you to talk about it to the person you're working with. There'll have to be one group of three. Maybe you three?' he said, nodding at Carol-Ann, Jo and Tess. 'This isn't a guilt trip; it's not meant to make you feel you failed at all. But until you recognise why marriage didn't live up to your expectations, you'll find it hard to move on. Right, you've got half an hour till we feed back and then you'll be allowed a well-deserved coffee.'

The students dispersed quickly – Rani with Tim, Natalie with Malcolm, plus the three girls, who dragged their chairs to the corner furthest away from William's kitchenette vantage point. Having just three groups rather than four made the hall look emptier.

He watched as they read through the categories. Rani began scribbling immediately, filling her page with tiny regular handwriting, while Tim frowned with concentration before putting down a single word or two under each heading. Malcolm finished within a couple of minutes, drawing lines through all the boxes on the right. He drummed his fingers on the clipboard as he waited for Natalie to finish, but she wasn't being hurried by anyone. She used a pencil and when she re-read her notes, even erased the odd word so she could rewrite it in block capitals.

William squatted next to Malcolm. 'You've finished already? I hope you haven't cheated like you did when you only thought of one song last week, instead of three.'

'Don't be ridiculous.' Malcolm scowled. 'I haven't written anything on this side about changes, because we were both entirely realistic about our expectations of marriage. Nothing changed for either of us. I told her my beliefs and my feelings and she was happy with them – she was too young when we married to have an opinion about most of it, in any case. So the only thing my response to this exercise has in common with last week is that for a second time, I am not clear how this is intended to help.'

If only bloody Malcolm had been the no-show. Aaron was arrogant, a bit too much swagger maybe, but at least he'd seemed willing to listen. Malcolm wasn't here to listen. He'd moved from the denial stage to anger and if he couldn't take it out on his wife, then William could be his whipping boy. Much more satisfying to direct your feelings onto a living human being than an absent wife.

'I can't predict exactly how each exercise will help, but a period of reflection *is* generally useful. Maybe it won't seem to help immediately, but you'll wake up one day and feel better. Or you'll be in your office, considering the latest garage extension application—'

'I only deal with major commercial applications at my level!'

God, he was hard work. 'The latest shopping centre, then, and you'll look up from the blueprint and something you talked about with young Natasha—'

'My name's Natalie!' she snapped back.

William sighed. One day she'd have a failing memory, too. 'Something you were discussing with young Natalie here will come back to you and it'll click. You'll make sense of it. How are you finding the exercise, Natalie?'

She looked at her notes. 'Uncomfortable, really.'

'Because you realise where you went wrong? I think it's always uncomfortable – the feeling that things were preventable.'

'It's not exactly that. It's strange, because on paper we're so right. We do ... I mean, we *did* have so much in common: the same beliefs, the same ambitions. But I can't make it work. *Couldn't* make it work.' Her voice sounded irritated, dissatisfied with her own inability to make things all right just because she willed it so.

William had the impression that most things and most people in Natalie's life fell into line straight away. No wonder she felt out of her depth when her marriage failed to do the same. 'You can only make it work if the other person wants the same. This isn't about blaming yourself. It's about recognising the joint responsibility for making a relationship work, and hopefully avoiding the same mistakes next time.' He tried to make his face convey wisdom, compassion and understanding.

It might have been easier if William had ever dared to allow himself to make mistakes again, but he was too scared. The longer he left starting over, the more impossible another relationship seemed. So he was desperate to get through to his students, the way a parent wants to stop a child making the same mistakes as they did, to prevent unnecessary pain, from grazed knees to puppy love.

'Perhaps you could both talk through what you've written down. You'd better start, Natalie; something might occur to Malcolm while you're talking.'

William's knees creaked as he stood up. He limped over towards Tim and Rani, who were already comparing their notes. 'How are you two getting on?'

They both waited for the other one to speak first. Some people were too polite for their own good. Finally Tim smiled at Rani, nodded for her to take the floor. 'Yes, we're finding plenty to talk about. It is interesting to go back in time like this, although I feel saddened by Tim and his wife.'

This was better, William thought. Anything close to a genuine emotion had to be encouraged. 'Do you think Tim's story makes you sad because it's similar to your own?'

Rani frowned, considering his question carefully. 'I think it makes me sad because it makes Tim sad and because Tim is a good person.' She blushed. 'Good people do not deserve bad things to happen. Tim does not deserve what has happened to him.'

William sighed. 'I've heard enough terrible stories in this room to know that unfortunately, being good or bad has nothing to do with it. It's about being human. If you're human, there is no escape.'

Rani nodded, satisfied with his explanation. 'When my marriage began to go wrong, I thought it was my fault. People told me it wasn't but I didn't believe them and I didn't believe they believed it either. And then when my husband went home—'

'To India?'

She stared at him. 'No, Leeds.'

'Oh. Right, of course.'

'Though it might as well be India. It was the end for my family; they said the right things but I felt them disapproving of me. Even my sons.'

'You've got two boys, haven't you, Rani?' William had been looking again at the questionnaires they'd filled in, his crib-sheets for the times when all their suffering merged into one long tale of woe.

'Yes, though they're hardly boys now. Rav is nineteen and Ajay seventeen. And then my daughter, Sunita, is eight, the baby of the family. Our little "mistake". Though I wouldn't give her up for the world.'

'Do you think your sons still disapprove?'

'Rav is my rock now. I couldn't manage without him. I think he sees what his father has done. And without his earnings we would have gone under. My husband ... well, he sends no money to me. He told me he wouldn't. The boys could pay for themselves, he said.'

'And your daughter?'

She looked away. After a pause, she said, 'My husband has

written her off as if she never existed. From the moment she was born, he blamed me for adding another burden to his life: as though he'd had nothing to do with it. So to the boys, he sends letters, and a cheque on Ajay's birthday – which he told Ajay not to tell me about. But to Sunita, nothing.' Her face was angry now. 'He never had a very high opinion of women.'

Tim stood up, patted her shoulder awkwardly. 'Rani, that's terrible.'

'I accept it now. I find it hard to explain to her why her father isn't in touch, but the boys are very protective. Rav takes her out on weekends; he is a better father than his father ever was. And we have enough to live on. Not much more than that, but you know, human beings are resilient. Look at you and your situation. We have to remember we didn't bring this on ourselves.'

'You're a strong person, Rani, to cope with that kind of rejection.' William said. 'How are you finding today's session, Tim?'

Tim shrugged. He didn't seem at all comfortable talking about feelings, but that didn't mean he didn't have them. That was the mistake so many women made, thinking that because men couldn't demonstrate or explain the pain they were feeling, it must mean they were less capable of experiencing it.

It wasn't true. If anything, it was worse to see the Tims and the Malcolms trying and failing to express the hurt inside them. Where inside, William was unsure. Medically, of course, the heart had nothing to do with how people were feeling, yet the head seemed too distant from the whole-body suffering his students were undergoing.

'It makes me feel silly. Naive to have expected to be happy ever after.' He looked away, embarrassed.

William opened his mouth to utter something vague, something comforting to encourage more detail, more self-disclosure, but before he could speak, Rani said: 'You should never be embarrassed because you believed in love.' She put her hand on Tim's and smiled at him. 'You are a gentleman. If your wife did not appreciate that, then another woman will.'

'What, a single dad with two kids? No one is going to take *me* on. I'm hardly a good catch.'

Rani shook her head. 'Would you take on a single mother with children?' William thought she only just stopped herself adding 'like me'.

Tim thought about it, seeming to struggle. 'If you'd asked me a year ago, I'd have said no. No way. Someone who'd failed? Someone who couldn't hang onto the father of her children?'

Rani kept her hand where it was. 'But now?'

'Now I know no one's perfect. So maybe I would.'

William moved away quietly. He'd been trained for his role, had been practising for six years now, but he sensed Rani would achieve more than he could with Tim. It was moments like this that made a million moaning Malcolms tolerable and removed the irritation Aaron's absence had caused.

He wished there'd been a Rani there for him when he needed one. But then if there had, he'd probably have gone out of his way to hurt her. To invest in his own future was as pointless as giving George Best a liver transplant. He'd had his chances and he'd blown them. Now he was better off helping people who still had a chance of recovery.

Time to check up on the three women. From a distance they seemed to be getting on fine, fussing around Tess exactly as he'd intended, but when he approached, the conversation stopped.

'Don't mind me, ladies,' he said. Jo glared at him. She really wasn't in a good mood tonight. Of course, she was as entitled to be bad-tempered as everyone else. It just seemed a shame to distort her lovely face. 'Have you all finished?'

William peered down at their clipboards. There wasn't a single word written on any of their forms.

Jo pouted. 'We got sidetracked.'

'Right ... well, I mean. Um.' He felt unsettled by her. It wasn't that he was attracted to her ... no, actually, it was daft to pretend. He *was* attracted to her; what man wouldn't be? But he knew that with a good twenty-five years between them, there was no point dwelling on it. There was something else about her ... a familiarity, maybe? But he couldn't think where he'd know her from.

'I think it's great that you're getting on well, being supportive of each other. But you do need to restrict the amount of *freeform* activity you do in the sessions, or you'll fall behind. Maybe you want to go through it verbally?'

Tess stared at her feet, while Carol-Ann doodled in the margins – smiling faces, like her own. Jo sighed. 'OK, OK, if we must. Expectations, right?'

'Yes. Why not start with family, or maybe fidelity? They tend to be the big ones.'

Jo raised her perfectly arched eyebrows. 'I fell in love with Laurie because he meant security to me. My dad left when I was little, so it doesn't take a genius to work out that absent men had appealed for years. And there were plenty in my business to keep me occupied.' She gave a wry smile and her friends smiled back.

'And your business is . . . ?' William felt excluded.

'Telly. Sorry, thought you knew. TV news. Full of men trying to juggle a woman in every port. Actually, a lot of the women reporters are the same. Stable relationships don't tend to be top of the list of priorities for foreign correspondents.'

Jo's familiarity was beginning to make sense to William. He had a vague memory of a slight-looking blonde woman in a khaki jacket, standing in dangerous places, talking calmly straight to camera.

'I did my share of messing about. There was always someone to have fun with and a warm body is a lot more tempting than a grim single bed in the horrible hotels the newsdesk would book us into. I only let myself get hurt once . . .' She tailed off, checking the reactions of her audience. William sensed she was trying to judge how far she could go. 'And that was after I was married.'

Tess took a sharp intake of breath. 'Really?'

Jo blushed. The colour of her cheeks just made her eyes look bluer, William thought. Then he blushed himself. Fortunately, the others were preoccupied waiting for Jo to expand on her story.

'I know it sounds bloody awful. I feel a fraud coming here, really. Wondered if I was allowed, when I'm the one in the wrong. But ... I *am* still hurt. I am still disappointed, disillusioned, all of that.' She looked down. 'Anyway. We were talking about expectations, and in my defence, I expected to be married for life, to be faithful, to stay totally and utterly in love with Laurie for ever. I wouldn't have done it otherwise.'

'Did you talk about what you both expected before you got married?' William asked.

'No. But I knew enough about what we'd both experienced – Laurie's parents split up when he was little, too – to know that we weren't going to go lightly into marriage. I suppose the trouble was that neither of us had seen it done successfully. It was like ... I dunno, an actor trying to perform Shakespeare if all they've ever seen is bloody awful daytime soap opera. We didn't have a clue how to do it without melodrama.'

They sat in silence for a moment. William tried to think of something to say. 'Do you feel you were repeating a pattern, then? The pattern set by your parents?'

'I suppose so. Except fortunately we got out before we had any children that we could fuck up too. Whoever heard of a female foreign correspondent with kids? The blokes do it, of course, then they never see them. But it wasn't exactly an option for me.'

'Did you talk about having kids?' Carol-Ann asked.

Jo grinned. 'Yes. Oh yes. And not just to each other. We talked about it to *Hello!* magazine as well. Posed with my bridesmaids, looking every inch the broody bride.

'But we weren't thinking straight. What were we meant to do, fit in the pregnancies around international conflicts, then leave Laurie holding the babies while I jetted off to the next hostile environment? I thought the excitement would wear off – the excitement of the job, that is. I thought somehow that making a home would be more of a buzz than live broadcasts.'

'And it wasn't?' William asked.

'Nope. It was wishful thinking. I tried it, got a job based in the UK, but I used to sit watching the satellite feeds with reports from people who'd overtaken me and who were all round the world, and I was insanely jealous. So I decided to do one last assignment, one final attachment overseas, with Laurie's support. To get it out of my system, before I came off the Pill.'

'And?' But William already sensed the answer.

'The cameraman. It's almost always the cameramen. He got through my bulletproof armour quicker than a knife through butter.' She dared to look at Tess. 'I'm not proud of it. Not at all. I think maybe I was never really the marrying kind.'

William shook his head. 'Or not the kind to marry the man you did. There's a big difference.'

'Maybe.'

'Jo, have you ever heard the term Starter Marriage?'

'No.'

'Well, I'm not saying this is relevant, but it might be a helpful concept. A starter marriage is a bit like a starter home. It suits you at the time, but you're not going to spend the rest of your life in it. It's like a test-bed – marriage might well end up suiting you, but maybe not with the first man you try—'

Tess interrupted. 'You're saying people seriously go through a wedding knowing they're going to get divorced, as . . . some kind of rite of passage?'

'Well, no. I don't think anyone goes into matrimony planning for a starter marriage. It's more a case of couples realising in retrospect that that's what they did. And the whole concept of marriage, well, think about it. In the old days, we didn't expect to live much past our forties, so you'd only be with someone for a couple of decades. Now that life expectancy has gone up, you could be spending sixty or seventy years of your life with the same spouse. Is that realistic?'

'I thought it was,' Tess said, quietly.

Carol-Ann frowned. 'Maybe people don't have the staying power they used to.'

William said, 'Or maybe you could see it as a positive step. Even twenty years ago, a husband and wife might have felt obliged to spend the rest of their lives together, however miserable it made them and the people around them, because the shame of being divorced was too great. Now there are other options.'

Jo was nodding. 'You know, I remember how odd it was

when we came back to work after the honeymoon. We'd spent so long deciding on the dress, the flowers, the cake . . . And then life was exactly the same, apart from our rings and the big dent in our joint bank account. Maybe we really were that shallow.'

'Well,' William said, 'I don't think it's something to feel guilty about. It's just that it can be helpful to see a marriage in context with the rest of your life; with your past and your future.'

'Hmm.' Jo looked at her watch. 'Isn't it time for the coffee break yet?'

William bit his lip. There were so many other questions. How long had she stayed married? What had happened to the cameraman? And what was a hot-shot foreign correspondent doing in Birmingham? But she'd made it clear that her confessions for the night were over. 'You're right. Time to get the kettle on. You two are off the hook for now!'

Tess and Carol-Ann smiled weakly, but William knew they'd be catching up properly later without him. He'd brought them together yet he would never be a part of their lives.

Under his breath, he repeated one of the Californian slogans: *turn your jealousy into generosity before it turns malignant.*

Sometimes he found it hard to practise what he preached.

Chapter Fourteen

The plus side of Aaron not turning up is that we don't have to go to some smelly old man's pub. Instead we go to one of those funky bars that have sprung up around the Chinese quarter.

You could mistake us for any girls having a night on the town. Maybe Carol-Ann is a bit old for a Bridget Jones-style piss-up, but if you don't look too closely, we're the kind of impenetrable threesome that you see in every pub and club: clustered together, thick as thieves, briefing each other about the latest developments in their lives, then moaning about the fact that no man ever approaches them when they're on the pull.

As if any man would have the nerve to try to intrude on our coven.

'I knew you'd end up back at his place,' Carol-Ann says. She folds her arms in front of her waiting for the full story, which I'd been unable to tell during the session itself thanks to the unsubtle intervention of William.

'Am I that predictable?' I snap back. I suddenly feel irritated. Surely she hadn't so much predicted my 'night of passion' with Aaron as pushed me into it? Without her provocation, would I really have dared to respond to his advances? I feel myself shudder from my shiny conditioned hair to my stiletto-warped feet. I made a real effort tonight, but Aaron didn't even bother to turn up. It's not looking hopeful as the romance of the century.

'It's not that you're predictable,' Carol-Ann says, 'just that you both needed a bloody good seeing to, and as you were in the same place at the same time, it was karma that you should take advantage of a meeting of pheromones.'

'So how come he wasn't here tonight?'

Jo looks solemn. 'You know there could be lots of reasons.'

'What, like he woke up next to me in the morning and thought, oh bloody hell, if I never see her again in my life it'll be too soon?'

'No, that's not what I meant.'

'OK. So maybe he thought it was the worst sex he'd ever had and couldn't bring himself to come because I might want another go.'

Jo says, 'Didn't mean that either. Maybe he's worried that you think *he* is the worst sex *you've* ever had and that's why he chickened out of coming along.'

I think it over. It probably was the worst sex I've ever had, but to be fair to Aaron, that wasn't his fault. Of my three other lovers, I was in love with two – which does tend to make things look that bit rosier – and I can barely remember the details of my one-night stand with Andrew Potter at university, so he doesn't count.

Carol-Ann shakes her head. 'No, I don't buy that one, sorry. Whoever heard of a man thinking he was rubbish in bed?' She takes a big sip of beer. 'What *was* he like, anyway?'

I blush. 'I . . . look, isn't this all a bit weird? I mean, I hardly know either of you—'

Carol-Ann winks. 'Not as well as you know Aaron, that's true.'

I plough on. 'But we're all expected to spill the beans about everything: our marriages, our deepest fears and feelings—'

'Our one-night stands!' Carol-Ann interrupts. 'Yes, that's right. Better out than in. Put it this way, it's easier than telling your mum. Or, in my case, my bloody holier-than-thou daughter.'

Jo plays with the free matches in the ashtray. The packet is midnight-blue, with an embossed pattern of little stars. Our bar is so trendy it doesn't have a name, just a symbol, like the artist formerly known as Prince. 'You don't have to tell us anything, Tess, but you looked pretty cut up when he didn't arrive and at least we've met him. We might be able to throw a bit of light on things.'

She's got a point. 'All right then. It wasn't great. No, it really wasn't great. Then again the truth is, maybe it was. Maybe I'm out of touch with the way people do it these days. Maybe all that was wrong with my night of passion with Aaron was that he was Aaron. And not Barney.'

'Not your bloody philandering tosspot of a husband?' Carol-Ann pulls a face. 'I'd have thought that'd be about the biggest thing in his favour. Was it big, by the way? His thing?'

'Carol-Ann!' She's as bad as Mel. 'I really don't think...' Then I do think. What do I owe Aaron? He couldn't be bothered to call me. He's humiliated me by not bothering to turn up. 'Average, I think.'

Carol-Ann holds her two index fingers together in front of my nose. 'How average? By your own admission, you probably haven't got the experience to judge properly. So you need the benefit of our experience.' She casts a sly look at Jo, then starts to move her fingers apart, very, very slowly. 'Just say when...'

'Oh for God's sake,' I say, then watch as the fingers part hypnotically. I look to the next table, where two men are staring at Carol-Ann, frowning as they try to work out what the growing distance represents.

The gap grows ever bigger. Between her fingers, I can see Jo smiling. 'Bloody hell, Tess. Aaron has hidden depths ... or should that be lengths?' she says, as the distance approaches eight ... then nine ... then ten inches. Any minute now it'll be the size of an LP and he'll be gaining an unfairly generous reputation.

'STOP!' I shout, louder than I intended.

Carol-Ann freezes. The gap is implausibly large. 'Our Aaron is more than average, I'd say, Tess. Either that, or you've been a lucky girl in your choice of men.' Then the two of them collapse into giggles and I feel myself fighting the desire to join in.

'No, no. Hang on. It's nothing like that impressive. I was just a bit slow. Let me have another go...'

But they're laughing too much, so I raise my own skinny fingers at eye level – casting a quick glance at the two men, who are as hypnotised as I'd been – and concentrate hard. I try to remember ... was it only a week ago?

I've packed a year's worth of emotions into seven days. Exhilaration, lust, fear, shame, worry, exhaustion, jealousy, paranoia, relaxation, expectation, disappointment, anger, all washed down with a heavy dose of grief. That's the one that's always there, however hard the other emotions fight to hijack my brain.

I look at the fingers and decide to stop moving them when they're about six inches apart.

'There you go.'

Jo raises her eyebrows. 'Erect?'

'Erect.'

Carol-Ann nudges me. 'I think we can safely conclude that Aaron is truly average. You're better off without him.'

I grin. It's silly and insulting and rather pathetic but it makes me feel better. Not much, but a bit. Baby steps. 'I'll drink to that!'

A couple of hours later we get a cab to Carol-Ann's place.

'Shh...' she says, creeping through the front door like a naughty teenager. We giggle. We've been giggling all night since trying to work out how all our various exes measure up. Then we giggled over men's bad habits – from farting to fucking around and everything in between. Then we giggled over the barman's cute bum and how it compared to bottoms belonging to different customers. It felt faintly hysterical but enjoyable too.

'Georgie's about a hundred times more strict than my dad ever was,' Carol-Ann whispers. We tiptoe through the hallway of her semi into the living room. She switches on the one ceiling light and we blink.

The room is cosy and cluttered, with burgundy-stained wood cabinets lining one wall. Behind the glass doors are photographs of a little girl growing into a bigger girl and then a surly teenager. There are trophies, too, cheap-looking alloy figurines featuring leotard-clad gymnasts in uncomfortable-looking positions.

'She was great at sports,' Carol-Ann says. 'It was the only thing her dad took an interest in. Claimed he'd been a bit of an athlete in his day. Huh.'

'It's a bit bright in here, Carol-Ann. Have you got any

candles?' Jo's eyes are glazed; she's probably the most drunk, as she doesn't seem to have a job to go to next day. There are still plenty of secrets to our own TV celebrity.

'No, I haven't, sorry. We only just got candles in the Midlands. If we want mood lighting, we use the telly with the sound turned down.' She turns round from the end cabinet, where she's pouring three glasses of port. 'But then you wouldn't really know that, would you? You're not from these parts.'

Jo accepts her drink, takes a sip and makes a little hum of pleasure. 'You're very direct.'

'Down the hatch, girls.' Carol-Ann moulds herself into a huge beanbag opposite me and Jo on the rose-patterned sofa, then says to Jo, 'There's no bloody point in being coy after all we've confessed to, is there?'

Jo nods, thinking it over. 'OK. I'm here to look after my mother. She's got cancer.'

Whatever explanation I've been expecting – exotic Brummie lover, undercover assignment infiltrating the Digbeth under-world, a relaxing sabbatical in Solihull – it wasn't that. 'Oh, Jo. I'm sorry.'

'Yeah. It's shit. Though she's getting better. It's a slower process than I'd imagined. I thought you got cancer, they whipped it out and then you either lived or died. Which is true, of course, but I didn't expect this many ups and downs.'

'Have you got any brothers and sisters?' Carol-Ann asks.

'No. There's my aunt, but she can't seem to shift her arse to see Mum, even though she only lives in Nottingham. My mum's got quite a few friends from yoga classes and all the other holistic stuff she's into, but she's really retreated in on herself since the op. And I never went to school round here or anything – Dad paid for me to go private, after they got divorced – so the survivors' course is pretty much the extent of my social life. Cheers!'

There's so much I want to know, but she's obviously not going to say any more. Suddenly the gap between the course's enforced intimacy and *real* friendship built up over years seems a hundred times bigger than the penis-sized gulf we were measuring in the bar.

All I can manage is a feeble, 'If there's anything I can do . . .'

'Well, you can stop looking at me like I'm a charity case for a kick-off. It's my mum who's ill, and while it's pretty miserable for both of us, it's not going to help me or her to bore everyone rigid with it on the odd occasion I do get to go out.'

'Right,' I say, wondering whether she's really as hard-nosed as she seems. Maybe her work's done that to her. I suppose you don't get to be a foreign correspondent without developing a shell to keep the traumatic stuff out.

She must realise what I'm thinking because then she says, 'Sorry. I know that makes me sound like a total cow. I suppose I don't find it very easy talking about it because I get so few chances. At home we kind of pretend it's not happening and I try to do that in the outside world as well.'

There's an awkward pause before Carol-Ann springs up and goes over to the stereo. 'I think we need a bit of music, girls. What do you think? Some of William's top choices for the broken-hearted? I've got plenty of soul, or there's a few of Georgie's CDs.'

What do I want her to play? I'm not sure what my musical tastes are, or my tastes in anything, for that matter. Nothing is certain any more. I have no identity of my own, no boundaries to kick against. It's frightening.

Or maybe it isn't . . . maybe it could be liberating. I go over to her and start rifling through the racks of CDs. 'Eeenie . . . meenie . . . minee . . . mo!' I pick out one at random, by someone I've never heard of. 'What about this one? Goldfrapp. Is that the band or the singer?'

'Search me.' Carol-Ann puts it in the little tray and it clunks shut. Strange soulful rhythms and instruments begin to leak out of the speakers, quiet at first, so she turns up the volume and a woman's pained voice – half singing, half whispering – reverberates around the room. It isn't the kind of music I'd choose, but there's something about the intensity of the sound that seems right for this time of night.

'This is different,' I say. 'Are we officially cool now?'

'What the fuck—?' The teenager from the photographs bursts through the door. The expression on her face suggests she isn't finding the music so invigorating. 'For God's sake, Mum, you know I've got a bloody early start tomorrow.' She's clearly inherited her mother's love of colourful language.

'Georgie, don't be such a spoilsport,' says Carol-Ann, turning the sound down a tiny bit. 'And aren't you going to say hello to my new friends?'

Georgie seems to notice us for the first time. 'Oh . . . hi, sorry, didn't see you there.'

Presumably her mother makes a habit of coming home late, raiding her CD collection and shaking the house down with the latest sounds.

Jo and I murmur a greeting. Georgie is prettier than the photographs suggest, with her mother's doll-like features and auburn hair. A kind face, but one that is currently torn between expressing her irritation and maintaining good manners. The manners are just about winning – it's an attitude that I, as Tip Top Tess, can only applaud.

'So what do you do, then?' I fall back on the question that has served the Queen so well during her decades of tea parties and ambassadors' receptions.

'Work in the ambulance headquarters, in the control room.'

Jo perks up. 'That must be exciting.' Georgie stares back. 'Sorry, I don't mean . . . I mean it must be a very responsible job. I used to have to ring our local ambulance HQ every couple of hours when I was a trainee reporter. They always seemed to be having a good time.'

Georgie sneers. 'Reporters! Huh. We get them trying to get through all the time when we're in the middle of big incidents. It's like, what do they want us to do first – get sick people to hospital or deal with their stupid questions?'

'Oh stop bloody moaning, Georgie,' Carol-Ann says. 'She's like this all the time. Sanctimonious. You're meant to have grown out of your adolescent moods by now. God knows how her future husband's going to deal with it.'

'Yes, your mum tells us you're getting married,' I say, desperate to find a way to reduce the tension. 'Is he an ambulance driver? That'd be romantic.' It nearly sticks in my throat. I don't believe in romance any more than I believe in Santa or honest politicians.

'No, he does exhausts in Kwik-Fit. I'm sure Mum's told you as well that she doesn't approve.'

'Well,' I say, 'I suppose it's natural for any mother to worry about her little girl, and to find it hard to accept that she's no longer a little girl and can make her own decisions.'

'Mum's just bloody jealous that I've got the chance to do it right, unlike her who cocked it up with my dad. It's *sad*.'

Carol-Ann reacts like she's been slapped. 'It's exactly because I made mistakes that I don't want you to do the same.' It's an argument they must have had a hundred times, but like all mothers and daughters, they have a gift for wounding each other in the fewest possible words. Like one of those slogan competitions – Complete the phrase in fifteen words or less: *You are the most useless mother/daughter (delete as applicable) in the world because . . .*

'So I should take advice from some withered old bag who hates all men?'

Carol-Ann opens her mouth to reply, then seems to lose all her energy and shuts it again. She turns around to switch off the power to the stereo. When she turns to us again, she is trying to smile. 'I'm pretty sure no one except us is riveted by our ongoing feud, Georgie. And as you said, you've got an early start tomorrow.'

Georgie glares back. 'Nice to meet you both,' she says, polite as Alice at the Mad Hatter's tea party, before turning on her heel without another word to her mother.

'Children are overrated,' Carol-Ann says. 'Now, anyone fancy one for the road?'

Chapter Fifteen

At least Georgie has the excuse of being a teenager. At thirty-five I'm no better at dealing with my mother than she is at dealing with hers. With Barney around, it was easier – he was my shield against her worst excesses. Having a husband showed I was a grown-up, showed I had managed one of her ambitions for me, even if he wasn't quite the calibre she'd hoped for. But without him, the prospect of a family party is about as tempting as a baby shower with the Curved One.

So far this year I've not been home at all. No one's dared to push, to lay the guilt trips on me or suggest 'it might help to come and stay'. They know as well as I do that that'd be a lie. But my dad's sixty-fifth birthday is a three-line whip. It's hardly his fault that my husband's chosen to leave in the year Dad reaches retirement age. In our family, 'events' – weddings, birthdays, christenings, funerals and especially Christmas – are sacrosanct. We feel the need to maintain this sepia-tinted pretence that everything's cosy and rosy and nice. Who knows, maybe my mother actually believes it. Perhaps she's watched so many ham actors in countless soap opera celebrations that she's convinced we're enjoying ourselves when we too are just pretending.

Like every soap household, we have a script. But ours isn't written by some overpaid screenwriter. Instead, it's evolved from freeform improvisations into a set of exchanges that permit little deviation from the routine. As I turn off the motorway to head into Cheltenham, I am trying to remember my lines. I should know them off by heart, but I don't have any idea whether I can carry it off this evening. I don't have the energy for my usual Oscar-winning performance.

Even my parents' house puts on an act. Outside it's a chocolate-box country cottage that's somehow been picked up by some Wizard of Oz-style hurricane, and dropped intact just off the race course.

Inside there's enough chintz to restock the Laura Ashley warehouse. The walls are primrose and buttermilk. Little dishes of colour-coordinated pot-pourri crowd together on every flat surface. But if you look closely enough, the cracks are there. Damp is bubbling away just above the skirting boards on the ground floor, breaking through the smooth paintwork. The floral print curtains have faded where the sunlight hits them and the pot-pourri is dulled by dust.

'Hello, darling,' my father says when he answers the door. He's wearing a novelty birthday jumper of the kind pioneered by regional weather presenters. I don't know where my mother gets them from, but this one features a man holding a surfboard to cover his groin; the lower half of the background is sand-yellow, the upper half sea-blue. The man has extra-curly black wool knotted onto his head and chest.

'Nice jumper,' I say. 'Very brave of you to wear it the day before your birthday.'

He smiles. 'Apparently it's a special one they do for people who're retiring. Sailing off into the sunset, you see.' He wears them without protest, though my mother must realise how humiliating they are. The rest of the time Dad is a snappy dresser for his age.

I follow him into the hall and a feeling of exhaustion overwhelms me. 'You're planning to live out the twilight years on Bondi Beach, then?' This is unlikely, given that my mother's definition of an ambitious trip would be to take the hydrofoil rather than the ferry to the Isle of Wight.

He looks down at the jumper. 'At a push it could be Torquay.'

'Only after a couple of decades of global warming,' I say. He grins at me. We've always done this, joking and bantering and trying to impress each other with our mutual cleverness. My mother never joins in. I think this makes me do it all the more.

'Is that you, Tess?'

We freeze behind the living-room door at the sound of her voice. 'It's good to see you, Tip Top,' my dad whispers. 'We've been worried.'

There's no natural light in the hall but I can see his eyes are shining – with tears? Surely my witty, dry old man isn't getting gooey with age. Emotional incontinence would, for him, probably be more humiliating than the kind below the waist. A vision of him in a bath chair weeping to *Watercolour Challenge* and *Emmerdale* springs into my mind. I go into the living room to distract myself.

'You're looking thinner,' my mother says as soon as she sees me. 'You haven't been eating properly. I don't know, you're like one of those models for heroin and yet your sister can't seem to stop stuffing herself. Why couldn't I have ended up with two average-sized daughters? I didn't have a clue what to buy for tea, but then looking at you, I don't suppose you'll eat it anyway.'

She pauses for breath. 'Hi Mum,' I say, forcing some brightness into my voice. 'You can put some extra sugars in my tea if it makes you feel better.'

'It's not funny, Tess. You're not going to help yourself by starving and you're not going to stand any chance of persuading Barney to come back if you don't take care of yourself.'

I dislodge Maurice, Mum's Persian cat, and sit down on the pouffe next to the patio doors. I haven't told them about the Curved One's baby. I suppose I will have to break the glad tidings at some stage but the thought makes me feel drained. 'I'm fine. I haven't lost any weight: I'm just tired after my first week back at work after half term and it makes my face look thinner. You look well, though.'

I try to spin out the courtesies for as long as possible, because once those are finished, I have nothing to say to her. At least Suzy and her kids will take the attention away from me once they arrive. Poor Suzy should be the thin one, the amount of running around she does after her two, not to mention her husband, the Strong-Silent-Patrick, but as her drugs of choice are fat, sugar and caffeine, her figure has expanded faster than you can say Plain Chocolate HobNob.

'Well, that's a miracle,' Mum says. 'I haven't been sleeping because of you and your . . . situation. I've no idea what to do.'

This is unlike my mother. Usually her disapproval is subtle, expressed in harassed gestures or through phrases like 'nothing's the matter' and 'I'm fine', uttered in a voice that leaves no doubt that the opposite is true. We're left in the dark about exactly what the problem is; whether it's something we've said, or something we haven't said; something we've done, or something we haven't; or simply a combination of the many unspecified disappointments life has thrown at her.

'There is nothing you can do, Mum. We're adults, Barney and me. You just have to let us get on with it.'

'But you're not trying hard enough,' she moans. 'You can't give up this easily. Marriage isn't supposed to be easy. It's a test.'

'Fine. Fine, well, so we've failed the test. Like I've failed at most things. You going on about it is not going to change a thing.' I know I should ignore it, rise above it, try harder to understand the upset that's making her so uncharacteristically explicit about her pain. But I am angry.

My father shifts from foot to foot. 'I don't want this today. Tess, Dorothy. Don't spoil things.'

She glares at him. 'As if you'd understand.'

He looks down. 'I just don't think it helps anyone.'

My childhood was full of these mysterious exchanges, hinting at things I didn't understand. Now I try to ignore them.

I take a couple of deep breaths, attempting to diffuse the adrenalin that's flooded my system in response to my mother's comments, and when the oxygen's worked, I take control again. 'I'll make some tea,' I say and leave them to their well-rehearsed sniping.

My sister and clan arrive late and harassed, accompanied by a slight smell of sick. Rosie always copies her older sister, Kim, which almost always means more hard work for Suzy. I suppose it might pay off if Kim turns out to be a swot when she starts school in September, but for now the imitative behaviour involves vomiting on any car journey outside the Southampton city limits, spreading my sister's one good Estée Lauder lipstick across their unblemished faces as if it's a Crayola crayon, and taking off their clothes in public.

And they say boys are harder work.

I never, ever copied Suzy, because our roles in life were so clearly defined. She was the pretty one, I was the clever one. Her job was to wear frilly frocks and mine was to bring home brilliant reports. It's probably why we never argued and still don't – we just weren't in competition with each other.

I race up to join her in the bathroom as she strips off Kim and Rosie's clothes – of course, this is the one time they don't actually want to be naked, so they're fighting every attempt to remove their sick-stained T-shirts.

'How's it going, big sis?' I ask, giving her the longest hug possible before she gets stuck in to cleaning them up.

'All the better for seeing you,' she says, wiping her reddened face. 'You look skinnier. Suits you. It's bloody unfair; the opposite happens to me when I'm miserable.'

'It's the D-plan diet. Get divorced and see the pounds fall away.'

Suzy really isn't that fat, maybe three stone heavier than she was before she had the kids, and though it means she sweats a little where the bulges meet, it also means her face is perfectly preserved. Wealthy women of a certain age pay to have fat injected into their wrinkles but her skin is almost unlined, puffed out from the inside, and despite exhaustion and her fortieth birthday approaching, she's still pretty in a youthful way. Even her hair shines. In childhood photos, she always looks like she's standing in the sun, and I look like I'm in the shade.

'Hello, Auntie Teff,' Rosie cries, leaping into my arms. I kiss her back, trying not to breathe through my nose, before joining the queue for help from my overburdened sister. I need to get all my frustration off my chest. 'I don't know what I'd have done if you'd been ten minutes later.'

Suzy wets a flannel and tries to wipe her wriggling eldest daughter down. 'Hold still, Kimmie. The stiller you are, the sooner you can go downstairs to Nanny and Grandpa.'

I carry on, knowing from experience that I'll have to pack all the facts into the short silences when the girls aren't chatting or shouting or whining. 'You'd have thought Barney leaving was something I'd arranged on purpose, to wind her up.'

'You're done,' Suzy says, patting Kim on the head. 'Get Daddy to find you a clean top from the bag before you get cold while I sort Rosie out.' She turns to me as she rinses out the flannel, time for my share of her attention. 'She's not very good at showing how she's feeling, Tess, you know that by now. But every time she's called me since it happened, she's been asking me for advice on what she should do. How she can help. She feels it's out of control and she doesn't know how to deal with that.'

'*She* feels out of control? How does she think I feel? My husband's gone and he's been shagging around—' I look down at Rosie. 'Sorry. But Mum's got no idea.'

Suzy gives me a strange look. 'I think you'd be surprised.' Then she turns to Rosie before I can interpret her expression. It's that feeling again, the one youngest children the world over recognise, of being out of the loop.

'What?'

'I just think she knows you better than you realise. And more about real life as well.'

'I doubt it.'

'Urrrrghh,' Rosie says as Suzy scrubs away at her neck, chin and hands. 'Lemme go, Mummy, lemme go.'

'OK, you're fit now.' Suzy lifts her out of the bath and gives her a quick cuddle before Rosie runs out of the bathroom, laughing. 'Look, I'm not pretending she's going to turn into some earth mother and sort your life out. But she's not as . . . I don't know, not as sheltered or protected as you might think. Anyway, never mind about her, I want to know how *you* are.'

Where do I start? 'Up and down like a bloody yo-yo.'

'And the stupid bitch?'

'Still pregnant, as far as I know.'

'Oh, Tess.' We have another hug.

'You smell quite bad, Suzy. Hope you've brought a spare T-shirt for you as well as the girls.'

'Oh yes. Goes with the territory,' she says, splashing her face. 'At least you don't have to plan every trip out of the house with military precision, Tip Top.'

'I guess I never will have to, now.'

She looks at me. 'Don't be daft. It's not too late to have your own.'

'At thirty-five? To meet someone, know them well enough, do the fun stuff before breeding? It's not going to happen, is it?'

'I was thirty-three with Kim.'

'Yeah, I know. But . . . well, I'm not exactly keen on blokes at the moment. I don't see myself wandering back into a relationship for a long, long time.'

'Te-ss! Su-zy!' My dad's calling from the bottom of the stairs. It's like being teenagers again, told off for hogging the bathroom.

I kiss her on the cheek. 'Don't mention the baby, yet. I'm not up to all that.'

'It's your choice. But keeping it a secret isn't necessarily going to make it easier in the long run.'

'Oh, you're so sage,' I say, giving her the cue for one of our sillier jokes from years back.

'And you're so onion.'

I finally lose the plot over dinner. Dad's chosen his favourite pizzeria, a basement restaurant with comedy giant peppermills and little plastic packets of tasteless grissini bread, which Suzy and I loved as kids, and Kim and Rosie now adore too. It's the perfect place to take two rug-rats. The noise levels mean their chatter simply adds another high-pitched note to the cacophony. The tables are wipe-clean and the plates could withstand a nuclear holocaust.

But the happy family scene – five adults trying to contain and entertain two children – wouldn't stand up to much scrutiny. We're all trying, except my mother, to keep things civil but I am not sure any of us want to be here. We've talked about holidays: Brittany for Suzy and her lot, the Isle of Wight for Mum and Dad, nothing planned for me. I don't mention that I suspect I'll end up spending August surrounded by packing cases, moving into a flat that makes Aaron's look like a palace. We've talked about work: the plans for Dad's retirement party, Patrick's franchising ideas for his dinghy club (of course it was Suzy who told us, because Patrick's incapable of finishing a sentence without clamming up), my fun-packed summer term. I don't mention that the hall, the staffroom and my classroom fall silent whenever I walk in. I suppose most teachers would be celebrating that kind of effect on their pupils. But it's not a productive silence – it's the silence of a cat stalking its prey, watching closely for the optimal moment to pounce. They're waiting for me to dissolve in front of them, like I did before half term. Children have short memories for most things, but a teacher losing the plot is the stuff of legends.

When we've run out of topics, we let the children fill the space with chattering about the horribleness of olives and the lovely frilliness of the waitresses' aprons. Then my mother drops her bombshell.

'We thought we might go back to Holden Hall for Christmas. As a family.'

I nearly choke on my pizza. My mother is smiling at me expectantly, my dad grins nervously and Suzy has found something fascinating to dissect on her plate.

I take a deep breath. 'Right. What made you think that was a good idea?' It comes out blunter than I'd hoped, but is still a lot more measured than what I want to say, which is WHAT THE FUCK??

'Oh,' she says. 'So you're going to be like that, are you?'

Dad is looking at me now, waiting. I try again, determined not to add guilt at causing a scene at his birthday to the already overwhelming list of things to regret in my life. 'I'm just not sure why you'd want to go back to my wedding-reception venue.'

'Isn't it obvious?' my mother says.

'No,' I say, congratulating myself on my restraint so far, 'it's not.'

'Well, it *obviously* wouldn't just be us going. You'd be invited . . .' she pauses, clears her throat, 'and Barney.'

Suzy's fork hovers in mid air and at last she looks at me. I wonder if she was in on it: judging from her expression – part sympathetic, part curious, but not surprised – I guess she was. But I should know more than anyone that when my mother gets a bee in her bonnet, she's unstoppable.

Even Rosie and Kim have stopped nattering, sensing that something interesting is about to kick off.

My father fills the gap. 'I know it seems a long way off, Tess. But Christmas has a habit of bringing people together . . . and your mum . . . we thought it might help things along a little bit. Oil the wheels.'

Do you ever wonder whether your parents inhabit the same planet? Whether somehow years of pretending that the tooth fairy and Father Christmas and Hilda Ogden do exist has interfered with their perception of reality?

It ought to be obvious to anyone with half a brain cell that Santa, his elves and the entire fleet of bloody reindeers are more likely to turn up for Christmas at Holden Hall than Barney. Especially as by that time he will have his own miracle baby to stow away in the manger.

'Oil the wheels?' I once went on a conflict-handling course run by the education authority – how to bring peace to classrooms inhabited by junior delinquents – and the only useful trick I learned was that to buy yourself time, you should repeat what the other person has just said.

Dad takes this as encouragement. 'Yes, love. I mean, when your mum first suggested it, I did wonder whether it might be a bit . . . what's the phrase I keep hearing the lads say at work . . . full on. But it could be what you both need, to remind you of what you had. What you could still have . . .' He tails off uncertainly.

My mother picks up the baton. 'And what better way to show that we're all on the side of your marriage.'

I have often wondered what my mother does during the day and now I know. She watches *Trisha*. No one outside a TV studio uses language like that.

'On the side of our marriage?' I repeat the words flatly. How do I begin to tell them how wrong they are, how the chances of reconciliation disappeared before we even knew there was something to conciliate – with a burst condom, a missed pill or a broken promise to be 'careful'?

My sister tries to rescue me. 'You don't have to make any decisions right away, Tess.'

My mother's already shaking her head. 'Well, you say that, Susan, but Holden Hall gets booked up very quickly. The Cotswolds are *very* popular at Christmas. So I made an enquiry last week for connecting rooms for you and the children, twin for me and your father, plus the honeymoon suite for Tess and Barney and they said they couldn't guarantee availability. They let me reserve the rooms for now, but can only hold them for a fortnight.'

'For a fortnight?' This time I can't keep the anger out of my voice: Rosie's face goes pale.

But Mum chooses not to pick up the signs, which are so obvious I might as well have them flashing in neon lights on my forehead. 'I know. It was good of them, I thought. It was because we're loyal customers. So have a think and then give me a call perhaps when you've had a chance to talk to Barney.' She thinks about it for a moment. 'Or if you think it'd be better, I could talk to him.'

'You? Talk to Barney?' I rummage about in my handbag and pull out my mobile phone. 'Tell you what, Mum, why don't you do it right now? No time to waste, after all.'

'Oh. Well, I don't think here in the restaurant,' she says, but then she sees my expression and reaches across the table to take the phone. But Suzy beats her to it.

'Stop this, Tess. You're going to have to tell them.'

'Tell them what?' my dad asks.

'There's a complication,' I say brightly, as if I am explaining that there are roadworks on the M5 which will necessitate a detour via the A38 on my journey home. 'You see, if you invite Barney you'll need a cot.'

My mother looks confused, then breaks into a smile. 'You mean . . .' she says, and points at my stomach.

I know it's cruel but I have had enough of her meddling, her interfering, the refusal to listen. 'A cot. And an extra bed. The cot will be for Barney's firstborn. And the bed for its mother.'

Chapter Sixteen

Dad gets it straight away. Mum is floundering.

'But that's wonderful news. Why didn't you tell us before?' Then she looks down at the half-empty glass of red wine next to me. 'Should you be . . . ?'

Does she expect me to draw her a diagram? 'It's not me.'

'What—?' She searches for clues in the responses of the other actors in our cosy little scene, as if she's wondering why they're not ordering champagne, climbing onto the tables and generally celebrating the addition to the Marshall dynasty.

Meanwhile my father looks like a junior doctor on his first day in casualty, unsure who to attend to first. 'Tess . . . Dorothy . . .'

My sister steps in. 'Mum, it's Barney's girlfriend who's pregnant, not Tess.'

Even this uncensored, unvarnished version of the truth takes a few moments to sink in. Then my mother's face changes. She seems to lose her grip; her mouth droops and her eyes glaze and I think for a moment that she's going to fall headfirst into her carbonara.

She's realised that Father Christmas doesn't exist.

Dad leans forward to steady her, gripping her shoulders. 'I don't know what to say, Tess.'

I wish he was holding me, not her. Who needs him the most? I suppose it's always been like that, a competition. And however much Dad and I played games together, ganged up against her and Suzy, I always knew he'd choose Mum over me. And that Mum would choose Suzy over me, too. I was no one's first choice.

I taste salt in the back of my throat. Crying won't help, but logic isn't too persuasive right now.

My father keeps his left hand on Mum's shoulder and motions for a waiter with the other. 'The bill, please, and perhaps some doggy bags for the leftovers,' he says, before turning back to me. 'It's a bit of a shock. I think perhaps we ought to get ourselves back to the house. Then we can talk or ... whatever.'

Even the girls don't complain as we wait, saying nothing, for the waiters to do their thing.

It's only quarter to nine when we arrive back at the house. The children go to bed, along with Patrick. It makes no difference; even when he is there, you'd hardly know it.

The four of us – the core of the Marshall family – end up in the dining room, on the four sides of the table like a bridge party. My mum is still acting dazed and I wonder quite what we're doing this for, why we can't just return to our charade that everything's fine. I want to cry out, 'Leave me alone with this! A problem shared is not a problem halved for me.'

Instead I say, 'I was going to tell you once I'd got it straight in my own head.'

'But Suzy knew already,' Mum says. For once she doesn't sound bossy or angry or resentful; just hurt.

'I didn't want to tell you two on the phone.' Or at all.

'But . . .' Mum tails off.

'It's out now,' Dad says, 'and what matters is how we can help you. Is this the bottom line, then, Tess? I take it this is the girl he left for?'

I nod. The thought of Barney with a harem of women fighting for his genetic material almost makes me laugh. Almost.

'It won't last,' my mother snaps. 'He's hardly got what he bargained for with his bit on the side, has he? He'll be back with his tail between his legs before long. They all come back in the end.'

I wonder what makes my mother think she's such a bloody expert. Watching *Trisha* again, I suppose.

'Perhaps, Dorothy, perhaps. Would you take him back, Tess,

if it didn't work out with this girl?' My father, ever practical, wants to know how the land lies before he pronounces his verdict.

'No.'

'Are you sure?' says Mum. 'Most things can be made to work, if you put enough effort in. Even the baby doesn't have to rule out getting back together. Especially after seventeen years.'

Bloody hell, that's the first time my mother has recognised how long we were together – usually she only ever acknowledges our married years as being legitimate. 'Really?'

'Yes,' she says, getting into her stride. 'Every marriage goes through its ups and downs.'

Or just downs in the case of my parents. Maybe I had lower expectations than Barney anyway and he saw what I didn't: that our marriage wasn't making either of us happy.

'I'm sure. But there's a difference between ups and downs like you've had, and this. I don't believe for one minute that either of you would have put up with the other being unfaithful.' That ought to shut them up. For once, they can't pull rank or do that irritating parental thing of telling you what mistakes they've made and how you can avoid them.

My mother looks straight at me. 'Your father has had four affairs. That I know of. I'm still here.'

When you have an accident – drop a heavy object on your foot, spill red wine on your cream silk-upholstered antique sofa, drive your newly serviced car into the back of the one in front because you were retuning the radio – you spend so long going over and over those last few moments, wanting to replay them: just ten seconds would be enough.

I feel like that now. I know that what my mother has just said will change everything. Not just the present and the future but the past.

'Dorothy,' Dad says and lays his hand on hers. There's no protest, no defence. She leaves her hand there and when she looks at me, there's an air of defiance.

'You think I'm a cold fish, don't you, Tess? Humourless. It's something I've accepted over the years, to protect you. Where was the sense in telling you and making you hate both your parents? But you're a grown-up now and I'd rather you were a grown-up who sees the world for what it is and has the chance to save her marriage, even if that makes you think less of us.'

It's quite a speech for my mother. I wonder if she's planned it for years, or perhaps every morning as she watches the lowlife of Britain purging their souls. But I don't know what to say.

Suzy is biting her nails. I haven't seen her do that since she got through ten bottles of Stop 'n' Gro over a single weekend when we were teenagers. I stopped by deciding one morning that I didn't want to have horrible hands. She got the looks but I got the willpower.

'Did *you* know?' I ask her.

'No one ever told me directly. But I kind of worked it out. Things changed between them, Tess. I couldn't put my finger on what or when, exactly. All I know is that around the time I moved up from infants into the juniors, I couldn't sleep at nights. Not for months and months. I used to lie in bed awake, terrified they were going to split up. Wondering who I'd go with and if they'd make me choose.'

'Oh, God.' Mum stares at my sister. 'We thought you were being bullied.'

Suzy shrugs. 'I couldn't *say* anything. If I said the word divorce out loud then it might make it happen, put ideas in your heads. But four times?'

'I'm sorry,' my father says.

My sister groans. 'You're sorry, but you still had *four* affairs? It doesn't really wash, does it, Dad? You didn't just hurt Mum – that's bad enough. But you also put our whole family at risk four different times.' She stands up. 'I don't want to look at you. I'm going to bed and I don't want to see you tomorrow so please don't try to talk to me. We'll be going straight home as soon as the girls have had their breakfast.'

'I'm sorry,' he says again. My clever, witty, verbally gymnastic father is reduced to the same two words. But I don't see how he can expect us to believe that he means it.

The remaining three of us wait, not knowing what to do next. Eventually my mother says, 'I wasn't planning to do this, Tess. It's what you said. I couldn't let it ... I wanted you to understand that things are never easy, but they can be worked out.'

I wonder if that's really true or whether somehow she wanted to sabotage the relationship Dad and I have had for so long. It must have been torture seeing how he could do no wrong, how I took his side and how the two of us together laughed at her, barely behind her back. We were as bad as playground bullies. But why break her silence now?

The sound of the door to my sister's room closing finally triggers my mother to do something.

'We'll go to bed now,' she says and my father instantly obeys her, standing up, while he shoots me the occasional glance, trying to test my reaction. 'But if there's anything you want to ask . . . it's only fair that you should know anything you feel you need to be told.'

I shake my head. Part of me wants to go up to her and hold her, let her know it's all right. But it isn't. I stay sitting bolt upright in my dining chair as they leave the room.

'I really am sorry,' Dad says, very quietly, as if even he is aware that his contrition beggars belief.

The house moans in protest as they go upstairs. The boiler fires up as my mother washes her face with soap and water in the en-suite. Then I hear the strange rattling in the plumbing as Dad flushes the toilet. These are the sounds of my childhood. Only when the door to their bedroom squeaks shut do I fetch the duvet and pillows and lie down on the sofa. I don't have the energy to brush my teeth, remove my make-up or change into my pyjamas, so I lie down fully clothed.

But everything is too loud for sleep. The noises of the floorboards and joists and whatever else settling down for the night seem as loud as a student party. Beyond that, whispering fills my head. Mum, Dad, Suzy, Patrick, all talking about the last hour, murmuring wildly different versions of one single conversation that will influence every family gathering from now on. Speaking the words will set their personal accounts of the moment in stone.

I have no one to whisper to, so instead the whispers are in my head. Who were these women my father slept with? Neighbours, friends, his secretary, maybe ... When? Most of all, why did he do it – not once but four times? Why did Mum put up with it? And why didn't I realise?

After an hour – or it could be only ten minutes; night plays tricks on you – I get up, find my father's whisky bottle and pour myself a tumbler. Gin and tonic's for socialising, Grand Marnier because I like the taste, but whisky is medicine. It catches in my throat as I swallow, but if I drink enough, it will all stop hurting.

I wake up to the patter of feet running down the stairs.

'Auntie Te-ess! Wake up!' Kim bursts through the door. 'Phewey, it smells horrible in here! Like Grandpa ...'

She's right. The smell is coming from me. There's a damp patch of Scotch on the duvet near my waist – I must have fallen asleep before I finished the whisky. I look down at my hand. It's still gripping the tumbler.

'You're right, lovely. I'll open the window in a sec.'

Rosie jumps onto the sofa next to me and gives me a big kiss. 'Morning, Teff,' she says.

Kim switches the TV on. 'Mummy won't get up. Daddy says she's tired but I think she's got angular.'

'Angular?'

'Drinked too much.'

'Ah ... a hangover.'

'Have you got angular, Auntie Tess?'

I move my head tentatively from one side to the other. 'No, I don't think I have.' She pulls open the curtains and a weakish light hits my face. 'Maybe your mummy just isn't feeling well.'

'Maybe she's having a baby. Hope it isn't a boy baby. Eurgggh.'

Rosie dutifully echoes her sister's groan.

'I don't think your mummy's having a baby, girls,' I say. Just for a moment, I wonder if Dad might have had another family. Do I have a brother or another sister I don't know about somewhere?

I dismiss that idea. My dad – in his new incarnation as a savvy, spivvy adulterer who cheats on his wife and kids but maintains his position as adored head of the family – wouldn't be stupid enough to get a mistress pregnant.

Perhaps he should have given Barney a few tips on playing away.

'Hungry,' says Rosie, exposing her tummy and rubbing it, in case I miss the point.

'Come on, girls,' I say, getting up very slowly. 'Let's get us all some breakfast.'

Chapter Seventeen

Even the M5 looks different this morning.

The sun is shining, it's perfect weather for putting your foot down and it's still too early for the Sunday drivers. But the pleasure of trying to beat my personal best from Cheltenham to Birmingham has disappeared. All I want is to be home, but I know it won't feel like a haven any more. Nothing will be the same again.

I didn't get to talk to Suzy properly. Patrick came downstairs just after the girls and tutted over their choices from the individual boxes of sugary cereals my parents stockpile before they visit. 'They'll only make you sick,' he muttered as he snatched the bowls away. He frowned at me as I followed him into the kitchen. It was obviously all my fault.

'How is she?' I asked him as he scoured the contents labels of the brightly coloured packets.

'Upset. But she's strong. And it's history, after all.' Patrick is the dictionary definition of 'no-nonsense' but he is a good if slightly Victorian father and is someone Suzy can rely on. That, it now seems, is the rarest commodity of all in a man.

'It's still a shock, Patrick.' I thought he probably needed it spelling out; he isn't someone who takes a hint and I knew Suzy would need TLC. 'I think the girls have picked up on it, too.' We both peered through the serving hatch, where Kim and Rosie were singing along with a loud, green-headed monster on TV.

'Doesn't seem to be worrying them too much.'

'That's what my parents thought about Suzy,' I said.

Patrick pulled open the packs of cereal he'd chosen – the most fibrous, brown and tasteless of the selection boxes. 'Look at all this packaging. It's so wasteful. No, if I know my daughters, they'll have forgotten about it by the time we get back to Southampton.'

I had a sudden premonition of the girls as teenagers, arriving on my doorstep with hurriedly packed weekend bags, complaining that their father didn't understand them, that he never listened, that he couldn't care less.

He went back into the living room, put the bowls on the dining table. 'Girls, girls, no watching TV over breakfast. Come to the table; your food won't go down properly if you're slumped on the floor.'

There were a few token moans but soon the cereal shut them up, as they tried to munch the 'bite-size biscuits' into something digestible.

When Suzy appeared a few minutes later, we didn't mention what had happened, just hugged until the girls started pulling at our sleeves.

'I'll call you, Tip Top.'

'Right,' I said. 'Love you.'

'Love you too.'

I watched as Patrick's people carrier scorched away, then I dragged the duvet upstairs and locked myself in the bathroom. First I tried to sponge off the whisky. It made the whole room smell of Christmas. Then I stood under the shower, trying to direct the dribble onto the part of my body where the tension was located, but then I realised it was all over, head to toe. I came out and sat on the toilet, reading Dad's copies of *Private Eye* until I guessed the coast was clear.

I collided with my mother as I left the bathroom. 'Is Dad playing hide and seek then?' I said, a weak attempt to lighten the mood.

'What have we come to, Tess? Your dad won't come out after what your sister said last night.'

'I'm sure it's just the shock,' I said, feeling far from sure. She nodded and went ahead of me down the stairs. 'Is Dad awake?'

'Hasn't even slept. I'm making him a cup of tea. He didn't know if he should come down while you were still here.'

I thought about him skulking in the bedroom, my fearless

father suddenly afraid of me. I turned round. 'I'll go and see him.'

I stood outside their bedroom door, listening. Was he crying? Or was it all a pretence of remorse, for my mother's sake? I knocked. 'Dad, it's me. Tess.'

I heard nothing. A horrible image of him lying in the bath, wrists slashed and bleeding to death while my mother made a brew, came into my head. I didn't believe Dad was capable of that, but then I hadn't believed he was capable of cheating on Mum either.

After a good two minutes, the door opened. 'I'm so glad you haven't gone home without giving me the chance to explain,' he said. He looked exhausted and smaller, swamped by a tartan dressing gown, like a hospital patient.

'I don't want an explanation, Dad. I don't want to talk about it at all, but I didn't want to leave without seeing you.'

'I'm a stupid person, but I didn't mean to hurt anyone. We were going through a bad patch, your mum and me, and—'

'Don't you mean *four* bad patches?'

He blushed. 'Your mother found out about the third, and then I told her about the previous two. They'd all been in the space of a year. I thought it'd make her more likely to trust me again. Because I'd come clean.'

'And the fourth?'

He opened his mouth to answer, but then I held up my hand. 'No, forget I asked. I told you I didn't want to know and I meant it.'

'Tip Top . . .'

'Don't!' The nickname seemed so childish, a souvenir of a time when I was Daddy's girl, but now as redundant as my Sindy doll or the Mousetrap boardgame with half the plastic bits missing.

'Is there anything I can do?'

I thought about it. I needed time to adjust to this new version of our family history. 'No. I'm going now. I will ring, I promise. But maybe not for a while.'

'You didn't need this now, did you?'

'Or ever.' I reached across to him, kissed his cheek and pulled away before he could hug me. 'Happy birthday, Dad.'

'Drive safely,' he said.

I press the accelerator to the floor. The car whines its resistance before responding. The motorway's so quiet that I'm doing ninety in the slow lane. I feel light-headed – perhaps I'm still drunk from the whisky.

The lines between the lanes are hypnotic, and as I stare into the distance, I imagine what would happen if I were to drive ever faster, pushing the car so hard that its whine turns into a scream, until a motorway bridge appears a long way in the distance.

In this other world I imagine myself steering carefully and purposefully towards it . . . for my other self there is no going back.

A fraction of a second before my other self collides with the bridge, I shut my eyes and wait for the impact.

When I open them again, the motorway curves in front of me like the road to heaven. I feel more tears behind my eyes – I've cried more in the last five months than I have in the previous thirty-five years – and slow right down. The sign for Strensham services comes at just the right time.

I splash water onto my face in the toilets and when I look up to the mirror I see that holding my head down has brought some welcome colour to my pasty cheeks. My eyes are alive. Wired.

I buy a posh coffee and a stale croissant in the empty cafeteria and sit down right next to the window. A couple of lorries race silently past the triple-glazing.

Where do I go from here? I never thought my parents had the ideal marriage, but it was familiar, a baseline from which to build my own. The temptation to use my father's infidelity to reinforce existing evidence that all men are indeed bastards is enormous, but somehow my near-death mirage has shown me this isn't the route I should take.

I think of Aaron for the first time in twenty-four hours. Before the logical side of my brain has time to intervene, I reach for my mobile and dial his number.

We've arranged to meet in Cannon Hill Park, but I wouldn't be surprised if he doesn't turn up. I used Mel's old trick of putting 141 in front of the number so he couldn't know it was me, and when he answered and realised who it was, he didn't sound exactly thrilled. I then used a trick of my own, the one I always pull on the kids at school when I want them to do something they'd rather not – I speak with such force that the idea of going against my orders doesn't seem possible.

But agreeing on the phone, and turning up in person, are two different things. And there's still the matter of why the hell I didn't call Mel, or Roz, or even Carol-Ann, instead of this man I don't know at all.

Maybe it's because, like me, he is hurting right now. Because he knows what it is to be lied to. Or maybe it's because I've decided I'm fed up with never getting the truth from the men in my life.

I find a bench overlooking the boating lake. I'm testing myself: it's proving to be a weekend of facing up to stuff I've been avoiding. I feel a bit shaky looking into the water so I concentrate on the families messing about, threatening to push each other in: a scene that must have been repeated every weekend since Edwardian days. When I first moved to Birmingham, I couldn't believe how green it was. I was expecting soot-grey and tarmac-black, with perhaps the odd flash of red bricks and tiles. But as soon as you left behind the motorways and the grim tunnel network of the city centre, there were Parisian-style boulevards dwarfed by massive trees, and parks as big as small towns.

How many of the mums and dads are living the lie, like my father did? And is it better to pretend, to preserve the family at all costs? Or should they be cruel to be kind, split up and ship out, so kids know the truth about love as early as possible?

I sense his presence a fraction of a second before he says, 'Hello, Tess.'

'Aaron.' I grant him an acknowledgement, nothing more, and he sits down, a good two bums' width away from me. He's bigger than I remembered, more masculine somehow, though not necessarily more attractive. Seeing his clothes in daylight doesn't help: they're as worn and uninspiring as his studio flat. I like the idea of his loucheness much more than the reality – he's crossed the line from cool into seedy. The thought that part of him has been *inside* part of me makes my stomach turn over.

'I was going to call but . . .'

'But?' I look into his eyes. The blue seems to have gone: in this light they look as grey and hard as concrete.

I'm not being awkward, I'm genuinely curious. Is he about to give me the one-night-stand version of the 'dog ate my homework' excuse, or will Aaron surprise me and actually tell me the truth?

'I called up your number a couple of times, but then . . . don't know. Suppose I wondered what I'd say. I mean, it was nice . . . more than nice, obviously. But, you know, we were both pissed. For a while we wanted something to take our minds off the fact we were both having a shit time. It worked. Sure. But I didn't know if there was anything else *to* say.'

Quite a speech for a man. Even more astonishing, it makes sense. 'I don't know either, but I do know that it's about more than me. It's also about the people on the course – it changed the whole mood when you didn't turn up.'

He blushes slightly, looks away. 'Yeah. Sorry. It got to Tuesday evening and I couldn't see how I could come when I hadn't called you. It wasn't on. I bottled it. Didn't know how you'd react . . . I kind of reckoned you weren't the sort to scream and shout, but that made me feel guiltier.'

'We're both adults. You didn't give me any commitments, Aaron, but you did give a commitment to the group that you'd keep coming.' God, I sound so mature. I'm almost fooling myself.

'Don't tell me. I know, I know.'

Another man avoiding facing up to things, in the hope they'll go away. 'Do you fancy a Ninety-nine?' I say eventually.

We join the queue by the van next to the Midlands Arts Centre. Older kids slalom around the adults on skateboards and roller-skates, while the teeny ones have white slashes of Mr Whippy ice-cream across their chins and cheeks. It's where I imagined bringing the family Barney and I were going to create. The Botanical Gardens were our childless haunt, a model of sophistication and order, a place for romancing and kissing and talking about the future. But Cannon Hill Park was where we would go when our joint enterprise was coming to fruition. We'd revel in the chaos and the face-painting and try to race each other pushing the pram around the lake.

Will he be bringing *her* here?

'Penny for them?' Aaron says. It's a strange, old-fashioned thing to say and it makes me suspect that for all his cool and his facial hair, he's got a mum who tuts over his winter wardrobe, and a dad who tuts over the money he's spending on divorce lawyers.

'It's nothing . . . so, are you going to come back?'

'To the group?' He reaches the front of the queue. 'What are you having? They're on me. Least I can do.' He is joking. I think.

'An Almond Magnum, then. If you're buying.'

'An Almond Magnum and a standard cone, please.' We both watch as the frowning man pumps out the white cream like toothpaste and finishes it off with a flick of the wrist.

'Two pounds,' he snarls. He doesn't seem to be getting much job satisfaction from his life in the van. It's not surprising – the noise of the generator must be overwhelming after a while and the pastel pink and blue paint is peeling off in big flakes.

'I love this stuff,' Aaron says, then he leans into the cone and licks off the top swirl. He stares at me as he does this and lets the ice-cream melt on his tongue before closing his mouth. I realise with a jolt that this is meant to be erotic.

Cheeky bastard. One minute he's being contrite, the next he's working up to a repeat performance. A flashback to the night on his foam sofa bed makes me want to look away, as I remember his face, his staring eyes and spade hands, but there's a little bit of me that's pleased. *He wants to do it again. I must be OK.*

'It's tasteless.' I'm not really talking about the ice-cream.

'Exactly. It's full of air. Chemicals. Vegetable fats. No vitamins, minerals or anything healthy about it. Fantastic.' Then he leers again. 'It's all about giving in to pleasure.'

I crack the chocolate on mine with my teeth – the sound is

satisfying and I pick off the biggest jagged piece. 'Each to their own pleasure, I suppose. I prefer the posher variety.'

He pulls a face. If we're talking about sex rather than ice-cream, then I guess I've insulted him. But I'm pretending that we're talking about ice-cream.

We take the path towards the far side of the lake, dodging pushchairs and squirrels. 'You didn't answer my question, Aaron. Are you coming back to the group?'

'William wouldn't let me! Come on, I've committed a cardinal sin by not turning up, haven't I?' He pushes ice-cream down into the bottom of the cone with his tongue. I can't tell if this is also meant to be suggestive or if it's a childhood habit he's been unable to break. My sister used to do exactly the same thing.

'He's a good Christian. He'll forgive you. I suppose it depends on whether you *want* to come back. I mean, what else is there to do on a Tuesday night?'

He pauses as he finishes off the tiny triangle of cardboardy cone. 'Dunno. Can't say it's helped much so far. Except for the extra-curricular activities, of course. They took my mind off things for a bit.'

I ignore the double entendre. 'Maybe the group is like antibiotics. Won't cure you unless you finish the course.'

'Yeah, maybe. I always thought the worst thing you could catch from women was the clap. Never thought I'd need treatment for a broken heart.' He laughs, a short, hoarse sound.

'Have you heard any more from your wife?'

'No. We're still trying to work out who gets first prize for unreasonable behaviour.'

'Can't you just go straight for adultery? I would, in your situation.' Is that what I'm doing? Suddenly my lack of action so far makes me feel unsettled. With the joint enterprise between Barney and the Curved One presumably progressing fast, I could end up husbandless and homeless as well as childless by the end of the summer. Tip Top Tess has been caught napping.

'It's a bit complicated,' Aaron says.

'You have to try not to let your feelings get in the way.' It seems like the sensible thing to say, though it's the classic example of me not practising what I preach.

'Well. Women going down on each other doesn't qualify. Even if they use a strap-on dildo it doesn't count as adultery. There's no justice, is there?'

A piece of almond-embedded chocolate goes down the wrong way. I try for as long as I can to fight the urge to choke because I'm desperate to get the full story this time. But it doesn't work and I start to cough. 'Ah . . . ah, sorry, Aaron, uugh, ice-cream gone . . . ugh—' I point at my throat.

He looks sheepish. 'Sorry. That was a bit blunt, even for me. You all right?'

I wave my hand in the air, trying to indicate that it's all fine, as I fight to catch my breath. Finally I regain control of my respiratory system, as I feel the chocolate melt into my lungs. 'Can we sit down again?'

We find another bench, and when I've cooled down, I say, 'You didn't get the chance to tell me the full story before.' Because you were too busy sticking your tongue down my throat, presumably in a bid to prove you can still pull.

'Not much to say.'

Bloody men, again. Your wife announces she's gay and there's *not much to say*. 'Well, it must have been a shock.'

'Yeah . . .' He's being evasive again. 'It was kind of a friend of ours. A close friend. But I never imagined I'd be replaced.' Aaron stares off into the distance.

There's something about the way he says it, his reluctance to meet my eye, that makes me wonder. 'How close?'

His expression confirms I'm onto something. 'She was more Kitty's friend than mine. You know women.'

'Yes, being one, I would. And you had no idea . . . no signs that she might be . . .' What would Barney call it? Batting for the other team? '. . . that way inclined?'

He flushes. 'Shit, Tess, what is this, the third degree?' He stands up again. 'I need a drink.'

'A coffee in the MAC?' I'm not letting him get away with it that easily.

'Alcohol.'

We head for the bar. There's a hippy-style craft fair going on, plus a few stalls doing braiding and henna tattoos and some

183

peculiarly bad face-painting. For all of Birmingham's rebirth, the MAC still has the aura of a 1970s youth club, with distressed wood on the windows and scuffed skirting boards. Aaron should be in his element. But at least it serves alcohol in the afternoons.

Aaron attracts attention immediately: this is a man who knows his way around a bar. 'Vodka and lime. A double. And . . .'

'A beer. Bud or something. Listen, I should get these. You got my ice-cream.'

'The ice-cream that nearly killed you! Bugger off, I'm getting them. It'll make me feel more macho.' He grins at me. I think he's taking the piss out of himself, a quality that instantly makes him attractive again. I am so malleable it's untrue.

The table wobbles as we sit down. I hold up my bottle to clink it against his glass. 'So, you were saying?'

'Was I? Yeah, I suppose I was.' He takes a swig of the yellow-green drink, wincing at the sourness. 'Listen. Tess. Don't take this the wrong way, but . . . I kind of figure you've led a bit more of a sheltered life than me.'

Is he talking about my sexual abilities? How can he tell? 'The wrong way, in that you're not meaning to be horribly patronising – is that what you mean? I've been around; I know about ladies who love other ladies, men who love other men and men who love farmyard animals.'

He takes a deep breath. 'What about men who don't know what they've got till it's gone? Who push their wives into doing stuff they don't wanna do, and then complain when it goes tits up? Literally, tits up.'

'I don't know what you mean.'

'Look. I've always had . . . an appetite. Booze, music, drugs. And sex. They go together, don't they? But the other three were just a way of passing the time until I discovered sex. Kind of like my hobby, really. I wasn't the type to get married. That's why I left it so long.'

'Right.' I'm not sure I like the way this is going: if sex is a hobby, what am I? The tunnel in his model-railway set? A stamp in his collection?

'But when I met Kitty, I knew she was different. Cute,

obviously. What the newspapers would call a healthy sex drive. But not . . . tarnished by life, like so many of the women I met. She was knowing *and* innocent. Does that make any sense?'

It makes no sense at all to me – except that I suddenly start wondering if I'm tarnished – so I stay quiet.

'We had a blast. I realised what they meant about sex being better when you're in love. Drew the line at calling it *making lurve* though. What's wrong with calling it fucking?'

He looks at me like he's expecting me to answer. I shrug. Certainly his technique was much closer to the latter than the former.

'I'm getting a bit carried away, Tess, sorry. Last thing you want is me banging on about my ex. To cut my long story short, we had fun. Then I pushed it too far. Said we should try everything once, even when she resisted.'

'You *forced* her into something?' My mouth has gone dry. Am I sitting opposite some kind of rapist? A rapist I have already slept with . . .

He shakes his head. 'No, not like that. God, no. It was more . . . mental pressure. Look, I wanted a threesome. She didn't. Looking back now I wonder if she knew, somehow, what might happen and that's why she held back. Most of us are supposed to be bisexual to some degree, aren't we? I was so smug I just assumed she was scared I'd go off with the other woman. Kind of ironic, the way things turned out.'

Finally I get it. 'And the third person is your wife's new lover?' He nods. 'Shit.' I don't know what else to say. My sympathy is ebbing away.

'You think I got what I deserved, don't you?'

'No, I don't . . . well, I do a bit, if I'm honest.'

He drains the last of his syrupy drink, slams his glass down on the table, which wobbles more dramatically than before. 'You want to know something, Tess? So do I.' He stares at the floor. 'So do I.'

Lesson Four

Back to the Future

William's moods had always been mercurial. When he was a little boy, he'd been nicknamed Billy Barometer by his uncle Jeff, because the slightest change in the weather would change his behaviour. A glimpse of sunshine would have him turning cartwheels in the backyard until he was sick with dizziness, while the first icy north wind of the autumn would trigger a sulk of Cold War proportions.

The weather still had a powerful effect, but other things were now just as likely to cause a change of disposition. The newspaper seller smiling or frowning, the music on Radio Two (William was especially angry about the increasing tendency to play chart music. Surely that was what Radio One was for?).

Today it was an early arrival that put a spring in his step. Aaron was the last person he'd expected to see, but his appearance made William feel all-powerful. The hippy had tried to break free, but in the end the only path to salvation came via St Gabriel's on a Tuesday night.

Not that William was about to make it easy for the prodigal son.

'Can I help you?' he said to Aaron, showing no trace of recognition.

Aaron was suitably taken aback. 'Um . . . well, yes. Listen, I'm sorry I didn't make it to the last session. The thing is, I . . .' he looked upwards, as though the excuse he was seeking was floating somewhere on the ceiling of the church hall, 'I think the intimacy of the classes . . . well, it freaked me out a bit. That's why I bottled it last time.'

William worked hard to suppress the smile of satisfaction he could feel appearing on his face. 'And . . . ?'

'And?' Aaron was trying to fathom what else could be expected of him. 'Well, I suppose, I think that ... it would be good if I could come back.'

'Come back?' William had no intention of offering an olive branch. If laziness and lack of courage had got Aaron into this mess, he needed to show he could be capable of more moral fibre before he'd be allowed back into the fold.

Aaron stared back. 'Yes, come back. What else do you think I'm here for? I think I'm on the right track and I'd like to stick around.'

'And how do you think the others will feel? I know how they felt last week. Let down. Why should they believe that you won't let them down again?'

Aaron shuffled his feet. 'We all make mistakes.'

William turned back towards the cupboard, where he was refilling a metal 'Country Diary of an Edwardian Lady' canister with supermarket economy teabags. He held one up to Aaron. 'They come in all shapes and sizes, now, don't they? Round ones, triangular ones, ones with scientifically engineered perforations. These old-fashioned ones make tea perfectly well. Like the ones with the chimps. I don't know why they had to get rid of the chimps, either. What do you suppose happened to them?'

'The chimps?' Aaron blinked in confusion.

'Yes. I hope they went to a good home. Did you know they have ninety-nine per cent of our DNA?'

'No, I didn't.'

William shook his head. 'I didn't think you would.'

'So?'

'So what?' William asked.

'So am I back in the fold? Am I forgiven?' Aaron's voice betrayed his impatience, and he seemed to be angling his body back towards the door.

'Oh, that.' William pushed the top back onto the canister. A few rust flakes fell onto the work surface. More cleaning up. 'Yes. If you really want to come back. Of course, if any of the others veto you, I will have to go with that. But I won't suggest it, if you see what I mean.'

Aaron nodded. He still looked grumpy.

'Why don't you make yourself useful, while we wait?' William suggested. 'I could do with a cup of tea.'

'Right. Tonight we're back at full strength – welcome again to Aaron – which is good stuff. We're going to do a bit of proper group work tonight, as we're getting to know each other better. Because if two heads are better than one, then imagine what we can do with eight!' William smiled encouragingly, though he knew the words 'group work' would have struck fear into some of his students.

People were strange. That was the most consistent finding after nearly a decade at the emotional coalface. In the three minutes it took the ageing kettle to boil to make the tea, Aaron had told William more than he needed to know about his break-up: the threesome, the jealousy and the final humiliation of being dumped for someone without a penis.

William couldn't remember knowing any lesbians when he was growing up, but now the world seemed to be full of them, including the predatory ones who targeted married women. Perhaps it was a generational thing. He blamed the media. Or maybe it was the government. Or the water board: maybe it was all those female hormones swilling around in the sewers because so many women were on the Pill. He'd read about it in the *Daily Mail*, but there'd been no conclusion about what effect it was having. He made a mental note to buy a water filter.

'What we're going to do tonight is work out what we think makes a relationship work, and what makes it break down. But not just your own. That's why for homework I asked you to try to come up with examples of relationships you remember from when you were little, because the chances are that your childhood experiences have had more of an impact on your view of the perfect marriage than you think.

'So you're going to start off in twos – choose your own partner – and I want you to take these packs of Post-it notes. First of all have a chat about the two relationships you've thought of, the good one and the bad one, and then I'd like you to scribble down the positive and negative qualities on different-coloured stickies. Let's see . . . yellow for good, green for bad. Choose an area of wall to stick them on and we'll come back together in . . .' he looked at his watch, 'forty-five minutes?'

William watched as Carol-Ann made a beeline for Aaron – was she just nosy about his absence last week, or was there something more? Jo and Tess had disappeared into the furthest corner before he could say 'happy ever after'. He felt the bitterness rise up in him again and tried to ward it off again with the Californian anti-jealousy mantra. But it wasn't helping, so he turned his attention to the rest of the students. Rani was pairing up with Natalie, while Tim, who already looked exhausted, with circles of sweat under the arms of his supermarket uniform, drew the short straw. Having to listen to dreary old Malcolm was hardly likely to lift his mood.

William couldn't face it either, so instead he sidestepped towards Rani and Natalie. Natalie was still the most mysterious of his students. All the others he could summarise in a sentence. After the evening's revelations over tea, Aaron was henceforth the pervert who'd been hoist by his own petard, so to speak. Carol-Ann was the victim determined not to be victimised. Malcolm was the epitome of misplaced self-righteousness. Tess was suffering from the worst disappointment of her life, while Tim had spent his life knowing that one day he'd be disappointed and was gaining a strange satisfaction from finally being proved right. Rani was a coper, the ultimate mother figure in a family that had lost its patriarch. Jo was probably the most sorted, but then again she'd been the only one who'd made the choice to leave.

Which left Natalie. The notes on the questionnaire told him only the bare facts: a new baby, some irreconcilable difficulties and a trial separation, though she and her husband were living under the same roof for now. An enigma in designer clothing. It was time he found out what made her tick.

'Mind if I listen in?' he said, as he pulled up a chair. 'Check you've understood the task?'

They both looked relieved that he was there, which made William feel useful rather than nosy. He'd provide a psychological helping hand. If a trouble shared was a trouble halved, then a trouble shared among three must be even better. Except when it was a threesome of course. An image of Aaron servicing two women suddenly leapt into his mind. To banish it, he asked: 'So, which of you two has a story about marriage that you remember from your childhood?'

They sat in silence. Natalie's was the pouty silence of a child used to getting her own way, Rani's the silence of a long-suffering mother, waiting patiently for a toddler to fall into line. They'd worked together quite happily before, so William knew the exercise must have hit a nerve.

'Natalie is finding the exercise difficult,' said Rani.

'Right, well, let's see if I can help. It doesn't have to be your parents. It could be the next-door neighbour. Your grand-parents. Your teacher. Anyone, really.'

Rani's smile had the serenity of the Mona Lisa, but it sent a clear message to Natalie. *I don't give up easily. I have more willpower than you do and you're going to do as you're told.*

Natalie pursed her lips, then spoke, sounding more resentful with every word. 'OK, OK. Why not go straight in for the kill? My mother and father were ... are averagely happy. She wears the trousers, which seems to suit them both. Only a fool would try to outmanoeuvre her and although my father is weak, he's not a fool. But he is not her equal. I don't know what that tells you, but they're no better and no worse than anyone else. There's no family history of divorce, if that's what you're looking for.'

'It's not like cancer,' William said, as gently as he could. 'I don't think divorce is hereditary. If it runs in families, then it's because people haven't found out how to break away from damaging patterns set in childhood. That's why we're talking about it here: not to lay blame, but to see a way forward. It's not my role to tell you what was wrong with your parents or your childhood or even your marriage – you draw your own conclusions.'

But it didn't stop William drawing some of his own. A woman so in control that, despite a small baby and a divorce looming, she was faultlessly made up and gorgeously groomed. So that would be her mother's side ... and her father's side? William speculated that perhaps Natalie had followed her father's lead in choosing a more powerful partner, someone who wanted her to be well turned out, toned to perfection and successful. But only as an accessory. Never as the main attraction.

Of course, it was idle speculation, but William's idle speculation was often right.

'My conclusions are that my break-up has nothing to do with my parents and everything to do with being wrong for my husband. Or him being wrong for me. Or both. Yes, it's probably both, though I seem to feel all the guilt.'

William tried to conceal his frustration. Her resistance made him tired. 'Fair enough. But if you think you'll want another relationship one day – and after all, most of us do – then it can be helpful to think about avoiding the same mistakes.' William picked up the Post-its and unravelled the cellophane. 'That's where these come in handy. Don't judge what you're feeling, just write down words: the things that are good, the things that are bad. To *you*. It's probably different for everyone. You might see "balance" in a relationship as important, while Rani here might see it as a bad thing. As, I don't know . . . unnatural.' He froze. Was he being prejudiced? Assuming that just because she was Asian, she'd want to play the little wife to some all-powerful husband? 'Not that I think that's what you think, of course, Rani.'

Her smile was as serene as ever, but her eyes seemed to be laughing at him. 'As a matter of fact, I do think that strengths and weaknesses are what make a marriage work,' she said. 'It is just that it tends to be the woman who has all the strength, and men who have all the weaknesses. Because the woman knows in the end that she is the one who can be left holding the babies and the man knows she has that strength and is intimidated by it. I have seen that in every marriage, no, in every relationship I have known. Equality is a fine ideal but I have not yet seen it in reality.'

William nodded. 'So it's always women who hold the cards?'

Rani shook her head. 'No, no. Because while women have the strength, men think they have power. They confuse the two.

They do have the physical strength and often the fear of that is enough to keep a woman in her place.'

William's domestic-violence antennae twitched. It was horribly common. He suspected there was a problem like this on at least one course in three, though it was so hard to get through to the victims. He prepared a solemn look, opened his mouth to deliver a carefully worded speech about how the help was all there, should a woman need it, when she slapped his outstretched hand.

'Not me, silly! No one would try that on with me.' She raised her eyebrows at Natalie, who had the look of someone who wanted to be anywhere but here. 'And you said you would not be jumping to conclusions. But that is men. Always jumping to conclusions. Unlike women, huh? We are the ones who will avoid the most obvious conclusions in the world until they are staring at us in the face and virtually baring their backsides at us.'

'At the same time?' William tried to lighten the mood. 'Conclusions must be very agile things. So, Rani . . . what about you? Any positive words you'd like to jot down?'

She frowned. 'I must sound very bitter, but I do believe in love. So that will go down.' She picked up a pen and the yellow Post-its and wrote *love* in beautifully neat handwriting. Then she drew a little heart in the corner and peeled off two more pages. 'There . . . and I have seen respect and kindness, from my parents. But on the bad side . . .' she reached for the green pad, 'there is dependence – for money, for security. And there is jealousy. Of the other's life. Particularly from my mother. She wanted more freedom, but only my father had that.'

'And do you think you've had more than her?'

Now her eyes were brighter than ever, circles of amber burning out of her face. 'I have not, until now.' A hint of tears magnified tiny flecks of yellow. 'But I will. And I will make sure my daughter has more than me. This is how it goes, isn't it? The next generation has a better life than we did, and so it continues.'

'Your daughter's a lucky girl.'

'Really? Even with a father who does not want to know?'

William thought about it. 'It's not ideal, I'll admit. But better a mother like you than two inadequate parents.'

She beamed. 'Thank you.'

'My pleasure.' He looked at his watch. 'You're doing well, both of you. But I still want to see at least . . . oh, thirty positive and thirty negative points on your Post-its before we come back together in half an hour?'

As he stood up, Billy Barometer heard the creak of his knees, but Rani's energy had made him as skittish as he used to be on a sunny day in his uncle's backyard. He might not be up to cartwheels any more, but he could change people's lives.

Chapter Eighteen

'I could murder a balti,' Carol-Ann says, as we escape through the doors of St Gabriel's into the outside world. 'Anyone fancy a trip to Balsall Heath?'

'Fantastic idea.' Jo is already rubbing her hands together in anticipation. 'You up for that, Tess?'

Proper balti served as it should be – hissing and steaming and almost jumping out of a blackened cooking pot onto the stained, lipstick-pink tablecloth in a neon-lit restaurant along the Ladypool Road – is exactly what I need after an allegedly therapeutic session dwelling on my parents' terrible marriage. But there's a drawback.

'I'd love to, but . . .'

'But bloody what, Tess? We won't accept any excuse except maybe a life-threatening allergy to flock wallpaper.' Carol-Ann is scary, even when she's only play-acting anger.

'It's just . . .'

It's just that curry crawls along the balti belt used to be one of our monthly rituals: me and Barney, Mel and James (though sometimes just Mel, if they couldn't get a babysitter), Sara and Ed. We'd always pace up and down the road, sussing out which of the garish signs and interchangeable wipe-clean menus held the key to our dining pleasure that evening. Our way of defying convention, now we'd become conventional in every other way, was never to eat at the same curry house twice.

I look Carol-Ann in the eye. 'I know it sounds incredibly wimpy, but going for a curry round there was something I always did with Barney. I feel a bit odd about going without him.'

'It's not wimpy; it's bloody madness. Let's face it, if you can have sex with a hairy hippy after fifteen years of only shagging with your husband, then committing curry adultery with a couple of girls will be a doddle.'

Jo smiles sympathetically. 'She's right, Tess. I mean, you can't spend the rest of your life avoiding everything you used to do together. Think how many things it'd rule out.'

'I know. I just don't feel very brave at the moment.'

'Bollocks,' Carol-Ann says. 'The world will look a cosier place once you've got a bhuna inside you. You'll be invincible.'

I give in. The alternative is another soggy delivery pizza in front of the telly – I've eaten all the gourmet stuff that Mel and Roz had donated over half term and have regressed to my terrible takeaway habits.

The curry convoy takes off, and as I drive behind Carol-Ann's beaten-up Micra, I wonder if the survivors' course is really doing me any good at all. It feels like yet another obligation on this long list of things I do because someone else talks me into it. First it was Mel, making me feel guilty for not getting on with my life. Then William with his guilt trip on the first night, telling us we'd rot in hell if we didn't turn up to every session. And now I can add two new friends to the roll-call of people who'll lecture me for being too miserable or for failing to see the opportunities for personal growth presented by my husband leaving me for his impregnated younger model.

Maybe I've had my chance and I blew it. I've had friends who never, ever get lucky with men – endlessly chasing the latest dreamboat who invariably turns out to be a nightmare: a philanderer, a conman, an armed robber. At least I had seventeen years before my dreamboat turned into a villain.

Dreamboat? That ages me. It's a word they used in *Jackie* to describe David Cassidy or David Essex or David Soul. *That's* where I went wrong! I should have married a man called David. If only I'd read the problem pages more carefully.

What would they say to me now, those teen agony aunts? Paint your nails in front of the telly with your mates, then dry your eyes and nip down to Boots to buy some lip gloss and new sparkly tights and try again. Plenty more fish in the sea. Only this time pick a fish called David. He won't turn out to be a piranha.

I park up next to Carol-Ann's car. She forces her hand into mine and starts to frog-march me along the road. 'There's only one bloody decent restaurant along here; with the rest of them you might as well use sauce out of a jar. Khalid would never forgive me if I took you anywhere else.'

I open my mouth to say that seems pretty unfair, since we've rarely had a bad meal down here, but then I remember that there is no 'we' any more. Instead my senses are hit by a breeze carrying so much spicy promise that I am rendered speechless.

Curry-scented summer is one of Birmingham's highlights. The first trip along Ladypool Road without a coat is like the first sighting of a swallow: a sign that winter's over. But as I follow Carol-Ann and Jo towards Khalid's Balti Kingdom, the wafts of cardamom and garlic make me feel cold inside. No wonder nostalgia sounds like a medical condition. It's as uncomfortable, unpredictable and inconvenient as piles.

'Carol-Ann!'

As we step through the door into the purple-lined restaurant, a small, grey-haired man who was sitting by the door playing cards leaps up to embrace her. 'Khalid, you're looking bloody brilliant. How's Mariam?'

'Very well, yes. You? And your little girl? Yes?'

'Lovely, thanks. Not so little any more, I'm afraid. I told you she's getting married?'

The man slaps his forehead. 'No, is not possible. She is twelve, thirteen now?'

'Nineteen.' She grins. 'I can't believe it either. Can I introduce you to my new mates, Khalid? Jo and Tess.'

We wave obligingly.

'A pleasure to have you here in our restaurant. Will you take a seat, please, and I will bring you poppadoms.'

We sit by the window, in front of a large family group. Carol-Ann nods towards them. 'You always know that a curry house is kosher when you get Asian people eating here.'

Jo chokes. 'Kosher? Sure that's the best word?'

I know it's her idea of a smart joke but I feel uncomfortable. If

I'm honest, I think Jo is a bit of a snob. But Carol-Ann just stares back. 'What?'

Jo's cheeks go pink as she realises she's going to have to explain. 'Well, you know. This is ... well, it's probably a Muslim restaurant. And you referred to it as kosher.'

Carol-Ann shrugs. 'Whatever. It's a bloody figure of speech.' She peers at the menu that is sandwiched onto the table by a sheet of glass.

I stare at the list of dishes. My boast in our years of curry-tasting was that I'd had more chicken balti dhansak than anyone else I knew – it was the benchmark dish by which I judged every restaurant.

Khalid puts down a silver tray of pickles and a big basket of poppadums. Jo reaches straight across the table to puncture them with her finger – the noise breaks the awkward hush, but makes me feel strange: cracking the poppadoms was always Barney's job. I decide to break with tradition. 'I'm having the lamb dopiaza, I think. What about you guys?'

Carol-Ann pulls a face. 'I thought we could have Khalid's balti banquet. Fantastic.'

I take a bite of the poppadom. It's stale. The onion in the chutney dish has gone dry and the mango chutney is streaked with yoghurt, presumably because the customers before us got over-enthusiastic in their dunking. I start to wonder about Carol-Ann's tastebuds.

'I don't think I'm that hungry.'

'Bollocks. Think of it as aversion therapy or something. It's a stage you've got to go through. You've done the first shag outside your marriage, now it's time for the first curry. You might as well make it a bit more satisfying than your experience with Aaron. How about you, Jo? Fancy it?'

Jo doesn't look keen either, but I think she's trying not to rock the boat. 'OK. Yeah, it's still pretty cheap.'

Khalid is hovering so I give in and agree to the banquet plus three Cobra beers. When he's gone, I ask Carol-Ann how the wedding plans are going.

'Don't bloody ask me. Georgie knows not to bother to get me involved in dresses or music or anything. Thank God she's changed her mind about a church wedding, so I don't have to give her away. No, I'm doing a few rounds of sandwiches for the reception and sorting out the hen night and that's her lot. You two are coming on the hen night, aren't you?'

I don't remember being invited. 'Why would she want us there? We don't know her, and we're far too old to be any fun.'

'Never mind what my precious daughter wants. I need some company too. It's on Saturday. Go on, it'll be a laugh. And when was the last time you were out on the pull? You're out of practice, Tess.'

I look at Jo, who is studying the label on the beer bottle. It's not as if I can claim I have a better offer because I don't. 'I'm not in the party mood.'

Carol-Ann sighs. 'Look. I know what's happened to you is shit. I know your husband is the worst man who ever lived. I know you're scared and lonely and worried. But you've got to help yourself. It's not fair but no one likes someone who moans non-stop, however good their reasons.'

How dare she? 'Right. Well, thanks for that. I will of course take your advice and now I instantly feel like painting the town red. Cheers.' I take a massive bite from the poppadom, if only to stop myself saying something I might regret. It sticks to the inside of my mouth.

She looks at me. 'I know it's hard, Tess, but you've got to start getting yourself back together, having fun. Pretending. If you pretend things are OK, you'll begin fooling yourself soon enough.'

'It's so hard . . .'

Jo puts her hand on mine. 'I know, Tess. You take your time. It's not a race to be back to normal.'

Carol-Ann shakes her head. 'You can say that, but it won't help. Sooner or later her mates will just get cheesed off with her being boring and no fun and stop ringing and then she'll get even more depressed.'

'Not her real friends.'

I finally manage to swallow the last of the poppadom and put my hand up. 'Hang on a minute. I am here, you know.'

They both glare at me, irritated that I've interrupted their conversation. Carol-Ann breaks her bit of poppadom into four pieces no bigger than a postage stamp, and dips each one into a different dish of pickle. One in the mango chutney, one in the raita (which I now notice is a disturbing day-glo green), one into the ageing onion and tomato, and one into the lime pickle. 'I love this one; it's not out of a jar. Mariam makes it all herself. The point is, Tess, that life stinks but the longer you put off getting on with things, the harder it gets. You get out of practice at being happy and having fun, and it takes that much more effort to persuade your mates that you're worth having around again.'

'You've got a very dim view of human nature,' Jo says, though I think she's probably got lower expectations of people than Carol-Ann.

'I'm just realistic. I'll prove it, too. Tess, how many of your married girlfriends have you seen since Barney left?'

I feel sick. 'Mel . . .' I don't intend to tell them that Mel's not married, because, after all, she might as well be. 'Roz . . .' Even though she also happens to be my boss. 'Suzy.'

'Isn't Suzy your sister?' Carol-Ann asks.

I nod, caught out. I don't have the energy to dredge up more names, as I know there aren't any. My social life for the last six months has consisted of muttering the answers to quiz-show hosts who will never answer me back, however many times I get the questions right.

'I don't mean to be nasty, Tess, but friends take as much work as a marriage, and the advantage of making the effort with them is that they stick around because they want to, not because of some bloody meaningless certificate,' Carol-Ann says.

I think about my friends, or the people I thought were my friends. Maybe she's right. I paid them too little attention, so it's no wonder they're not interested. 'I haven't been much of a laugh lately, you're right.'

Jo shakes her head. 'Don't feel you have to be the life and soul. It's unrealistic. I mean, we're all different – people think I'm a hard bitch because I walked out on Laurie, and I lost friends over it, but you have to be true to yourself. And it's easy for you to preach, Carol-Ann, but it's years since you split from your husband, and you'd fallen out of love with him God knows how much earlier than that.'

'True. But you're missing the point. Tess has got to come on Saturday; it's the ideal chance to practise putting on a brave face. Go on ... you only have to stay for an hour.'

The starters arrive and we put our conversation on hold while Khalid places little plates of greasy onion bhajis and pakoras and samosas in front of us. The gap gives me time to think. Can I afford to stand still? One party suddenly seems to represent the gateway to the future. Do I stay where I am out of fear, or take the risk?

'So?' Carol-Ann asks, when Khalid moves away.

'OK, I'll come. But I am not dressing up.' And I won't enjoy myself, I know that already. It's something to be endured for the future, like going to the dentist.

'Bloody right answer! What about you, Jo?'

'It's not really my cup of tea ...'

'Oh, not you as well. If Tess can do it with her heart well and truly broken, you've no sodding excuse. And you deserve a break from your mother.'

Jo takes a bite of a samosa and immediately spits it out into her napkin. 'That is foul. Are you sure about this place?'

Carol-Ann breaks a bhaji apart with her fingers, the oily residue staining them crimson. 'Bollocks. This is fab. Just because you can't appreciate *authentic* Indian food. Are you coming or not?'

'You'll never let me hear the last of it if I don't, will you?'

'Ha! I take it that's a yes, then.'

'Yes,' Jo says resignedly.

'Let's toast to it,' Carol-Ann says, holding up her glass of Cobra. 'To a summer of fun ...'

'To fun,' I say, like it's a new word in a foreign language.

'To fun,' says Jo, the sarcasm barely disguised.

'And to survival,' Carol-Ann adds. She has to have the last word.

Chapter Nineteen

I only realise when Carol-Ann holds up the mirror after she's finished with me just how different our ideas of *subtle* make-up really are.

'There you go. You look less like a bloody washed-out cancer victim,' she says. Then she blushes. 'Sorry, Jo. I didn't mean anything . . .'

Jo shrugs. 'Forget it.'

What I look like now is a child's painting of a clown – broad, primary-coloured brushstrokes highlight my eyes, cheeks and lips. All that's missing is a red ping-pong ball on the end of my nose.

'Do you like it?' Carol-Ann asks.

'No. I look grotesque.' I'm sure I can be honest with Carol-Ann: she's blunt with everyone else, so she's the last person to take offence.

'Oh,' she says. 'Oh. Well, there's no bloody need to be like that.'

Sometimes the enforced intimacy of the group makes me feel I know my fellow 'survivors' much better than I actually do. 'Sorry. I didn't mean to be offensive. It's . . . I don't know, it's a really . . .' I take the hand mirror and pull faces at the strange person who is responding in kind in front of me, 'a really *different* look. Unusual.'

I've been here an hour now and I feel like Sandy in *Grease*, at the Pink Ladies' sleepover. I suppose I could do with a transformation. My skin is dull and my hair is longer than it's been in ten years, the weight of the strands pulling it down flat on either side of my face, leaving me looking slightly thin on top, like a balding pensioner. So Carol-Ann has gathered it up in a big bunch and then affixed it to the crown with half a can of Elnett hairspray and some diamante hairclips.

Jo steps back. 'Looks better from a distance. Which, if you're as determined as you say not to let anyone try to pull you, could be an advantage.'

The doorbell rings. 'That'll be the cab,' Carol-Ann says. 'So you're going to have to like it or lump it.'

Downstairs, I pull my coat on and check myself out in the hall mirror. Carol-Ann systematically removed my clothes as soon as I arrived and then attempted to put me back together as someone her Georgie would not be embarrassed to be seen with. 'We have the technology to rebuild you,' she said, raiding her daughter's room for tops and trousers and jewellery like my pupils would wear on a night out at the pre-teen disco. 'You're so bloody tiny, you should wear more cool stuff; it'd make you look years younger.'

I'd opened my mouth to protest that I had no desire to look years younger. Unlike my friends who fretted about passing the thirty mark, I'd felt relieved. At last I could get away with the look I had always coveted: practical, sensible, with the odd foray into something approaching elegance.

But now the mirror makes me wonder. It's not a bad look – hip-hugging jeans with white streaks down the front of the thighs, as though I was cleaning the bathroom in them and had an accident with the Domestos. Which, apart from anything else, is highly unlikely these days; I can't remember the last time I applied bleach to anything. With the trousers, I'm wearing a little plain green sleeveless top – Jo told me it's called a 'shell' top – which is close fitting and slinky, with a high neck that she says is only an option if you're flat-chested. At last, a reason to celebrate my non-existent cleavage. It's simple and un-girly so suits me better than the few frilly 'party' items in my wardrobe that I've felt obliged to buy over the years for weddings, Christmases and birthdays. I do look younger, and in the subdued lighting of the hall, the make-up looks better than I thought it did. I tug at the top – it's too short and the jeans are too low, leaving a good six centimetres of exposed midriff.

'Don't pull it out of shape,' Carol-Ann says. 'It's meant to show off your tummy. Christ knows, if I had one as flat as yours, I'd wear a bloody bikini on Broad Street.'

The taxi drops us off at the Mailbox, transformed from the old postal sorting office into a solid block of retail outlets I'd never have believed Birmingham could support: Harvey Nichols, Bang and Olufsen, Armani. We walk through the centre past the closed shops towards the bars at the back and I keep catching glimpses of myself. The look's definitely growing on me – but then I curse myself for being silly. I am thirty-five. That's all there is to it. Too old to be at a nineteen-year-old's hen night. I should be sitting at home with a boring husband, a DVD and a winebox.

But even boring husbands need more attention than I gave mine. If I'd concentrated on him rather than the state of the kitchen floor and the bathroom taps, maybe he'd still be here.

We walk into the bar, the three of us making a grand entrance like a poor man's Charlie's Angels, and to my surprise we do get a proper round of appraising looks from the guys around the bar. I have felt invisible for the last six months. No, make that six years. Or even sixteen.

Of course, they're looking at Jo – even in jeans and a bulky Eighties-style parka jacket, she projects star quality, and some of them might recognise her from TV. Apparently she cut her teeth in the Midlands, covering school fires and planning rows for local radio and telly news, until someone plucked her out of the ranks to go national.

But as she orders our first round – three Kir Royales, from the '*House Cocktale Special's*' blackboard behind the bar – I do have to admit that a couple of men are still checking *me* out. OK, so they're the kind of Neanderthals I wouldn't want to talk to, never mind date, but it's a shock and almost flattering.

'Cheers, Jo.' Carol-Ann takes her drink and holds it up to do a toast. 'Dunno what we're toasting; as far as I'm concerned there's nothing to bloody celebrate about my daughter making the biggest mistake of her life. To singledom?' she suggests, clinking glasses and shooting a defiant look in all directions. 'Now where is bloody Georgie?'

I look beyond the dodgy clientele for the first time. It's a strange bar, too brightly lit to be relaxing, but then if the point of coming here is to be seen, then mood lighting would be the wrong approach. It's decorated in primary colours and the centrepiece is a sunken area in the middle of the room, with an aluminium-coated chimney stretching to the ceiling. We walk around it and see a full open fire burning at its heart, although it's June. The flames are purple and green as well as red and orange and I wonder what chemicals they're burning to get that effect. I open my mouth to ask the girls what they think and then realise that my Key Stage Two science curriculum questions may not be their idea of suitable conversation for a hen night. I don't think I ever had the art of small talk sussed and any skills I did have in that direction are severely out of practice.

'Can't see them. Seems a bit old in here for Georgie,' Jo says, and she's right. There are lecherous middle-aged men in every corner, some alone, some with mirror-image partners in crime, and some accompanied by raddled-looking women in revealing tops. The music is upmarket airport muzak and people are swaying along lethargically. I feel quite young.

'There they are!' Carol-Ann points towards the back of the bar, where a set of steps lead up to a shadier area. Jo and I follow her through the maze of tables attracting more looks, most of them directed at Carol-Ann, and we finally find Georgie and half a dozen mates as far away from the pseudo-fireplace as you can get. They are almost hidden by an incongruous Bedouin tent affair, which drapes around a circular table. We hover at the edge of the table, waiting for admission to Georgie's lair.

'What the hell are you wearing, Mother?' Georgie says, as Carol-Ann removes her coat and reveals huge expanses of freckly shoulders. Her scarlet top is sleeveless and halter-necked, with a bamboo-look ring at her throat where all the Lycra material gathers. It is an ambitious look for a fifty-one-year-old woman but I do think she carries it off. Georgie obviously doesn't agree.

'The sorts of clothes a woman should wear to a bloody hen night,' Carol-Ann replies and I look at Georgie's outfit. It's the kind of thing I would have worn, if I'd had a conventional hen night. Pretty but unflashy blue cotton blouse, with a coral necklace and matching earrings. On her head are a pair of red glittery horns, which she straightens in irritation.

'Oh, that's it. Slag me off on my own hen night. Cheers, Mum. You want me to dress like a tart so I can presumably start cheating on Paul before I even say the vows. I think I'll leave that to your generation.'

Their eyes lock like two wild animals, oblivious to everyone else. Jo coughs. 'Can we sit down?'

Georgie is the first to shake out of their staring competition, though I can see from Carol-Ann's eyes that she regards her daughter's politeness as surrender. 'Yes, of course. Sorry.' Georgie frowns slightly when she realises I'm wearing her top, but then grins. 'Hey, that's suits you much better than me. Budge up, girls. Let me introduce you to everyone . . . this is Louise, this is Karen . . . this is . . .'

As she recites names I know I'll never need to remember, I study them. They're a conventional-looking group of girls; I'd guess most of them probably work alongside her in the ambulance service or are old schoolmates, the sort of unspectac-ular pupils who never cause the teachers any trouble but are instantly forgotten the moment they walk out of class into the real world.

They've gone through the motions of a hen night – as well as the horns, there's a pile of wrapping paper in the centre of the table with gifts nestling in the centre: a pair of chocolate buttocks, a purple g-string with beads on the bit that goes round your bum, a cartoon-illustrated *Kama Sutra* book, and a wind-up clockwork willy. But two of the women are drinking Diet Coke, while the rest sip slowly on their glasses of unidentified blue cocktail or Bacardi Breezer. There's none of the raucousness I'd have expected.

'So how are the preparations going?' I ask Georgie. She's wearing too much make-up, badly applied, and it's a shame because despite the odd spot I can see bumping under her foundation, she's got that glow women lose somewhere around their late twenties and spend the rest of their lives and a large proportion of their disposable income trying to get back.

'OK, thanks. I mean, the register office is booked and then

Mum's talked the brewery into letting us hold the reception there.' She raises her eyebrows. 'I've given her strict instructions for the party, but she'll do her own thing anyway.' The look on Georgie's face – like someone's just let out a huge fart – suggests that Carol-Ann's 'own thing' couldn't be further removed from her daughter's wishes.

'I'm sure she'll do what you want,' I say, trying to sound more confident than I feel.

Georgie raises her eyebrows again. 'What about you guys? How is your therapy stuff working out?'

'It's interesting.' And, of course, painful, contradictory, helpful, useless, inspiring, depressing. But somehow I don't think Georgie wants to hear this on her hen night.

'Mum doesn't really say anything about it.'

'No. Well, we've all taken a vow of silence, you know. It's confidential.'

She nods, is quiet for a moment. 'But . . . I hope it's OK to ask this: is it helping her, do you think?'

I take a sip of my drink, trying to formulate an answer that will please Georgie but also contain some semblance of truth.

'Sorry,' Georgie says. 'I didn't mean to overstep the mark.'

'No, you haven't. Honestly. I suppose . . . I think, you can lead a horse to water and everything. The guy who runs the course, he said we won't always see progress as an obvious thing. It's more like snakes and ladders. And your mum isn't in nearly as bad shape as some of the rest of us!'

Georgie doesn't look like she's understood a word I've said, which is not surprising. I wasn't exactly crystal clear. I try again. 'She'll be OK, Georgie. We all will. Now would you like another drink?'

As I return to the bar, sensing the attention I'm getting as I totter in my borrowed kitten heels, I realise that for the first time, I do believe it. We will all be all right.

I'm on my third Kir, starting to enjoy the feeling of exposing my tummy to the world, when two men sidle up to me and Carol-Ann. I reckon they're closer to my age than hers, though it's hard to be sure which side of forty they're on. One has sandy-red hair, wrinkles that do actually look like laughter lines and bad teeth. The other is flat-faced and greying. Neither is my dream man, but Carol-Ann's just been telling me I need to rehearse being chatted up, so I turn my body to allow them to talk to us.

'Hello, ladies,' the red-haired one says. 'You enjoying yourselves tonight?'

'Yes, thank you,' I say. I sound like a small girl at the Sunday School summer picnic.

'Yeah, we're gearing up for a big night,' Carol-Ann says, flicking her hair, then fixing Flat-face with a long stare. 'How about you? Haven't seen you in here before.'

This is probably because she's never been to the bar before, but I suppose these white lies are part of the game. The men nudge each other.

'We're celebrating,' says Flat-face.

'That's a coincidence,' says Carol-Ann. Flick. 'So are we.' She licks her lips. I can't believe how blatant she is.

'Right. Yeah, what's the occasion?' Red-head is feeling sidelined.

'My . . . a friend's hen night.' Carol-Ann points at the party, which is proceeding quietly behind us. One girl is in tears and the others are clustered round her, glad of something purposeful to do.

'Nice,' Flat-face says. 'I suppose you could say he's at the other end of the scale.'

'Yeah,' Red-head interrupts. 'My divorce came through last week.'

Carol-Ann and I exchange smiles. She says, 'Now that *is* something to celebrate.' She holds up her glass to them, then stops. 'I can't toast you with an empty glass.'

Flat-face seizes his chance. 'We can soon put that right. What are you having, girls?' But he's only looking at *her* when he asks.

'Well, I always say, if you've got something to celebrate, you might as well do it in style. With a bit of fizz . . .'

'Right,' he says, a worried look flashing across his face before he recovers. 'Champagne, yes, of course. Gotta do it in style.' He downs his pint, taps at Red-head's elbow to direct him back to the bar. 'Back in a moment, ladies.'

When they're out of earshot, Carol-Ann says, 'Bless them, eh? You've got to make a bit more effort than that, though, Tess, or they won't think you're interested.'

'That's just it. I'm not.'

She grins at me. 'Neither am I.'

'But you're flirting like crazy; poor bloke thinks he's in there.'

She shrugs. 'Don't be silly. It's just a game. They know the rules and we can make them feel special. Who are we to deny them a good night out? They deserve a bit of fun. And so do you.'

Chapter Twenty

From what I remember, when I was last into being chatted up, the way to a man's heart was to dress like Madonna and rave about The Cure, Spear of Destiny and Manchester United.

Now it seems the goalposts have shifted. I'm sitting on one of the upstairs sofas in Bobby Brown's nightclub with red-headed Tom, discussing what constitutes unreasonable behaviour.

'She complained about how often I cut my toenails,' he says, squinting at my chest. Maybe he's hoping that if he wishes hard enough, my boobs will get bigger. 'Can you believe that?'

'So what did you put on *your* petition?' I am genuinely interested. I've still done nothing about mine and even though I am finding Tom increasingly repulsive, I did promise Carol-Ann I'd make the effort. She's disappeared onto the dancefloor with flat-faced Brian.

'I wanted to put about the bathroom and how she always hogged it when I was desperate to go, just to wind me up, like. But my solicitor thought it was too trivial. Like, how trivial are toenails?'

'Pretty trivial,' I agree. I can see how hard it would be to explain the reasons why a marriage fails in bullet-points on a blank sheet of A4 paper. All that personal, private suffering somehow has to be reduced to facts that lawyers and judges would understand. This is what lawyers do: change pain to mundane in one easy step, at £150 an hour.

I think of Sara. How she'd mocked the whole thing at *my* hen day. She'd already got five years of matrimonial work under her belt by then, rising higher and higher up the slippery pole towards partnership, and she made no secret of her contempt for the whole institution. Working at the sharp end of divorce and custody battles had given her a very warped view of relationships.

'I don't understand why you'd want to spoil a perfectly stable relationship with a legal arrangement designed for another century,' she'd said, as she pulled on her fluorescent boiler-suit. It fitted her long body rather well. Mine dwarfed me, while Mel looked bulky rather than buxom in hers: to get one big enough to fit round her chest meant it was enormous everywhere else.

I decided to have a go-kart race instead of a classic hen do precisely because I hated the rigmarole that Georgie and her friends are acting out tonight. Stupid T-shirts with rude slogans, bumper packs of condoms, L-plates attached to the back of some tarty outfit the bride-to-be feels obliged to wear, whatever her normal fashion preference. It all seemed profoundly pointless. I already felt like I was going along with the whole white wedding thing for the sake of other people: our parents, our friends, our colleagues. The hen night was something I was going to do for myself.

'Well, legally speaking, being married must be what you'd advise,' I'd said, looking down at the race-track with a growing feeling of nausea. I couldn't tell for sure, but I thought it was probably nerves about riding the go-kart rather than second thoughts about getting married. 'Makes things so much more straightforward if either of us should die suddenly. In a go-kart pile-up for example . . .'

'Yes, but I've seen so many people who live together quite happily and then decide, "Oh well, we've been together since the year dot, might as well head down to Pronuptia, do the decent thing." And that's when it all goes pear-shaped. It's the whole "till death us do part" bit that freaks people out. Especially men. And especially if people aren't one hundred per cent sure.'

'But *we* are.' About each other, even if not about the whole Big Family Wedding.

'Hmm.' She gave me a classic Sara look at that point. She always had a very distinct way of seeing the world and when she disagreed or objected to something someone had said, it showed in her face. She couldn't help it. I wondered whether this would be the one obstacle to her promotion at work. She looked away, pretending to fiddle with the zip on the boiler suit.

'What's that supposed to mean?' I realised I'd just shouted the question and all the other 'hens' were looking at me. I lowered my voice. 'If you've got something to say, Sara, you might as well come out with it because we can all see you've got the hump about something.'

'It's nothing personal . . .' she sniffed, but as soon as she said it, I realised it was *absolutely* something personal. 'I kind of wonder how anyone can ever be one hundred per cent sure about anything, which I suppose is exactly my objection to marriage in the first place. But I guess you and Barney will be fine. He's a great bloke. The odds are in your favour, statistically. Just.'

'Do you want another drink?' Red-headed Tom's question drags me out of the timewarp. He's not really getting the attention he deserves on his special night.

'Yes, that'd be lovely.'

As Tom trots off to the bar, I look around. Bobby's hasn't changed. When I first moved to Birmingham, it was the height of cool. We worried about being turned away because we were under twenty-one and reeked of studenthood, but they still let us in, and looking at the youngest dancers here now, I can understand why they weren't too harsh at enforcing the age rule. That freshness is irresistible, especially to the creepy hangers-on we used to rely on to buy our drinks for us when we ran out of money.

Tonight, as me and Jo and Carol-Ann crossed the canals to get to the club and then joined the queue, we worried that we'd be turned away for being too old. The bouncers certainly looked confused by our group – a hen night of quietly spoken girls in their late teens and early twenties, plus two thirty-something women with too much make-up, two pissed guys in their forties (we'd established that much in the bar) wearing lounge suits and ties, and a fifty-something diva with more energy and gumption than the rest of us put together.

'Evening, girls . . . er . . . ladies . . . and gents,' one murmured as we stepped inside.

I couldn't quite face the writhing mass on the dancefloor, so we've been sitting in the lounge area for a good hour now, talking through the highs and lows of Tom's divorce. They've mainly been lows.

He returns with the drinks – in the absence of Kir Royales, I am attempting to recapture my youth through the elixir of Bacardi Breezer. Alcopops didn't exist when I was a teenager, so I'm making up for lost time.

'What about you, Tess? How long before you're footloose and fancy-free again?'

Never. That's what I want to say. I can't imagine ever feeling footloose again, though that could be partly because I've never understood quite what it means. 'Hasn't quite got that far yet. I mean, I know the divorce is definitely going to happen, but I've been a bit slow off the mark in replying to letters, that sort of thing.'

'Well, you know why that is, don't you? You're in denial, like. Natural, it is, but you're going to have to let go sooner or later.'

He puts his drink down and I have a premonition of what is about to happen. I wince. He leans across with his mouth open like a guppy. I catch a wave of mild halitosis just before he tries to hermetically seal his lips around the outside of mine. My mind flashes with conflicting thoughts in the fraction of a second before he inserts his tongue ... Isn't this what he needs? But then you're not a charity for unwashed causes. Why should it be you? But then at least he's not playing the sympathy card like Aaron. But then again, you don't fancy him and you did fancy Aaron a bit. Exactly, and look what happened there ...

And then a strange thing happens. Tom pulls away. 'I'm sorry, I'm being a bit forward, like. You're a lovely girl, Tess. Lovely. But I'm a bit drunk so I hope you'll understand.'

It's the most heartfelt speech he's given all evening and I can feel my resolve weakening, but then Aaron pops back into my consciousness. How do I know Tom doesn't have the same kind of hidden shallows? Perhaps the toenails were the least of his ex's worries. He could be a liar, a snorer, a wife-beater.

That's the trouble with nightclubs. What you see is very rarely what you get.

'I do understand,' I say, trying to look convincingly sorry. 'I wish you'd found someone a bit more straightforward for tonight. You deserve to celebrate with someone who doesn't have a million issues of their own to deal with. Someone young.' I look around. 'You could probably still get lucky and find her in here. I wouldn't mind.'

He smiles. 'Maybe I already did get lucky.'

I manage to disguise the sigh that's trying to escape my lips. 'Perhaps. I do wish you every happiness, you know, Tom.'

He doesn't register the finality of the statement. Instead he starts rummaging around in his pockets. 'Have you got a pen?' he says, as he pulls out a piece of tissue.

'No. Why?'

'I . . . let me just . . .' He disappears towards the bar. I look at my watch; it's ten past one already. When I look up again, the barman is shaking his head and Tom is waving a five-pound note at him.

Tom comes back. 'I know they've got pens, like, they must have behind the bar. But they say people promise to bring them back and they never see them again.'

He looks so glum that I relent and find the pen I've known all along is in my handbag. 'I've found one.'

'Great! Tess, I really would like to have your number. If that's OK.'

'But . . .'

'Or I could give you mine. You know, you might need advice from someone who's been through it all, with the paperwork and all.' He tears off a piece of tissue and writes his number in huge letters, as the ink bleeds through, merging one figure into another.

I take it, and make a show of putting the scrap in my purse. I'm not going to tell him that there's no way I will ever call it. 'Shall we go to look for your friend?'

We work our way through the sweating bodies towards the part of the club where we last saw them. Georgie and her friends are standing on the steel staircase overlooking the dancefloor, drinking Smirnoff Ice and looking more relaxed – or possibly just more pissed – than they were before. A couple of spotty young lads, drawn by the obvious potential of a hen night group, are hovering around the girls, trying to impress with their dancing, but they're making no headway at all.

'Have you seen your mum?' I shout in Georgie's ear.

She raises her eyebrows and points towards the far corner of the dancefloor. The speakers are pounding out 'Music Sounds Better With You' and I can just make out a flash of scarlet and an expanse of flesh. Her back is to me and two hands are circling her waist, testing her reaction by lingering on her hips. She doesn't seem to be objecting.

Tom is standing awkwardly at my side and I wonder if he's wishing he'd gone for Carol-Ann instead of me. Then I remember our third musketeer.

'What's happened to Jo?' I ask Georgie.

'WHAT?'

'JO – IS SHE STILL HERE?'

She shakes her head violently, as if even gestures need to be bigger to be understood above the noise. 'WENT HOME . . . HOUR AGO, MAYBE MORE.'

'ME TOO. HAVE TO GO,' I shout. 'THANK YOU. LOOK AFTER YOUR MUM.'

I turn to Tom. 'GOT TO GO. LOOK AFTER YOUR-SELF.' The great thing about nightclubs is that they make you edit your speech down to the essentials, because your voice can't stand the strain of a long conversation.

He takes out his mobile and mimes dialling a number, pointing to himself. 'CALL ME,' he mouths.

I nod, wondering if it counts as lying. As I leave the club, I have mixed feelings – proud that I've had a proper night out, but deeply relieved that I'm getting out before the slow dances. I never want to be clubbing age again.

I walk towards Broad Street and manage to hail a cab straight away, beating the girls in their sequinned mini dresses and the men running into the centre of the road to try to stop taxis in their tracks. Perhaps I just look too old to vomit in the back seat.

On the way home, I unwind the window and pull out the

piece of tissue with Tom's number on it. It's not that I think I'm better than him, it's just that there's no point. I am not ready for anything, and definitely not for nursing someone else through the aftermath of a split.

I wait until the taxi gains speed and then throw the fragment of paper out of the window. I don't look back. Maybe Tom was my future, but I doubt it. I just hope no one saw me. Littering is not a Tip Top Tess thing to do.

But there is one phone call I do intend to make. I just have to wait until the morning to make it.

'Hi.' Sara sounds brusque, in the middle of something. But then she always sounds that way.

'Sara, it's Tess.' I've waited until ten a.m. to call. Still too early for most of my friends, but by this time on a Sunday morning, Sara will probably have run five miles, scanned all the papers and the supplements to keep abreast of current affairs, and bought the ingredients for a healthful breakfast of bircher-muesli and freshly squeezed pomegranate juice to be taken back to Ed in bed. After all her protests against the institution whose constant failure pays her massive mortgage, Sara finally got married two years ago.

'Tess.' She makes my name last for three syllables, each one at a lower pitch than the last, and I can hear in her voice irritation, frustration, doubt. There's certainly no hint of pleasure. 'How are you?'

How do you think? 'Well, you know how it is.' I have been sitting in my dressing gown since six, drinking coffee and waiting for the right time to call. Now that I've got through, I don't know what exactly I want to get out of the conversation. 'Long time no hear.'

I hear her breathing at the other end of the phone. The warehouse conversion where she lives with Ed overlooks the city-centre skyline – it was one of those places that seemed desperately overpriced only a couple of years ago, but has doubled in value. Shrewd should be Sara's middle name.

'Yes. It's been a busy time . . . and an awkward one.'

I guess she means awkward because she's been stuck between

me and Barney. But she should be the expert at managing tricky situations after all. 'I called because I missed talking to you. I didn't want to let our friendship slip,' I say.

'Yes. I understand. It's always horrible, trying to divide up the friends like the fixtures and fittings.'

In that one comment, I realise who is getting Sara as part of their settlement. I don't know why I hadn't worked it out before. 'Have you seen Barney lately?'

'Well, we work in the same building, Tess.'

'Socially?'

'Tess . . .' Her voice has moved into official mode, the patronising tone she must use with particularly obtuse clients. Repeating their name is probably one of her tricks, too. 'I've found it very difficult to know how to handle this. But at the end of the day, I was Barney's friend before I was yours.'

'Right.' And that, I suppose, is what it amounts to. Centuries of sisterhood go out of the window when you're dealing with solicitors. Friendship has to be weighed up and meted out in the most impartial fashion, with Sara in charge of the scales of justice.

'I don't really see Mel much any more,' she says, as though this is some kind of consolation, and I understand suddenly how much has been going on behind the scenes without me knowing. A history dating back to the first term at university has been rewritten; the subject decisions we made on our UCCA forms before any of us had even met – me and Mel choosing airy-fairy humanities, and the ever-practical Barney and Sara picking Law – now determine the future. Like at school, where everything from TB vaccinations to cartons of milk was given out in strict birth-date order.

'That's a shame.' I hold the phone clamped to my ear, wishing I hadn't called. But at least I know now. 'I'm sorry it's come to this,' I say and then realise I'm not sure I want to apologise for a situation that would never have been of my choosing.

'Yes,' she says and I hear reproach this time. 'It is a shame.'

'Sara . . . you remember the go-karting?' She ought to, after all. She was the one who was so determined to win that she gave one of my colleagues whiplash as she tried to overtake her at the finishing line.

'Yes.' I can imagine the pile of pomegranates sitting impatiently on her marble worktop waiting to be squeezed. She is leaving me in no doubt which she sees as the greater chore.

'Did you know? I mean, did you have a . . . premonition that it was going to end this way? You said . . . well, you tried to tell me that maybe it wouldn't quite work.'

'Did I? Listen, Tess, I don't remember that much about it.'

I feel disappointed somehow. Perhaps I thought if she'd seen it coming, she might have been able to make me feel better. 'I see.'

'The thing is, if I'm honest, I never quite saw the two of you together. Barney was always kind of a . . . free spirit, and I think perhaps you made him grow up too quickly. Maybe that's what I was trying to say. I wish I'd said it better.'

'But . . .' But I wasn't the one pushing to move in together, to join the establishment, to lay the laminate. Was I? 'I thought he wanted to.'

'Yes. Maybe he did. But I don't think he wanted to be treated like your dad.' She stops. 'Sorry, that sounded worse than I meant it to. I just think that . . . well, it doesn't matter now, does it?'

'No, it does. Tell me, Sara. I do want to know.' I think I do.

'OK. You asked for it. I think you took him for granted. You were very lucky to land him, Tess, he's a great bloke. Or was. The Barney we all knew would never have cheated on you.'

'But he did.' My voice sounds very small.

'Sometimes it's easier to blame someone else, Tess. But if he changed, he probably wasn't the only one.'

I sit down in the hall chair. Now I don't want to carry on the conversation either. 'I suppose we've all changed. Look, Sara, I'm sorry to have bothered you. I guess I never was very good at taking the hint.'

'No,' she says. 'You never were. Goodbye, Tess.'

I open my mouth to reply but the phone clicks before I speak. It's probably better that way.

Lesson Five

From Little Acorns

'How many of you feel like you're living in the past?' William cut through the group's chatter with his loudest voice. Session five was time to get even tougher – now they'd passed the halfway mark, he had to take no prisoners, if his students were to walk out the door at the end truly ready to take on the world.

'I'm to blame, of course, in some ways. It's exactly what I've encouraged you all to do: to look back at the mistakes and to learn the lessons. But there comes a time when you have to move on.' And if anyone should know that, William thought, he should. Maybe he'd even manage it himself one day.

The students trusted him now. They even did their homework. Tess, Carol-Ann and Jo had already been showing each other cartoons and giggling.

'So today we're going to start living in the present. And the future. And that means talking about kids. Because if you have them, then you can't totally turn your back on the relationship that created them. But you can reinvent that relationship, for your own sake and that of the kids and, in fact, everyone else who knew you in your previous, married incarnation. Colleagues, friends, parents. Which is why those of you without kids shouldn't think you're off the hook.'

He sat down in front of them. 'Let's see the homework then.'

No one ever wanted to go first, so he'd have to nudge one of them into action. He scanned the front row.

'Tess? Would you like to kick off?'

She frowned. 'I haven't been able to bring a picture.'

'Well, are they characters we'd know about anyway?'

She laughed. 'Yes, I guess so. I don't know how significant it is, but we always used to see ourselves as Barney and Betty Rubble. Because of Barney's name, really. Nothing more involved than that.'

'Hmm. That's not quite what I had in mind, but we can work with it. So ... *The Flintstones*. What really happens below the surface, do you think? It's a funny family scenario on the face of it, but there are conflicts there. Between Betty and Barry—'

'*Barney!*' Tess sounded more irritated than she had a right to at his error. So he didn't have an encyclopaedic knowledge of rubbish American TV programmes. So what? It was hardly what they came to him for.

'Barney, yes. What's happening in *The Flintstones* is the embodiment of conflict within two marriages. Or perhaps of a man who's closer to his work colleagues than his wife. So does that ring any bells, Tess?'

She flinched, but shook her head. 'I'm sure that's not why I chose it.'

'OK. Well, fair enough. It doesn't work every time, but there again yours is a bit of a cheat, isn't it, because you didn't pick it to represent your marriage. I could tell you off for not doing your homework properly—' She scowled at him. 'But I won't. Do we have another volunteer?'

Tim raised a tentative hand.

'Great, Tim. Go ahead.'

He opened the folder and pulled out a small, creased piece of paper. 'I used to have this inside my locker at work. It's from the *Love Is ...* series; do you remember it? Mine says *Love is ... never going to bed on an argument*. We believed that, you know. We took it so seriously that even if we argued late at night, we'd make the effort to make it up, have a back rub or make love or whatever. It was hard, mind you, with the hours I was working, but we managed it. Then the kids came along and we were too tired to argue, never mind make an effort to get along.'

William tried to think of the best way to respond. 'I suppose the lesson from that one is that life is never as cute as the cartoons. Which is my point, in a way. Hang on to the cartoon, Tim. We'll come back to that a bit later on. So, anyone else?'

Sometimes it was harder than others. The point he was trying to make was that relationships between men and women could never be seen in two dimensions, and that over-simplifying the 'history' for kids or anyone else could be counterproductive in the end. But it was the luck of the draw whether the cartoons they picked actually made that point, or a completely different one.

'Mine's The Simpsons, if that's any help,' Jo said. She waved a computer printout half-heartedly. William could see the bright-yellow flesh tones of TV's most dysfunctional family.

'Ah . . . Marge and Homer?'

'No. Bart and Lisa. We were more like brother and sister. That was the trouble.'

William felt a sinking feeling. 'At least you know where it went wrong. So . . . anyone else have a cartoon they want to share, before we do a bit of smaller group work?' He'd have to leave the moral point of this particular exercise until the end of the session, if he bothered at all. The first time things had strayed off course, he'd panicked, wondered if he ought to return to the very strict lessons of his former Californian mentors. They'd been insistent that no more than half an hour should pass without imparting a homily that could have rounded off a particularly sickly episode of an all-American sitcom.

But then he realised that, somehow, the lessons that the students needed to learn always emerged despite the muddle and chaos. The Yanks had plenty of complex, academically proven theories, but all they needed was a little more faith in human nature.

'I couldn't decide if my marriage was more Road Runner versus Wile E. Coyote, or Tom and Jerry.' Carol-Ann was grinning as she spoke. She had nothing to lose, William supposed. Having a dead spouse meant she'd won the war, though it probably felt like there had been nothing left to fight for.

'You don't have to have a final answer. But what made you think of those gruesome twosomes?'

'Well, they always seemed locked in this eternal bloody battle that they'd forgotten the point of. Which was pretty much how it was for us . . . when we were getting on well.' She paused. 'I knew the game was over when we didn't even row any more. But then you don't see many cartoons with the two main characters living in the same house and ignoring each other. It doesn't have the same level of humour, does it?'

At last, William thought. The point of the exercise, spelled out beautifully by Carol-Ann. He'd been right about how much she'd bring to the group. 'Thank you, on behalf of all of us. It's funny how such a simple task can bring about such powerful responses. You see, it doesn't really matter what cartoon you chose to represent your former relationship. There's an element of fun about it, but my real purpose is to explain why it's so dangerous – as well as tempting – to view your ex only in black and white, or to see the whole thing as some kind of primeval fight of good against evil.

'We all tell stories about our past, and the nature of storytelling is that it simplifies things. A fairy story about two slightly plain sisters and a mildly menopausal stepmother trying to do the right thing towards her grumpy teenage stepdaughter wouldn't have worked. Hence, Cinderella is reduced to good and evil, selfish versus selfless, beauty versus ugliness. But the danger of starting a story like that about your marriage is that as the years go by, the fable you've created becomes more and more exaggerated. When you demonise your ex, your kids will resent it sooner or later. And it kind of leaves you with the emotional equivalent of blood poisoning: it affects the way you see your world for ever.'

They looked confused. 'Bit of a speech, I know, but it's a subject close to my heart.' William took care never to refer explicitly to his personal life, so any hint caused a ripple of interest in his 'congregation' – and he could tell that this snippet would have the usual effect.

'What I'd like you to do now is to get into fours to go through this worksheet about children and family and friends and their response to what's happened. Now I know that generally I let you be grown-ups and choose your own partners – after all, that's what got you into this mess in the first place – but because we've got a mixture of parents and non-parents, I need to make sure we're balanced. So let's have . . . Tim, Natalie, plus Tess and Aaron in one group. And Carol-Ann, Rani, Malcolm and Jo over here. It should take you roughly forty minutes, then we'll come together for coffee and biscuits. I've even brought chocolate digestives to celebrate getting past the halfway mark without any casualties.'

He gave each person a handout and turned back towards the kitchenette, counting the seconds until the groups erupted with speculation about his own romantic history. It was a shame, he thought, that their imagined versions would probably be so much more vivid than the non-existent reality. But he couldn't let them know what his home life was really like. It was important that they believed he was a success story, otherwise why would they trust him? Would anyone buy a miracle diet from a twenty-stone man?

After allowing them to speculate about him for a couple of minutes – and treating himself to a couple of chocolate digestives to pass the time – William headed back towards the students. He felt bad about saddling Carol-Ann, Rani and Jo with Malcolm, but he didn't feel guilty enough to listen to his moaning. Instead, William headed towards the left of the hall, where Tim was talking more animatedly than he ever had before.

'. . . And Anya said to me a couple of weeks ago, "Daddy, you're too cross, if you weren't so cross, Mummy might still be here." And I wonder if she's right. I lie awake at night and I think, when did I get cross? When did we stop living by the *Love Is . . .* cartoons?'

The others, William realised, were silent because they had no idea what to say. At least here he could prove his usefulness.

'Is Anya angry all the time, Tim?'

He blinked. 'I don't know. No, not really. Sometimes I think she might be forgetting about her mum – when we're playing on the swings or I'm tickling her. Then she seems happy. But I feel so tired looking after them, ferrying them about and everything, that I hardly ever have time for the good bits. And then I feel even worse, even more inadequate. It's definitely hit Anya the hardest.'

'How old is she?'

'Seven. And Lily is four.'

'They're lovely names,' Tess said. She looked wistful, but a little better than last week, William thought. No kids, and if he remembered her answers to the questionnaire right, the wrong side of thirty-five.

'Thanks. Yes, they are. By the time Lily was born, the name was about the only thing me and Karen agreed about. I suppose, when I look back, she was trying to warn me about how fed up she was. I was too stupid or too knackered to notice. But I wanted to provide for them, you know, to look after my girls. So now I'm clueless about how to make my daughters happy and my best girl, the girl I always wanted to look after for ever, has gone, because I wasn't good enough.' He wiped his eye with his shirt, but little tears kept appearing, to his obvious embarrassment. 'Sorry.'

William wanted so much to take the pain away, but he knew he couldn't do it for Tim. He could, however, give him the tools. 'Tim, what I was saying before . . . well, it doesn't always happen the way I described it. You know how I was saying that we often demonise our other half, to make things simpler for ourselves and the people around us?'

Aaron was nodding. 'It's what I've done to my ex, mate,' he said, proffering a grubby-looking handkerchief.

'But it can be just as bad to go too far the other way: to blame yourself and not to recognise that a partnership is just that – there is equal responsibility for making things work and for making things fail. It takes two to go from husband and wife to petitioner and respondent.' William glanced over at the other group, where Rani was talking. He remembered her hint about domestic violence, followed by her vigorous denials that she'd been referring to her own situation. 'In most cases, anyway. The only exception would be where one partner is abusing another, of course.'

'Really?' Natalie stared at him. 'So it's always one person's fault in those circumstances?'

He couldn't read her expression. He tried to summon up the details of their conversation at the last session and could dimly recall a powerful mother, a weak father. Perhaps her mother's strength had included physical acts. He shuddered. Although

223

he'd come across cases where it had been the woman who'd been the aggressor, it felt so unnatural somehow. 'I do think that violence is never an appropriate response.'

'So it cancels out any provocation by the other party? Always?' Her voice was blank, stripped of any emotion, as though she was commenting on the likelihood of the next test at Edgbaston being rained off.

'It doesn't cancel it out. But there is no excuse for hitting your partner. Ever.'

'You were the one who said nothing in relationships was black and white.'

'But I never laid a finger—' Poor Tim was distraught.

'No one is saying you did, Tim. I promise.' William gave Natalie a questioning look. 'It's an interesting debate that perhaps Natalie and I could continue over coffee. What I was trying to say was that, yes, it's as bad to see yourself as the guilty party as it is to see yourself as an injured innocent. No one is wholly innocent – not even your children, who will play with your emotions quite deliberately, because they are confused by their own.'

'It's true, Tim,' Tess said, leaning forward to touch his hand. Women seemed to feel the need to do this all the time with Tim. Lucky sod. 'The kids in my class at school are terrible. I have divorced parents coming to me with horrible stories of them playing Mum off against Dad. The same guilt trip laid on each parent, but of course they don't speak to each other any more, so they never know. I have to say I get the impression the kids learned the game-playing from what they saw their parents do.'

'Very astute, Tess.' William wondered if Tess and Tim could be this course's happy ending. She was too sensitive for the likes of Hairy Aaron and he'd never go after someone as conventional as her. As for Malcolm, he wouldn't wish that on anyone. 'The point she's making so well is that children learn from what is going on around them, so it's only fair to try to tell them as honest a version as possible of what happened. You can end a marriage, but you can never walk away from the fact that you both made those children together.'

'She has,' Tim said quietly.

'For now, Tim. If I were a betting man, I'd gamble that she'll come back.' William saw the hope in Tim's rabbit-pink eyes. 'Perhaps not to you. Sorry. But there are very few women who can walk out of their children's lives for good. My experience in the group suggests that men don't always find it as difficult.'

He caught Natalie's eye. She looked sadder than he'd seen her before, a chink in her Juicy Couture armour. William felt a familiar pang of guilt at being part of the weaker sex.

'Let's take a look at the next section. So to continue the cartoon theme, let's look at How to Avoid Becoming the Addams Family.'

Chapter Twenty-one

Carol-Ann lights up a cigarette as soon as we leave St Gabriel's, though it's drizzling and she has to try three times before the flame catches. 'Shit, that was a bit bloody intense. Who's going to join me for a therapeutic pint?'

'Yeah, I'm up for it,' Jo says.

'I can only manage a quick one,' I say as we huddle outside the entrance. 'Are you happy with a quick one, Carol-Ann? Or did you get one of those the other night?'

I still have no idea whether she went above and beyond the call of duty to make flat-faced Brian's weekend. The morning after the night before on Sunday had been another reminder of the strange limitations of our new friendship. I hadn't felt I could call her for the gossip, the way I would with Mel. Not that I've even felt like calling Mel lately. The burst of optimism I felt at Georgie's hen night proved as short-lived as a heatwave in Halesowen.

'Very funny,' she says and I can't tell whether she's grinning because she's misbehaved or because she's amused by my curiosity. 'Anyway, never mind me, what happened to Her Ladyship?'

Jo blushes. 'I just got tired and I don't like to leave Mum on her own all night. Plus you two abandoned me with a bunch of teenagers, if you remember.'

'You could have had your pick of Birmingham's finest men, if you'd tried. Might have done you good. Right, one drink in the pub, then?'

We return to the dump where we went the night I pulled Aaron. Or he pulled me. Tonight he was hovering around at the end of the class waiting for his invite to the pub, but he didn't have a hope. Men can be so stupid.

'So did you, then?' I say finally when we sit down with our drinks.

'Sleep with him? No. He was happy enough with a hand job.' She waits for my jaw to drop as far as it'll go and then sticks her tongue out at me. 'God, you're gullible. I had a snog that lasted about half an hour, took his phone number and then got a taxi home with my darling daughter.'

'Wasn't he terribly disappointed?'

'No. The great thing about men like Brian is they don't expect anything, so they never get pissed off. He got a little grope with a woman in her prime, which is more than he could have wished for at the beginning of the evening. I'm sure he got what he wanted in his head, and his right hand probably finished the job much more effectively than I could have.'

'Carol-Ann!' Sometimes she's too coarse for my liking.

'Don't be disapproving; you sound like Georgie. And we know you're not exactly a nun. What happened to yours? Tom was by far the more deserving cause.'

'He wasn't right.'

'Ha! They never are, darling. But he didn't seem too bad. Generous.'

'And ginger.' I think she must have forgotten what he looked like. I wish I could.

'Now we're being gingerist. I hope he did at least try it on. Man on the night of his divorce, he had to give it a go.'

'He was a gentleman. And he gave me his phone number.'

Jo looks up from texting someone on her mobile. 'Have you called him?'

'I threw the number away,' I tell her, embarrassed.

To my surprise, Carol-Ann raises her pint glass to me. 'Good on you, Tess! Sometimes you've got to do that, just to make yourself feel wanted. I mean, I know he was a bloody red-head and everything, but apart from that he was OK. Turning down an OK bloke is good for your self-esteem.'

'I'm rubbish at saying no,' Jo says. 'I mean, take your

situation, snogging that bloke for thirty minutes. I'd be feeling a bit too turned on to send a bloke away without doing the deed.'

'Oh, and to look at Her Ladyship, you'd think butter wouldn't melt . . .' Carol-Ann's words sound jokey, but she's fooling no one. 'That probably explains why you never quite made it into the second year of your marriage, doesn't it? Some people should never bother to get married.'

I don't like the way our threesome is progressing. It feels more like the back of the bike sheds than a support group. 'Maybe *no one* should bother with marriage. It's not like any of us are terrific adverts for the institution. But then maybe Georgie will prove us wrong.'

'I bloody doubt it. Can't see any daughter of mine being a natural in the matrimonial stakes. And he's a loser.'

Jo's mobile phone beeps; she looks at her newly arrived text message and sighs. I think she's keeping something to herself, but then there's no law saying she has to bare her soul the way the rest of us do. 'Georgie's a sweet kid, considering,' she says. 'You shouldn't write it off before she's walked up the aisle. I feel like drinking to Georgie. We might be lost causes, but let's give her the benefit of the doubt. To Georgie.'

'To Georgie,' I say, holding up my glass, just to show willing.

Carol-Ann knows when she's defeated. 'To Georgie . . . and all the other mugs who believe in love.'

The reason for my early departure is that I have to pack for the Outdoor Adventure. God help me.

It was Roz's suggestion originally. When it became clear during that first year that it'd take more than my fervour for hygiene and her command of discipline to get the kids and teachers working as a team, she'd done her research.

'Outward Bound is the answer!' She'd come striding into the staffroom with a handful of brochures depicting middle-aged men abseiling and sitting round campfires. 'If it can work for captains of industry, it's bound to work for Old Oak.'

I'd felt a sinking feeling even then. My body has never been built for the outdoors. I don't mind a bit of a country walk and I'm more than happy to spend hours on a beach on a sunlounger provided the temperature stays above twenty-five degrees at all times. But tackling an assault course – especially being watched by a horde of giggling ten-year-olds – was pretty much my worst nightmare.

Of course, water is my worst nightmare now. But this was 1996, three years before the Worcester Incident and six weeks before my wedding. Life was full of possibilities so I decided to go along with it, for the good of Old Oak. We took a decision to take Year Four and Year Five, leaving behind the terrorist faction also known as Year Six, and the kids were so excited to get away from the clutches of the bullies that they weren't remotely interested in my failure to master the climbing wall. And the weather was gorgeous, so on three out of the four days I managed to sneak away to the forest, where I spent a couple of hours watching the shadowy patterns the leaves made on the earth and drinking from the hip flask Barney had given me as a present before I left. He'd filled it with my favourite Grand Marnier and I remember thinking that the only way to make the scene more perfect would be to have him there. We could have stripped off and made love in a glade, warmed by the sun and the orange-flavoured liqueur.

In reality, of course, it's unlikely Barney would have bared his already generous behind for a spot of woodland action. We'd cut out most of the adventurous stuff years before, which had seemed no great loss. The combined risks of insect bites, sunburn and discovery (with the possible repercussions for our joint careers) suddenly seemed to outweigh the extra frisson of doing it as nature intended. The final nail in the coffin of our al fresco desires was Mel's story of doing it down by Edgbaston reservoir, rolling about properly like they do in the movies and ending up with her pride-and-joy leopardskin coat covered in dog shit.

The very last time we made the effort was on honeymoon in Sri Lanka. Determined to act like proper newlyweds, we had sex in the sea in an area of beach a mile or so up from our hotel. We lay down in a shallow bit and managed a few goes before the motion dredged up all that lovely white, fine sand with obvious high-friction results.

I was so sore that we couldn't do it again for a week. And the water washed the SPF 25 off Barney's back, so that it burned and blistered and cracked and seeped all the way through the honeymoon.

After that first year of Outdoor Adventure (the school version, not the one for married men and ladies), Roz appointed Juliet, an upper-crust sports fanatic, as our PE co-ordinator. She's led the trip every year since then, to my relief. But this year there's no getting away from it. My class is Year Five, and as their teacher, I have no excuse.

Even worse, we're going to some new place in Gloucestershire rather than our usual location. 'Higher child-to-adult ratio *and* more challenging than the last one,' Juliet told us during our briefing session last week. 'Challenging' is easily the most ominous word anyone could use in connection with an outdoor pursuits centre, especially when the weathermen are forecasting non-stop rain.

I let myself into the house at about ten p.m. and find the usual pile of pizza and curry fliers. I am probably now on some priority mailing list of sad people who use delivery services more than three times a week. I am constantly trying to balance the reliability of my usual supplier with the uncharted excitement of a new menu – how will the addition of green rather than black olives enhance the subtle flavour of the Popeye Special? What difference might it make to the experience to substitute 'cheesey garlicky creamey sauce' instead of my usual herb and tomato on the base of my American Hot One?

I scoop them up and then I shudder at what lies beneath. A vellum envelope. A thin one.

Thin envelopes are so much more menacing than thick ones. Thick ones offer so many possibilities. Congratulations, you've got the job and here is your new contract and a lovely thick booklet all about our fantastic policies and facilities.

Here is your mortgage on your dream home; please also find enclosed our structural survey which confirms you are undoubtedly getting a bargain and in fact it was such a pleasure for our surveyor to look around your palatial new abode that we have refunded the fee.

We're delighted to confirm your reservation in our five-star hotel and can also confirm that you are booked into our honeymoon suite, with complimentary fruit, flowers, champagne and Belgian chocolates and a postcard sunset at 7.18 p.m. every night, to be viewed naked in your private plunge pool overlooking the Indian ocean. Hummingbirds optional.

Instead, the thin envelope is as mean as Scrooge. It says all it needs to in a couple of stingy lines. In fact, it's surprising that the sender hasn't used a compliments slip to save on paper.

No, of course you haven't got the job, you upstart. Don't bother to ask for feedback on your interview performance unless you want to listen to twenty minutes of us laughing a lot.

Why the hell would we mortgage a tumbledown piece of shit like this, even if it is all you can afford? Especially when it's clear from your choice of accommodation that you have no judgement whatsoever.

Unfortunately we are unable to take your booking because you are lowlife and we have a policy of never accepting honeymoon reservations when it's clear that yours is nothing but a Starter Marriage.

I open the envelope carefully, afraid that the contents will leap out and bite me on the nose. The message is simple:

Dear Mrs Leonard,

Further to my letter of 31 May, I have yet to receive a response regarding the valuation of the joint property, 107 Victoria Terrace, B17.

My client is anxious that this should proceed as soon as possible; therefore I have provisionally arranged two valuations, with Scott and Co. and Marchant's, on Monday 24 June, at 4.45 p.m. and 5 p.m. If these times are inconvenient for yourself, then please could you arrange for your legal representative to contact my office or for keys to be dropped off at the agents, which are both situated on the High Street.

Your co-operation in this matter is appreciated.

So Barney is in a hurry, is he? A small matter of his girlfriend's no doubt increasing girth. He always fails to appreciate the urgency of anything until it's right under his nose and I suppose the Curved One's biggest curve of all is now leaving him in no doubt that while most things can wait, a baby certainly won't.

I put the letter in my handbag. So much to look forward to – four days of hell in rural England's answer to a hard labour camp, followed by the first stage in the loss of my home, presided over by a couple of slimy estate agents.

I take a glass and a bottle of Grand Marnier and go upstairs to pack, throwing stuff into my rucksack without caring what. If I pack badly enough, I might suffer exposure on a hilltop, catch pneumonia and solve everyone's problems, including my own, overnight.

Chapter Twenty-two

The school car park is ablaze with neon-coloured man-made fibre – not the most soothing sight for a woman with a scorching hangover. The kids are already dressed for whitewater rafting, even though the biggest physical challenge they'll have to face in the next few hours will be not throwing up in the coach.

I'm far from convinced I'll manage it myself. Maybe I should change into my waterproofs too. I'm pretty wet already – the weather hasn't improved and the forecast on the radio as I drove in was the pits. But sunshine would make me feel more miserable still.

'Everyone on the coach, come on.' Even my own voice makes me wince. I wonder if I could talk the driver into letting me make the journey in the baggage compartment.

'You don't look very well, miss,' Sanjay says. That little bugger is too bright for his own good sometimes.

'Really? I'm fine. Which is more than you'll be if you don't get on board before I count to ten.'

He frowns. I'm not normally this strict, but there's already a sense of hysteria among the group and it's only seven thirty a.m. If they don't calm down a bit, there'll be tears before we hit the M5 and they might be mine.

Juliet's voice is as loud as you'd expect from a woman who was probably born wearing crampons. 'Right, I'm not telling you lot again. On that coach now, or I'm taking your luggage off and you can sit outside Mrs Mead's office until Saturday doing extra maths while the rest of us are having fun.'

For a moment I wonder if that tempting offer extends to me. Only in my dreams.

I climb resignedly onto the coach. Craig appears from

somewhere in the throng to lumber on behind me. He looks bigger than ever in an old-fashioned cagoule that's stretched tightly across his arms and stomach. As I take my seat at the front, he stands with his grubby hands open in a silent appeal to invite him to sit alongside me. I can't let him, partly because it really wouldn't do him any favours, but mainly because I know the smell of him would definitely make me vomit. I turn my head very slightly to indicate no and he looks down, then shuffles past me. I know he'll be sitting on his own while the other kids sing and mess about. Get used to it, Craig. We're all on our own in the end.

Juliet skips aboard and vaults over me to take the window seat. Finally Derek the driver gets on too, smelling strongly of nicotine. We always get his company in when we've got too many kids for the minibus. He's a decent bloke but he has to stop at least every ten miles for a fag break. It's going to be a long journey.

'Fantastic weather for it,' Juliet says, wiping a clear patch of the steamed up window with the sleeve of her Gore-Tex jacket. I'm sure she's even more excited than the children.

'Are you serious? We'll be lucky not to be buried alive in a mudslide.'

'Don't be daft. Honestly, it's so bonding for the kids to get properly stuck in together: sleeping in bunk beds, the sound of the rain on the roof, mugs of hot chocolate all round after a brilliant day getting as wet and as messy as possible. They'll never forget it.'

I shiver at the thought. As the coach lumbers its way out of the car park, leaving bedraggled parents in its wake, an eerie silence descends. For all their bravado, it's the first time some of the kids will have been away from home for more than a sleepover – the littlest are still only eight years old. At least while Juliet is leading the troops from the front, I can trail back with the smallest children. I understand how it feels to be cast adrift.

'Fancy a bit of this?' Juliet asks, proffering a bar of Kendal Mint Cake. 'I know you can get much healthier energy bars and all now, but this really reminds me of my first expedition with my parents up Snowdon. Fantastic trip, truly, and it was this stuff that kept me going.'

'Thanks.' Dubiously, I snap off a piece but as the sugary mint melts on my tongue, I feel a bit less sick. 'How old were you?'

'Seven I think. Or was it six? It was January, I know that, because they'd bought me climbing boots for Christmas. I thought I was going to die as we headed up towards the top; I remember crying and moaning and trying everything I could to get them to abort the expedition. But they weren't having it, and, you know, it was the making of me.'

Parents have a lot to answer for.

Murmuring has started again behind us on the coach. 'God, they sound miserable, don't they? We'll soon have them sorted.' Juliet climbs over me into the aisle. 'Right, chaps. We're going to have a sing-song. And none of your Britneys and your Blues, thanks very much. Anyone know "One Man Went to Mow?"'

I catch sight of the driver's expression in his mirror. I can see that he's looking forward to this even less than I am.

Five fag breaks, one case of travel sickness and two and a half hours later, we arrive at the River Cross Adventure Centre. The coach has to weave down a country lane to reach the entrance and we see it first from a distance, an orange-roofed farmhouse that has grown ugly extensions spreading like tentacles through the grounds.

When we finally reach the front courtyard, Juliet jumps out of the coach like Lara Croft and springs forward to the front door of the main building. It looks a little bit less bleak in close-up. A lazy dog that looks like an Irish wolfhound with a shaggy perm appears from nowhere and nuzzles her hand. Rainwater splashes off the porch roof straight onto Juliet's head but she doesn't flinch. She's probably enjoying the fresh air.

The kids have been singing and screaming and giggling quite happily, but now we're here, in the land that Sky Digital forgot, they're subdued again. After a couple of minutes, and a couple more knocks on the door by Juliet, a man appears on the doorstep. From this distance, all I can see is that his hair is very short, almost shaved, so he's either going bald or he's taking the whole adventure thing way too seriously by going for the squaddie look.

He rushes out when he sees we're outside and runs up the steps to the coach. Oh shit, another ludicrously keen sporty type, with more energy than is good for him or anyone else.

'Hello, guys! I'm Robin. I can't tell you how pleased I am to see you guys. How was the journey?' His voice is confident and his accent is hard to place, though if I was a betting woman I might guess at the Cornish end of the West Country. But my biggest worry is the way he's addressing the whole group, always a mistake. I cringe inwardly for the poor man, wait for him to blush and withdraw at the lack of response from our streetwise charges.

But then something strange happens. They answer him. All of them, at once.

'Wicked!' 'Cool!' 'Too long, and Joanne was sick all over me.'

It's very odd, but they're clamouring to talk to him. I take another look. Beneath the borderline bald forehead, there are two very deep-set brown eyes, a Roman nose and a mouth so full of teeth that his front ones are protruding. He's not good-looking by any definition, but the kids like him instantly. Perhaps he's got hypnotic powers.

'Great! Well, we'll have you off the coach in no time and show you your bunks and then meet up in the kitchen for some cookies. You're going to work them off later, though! First of all, I want you lined up outside the coach, in alphabetical order by surname. One queue of girls, one of boys. OK? You've got two minutes.'

They follow his instructions like he's a Territorial Army version of the Pied Piper. I wait until they're all off before I step down from the coach. However weird I find this hold he has over the kids, at least it means I should get an easier ride. The brochure promised an adventure leader for every eight children, so maybe no one'll miss me while I get some kip.

'You must be Tess,' he says, holding out his hand. I shake it. It's almost too firm, but his palm is warm and when he adds a big smile, I feel myself coming under his spell too. I pull away.

'That's right. I gather you're Robin.' I'm trying to sound cool and disinterested, but as his smile lingers I feel I'm being gratuitously rude. 'Sorry if I sound knackered. Been a bit of a journey and I didn't feel too hot this morning.'

'Hangover or morning sickness?' he asks, then when I fail to laugh back, his face turns apologetic. 'I can't believe I just said that. I don't get enough female company out here. You ought to humour me; I'm hopeless.'

'Right.' I look around. My rucksack is on the edge of a puddle next to the coach. 'I need to rescue . . .' but before I complete the sentence, he's picked it up with one hand and is carting it off into the house.

'Allow me to show you to your luxury en-suite accommodation, Madam. And welcome to the River Cross five-star resort.'

It's not exactly luxurious, but to my surprise he wasn't kidding about it being en-suite. Well, I share the bathroom with Juliet and there's a door from each of our rooms leading into it – could be embarrassing, though I can't imagine her blushing at anything. The shower is forceful enough to wake the dead, so I go back downstairs feeling, if not a new woman, then at least a less hungover version of the old one.

The kitchen is functional. No farmyard table like Roz's rustic effort. Instead, there's a long formica-coated trestle. On top are jugs of squash and milk, rows of metal camping mugs and a few chipped plates loaded with biscuits that have either been bought from a supermarket's 'authentic country-style range' or are homemade. Knowing how little we paid for the accommodation, I suspect they're the latter. I wonder where Robin's wife is.

Above my head I hear the clatter of the kids heading downstairs. I grab a cookie before they come down and hoover them all up. When I bite into it, the chocolate chips are gooey. They must just have come out of the oven.

Robin walks in, followed by the dog. He grins again. Maybe they put Prozac in the water supply around here.

'Did your other half make these cookies? They're really good.'

He gives me an odd look. 'So you don't believe a man could bake? That's a bit sexist, isn't it?'

Whoops. I seem to have struck a nerve. 'Sorry, didn't mean . . . you're a good cook, then.'

'Actually, they were made by the lady of the house.'

I turn around and there is a teenage girl. 'Hi,' I say, trying to work out the dynamics of the house. Maybe they do things differently in the countryside, but she looks suspiciously young to be his wife.

'My lovely daughter, Charlotte. Charlotte, this is Tess, one of the teachers from Old Oak.'

'Hi,' she says, taking me in with the big brown eyes that I now realise are exactly like her father's.

'Hello,' I say. 'Great cookies. But I hope your dad doesn't make you do all the cooking.'

'No, we've got a housekeeper. I just do the bits I enjoy.'

Her father goes over and puts his arm around her skinny shoulders. She's less solidly built than him, but almost as tall. 'She's brilliant with the younger kids as well. Couldn't hope for a better assistant.'

I wonder where her mother is? The outdoor life is all very well, but I can't imagine any woman abandoning her daughter so far from civilisation. Then again, Tim's wife didn't seem to have any qualms about deserting the whole family. Robin seems to be coping without a wife much better than Tim, it has to be said. There are none of the dandruff flakes on the scalp and white toothpaste tidemarks that lurk at the side of Tim's mouth. Robin looks and smells as though he's just stepped out of a pine-scented hot bath.

'Da-ad!' She blushes. 'Come on, Wirewool,' she says. The dog ignores her, so Charlotte shrugs and saunters off. The kids arrive en masse before I have a chance to ask Robin any more about the set-up. I'm surprised by how important it suddenly seems to me.

It's still raining when we've polished off the cookies. I could very happily stay in the steamy kitchen, drinking tea and rubbing Wirewool's stomach, for the next three days, but I have a feeling that's not an option.

'OK, guys. How were the cookies?'

The murmurs of pleasure are just about all the answer Robin's going to get for now. I think the kids feel the same way as me about sitting tight; as sickly-looking townies, our usual response to the downpour outside is to switch the central heating up. If only it was a democracy.

'I'll take that as compliments for the chef, shall I? But before you get too comfortable, I'm going to explain what we've got planned for you while you're here at River Cross. In a minute, I want you all to go back to get changed into your wet weather gear and we'll meet outside with a couple of my colleagues here for some games, just to get you all revved up. That'll go on until it's time for lunch, and then we're going to get you all nice and wet when we do some raft-building and kayaking. And I know you've all been practising your moves in the swimming pool, haven't you?'

Only Juliet responds – and she's probably canoed single-handed up the Amazon. She wasn't too huffy about me opting out of all watersports – before I agreed to come, I'd warned her that I wasn't up for anything involving rivers or currents or splashing and she'd assured me it'd be fine. And there's no shortage of super-fit safety types on hand to allow me to bunk off when the going gets tough. Just the thought of canoeing makes me want to throw up those lovely chocolate-chip cookies onto the trestle table. I dig my fingernails into the palms of my hands to control myself.

'Don't be nervous! It's going to be a real treat. You'll love it. And the non-swimmers will be dead jealous – though we'll have brilliant stuff for them to do too. Then tonight we've got some bangers and mash and a bit of a sing-song. Over the next couple of days we've got some archery, a treasure hunt, orienteering, mountain biking and the highlight of the whole trip, a moonlight walk. How does that sound?'

Juliet starts whooping and after a bit of hesitation, a few of the kids join in. Even the force of Robin's personality can't quite overcome their natural uncertainty. Home feels like a long way off.

'Right. See you back down here again in twenty minutes ready for a good soaking in the rain. You're all going to love it!'

Wrestling forty-odd overexcited children back into cagoules and waterproofs is a tough job, but someone's got to do it. Me and Juliet, to be precise; Robin and his sporty sidekicks disappear with murmurs of 'got to get the equipment ready'. The kids are so hyper they've regressed to squabbling toddlers, playing tug-of-war with their macs, and pretending not to know which wellies belong to which child.

Finding something suitable to wear myself proves even more stressful. My Grand Marnier liqueur-fuelled packing last night has left me with the world's most unsuitable adventure kitbag.

I get away with it by the skin of my teeth for the team-building games, even if Sanjay does draw attention to the clash of colours. Lime green jacket (my own), orange waterproof trousers (Juliet's spare pair, so way, way too long for me) and a slightly pinching pair of dusky-pink walking boots with fluorescent stripes (supplied by Robin from a cupboard full of spares).

But with lunch under our collective belts (toad in the hole and gravy, the ideal comfort food for a rainy day in rural Gloucestershire), the time for canoeing is rapidly approaching. Of course, I've already got special dispensation from Juliet, but suddenly things seem different. For all my pathological terror of being submerged, I don't know if I want to let Robin know what a prize wimp I am. Sitting here opposite him as he dispenses endless food and joie de vivre, I am rapidly reassessing my earlier judgement of him as an uglier version of Jean-Claude Van Damme. Now he's reminding me of a funnier version of Russell Crowe.

If only Worcester had never happened.

Chapter Twenty-three

The Cole, Murray, Tilbrook rowing boat race was meant to be fun. A jolly for legal partners, would-be partners and their other halves. *A little R and R, a chance for us all to get to know each other better away from the office.* And, given the firm's unofficial motto – fit in or fuck off – it was no doubt a chance for the bosses to get a better idea of exactly who could do the former, and who should be encouraged to do the latter.

As Mr Toad had it, there is nothing so much fun as messing about on the river.

The river in question was the Severn and the day was the sort that made you believe global warming was not only a reality, but something we should be celebrating, at least once we got out of sticky Birmingham. We drove down the motorway in convoy: me and Barney with Steve, his pompous deputy, and his silent little wife, Amanda, in one car, with Sara and some fly-by-night boyfriend she'd rounded up leading the way in her Racing Green MGF.

'It's a smashing idea, this, I think,' said Steve from the back seat. He'd entered into the spirit of it, with a boater and flannel trousers. I was nominated driver, so that Barney could get pissed and bond with his colleagues unhindered while I supported him from the sidelines. It wasn't that different from my brief experience as a cricket girlfriend to Ian, when I'd spent the summer before our A-levels on numerous village greens, reading my history revision notes and trying to avoid being pulled into the pavilion to help with the tea. There was something so *Victorian* about the women doing all the work – spreading endless sandwiches with cucumber or potted meat, filling enormous urns of hot water, cutting the tops off fairy cakes to fill them with cream and then replacing the tops in the shape of butterfly wings – while the men strutted round the field looking so proud of themselves. In those days I was a feminist.

But by the time of the boat race, I was a pragmatist. And a wife. The rules were different for Sara; she was allowed to be cool and modern and even to wear short skirts when the occasion merited, because she was on her way to being a partner. My role was different. I had to perform. My job was just about acceptable – a teacher was harmless enough as far as the partners were concerned, though Barney had conveniently forgotten to mention I'd become deputy head. That sounded far too *political* somehow, especially when I didn't have the good sense to work in the private sector.

So today I was going to be – what did they call them? – a consort. One step down from a geisha, really. Speaking when spoken to, sipping demurely on orange juice and then driving people back to Birmingham without complaint. I no longer resented it. In fact, after the effort at work of bossing around caretakers and governors and a dozen other would-be alpha males, my weekend role was quite relaxing.

It took a sweaty hour to get to Worcester and we parked up at the riverside. There were thirty or so people there and Marcus, one of the senior partners, was marshalling people into the boats, little flat wooden affairs that each held four people. The water looked murky, the pleasure-trip traffic on the river having churned up so much mud that there were no reflections, though the sun was relentless.

'Right, everyone,' said Marcus. 'Now, if you've ever done any punting – hands up the Cambridge posse, yaay – this'll be a doddle.'

A dutiful chuckle spread through the gathering. Cole, Murray, Tilbrook was dominated by the Oxbridge brigade; even though the company was based in Birmingham, appointing Sara and Barney from the city's university had been rather a daring move back in 1989. And judging from the turnout that day, the old school tie still ruled supreme.

'Everyone's to grab a coolbag for refreshments should you get a little thirsty on the way ... it should take forty minutes or so to reach the pub, then we'll be having some more beverages there, on the house, of course, but make sure you don't drink so much that you can't find your way back again.'

Despite angling to get a boat with Sara and her sporty-looking boyfriend, we drew the shortest straw of all and ended up teamed with two of the younger lads from the commercial law department. Though their chinlessness was no doubt testament to their extensive punting experience, their laddishness far outweighed that small advantage.

They were already drunk by the time we climbed into the boat and they looked at me with barely concealed hostility. 'Marcus, hey! I know you wanted to handicap us, but there was no need to go this far and put us in with a woman,' said the chubbier of the two, as he stepped onto the planked centre of the boat. It seemed to sink a further five centimetres into the water. 'No offence, Mrs Leonard, but you don't look the sort to have sea legs.'

Barney raised his eyebrows at me. 'No comments about my wife's legs, thanks very much, Geoffrey. I think you'll find *you're* the handicap with that big belly of yours. You're the only twenty-five-year-old I know with middle-age spread.'

'You're hardly anorexic yourself, Barney mate,' Geoffrey said, as he managed to squeeze his way along the boat towards the front end. It seemed an unwise place for the fattest member of our crew, but what did I know? He looked down at his T-shirt, which was stretched thinly across his stomach. We could even see the indentation of his navel through the cotton. He patted it affectionately. 'Buoyancy aid, that's all. So what's on offer in the way of refreshments then, Mrs Leonard?'

I was perched on the forward-facing plank that served as a seat, feeling like someone's maiden aunt. As the woman of the group, Marcus decided I should have custody of the coolbag and I undid the zip. Inside were eight small cans of Pimm's, a bottle of mineral water and a punnet of strawberries that were disintegrating in the heat, their once firm flesh turning pale pink and mushy against the plastic walls of the container. I felt like the same thing was happening to me.

'Pimm's! Yes!' Geoffrey held out his hands for me to throw him a can but I shook my head.

'I think we might be better sticking to mineral water until we get to the pub,' I said. I felt woozy myself from the heat and I hadn't touched a drop of booze, so I had my doubts about the wisdom of letting Geoffrey or his sidekick anywhere near it.

'Don't be a bloody spoilsport, Mrs Leonard, we're absolutely sober as judges, aren't we, Toby?'

Toby guffawed. 'Would that be as sober as His Justice Clifford the pisshead, or as sober as Circuit Judge "Gin Fizz" Fitzherbert? Ha ha, good one.'

I groaned to myself. At least the older partners had some manners. I threw one can at Geoffrey so hard that it nearly knocked him off balance, but we hadn't left the bank yet, so I didn't really care. Toby reached over for another and Barney smiled at me ruefully as we pushed away from the jetty and embarked on our voyage.

Once I'd realised that Toby and Geoffrey, despite their Pimm's-lout behaviour, were very competent rowers, I almost enjoyed the trip to the pub. The weather was so sultry that it was hard not to give in to the soft splashing of the oars in the water and the birds and dragonflies that dodged lazily out of our way as we approached. Barney managed to keep the boys under control with the odd threatening glance whenever their boisterous antics threatened to make us capsize, but otherwise he made enough jokes about girls in the office and the sexual habits of the partners and minor members of the local judiciary to keep them smiling.

Barney's chameleon quality was always one of his strengths. If he'd only had the dedication or the brains to go along the criminal law route, I could really imagine him swapping slang with the lags in the cells one minute, and dazzling the beak with his command of the English language the next. He seemed a bit wasted in conveyancing. But I wonder if that ability to imitate and ingratiate was also a sign of a weakness of character that I never spotted in seventeen years.

Our boat came in a respectable third, which brought a consolation prize of a bottle of champagne, with instructions that it was only to be drunk on the way back, to avoid annoying the landlord of the Anchor. The pub was pretty, its trestle tables already crowded with families and couples and a few hardcore Worcester locals with tattoos and intimidatingly short haircuts. But if they were put out at the arrival of a couple of dozen pissed posh people, then they were too relaxed or hot to try to initiate a punch-up. I managed to get a rubbery cheese sandwich from the kitchen and tried to get the boys to eat something, but they were too busy stuffing mouldy strawberries down each other's T-shirts and shorts to bother with food.

After an hour or so, Marcus stood up and gave three cheers to the other members of his winning boat – no surprise, I suppose, that the partners won – before explaining that we had another hour before we needed to board our crafts for the return journey. The company had hired a local hotel for an evening bash and Geoffrey and Toby were suddenly determined that they would be the first ones there. They shouted at Barney and me to get ready for the race back and when I tried to finish my Diet Coke, they pulled on my arm to get me back into the boat.

'All aboard the HMS *Toby*,' Toby declared as he stumbled towards the back of the boat. 'We'll show 'em who's the fastest team on the Severn seas!'

The two of them laughed so loudly that the boat began to wobble and I was sure it would take in water straight away, but somehow it righted itself. I tried to talk sense to myself: we'd managed to get to the pub in one piece, we were the same weight, same crew and the river was quieter than it had been earlier, as the sun was setting on us and the day trippers had already headed home.

And if nothing else, the boys' competitive spirit would ensure we made it to the hotel before anyone else.

'Let's crack open the champagne, Barney!' Geoffrey slurred as we reached the centre of the river. I was beginning to feel chilly, though the alcohol was clearly keeping everyone else glowing with bonhomie.

I glared at Barney in case he was mad enough to agree. 'I think we should wait.'

'Don't be boring. We're thirsty,' Toby moaned.

I held up the mineral water. 'This is fizzy.'

He stared at me. 'God, I hope we never get as boring and grown up as your other half, Barney. Looks like carbonated water is her idea of splashing out.'

Geoffrey nodded. 'You're a teacher, aren't you, Mrs Leonard? It figures!'

I wondered if Barney would stick up for me, but all he did was shoot me a sympathetic look. 'Better grown up than soaked through, lads. It's not far now.'

We went round an island of reeds and I could feel the current was helping us, making up for the slackening performance of the boys.

'We should be singing,' Geoffrey said. 'Come on, guys. What shall we do with the drunken sailor?' His voice was deep, and as he started to sing, his belly quivered.

The others joined in and even I mouthed the words, to show willing. I was a bit stung by the grown-up comment. Sure, I was more grown up than these two juveniles, but then so was the reception class at school, in terms of common sense. If that was what public school did, then thank God for the state system.

'Oh-eh and up she rises, oh-eh and up she rises, oh-eh and up she rises, EARLY IN THE MORNING.'

And before we could do anything to stop them, the two boys stood up at either end of the boat and began to move towards the centre. 'Swap sides, SWAP SIDES,' cried Toby excitedly.

It happened so slowly after that. I remember looking at my handbag and wondering if I could hold it above my head as we went down to avoid spoiling the film in my camera. I saw the first sludgy water lap over the wooden sides of the boat, and just for a moment it looked like it was all going to be OK, that the water would be like champagne in a glass, the bubbles nearly pouring over the edge, but settling back at the very last minute.

'TESS!' Barney said as I looked at the water and realised there was no escape now; the boat was going under and if we stayed anywhere near it, so might we.

'Abandon ship!' shouted Geoffrey. Or maybe it was Toby.

I shut my eyes, took a deep breath and moved myself into the river. It wasn't a jump or a dive, more of a slump sideways. I wouldn't say that my life swam in front of me, but the time between being seated on the plank of wood with the water up to my knees, and being engulfed by the muddy, smelly Severn, seemed to last for ever. I felt sick and scared and then relaxed as I realised that if the current was going to take us away, there wasn't much I could do. Somehow it wasn't the fear of dying that made me feel more disgusted, it was the thought that we would drown in the horrible shit-brown eddies of a Midlands river, rather than the clear crystal tides of the Indian Ocean. That when my parents had to identify my body, my clothes would be streaked with silty stains and my teeth would be blackened by mud.

Enough of this defeatism, I told myself, and my feet began to pump in a reflex action, trying to tread water.

'Tess!'

I looked up and saw Barney, standing up. I felt my feet touch the riverbed, though it took my brain a fraction of a second longer to register that the stretch where we'd capsized was, at most, a metre and a half deep, and that my crewmates were now all standing up to their armpits laughing at my panicked expression. In my husband's case, I like to think he was laughing out of relief. But Toby and Geoffrey's faces were full of derision.

I could taste water and blood in my mouth – I'd bitten my lip and the reddened spit had dribbled down the right side of my chin. But my handbag was still wrapped around my shoulder. I couldn't quite believe what had happened. Even the sight of the edges of the submerged boat occasionally breaking the surface of the water seemed unreal.

'What the fuck do we do now?' Barney looked accusingly at the lads. He very rarely got angry but at least they had the grace to stop laughing.

We clambered onto the bank and the boys tried to pull the boat up but it was too heavy. The sun had definitely disappeared now and because we'd left the pub so much earlier than any of the other boats, we had no idea how long we'd be there. I made a half-hearted attempt to squeeze the water out of my clothes, but in the fading light I could see that they were stained with rings of dirt in tie-dye patterns.

Finally a cabin cruiser responded to our cries and waves. 'Had a bit of a setback, then, lads, have you?' said the man, as he pulled us on board and attached the rowing boat to the back of the cruiser with rope.

'Just a bit of fun,' Geoffrey said, happier now. 'Only Mrs Leonard here thought we were all going to be lost at sea.' He laughed and Toby joined in, mocking me with little squeals.

He looked at them oddly. 'It's not really something to joke about.'

It didn't stop them, though. I drove us all back to the hotel because the boys were determined not to let the accident and some wet clothes get between them and a bar-load of company-funded free alcohol, and they were in hysterics all the way about my silliness.

It wasn't until the Sunday when I switched on the local news and saw that two teenagers had been swept to their deaths just a mile further up the river that I realised I was no fool. A little way upstream and we could have been dragged under. And now all my nightmares revolve around water: weirs and whirlpools and waves all threatening to suffocate me. They say that death by drowning is an easy way to go, but I would fight it all the way.

I haven't been swimming now for four years. Even the inviting, harmless depths of turquoise hotel pools make me feel dizzy. But maybe I have been hiding from things that scare me for too long.

'Are you going to try to brave the canoeing, Tess?' Robin is dressed like a sea captain ready for a long voyage, in a yellow Berghaus jacket and massive over-boots. 'Why don't you just come down to watch, see what fun it is. You'll love it if you give it a try, I promise.'

I take a deep breath and follow him out into the courtyard at the front of the building. The one advantage I can see of my sudden enthusiasm to risk life, limb and humiliation to try to impress a man is that it suggests divorce is no longer the biggest of my worries.

Chapter Twenty-four

Down in the car park, even the brashest kids are clustered together like nervy convicts in a prison exercise yard, shuffling their feet and avoiding eye contact.

Robin beams at all of us, his arms wide open like an Outward Bound-certificated Jesus Christ. 'You all look like a wet week-end in Skegness. There's no need to be scared, you know. You're safer here than you were in the coach on the way down. As safe as houses.'

He's probably got a point, but it doesn't make me feel any better. Statistics usually reassure me, but I am beyond reason now. Real fear's like that. Which is why I want to shout at the kids, IT'S NOT GOING TO GET ANY EASIER. You might as well jump headfirst into the water now, while your bones are bendier and your skin's thicker and your heart will mend quicker.

They probably think that age makes you brave. I was like that when I was little. It was my argument against having to undergo most unpleasant things: going to the dentist, having injections, sleeping without a nightlight.

I became convinced that the magic moment would be my tenth birthday – hitting double figures would mean I would suddenly be a fearless creature, like Steve McQueen in *The Great Escape*. His valour in the face of the very worst behaviour by the Nazi camp commandos had recently given me all sorts of warm feelings in my tummy that I put down to an excess of Christmas pudding and a recognition of his amazing strength of will.

I woke up on 22 August 1978 and waited for a wave of courage to overwhelm me. I stepped out of bed and tiptoed downstairs. A huge black spider scuttled across the hall. I didn't flinch.

But I never had been scared of spiders.

I went into the living room, where Mum, Dad and Suzy were waiting with a small pile of presents.

'Hello,' I said, testing whether my voice had a new confidence, on account of my recently acquired pluckiness.

'Hi, Tess,' my dad said. 'Feeling braver? Hope so. Only we thought we'd test it out for you.'

'OK,' I said, though my mother disapproved of any Americanisms in my speech. That was quite daring, wasn't it?

'Yes,' he said and he was smiling like Santa. 'We've booked for you to have a filling at nine thirty. Now you're into double figures, it'll be no sweat, will it? So you'd better get on and unwrap your presents before it's time to go.'

In that moment I knew it had all been for nothing. As my big toe began to twitch – a nervous reaction I still feel before an appointment with the dentist – I realised that there was no age of fearlessness.

And now, as a fully fledged adult, I know it's not bravery, but fear of the future that forces you to do the things you hate. As a kid, I didn't care about my teeth falling out or catching TB, because those were things that would only worry you if you weren't going to live for ever. Now I know I'm not immortal, so I take the short-term pain (which now includes smear tests, travel vaccinations, MOTs and other terrifying features of grown-up life) because the alternatives are even scarier.

None of which explains why I am taking this entirely unnecessary risk, rather than sitting huddled around a jigsaw with the other non-swimmers.

'Right, we're going to walk down to the river; watch your footing as it's quite slippy,' Robin says, falling in alongside me, grinning. 'How are those shoes?'

'Yes, they're fine,' I say, even though they're now digging into the outside edges of both feet. 'So do you keep spare pairs in every size then? For idiots like me?'

'No. No, they used to belong to . . . someone else here.'

'They're not very worn. Did she get fed up with all the yomping?'

To my horror, Robin blushes deeply, then gives me a very odd look. 'Something like that.'

Oh my God, they must have belonged to his wife. That's why Charlotte is the lady of the house. Robin's wife must have left him because she couldn't handle the Spartan conditions.

I wonder if I should say something about my own divorce, show him I understand, but before I can, the river appears ahead of us, through a break in the woods. If I am honest, it's more of a creek, but to me it might as well be Niagara Falls. I feel winded.

'Tess, I hope you're not going to mind me mentioning this, but Juliet . . . well, over lunch, she told me that you'd had a bit of a bad experience.'

Silly gossiping bitch. How dare she? It's one thing for me to decide to confide in Robin for the sake of solidarity among the Dumped, but it's another thing to be told tales on by super-fit, super-perfect supercilious colleagues. 'I'm not sure why my personal life would be any concern of hers. Or yours, in fact.' It comes out sniffier than I intended.

He looks confused. 'Sorry? I don't . . . all she said was that you'd once had a nasty experience on the Severn and that it was touch and go whether you'd come down for the canoeing at all.'

'Ah.' My mouth hangs open as I add clueless to the range of expressions Robin has seen me make.

'Only I just wanted to tell you that I think it's really brave of you to even consider kayaking. No one's going to force you to do anything you don't want to. I knew as soon as I met you that you were a good egg. If you do give it a go, I'll keep a special eye on you, OK?'

He gives me a look that makes me melt; it's so sincere and caring and just . . . ooh, this is very odd indeed. Eat your heart out, Steve McQueen.

'OK,' I say, trying to seem brave yet vulnerable, winsome yet knowing. The contortion hurts my face.

Robin's sidekicks are already at the water's edge, marshalling the kids into groups by age and size, then placing buoyancy aids over their heads and giving them fluorescent helmets to wear. His team has an air of confidence, so that I can almost believe nothing will go wrong. But however much I can convince my logical side that I've been in more danger trying to cross Broad Street on a Saturday night, my irrational brain is swamping me with adrenalin. I can feel sweat forming under my arms, on my face and neck, even around my ankles, for God's sake.

As I step forward to grab one of the adult buoyancy aids, Robin punches me lightly on the arm. 'You'll be fab . . .' he says. 'Though you'll need one of these.' He reaches over for a safety helmet. A purple one. Oh yes, that'll go well with my lime-green, orange and pink waterproof combination. I feel myself blushing as I pull it over my head; I couldn't look less cool if I tried.

'Hey, it suits you!' And he smiles as though I've just added a gorgeous hat to a girly wedding outfit. 'Now,' he says, turning to the children, 'take a look in the water. Can anyone tell me what these are?'

Sanjay's hand is in the air faster than you can say watery grave. 'Canoes!' he shouts triumphantly.

'Ah,' says Robin. 'That's what *you* think. Sorry, it was a bit of a trick question. These are kayaks – invented by the Eskimos for hunting and fishing. But we're going to use them for fun.'

Sanjay frowns. He's not used to being proved wrong.

'Now then, first of all I'm going to show you the best way to get in, then we can all get onto the water and play some games. I know you're all going to be terrific.'

The water is calm but grey, reflecting the sky. It's impossible to tell how deep it is and I feel like I am tempting fate. I managed to escape drowning once; am I mad to think of doing it again? I try to concentrate on Robin's physique as he strides down the muddy pathway towards the biggest kayak. If that was me, I'd have fallen on my bum by now, but he looks unbreakable, like a cartoon superhero.

As he twists himself into the cockpit, I wonder if this is going to fuel still more nightmares, of being trapped upside down in a freezing current, trying to attract the attention of Robin while he's too busy comparing muscle tone with Juliet.

He paddles out a little way from the bank and waves at everyone. 'Right,' he shouts. 'Before we do anything else, I'm going to show you something.'

Then with an expert flick of the paddle, he flips the kayak upside down. I take a sharp breath and hear a few of the children do the same, as we count the seconds: one . . . two . . . three . . . four . . . bloody hell, this is getting worrying, surely he should have reappeared by now . . . five . . . six . . .

Suddenly, like Houdini escaping from padlocked chains, Robin swims up from under the water, his shaved head appearing first, then the red of his jacket. The kids clap and cheer as he wades ashore, pulling the kayak back towards the bank. He gives a little bow: I think Robin's a bit of a show-off at heart.

'I thank you! Right, apart from getting me nice and wet, there was a point to me doing that,' he says, his voice still booming, though he must be pretty cold. 'And the point is that whatever you might have seen on the news or heard silly grown-ups saying, it's pretty much impossible to get trapped in a kayak.' He looks straight at me. 'I'll just repeat that: you are NOT going to get stuck underwater. Now, in the old days, we used to make beginners capsize to prove it to them, but I reckon you're all sensible enough to get the message without having to do it yourselves. Unless anyone is burning to do it straightaway?'

He raises his eyebrows and waits. No one volunteers. The logical bit of my brain knows he must be telling the truth. I can see for myself that the cockpit of the kayak is so big that you'd just fall out of it as soon as the thing turned over, but still . . . I have pushed my luck before. The longer I stand here, the less sure I feel that I can go through with this.

'Right, guys, enough spectating. It's time to have a go. We're going to split into smaller groups. So if your buoyancy aid has a yellow ribbon attached, head towards Jack on my right; if it's green, follow Noel; if it's blue, then Graham will be teaching you this bit over to my left . . . and if it's red, stay where you are, because you're with me.'

I look down and feel momentarily elated when I spot the red ribbon. I wonder if he might have made sure I was in his group . . . but why would he have done that? It must be fear that's making me jump to illogical conclusions. And all it means is that Robin is going to see what a coward I really am.

Unlike the kids: they're already looking less nervous and moving down towards the water's edge as his confidence rubs off on them. I feel my toe starting to twitch, so distract myself by speculating about Robin's past. Military, certainly, judging from his posture and air of authority. I decide that only the SAS – or maybe the Paras, though are they the same thing? – could have turned out such a fine specimen.

Where has Robin kayaked his way out of danger? I picture him on African rivers and Canadian rapids, though I can't quite work out what missions he'd be carrying out. Top secret ones, presumably. Normally I am a stickler for the facts but the fear of having to get into that bloody plastic deathtrap is making me sloppy. If I can believe that he is some kind of superhuman rescuer, then maybe I can believe he will get me out in one piece.

'So, before you have a go yourselves, any questions?'

Sanjay's hand is in the air again. 'You know you said safety's the top priority, sir?'

'Yes?'

'How come you're not wearing a helmet?'

For the first time, I see irritation in Robin's face. Then something surprising happens. He looks at me and then he blushes, from the top of his helmet-less scalp, down to the tiny area of hairy chest just above his Berghaus jacket. If I didn't know better, I'd have thought he'd left it off deliberately, to look cool. But why . . . ?

'Well spotted, Sanjay. Just checking! Right, if there are no more questions, let's get going. We don't have all day!' He winks at me, as I hang back. 'Mrs Leonard? Are you joining in?'

It's the moment of no return. I feel my legs go heavy and my head go light. One by one, the children move forward to the tiny kayaks in a fenced-off stretch of river and climb inside them.

Then there is only me. Come on, Tip Top. You've survived Trial by Mother, your husband leaving you for the shallowest woman alive AND the weekly navel-gazing of William's course. This ought to be a doddle . . .

'No.' I can't look at him.

All I can hear is the sound of water lapping gently against the bank, then finally he says, 'OK. Well, why don't you stay and watch and if you change your mind . . . ?'

I stare at my feet, pinched and sweaty in their borrowed boots. I can't remember feeling this defeated since . . . well, since Barney told me he was going to be a dad. Except last time at least it was someone else's fault. This time I have no one to blame but myself.

I pull off my helmet and close my eyes. The sounds of the children's laughing and splashing seem to come from somewhere miles away, rather than a few metres from where I am standing. I hate myself for not joining in but that's the way I am now. Someone who watches from the sidelines. Safety first . . .

'Tess?' It's Juliet. When I open my eyes, the children are further down the river, they seem to be racing each other. I don't have a clue how long I've been out of it. 'My lot seem to have developed a collective crush on Jack, so I thought I'd come and see how you were all getting on.'

'I bottled it.'

'No point talking like that, silly! Everyone gets cold feet sometimes, but if at first you don't succeed—'

'Then you might as well give up.' I see the hurt in her face. 'Sorry, Juliet. I'm not having the best of days. Or years, come to think of it.'

'Don't be daft. I don't take offence easily. Do you mind if I go out there?' she says, gesturing towards the water.

'Yeah. I might head back myself in a while.'

She touches me lightly on the lime-green arm of my jacket, then bounds off. She's no sooner in the kayak than she's reached Robin's group and they open up the circle to let her in. For the first time, I notice that Craig is among them – bigger and bulkier than the rest, but on the water he seems just as agile, using his paddle to overtake Sanjay. I catch sight of his face and he's smiling. Maybe there's hope for him yet.

Which is more than I think there is for me. It's started to rain again, solid splats that fall in my eyes. That's my story, anyway. I decide to head back to the centre: at least Wirewool the dog won't judge me for my cowardice.

'TESS!' I hear Robin's voice. He sounds rather breathless and much closer than he should be. 'Hang on a tick.'

'Shouldn't you be with the kids?' I turn round and there he is, quite pink in the face.

'Juliet's qualified to lead a group – she suggested I come after you.'

Meddling cow. 'I'm getting cold.'

'I wondered if you wanted to talk about it. The water business.' He's next to me now, and though I try to pick up my walking pace, he keeps up without any trouble. He is, of course, a million times fitter than me so it's not a battle I am ever going to win.

'Look, I appreciate your efforts, but I've managed perfectly well for thirty-five years without knowing how to canoe or kayak or whatever it is.' But even as I say it, I can feel the tears welling up.

'I'm sorry, Tess, I can be a right clumsy sod at times. It's just that working with kids all these years, I've seen so many of them come here and be terrified by something: heights, or the dark, or water. And I suppose I've got a bit addicted to helping people face up to their fears. It's the best feeling in the world. But maybe it's given me ideas above my station.'

I stop walking. His face is so contrite and he looks so silly in that helmet that I feel a bitch for snapping at him. 'What about adults? Have you managed to cure any of them? I feel like a lost cause, to be honest.'

'No one's ever a lost cause in my book. Grown-ups find it harder, there's the risk of looking a fool or whatever. But, yep, I've helped adults as well.'

I peer back at the river. 'Is there anywhere a bit . . . quieter?'

He smiles and I feel an odd glow. 'Yeah, let's move up more towards the boathouse.'

I follow him towards where the river bends slightly and there's a large storage building where I guess they keep the kayaks. While he gets an adult one out, I wonder how he's managed to talk me into this. There's something about him . . . even the kids recognise it.

'Right,' he says. 'Before we even think about getting you

afloat, can you tell me what it is in particular that worries you about water? The cold? The current?'

I think about it. 'I suppose . . . I have these nightmares and they're always about . . . the boat turning over and then being trapped. I don't know, either the weeds or the current sucking me under, or the boat itself being on top of me and not being able to find the light.'

'OK. So what would be the worst thing that could happen to you in the kayak?'

I shrug. 'I know what you said, but it has to be capsizing.'

'I want you to trust me, Tess. Do you trust me with the kids, not to do anything that would hurt them?'

'Yes. Definitely.'

'Well, what I'm going to suggest . . . it's not what I'd suggest for everyone, but I think that you're an intelligent woman and you'll see the logic of it. I want to help you tackle it head on. By making you capsize.'

I feel freezing cold and my big toe twitches instantly. I shake my head.

'Tess, you said you trusted me.' He stands next to me, places his arm on my elbow. 'You are going to be totally, utterly safe,' he whispers, and I feel some of the heat from his body transfer to mine. He looks at me, his brown eyes as soothing as the Valium my auntie used to slip me the night before an exam.

'I know.'

'Would you just sit in it to begin with?' His voice is low, almost hypnotic, as he takes my hand to lead me to the edge of the water. The kayak is moving gently up and down in the water. I wobble my way towards it and find that I have to tell my legs a dozen times what they need to do, and even then they're misbehaving, refusing to work properly, fighting till the last minute not to do what I've spent so long avoiding.

'That's it,' he says. 'Now I'll hold it steady.'

I manoeuvre my legs into the cockpit, fighting the image that drifts into my head of an underwater coffin. I feel the movement of the kayak below me and concentrate on breathing very slowly.

'How does that feel, Tess?'

'Weird.' It's quite unlike being in the rowing boat. Lower in the water, but more stable without those little ex-public school idiots larking about. Almost like an extension of me.

'You're doing well. Can you see how big the cockpit is? That's why it's impossible to get trapped – if you were to turn over, you'd fall back out again and swim to the surface.'

'Hmmm.' I think I know what's coming.

'You're not going to believe me until you do it yourself, are you, Tess?' He's smiling. 'You saw me do it before. Would you work with me on this?'

Against all my better judgement, I find myself nodding – maybe because speech is so hard at the moment.

'Brilliant. Well, what I am going to do . . . when you feel ready and only then, I will tip the kayak over. I want you to stay as relaxed as you can, then once you've capsized properly, what I'd really like you to do is count to three slowly, like this . . . one . . . two . . . three . . . to prove to yourself that you can feel safe underwater. Then all you need to do is swim out from under it. Little tip – if you do feel like it's not natural, then imagine the kayak is a pair of trousers you're trying to take off . . . push it away like you'd push at a really tight pair of jeans . . . sounds silly, but it's useful.'

For some reason, the image of Robin removing his trousers makes me feel quite sweaty. But I manage to nod again.

'One last thing – if you swallow water or feel worried or anything, forget the counting and come up anyway. I'll be here to help if you need it. I'll count to five – any longer than that, and I'll get you out, I promise.'

'Right.' My fingers are digging into my palms and I've clamped my two rows of teeth together to stop them chattering. 'Right, let's do it?'

He gives me a questioning look. 'Now?' I nod and take a final goldfish breath, pop-eyed like someone being strangled, bracing myself for the cold. He moves across the kayak and with a movement so subtle I wonder if he's assessing my weight, he tips me over. Now I close my eyes.

Shit . . . bollocks . . . fuck . . . from somewhere else, the words I never use flood my brain. And then . . .

The water isn't quite as cold as I expected but it still makes my cheeks smart, and though my mouth is closed, my teeth ache. I begin to count in my head . . .

One . . .

I open my eyes and catch a glimpse of a clear, unfocused underwater world. A distance away, it's impossible to tell how far, I can see weeds and what looks like another kayak.

Two . . .

My lungs are tight from not being able to breathe, but I feel oddly relaxed. I AM safe. I can pull myself back to the surface, I can make it . . . knowing Robin is counting with me makes me certain that everything will be all right.

Three . . .

The current from what I'm now sure is another kayak sends a stream of water towards my face. My fringe is floating in front of my eyes and I feel light and fluid, like a mermaid.

Four . . .

I wonder how long I can stay under as I feel a tap on the kayak. It's definitely a case of feeling rather than hearing, as I can hear nothing under here except the pressure in my head.

Reluctantly, because it's too, too peaceful, I use the strength in my hands to push the kayak away and pop back to the surface, blinking at the light like a newborn foal, and through the water in my ears, I hear the applause. The first thing I see after the clouds is Craig, alongside me now in his kayak. But he looks different: rosy-cheeked, excited, maybe even happy.

'Well done, Mrs Leonard,' he says, clapping one chubby hand against the other that's holding the paddle. 'I knew you could do it.'

'Yes, well done,' Robin mouths at me, putting out his hand to help me back onto the bank. 'How was it?

'Cold! But something I should have done a long time ago. Thank you.'

'We could have another go?' he says, but sees me pull a face. 'No, fair enough. I think you've earned a break. The others are finishing off anyway. Shall we head back to see if we can get first choice of cookies?'

And Craig nearly capsizes his own kayak in his desperation to reach dry land.

Despite being soaked, I feel a glow starting somewhere in my tummy and spreading throughout my body. As Robin leads the way back to the house, I start to wonder whether Juliet's theory about the trip being unforgettable might not be that far from the truth.

Chapter Twenty-five

Fresh air is cruelly misleading. It makes your skin tingle and your eyes shine and your whole system feel about a thousand times more alive. It makes you feel invincible and incredible and as irresistibly dishevelled as Goldie Hawn in *Private Benjamin.*

Then when you finally return indoors, you check yourself out in the bathroom mirror and instead of the look you were expecting – lightly flushed and appealingly windswept – you resemble a refugee from a tropical typhoon.

It doesn't help that Juliet somehow looks exactly as I had thought I did. The water makes her high-spec all-weather gear cling lovingly to her long limbs and slim torso as though she's entering some sort of expeditionary wet T-shirt competition, while my jumble-sale combo drips all over the floor, dragging my clothes down and making me look stubby and sorry for myself.

'You did soo well,' she chirps as we strip off layer after layer in our shared bathroom in the teachers' quarters. The kids have been left to their own devices for ten minutes while we get ourselves sorted out and dried off, though there's precious little point. I'd guess that by the time we've finished removing their sopping clothes, marshalling them through the showers and drying *them* off so they don't catch colds, we'll be as wet as we are now.

'Yes. I did, really, didn't I?' I might not look it, but I feel exhilarated.

'Robin's so inspiring, as well. I'd actually read about him in one of the PE journals when he won this award for customer service. That centre we used to go to was so boring.'

'Well done,' I say, towelling my hair. My life sometimes seems a bit tragic, but at least I don't sit at home leafing through back copies of *Physical Education Today* or whatever it's called.

Juliet chuckles. 'Plus Robin's a lot easier on the eye than the whiskery old git at the old place.'

A nasty familiar feeling twitches in my chest. 'Fancy him, do you?'

She gives me a long look. 'No . . . not at all. God knows I've seen enough of these macho types to last me a lifetime at college. But he's quite sweet, maybe, for someone a bit older.' That look again, and then she turns to smother her face in what looks like goose fat from an industrial-sized pot of bargain moisturiser. High-maintenance is not a phrase anyone could apply to Juliet.

'There's obviously some unfinished business there, with his wife,' I say, as nonchalantly as I can.

'Yes, I was probing him on that one as well. Went very cagey. But his daughter seems sweet.' She gives her hair one quick comb through and she's transformed, from glowing round-the-world yacht babe, into coiffed English rose. There really is no justice in the world. 'So are you ready for the damp hordes?'

I peer at my own face. The all-over red effect has faded in places, leaving my complexion uneven, with sallow dry bits on the cheeks and brighter crimson patches on my chin and the end of my nose. Every woman teacher who comes to River Cross probably develops a crush on poor Robin. He was only helping me because it's his job. And though what I've done is a big deal for me, it hardly makes me Wonderwoman. Why would he find a lily-livered townie a tempting prospect?

I sigh. The very last thing I need right now is a case of unrequited love. 'Ready as I'll ever be.'

Now I've recognised the fact that I have as much chance of attracting Robin as I have of winning the canoe slalom or whatever the most difficult watersports race is at the Olympics, I start to enjoy myself.

The fresh air might not do much for my appearance, but it's making me feel so much more alive. Distance from our house helps, too. I'm going to have to get used to being somewhere else once the place is sold, so this is the first part of the second most painful separation of my life.

Most of all, I'm enjoying the company of the kids. Unlike maybe sixty per cent of the teachers I know, I actually like the little buggers, but I've forgotten that lately, under the mental cosh of paperwork and bureaucracy and staffroom politics. Seeing them here, away from the literacy hour and the numeracy hour and all the other directives that govern every moment of our everyday lives, they're being transformed, just like me.

'This is yummy,' says Joseph, the pickiest eater in my class, who is wolfing down some sort of veggie crumble. His sudden omnivorous urges have more than a little bit to do with the morning of archery and map-reading skills, followed by an afternoon's orienteering. Their appetites have grown along with their confidence. Even Craig is being allowed by the other children to sit nearby, at the end of a row near the door. He hangs around Robin, as if he's trying to draw some of that strength for himself. And it wasn't my imagination – that unsavoury smell that follows him everywhere seems to have disappeared since he got here. There's more than an element of magic about River Cross.

Maybe it extends to controlling the weather, because by some miracle the rain's held off so far, and if anything, it's looking a bit clearer for the moonlight walk.

'Guys?' Robin is now such a hero among the kids that all he has to do is tap the side of his mug with a spoon to get their attention. 'Guys, you're going to need all your energy for the next stage of our adventure, OK? It's the best bit, especially for anyone who likes picnics or campfires or being out and about after dark . . . but we won't be heading off for a couple of hours and the very best thing you can do to prepare now is have a nap.'

The kids groan and pull faces. After nearly two days of being grown-ups – sleeping away from home, refusing to clean their teeth if they don't want to, and peeling their own potatoes for tea – the last thing they want is to do something as babyish as go to bed in the afternoon.

'Now I know you're all feeling far too excited to want to sleep, but if you give yourself just an hour of shut-eye now, then you'll stand a chance of winning my special "who can stay awake the longest?" competition tonight. And let me tell you, it's hardly ever the grown-ups who win.'

I believe him. I slept better last night than I have for months and already I feel drowsy from the stodgy comfort food we've just bolted. I join the kids, who are grudgingly carrying through their dirty plates to be loaded into the dishwasher.

Juliet is already hovering around Robin. It seems strange behaviour from someone who claims not to fancy him, but maybe they're comparing notes on equipment or resting heart rates or whatever it is that gets sporty types excited.

I sidle up to them. 'I'm going to take your advice, Robin, and bunk down for an hour, otherwise I'll be sleep-walking this evening.'

'That's a shame,' he says and he genuinely looks disappointed. 'I usually have a little afternoon snifter around this time and I was just suggesting to Juliet that the two of you might like to join me? To celebrate what you've done this week.'

'Go on, Tess. We deserve it. You can sleep at the weekend.'

I look from one to the other, their faces as flushed and smiley as the kids', and shake my head. I don't want to get in the way of a beautiful friendship. 'Honestly. One drink and I'll be flat out and no use to anyone. Why don't I see you upstairs at seven, Juliet, then we can round up the troops together?' I smile at Robin, who now looks put out. 'Thanks for the offer, though. I really appreciate it.'

But when I get to my room, the sun comes out and shines through the gap in the curtains, and I don't sleep a wink.

The kids emerge bleary-eyed and irritable from the land of Nod, and I curse Robin's commitment to the outdoor lifestyle. Surely it would have been better to let the children get worn out and keep the night walk short and sweet. *Then* I might be up for a few drinks.

'Come on, gang,' he booms as he comes through into the entrance hall. His tanned face is glowing. I wonder if it's from the alcohol or from Juliet's company. Whatever: it's none of my business. 'We're going to separate out into four groups for the walk, according to your year. So half of Mrs Leonard's class – and Mrs Leonard – are coming with me on Robin's truly terrifying trek . . . whooo. The other half will be led by Graham. Then Miss Henderson's class will either be with Noel or Jack. So let's get this show on the road. It's going to be brilliant!'

The kids take a while to sort themselves out into their groups, while I walk over to Robin and Charlotte. She glares at me as I approach and I just catch him saying, '. . . because I want you to be at the back. That's why. You can help the stragglers along and at least you won't have to help us with the campfire or the cooking if they hold you up enough.' He turns towards me.

'But, Dad, I get bored with the fat kids—'

'I don't care. GO!'

Charlotte pushes past me, knocking against my shoulder and muttering under her breath about 'slavery' and 'minimum wage'.

'Touch of teenager trouble?' I ask. I'm really surprised he's taking our party rather than Juliet's, but maybe Noel wants a share of my lovely colleague's company.

'She's very good, usually,' he says, and I hear the confusion in his voice.

'And how old is she again?'

'Just turned fourteen.'

'Well, there's your answer then. You've been lucky that she's stayed on her best behaviour for as long as she has. She'll grow out of it in . . . maybe five years?'

His face falls back into his default grin, but around his eyes – stop it, Tess, don't look into them – there are still little lines of worry. 'I see enough sulky girls come on the courses here, but within a few hours they're knuckling down and getting on with it. But I don't seem to have anything like that control over my own daughter.'

'And you really don't know why that is?'

'I suppose they have to rely on me to look after them, so they're more likely to listen?'

I laugh. 'Nothing to do with your SAS physique and big brown eyes then?'

He blushes. 'Bugger off, Tess,' he says, so quietly only I can hear. Then I blush too. 'Come on, guys, let's get moving. We're

265

all going to wear one of these fluorescent bibs, just in case we lose any of you along the way. Plus there's a whistle attached to each one, which is only to be used in an emergency. If you get any ideas about wandering off, just remember it's first come, first served at the campfire. And we *are* planning to bake bananas in their skins.'

The evening is turning from intense green to amber and pink as we walk, thanks to the two days of rain and the thin sunlight that's filtering through the clouds. Even though I prefer my countryside steam-cleaned, shrinkwrapped and definitely dry, Robin's handily found me a pair of wellies in my size and there's something fun about tramping through puddles and stamping on the spongy grass.

The children's chatter eventually dies out as the walk gets tougher, up a slightly steeper track. Dusk falls suddenly and Robin pulls twenty small torches from his daysack. He hands them out, does a quick head-count and then lets the children play with the lights for a few minutes while they get their breath back. They shine bulbs under their chins and through their fingers and make ghostly noises, while Charlotte stands behind them, frowning and chewing at her nails.

Robin goes up to her, puts his arm round her. 'You all right, love?'

She shrugs him off. 'Fantastic,' she says, staring at the ground.

Robin sighs and claps his hands to get the attention of the group. 'Right, that's enough messing about. We don't want to let the torch batteries run down. I'll keep mine on, because I've got spares, but the rest of you, remember they're only to be used . . . ?'

'In an emergency!' the kids chant back.

'Cool! The most important thing now is that we beat the other team. It won't be easy because they've got the shorter route, on account of being smaller than you lot. But we can definitely do it if we concentrate and stick together.'

As if to emphasise his point, he pulls me forward to walk alongside him. 'So are you enjoying the walk, Mrs Leonard?'

I peer at the countryside below us, which looks out of focus in the fading light. The only sounds are twigs being stepped on and wellies sticking to muddy earth and the occasional hoot of an owl or a woodpecker or whatever kind of bird it is you find in the countryside. 'Yes, thank you. I feel more relaxed than I have in months.'

'That's good. You did amazingly before, not everyone would face their fears like that. Juliet was saying earlier that she thinks you look very refreshed. So do I.'

In the semi-darkness I can't quite make out his expression, but it seems an odd, not to mention, cheeky thing to say when he doesn't know me. Tip Top Tess can't quite bring herself to be rude to a near-stranger, but I'm happy enough to express my irritation with my colleague. 'I wish Juliet would stop meddling. It's really nothing to do with her.'

'Or me, I suppose.'

I don't say anything for a while. It's now completely dark, bar the moonlight, and I don't want to spoil the calm. 'I expect she's told you enough for you to know why things haven't been too good lately. OK, that's fine. I don't think I'd be doing the same in her position, but we're different people—'

'Tess, she hasn't been telling tales out of school; in fact, she didn't want to tell me anything but I—'

'You don't have to defend her. I just don't believe that the personal and the professional should overlap.'

'So you'd never mix business with pleasure, then, Tess?'

I wish it was light, then seeing his face might help me to work out what the hell he's on about. A tiny bit of me wonders if he might be flirting, but that seems too improbable, especially when he's heard my tales of woe courtesy of Blabbermouth Juliet. 'What, in a school? Not generally, no.'

'Shame.'

'It keeps things simple.'

We keep walking for a little while. My breathing is heavy as we go uphill, and the children are whispering again, giggling at the shadows. 'Tess, I do think I ought to put you straight on Juliet. It really wasn't her shooting her mouth off about your private life. It was my fault. From the first time I saw you . . .

well, put it this way, I wouldn't stop pestering her until she told me if you were single or not . . .'

I stop in my tracks. There is only one reason why he'd want to know. I chuckle nervously. 'But surely being called Mrs Leonard was a bit of clue.'

'But you're not wearing a wedding ring.'

I look down, cursing and thanking my naked finger in equal measure for giving the game away. 'No. I felt undressed without it at first, but now I don't even notice its absence.'

'I felt the same way, to start with,' Robin says.

My feet pinch in the wellies. Oh God. These belonged to her as well. I am literally in her shoes. She must have left in a hurry.

I want to know everything, the full heartbreaking story, but it feels wrong to ask with Charlotte around. Now I'm glad I took that nap, as I have a feeling I might be talking late into the night, round the burning embers of a campfire, under the light of the moon . . .

'Miss.' Sanjay chooses this moment to rush up to me and tug on my sleeve.

My feelings of benevolence towards all creatures great and small are in danger of disappearing at this moment, but I pour as much patience as I can into my voice. 'In a minute, Sanjay.'

'But, Miss . . . it's important.'

He is such a little drama queen but I know from experience that he won't shut up until he's had his say. 'Sorry about this, Robin. OK, Sanjay, what is it now?'

'Miss, it's Craig. And it's Charlotte, miss. We've been looking for them and we can't see them anywhere and what if they've been kidnapped by ghosts?'

Chapter Twenty-six

I freeze, but Robin's SAS training kicks in.

'All of you stop what you're doing. Stop walking! Let's have a head-count.' For the first time, he's not smiling, as he reaches the same conclusion as Sanjay: one missing child, one missing teenage daughter.

'Everyone switch on their torches, now. Listen to me. There are no ghosts, nothing scary out there at all, and Mrs Leonard is going to get you all to the campfire for some food and hot drinks while I find Charlotte and Craig. They've been a bit silly to wander off from the group, but they're fine.

'I want you each to find a partner to hold hands with. I'm going to show Mrs Leonard the quickest path for you all to take, which means you'll definitely beat the others and get your hands on the grub first.'

I follow him to the side of the path, trying to stop my teeth chattering. 'What the hell are they playing at?'

He holds his torch out in front of us so we can see each other's face. 'I don't have a clue, but I intend to find out. It's not like Charlotte; she might be stroppy but she's usually sensible. What about the other kid? He seemed like a loner to me and too fat to get too far on his own.'

'Yes. That's a fair assessment.' I struggle to think of something else useful to say. 'Could it . . . well, could they have fallen, hurt themselves? Or would Charlotte have gone after him if she'd realised he'd done a runner?'

'The path is safe, so long as you stick to it . . .' He wavers, as the significance of his own words strikes home. 'Listen, the fact that they've gone together is good news, Tess. Perhaps they both got cheesed off and decided to wind me up.'

'Are you sure you should go looking on your own?'

'I know this area very well. But the last thing we need is stressed-out kids, so I want you to get them to the campfire. Our trainee is down there; Keith. Tell him what's happened and send him after me, and all the other men when they arrive. They've got walkie-talkies because mobiles are as much use as a chocolate teapot round here, and if we can't find them in twenty minutes, we'll get help.'

'Help?' I am fast-forwarding to the moment when I have to tell Craig's mother that he's missing . . . or worse.

'We won't need it, Tess. I've had kids go missing before, and they always turn up.'

'But never your own.'

'No . . . never my own.' He moves the torch away from his face but not before I've seen the fear in his expression. 'Listen, do you see the campfire?' He points down the hill and I can see a red glow in the distance. 'The fastest route is to go absolutely straight, down this way. It should be fine underfoot, slow and steady does it.'

'Right.' The fact that the least outdoorsy teacher who ever came to River Cross is now leading a group across country proves the seriousness of the situation.

'You'll be fine, Tess. And so will Craig and Charlotte.' He squeezes my arm and I can't quite believe that it was only five minutes ago that we were flirting and blushing. The fear now makes me feel even closer to him. Too close. 'Right, you lot, get in your twos and follow Mrs Leonard down. And save some food for me!'

He turns his back on me abruptly and I follow his lead, charging ahead of the crocodile of children. 'Come on then, we'll be there in no time at all. But to help us on our way, who fancies a bit of a sing-song?'

Their silence speaks volumes, but I am not that easily deterred. I am Tess Leonard, sidekick of an SAS war hero, and we will fight them on the beaches. 'You remember the words from the coach, don't you? Let's sing as loud as we can, to let Keith at the campfire know we're on our way. *One man went to mow . . .*'

They start to join in, struggling at first to co-ordinate the singing with the marching. *Went to mow a meadow, one man, two men and his dog, went to mow a meadow.* Usually the strange grammar of the song – shouldn't it be *their* dog? – irritates me, but as their voices grow stronger and carry through the night air, I welcome the simple words and the simple rhythm because I know they will propel us back to safety.

Keith isn't quite as cool as Robin. In fact, his skinny, unlined skin drains of colour even in the orange glow of the fire he's been building.

'Right,' he says and does a funny little circle, like a puppy chasing its tail. 'Right, I'll get straight up there to join the search.' But then he stands still, unsure which task to prioritise first.

'Why don't you tell me what you were going to do next, and I can do it for you?' I suggest. 'Then Robin mentioned getting some walkie-talkies to take up with you. Maybe I could hang onto one if you have enough?' Suddenly I feel like the only grown-up for miles around.

'Right. Good plan,' he says. He shows me the bags of food: part-cooked jacket potatoes already in their foil, hot dogs, banana-shaped parcels which he instructs me to avoid leaving in the fire too long because the chocolate in between the slices of fruit will burn. There's a kind of platform where we can cook frying pans full of sausages. On the trestle table he's set, there are paper plates and napkins and ketchup and plastic boxes of ready-grated cheese for the potatoes. There are groundsheets and cosy blankets and huge umbrellas in case it starts raining again. And a big roll of bin bags. 'Don't forget to clear everything away or to get the kids to do it. We're an eco-friendly adventure company,' he tells me sternly.

It's so beautifully planned and executed. The only thing that could go wrong is not being able to find Craig and Charlotte. I feel like crying, but instead I turn away from the fire towards the children. 'OK, it's going to take me a bit longer than it would Keith to do this. But Keith's going now, AREN'T YOU, KEITH?' He nods violently and heads off, holding the walkie-talkies, a couple of banana packages in case the kids are hungry when they turn up, and a big torch. 'So I'd like you to take the groundsheets and spread them out five metres away from the fire. Then I'd like you to sit quietly until the others arrive. And because they're younger, I want you all to be very careful what you say to them. None of that silliness about ghosts or whatever. Craig and Charlotte have been naughty walking off, but they're going to be fine, and like Robin said, thanks to them, you're going to get your moonlight feast earlier.'

They do what they're told without any real fuss. I'm not sure whether they believe me any more than I believe myself, but they're pretending. If any of us stop pretending, the whole thing could fall apart.

When the leaders turn up with the other groups, they look around for Robin. I am so relieved to see adults I can confide in that I blurt it all out. 'Craig's disappeared and so has Charlotte and we didn't see them go and it's dark and cold now and what if we can't find them?'

Until now I've seen the three of them as nothing but over-muscled, under-brained Neanderthals – albeit Neanderthals with surprisingly sweet, patient natures – and now they get the chance to write me off as a hysterical bimbo. Noel leads me away from the campfire, which is burning well in spite of my ineptitude.

'You must try to stay calm,' he says. 'There is nothing you can do down here, but avoid stressing anyone else out. The kids' chances are fine, so long as we find them tonight. They won't have gone far.'

'But what if they've been abducted?' Even I know I'm not really making much sense.

'By who? There's no one round here except us. They'll have wandered off for a joke and got cold and freaked and lost—'

'Charlotte knows the area though; how can she be lost?'

'Things look different in the dark.' He looks at his watch. 'How long have they been gone?'

'I don't know. Sorry. Maybe twenty minutes.' I feel more of an idiot. What was it that Robin said about sending for help after twenty minutes?

'Sixty per cent of children missing on expeditions are found within the first hour, so the chances are that by the time we get up there, Robin will be on his way down. Did Keith leave you more than one walkie-talkie?' I show him the two I've got. 'Right. You hang onto this one and we'll keep in touch. If we need help, then one of us will be faster running down to the farmhouse to use the phone anyway.'

Then Juliet appears with the last few children. She sees my face and rushes over. 'Bloody hell, Tess, what's happened?'

Noel raises his hand. 'We'll get going.'

And then they're gone again, the men off to search, leaving the women to keep the campfire burning. Even Juliet looks thrown but she soldiers on, declaring the fire ready to cook on and organising a production line for hot dogs and potatoes.

We encourage the kids to sing and play running games around the fire to keep moving. And as the time passes, I become convinced that Craig was running away from something, from the other children, perhaps. I'd naively thought that the trip was helping him to relate to his classmates, but maybe all it did was emphasise his loneliness, his size, his difference.

'How long's it been since Noel and the others went now, Juliet?' I ask, not daring to look at my own watch. Maybe it hasn't been as long as it feels, because every second without news seems to last an hour.

'Eighteen minutes,' she says. 'But maybe they're heading down as—' And she stops, because we hear the sound we've been dreading most.

Sirens.

Jack and Graham come back to the campfire and hardly say a word.

'What's happened?' Juliet asks pointlessly. If there was any news, surely they'd tell us.

'We've been told to take the children back to the farmhouse. There's no sign of them, but that's good, in a way,' Graham says unconvincingly. 'Because if there'd been an accident, they'd probably have been found by now.'

We pack up the blankets and the children; as we start the walk back, Jack douses the fire behind us. It sizzles then dies. The farmhouse is closer than I'd thought: the trek must have been very circular, an optical illusion of danger. So where the hell are they?

A couple of police cars are parked at the front, and once we've set the children about getting ready for bed (not that any of us are likely to get any sleep tonight, but we're keeping up the pretence), a woman officer approaches me and Juliet.

'Can we talk to you about the young boy? We need to think about contacting his family.' She's red-haired, and has a permanent scowl. I wonder if it's an occupational hazard.

Juliet frowns. 'Honestly, do you really think there's any reason to worry them at this stage?'

'The boy's already been missing for an hour and a half. In the dark,' she adds, as if we can't see that for ourselves. 'I understand he has some kind of . . . special needs.'

'I'm his form teacher,' I say. 'It's not exactly special needs, more that he's rather a reserved child. Not very socially adept.'

She writes something down. 'Bullying?'

'Nothing overt, but the other children don't go out of their way to spend time with him.'

'Has he been having any trouble while he's been staying here?'

'Not that I know of.'

She looks up from her notepad. 'And do you think you would definitely have noticed?'

'I like to think so.'

As we search our emergencies file for Craig's mother's number, I keep thinking, *this isn't happening, this isn't happening*. But it is. I fight to be the one to tell her, rather than the policewoman, but when she answers the phone after eight or nine rings, I wonder if I am going to be able to speak.

'Hello?' she says, the irritation at being woken up or interrupted clear in her voice. I wonder what she's been doing with the freedom of three nights without Craig at home.

'Mrs Green? It's Mrs Leonard, from school.'

My tone cuts through all her bitchy bravado. 'Craig?' Her voice is high-pitched.

'It's not an accident or anything. I mean, we . . . Craig has gone missing during a walk we were doing this evening. But he's with the daughter of the course leader here, who's a very sensible girl, fourteen going on forty, and she knows the area back to front. We think he's with her, anyway.'

'How long?' All her bluster, her threats, are gone. All that's left is a voice so small I can barely hear it.

'Since about nine.' Somehow that sounds better than ninety minutes. So much can happen in ninety minutes. 'There are officers out searching for him. They're confident of finding him; the terrain is very easy around here. It's just we had to let you know.'

'Is there anything . . . ?'

'You ought to come, if that's what you want to do. Though of course, I'm sure he'll have turned up by the time you arrive. I spoke to the police and they can send round a West Midlands officer to escort you. Unless there's someone who can drive you down?'

'I can . . . I will try to get my husband. He's . . . out.'

I had assumed that there was no husband. 'Let me give you the number here, so you can get directions when you know what you're doing.'

I hear her making a note of it, then she puts the phone down without asking any more. What else is there to ask?

At eleven o'clock, Robin comes back.

'Anything?' I ask, though his face tells me my answer.

'I don't understand it.'

The policewoman plus a few other official-looking people have set themselves up in the kitchen, so Juliet and I lead him into the lounge area. It's still cluttered with jigsaws and comics left by the kids who decided not to take a nap before the walk.

'Let's get you a drink,' Juliet says, heading straight for the bureau in the corner. She pulls out a tiny key from the pen tray and opens a cabinet on the opposite side of the room. I remember their little tête-à-tête earlier on and feel even sicker. She pours him a large whisky, delivers it and then pours another two for us.

He holds the whisky so tightly that his fingers go white. But then the rest of him is pretty white, too. 'The lads said I should come back. I wasn't helping. The kids are either deliberately hiding, or . . . what if your Craig fell in the water.? Or jumped? Charlotte is trained in life-saving, and she'd have gone in after him. But in the dark . . .'

I think of my nightmares. Being pulled by the current, out of control, taking in water, all strength sapped by this greater force. 'But you said the river was safe.'

'The bits we use for kayaking beginners are as calm as a millpond. But further along . . .'

'Have you been along there? There'd be some sign, surely.'

'I don't know any more.' He sits on the edge of a battered sofa, pulls at the loose fragments on the worn arm. 'Has the kid's mother got here yet?'

Juliet shakes her head. 'It'll take her another couple of hours. Not that there's much she can do. She's quite a . . . difficult woman.' We both shudder.

I try again. 'Charlotte knows what she's doing. It's quite likely that they're hiding, isn't it? I mean, she was in a mood with you.'

'She's too sensible.'

'But she's also fourteen.'

What did I do when I was fourteen? I was never a rebel. Occasionally I didn't do my homework until the very last minute, or walked the dogs for half an hour longer than usual, wondering if anyone would notice. They never did. Tip Top Tess didn't like to create unnecessary fuss.

So now all we can do is sit, like patients in a doctor's surgery, not catching each other's eye or trying to intrude too much on each other's secret thoughts and fears. Our markers of time are another whisky, the odd question from the policewoman about the terrain and what food or equipment Charlotte had with her, a screech of tyres on the gravel outside . . .

It's ten past one, and Mrs Green has arrived. I brace myself. But instead of the harridan who sends teachers and children and cleaning lady running for cover, she looks shrunken, her face contorted with fear. Her husband is there too, the first time I've ever seen him. He is average in every way and hardly acknowledges his wife or anyone else.

I show them into the lounge and fill them in on the facts. Then the policewoman asks to speak to them in private, probably to run through all the questions that she's already asked us about Craig: is there any reason he might have run off? Is he unhappy at home? I wonder what she answers, wonder if she has the slightest idea what's going on inside her son's head. I thought I had an inkling, but now I wonder. After all, I thought I knew the man I married inside out.

When the policewoman's finished 'for now', Mrs Green refuses whisky but accepts tea. Mr Green has nothing.

No one is into small talk. The whisky makes my head feel huge and full of hot air, and the creaks and rumbles of the old farmhouse are the only sounds as I doze in and out of reality . . .

'Wake up, Tess!' Juliet's voice pulls me out of a disturbing half-dream about sinking. I'd hoped my session in the kayak had cured me. 'They've found them!'

The room is empty except for the two of us, but I somehow have a strong sense that Robin and the Greens have only just left. I try to read her expression.

'I don't know. They're alive, we know that.'

Of course they are. I feel my body relax slightly, but then the range of possibilities allowed by the word 'alive' occurs to me. A little dazed, confused but otherwise unharmed – or barely conscious, with fading heartbeats from the cold and the shock and injuries. 'Alive and well?' That's the phrase they always use in news reports.

She shrugs and I can see that she is as scared as I am. 'Alive is all they said. They're talking to the parents now.'

For the first time, I wonder why Robin hasn't called his ex-wife. Surely, however acrimonious their parting, she deserves to know what has been going on? Perhaps it's another feature of the SAS training, the ability to cut off all feelings for someone who is no longer in your life.

Or perhaps it's part of being a man.

We walk into the hall as the kitchen door reopens. The policewoman leads the way, and Mr and Mrs Green stare fixedly ahead as they follow her out into the yard.

'Robin?' As I speak his name, he looks at us. His face is

neutral, the expression of a man under interrogation, not giving anything away.

'She's OK.' He barks the words. I think he's only just managing to stay composed.

'Properly OK? Not . . . hurt?'

'She's fine. Cold. And stroppy. That's what the policeman radioed back.' He allows himself a smile.

'And Craig?'

'Not quite so good. He was fine when they spotted him, but he made a run for it when he realised they'd been found. Suspected broken ankle. They're stretchering him down and we're all going to the hospital while they get checked over.'

I think of Craig and Charlotte, River Cross Centre's very own Bonnie and Clyde, on the run . . . from what? Bossy father, callous children, reality? It would almost have seemed charming that they'd found a strange companionship under a moonlit sky, if it wasn't for the fact that Craig was so desperate not to be found.

As it is, I reckon that a broken ankle is the least of our worries.

Juliet and I go up to the dormitories to tell the children the news. Most of them are still half-awake and their reaction is muted, almost disappointed, as if we've given away the ending of a film halfway through.

'Heartless little buggers,' I whisper to Juliet, after we've collected together Craig's few things from the bunk nearest the draughty door to the bathroom.

'Funny, that's the thing I love most about kids,' she says. 'They're not hypocrites. I mean, what is he to them? They didn't like him before this happened; why would they pretend to feel any differently now?'

'I guess. Are you going to bed now?'

'Yep. It's been a long day, eh? The cops seem to think Craig's going to be OK and there's nothing we can do now. Try to get some sleep, and I'll see you in the morning.'

As I go through Craig's stuff in my room, I think about what Juliet said. Do I really care about him? If I didn't have a professional interest in his wellbeing, would I be shunning him too, for being different? It's hard to be around someone who doesn't play by the rules. Or even know the rules exist.

Maybe we're both loners and I'm hoping that if I look after him, one day someone will look after me. But life isn't like that. One good turn doesn't deserve another. I refold his clothes: M&S underpants for age thirteen to fourteen, a small pair of scuffed trainers, grubby T-shirt. It all has his tell-tale sweaty smell about it and that makes me want to cry.

Nothing makes sense any more. Robin's shy confession from earlier feels longer ago than my wedding, and though I feel exhausted, I know I won't sleep.

I check the front pocket of Craig's kitbag and pull out a piece of paper.

To Mum and Dad and Mrs Lennord.

I unfold the note.

I have had enough I do not want to go home I want to stay here and be like Tarxan in the woods live with the animals the kids are worse than the animals I dont care and if I die then its better than this I am sorry I wont see you again but maybe when I am grown up I will come back to visit Craig sorry

Craig never did see the point of punctuation.

Charlotte must have gone after him when he slipped away, trying to talk him into heading back. I tuck the note into my own bag for safekeeping.

I must have slept somehow, because when I wake up it's seven and I can hear the children already moving about. I know I'm going to hand the note over to his parents later, to help get to the bottom of why he went, but it feels like yet another betrayal for Craig.

Downstairs, Jack is serving up breakfast. There's no sign of Robin, but Juliet appears from outside as I wonder if I can force down any cereal.

'How are you doing? You look pretty grim.' She looks almost normal, except there are the faintest traces of shadows under her bright eyes.

'Yeah, I've been better. Have you heard from the hospital?'

'Everything's fine. The fracture's not too bad, but Craig wasn't very happy when his parents arrived, so they had to sedate him and keep him in.'

'And Charlotte?'

'Apart from a massive bollocking from her dad, she's fine apparently. They've kept her overnight for observation, just in case. I think they're going to wait until we've cleared out before they come back here. Shame we won't get the chance to say goodbye. I still think it's a great place, but I guess the two of them need a bit of space.'

I see the coach already waiting in the yard. I try not to look disappointed. 'You got Derek to come early?'

'Yep. I figured that this morning's final activities would be cancelled. I reckon we've all had quite enough adventure to last us till the end of term.'

I don't reply. But I can't help thinking that a little bit more adventure with Robin wouldn't have done me any harm at all.

Lesson Six

For Richer, For Poorer

Maybe it was the birds singing. Maybe it was the sunshine. Or maybe it was just that the improved weather meant William could switch off the ageing central heating with some confidence that he wouldn't need to try to get it working again before September.

Whatever it was, Billy Barometer was looking forward to the session, despite the fact that this one was always one of the angriest. Talking about money and lawyers always had that effect on people who'd gone through divorce.

'So, by now I'm sure I don't have to ask if you've all done your homework.'

He was fond of this group. More, maybe, than any of his previous ones. He looked at each person in turn. Jo stared back. She was beautiful, there was no doubt about that, but it was her spirit that he liked the most. Or at least, that was what he was trying to convince himself.

Tess and Malcolm looked away. Tess seemed a sweet person, a little bit buttoned up, but there was nothing wrong with that. Malcolm he could take or leave, but in a way his dogmatic attitude to everything made the others seem that much more human. Tim in particular, one of life's underdogs, was growing in confidence through the kindness of the others, especially Rani. Aaron had lovable rogue off to a fine art, and although William still wasn't quite sure what he was doing here, as he clearly wasn't going to pull any of the women, he added a welcome dollop of sex appeal to the mix. After all, sex was what so many of these traumas were about. The jury was out on Natalie, but Carol-Ann, who was currently giving him a huge grin because she'd done her homework for a change, was a riot. It was almost worth running the course for her alone. One day, he thought, it'd be lovely to chat about beer with her, a fellow enthusiast. It was so rare you found a woman who was partial to a pint.

'So, Rani, what is the worst, most unjust story you could find in the news this week?'

'I have not cheated, but it was a story I heard on the radio. It was about a father who climbed onto a motorway bridge dressed as Snow White, to protest about not being given access to his children. He stayed there for twelve hours, with his packed lunch and his banner, before the police brought him down.'

'Bloody nuisance,' Malcolm mumbled.

Rani turned to the others, trying to win them round. 'No, not at all. He was making a stand. This is a father who wants to see his children, but is not allowed to. Who wants a relationship with them, but is not allowed. It is always the children who suffer. I felt moved, because here was a man doing what I long for my husband to do with *all* his children, and yet he's denied what he wants by the jealous mother. And now he could go to jail. Imagine, prison, for wanting to see your children.'

William nodded. 'That does sound unfair, though his wife may have had her reasons. And probably doesn't have any spare time to protest herself. Can anyone beat that? Yes, Natalie?'

She picked up her handbag and William saw she was wearing a wedding ring this time. She must have forgotten to take it off before the session. Inefficiency wasn't really Natalie's style and she looked paler, less well-groomed than usual.

'I don't necessarily think it's a worse story than Rani's, but mine is about . . .' she pulled out a pair of glasses with a posh perfumer's logo on the sides, 'business, really. This guy worked with his best friend to develop a groundbreaking new computer product. Anyway, they spent all their spare time doing it, working through the night. Then they couldn't find anyone who wanted to buy it. Then the guy who'd thought it up, his child got ill and he had to pull out of the whole thing. There weren't enough hours in the day.

'The next *month* his friend sold the whole business to this huge multinational that had seen the potential of the program, wanted to market it themselves. And he didn't give his ex-partner a penny. Nothing. They'd agreed to share any profits, shaken on it, but that was worthless.'

Malcolm leaned over to take the cutting. 'Yes, I think I read about this; he took it to court, didn't he? But it seems all his friend has is a moral obligation to pay up, and that counts for nothing these days. No one does what they ought to, whether it's in business or in the home. Do you know my wife has just employed a solicitor to try to get her mitts on half of my money? Including the house. I mean, she never paid anything into the mortgage in twenty years of—'

William waved his hand to stop the latest rant by the course's answer to Victor Meldrew. 'Forgive me for interrupting, Malcolm, but you've very handily introduced the subject of today's session. Why do you think I've asked you to find these stories? Tim?'

'To make us feel less sorry for ourselves? Like my mother used to tell me about the starving babies in Africa when I didn't finish my tea?'

'Kind of . . . though I'm not trying to make any of you feel guilty. It's more that I want to get rid of one of the most damaging beliefs you can possibly hold. And that's the belief that *life is fair*.'

The group chuckled back at him. 'I know what you're all thinking. Who could be so silly as to believe that? No one over the age of six, surely. You gave all that up around the same time you realised that the tooth fairy didn't exist. What with famines and world wars and road accidents happening every day to people who've done nothing to deserve it. The thing is, we might all know the rules but we all think we are the exception. Think of that phrase, "there but for the grace of God go I". As though God chooses to spare us, personally. Or the way people interviewed on TV news in the middle of some horrible disaster will say, "I never thought it would happen to me." How many of us have seen bad stuff, from illness to marriage break-up, happen to other people, and looked for reasons why it wouldn't happen to us?'

William sat down, the clearest signal he could give that he was the same as them, that he wasn't immune from belief in his own immunity. 'It makes absolute sense, that's the thing, that in the face of all the other evidence, we hang onto the idea that there is some strange logic to the things that happen, a hidden justice system in life, because without it, it's hard to contemplate leaving the house or, more relevant to us, entering into a loving relationship. And after all, everyone who's ever got divorced knows that the legal system is pretty short on justice, so surely there must be a better version that's secretly governing our universe?' He smiled at them, to show this was a joke. They chuckled helpfully.

'What we don't realise is that accepting there is no justice system on earth – I don't claim to know if there's one in the afterlife – can be liberating. And not because it gives you carte blanche to do what the hell you like, or behave like an idiot. It's just that I know from my own experience that when you stop looking for reasons why you've drawn the short straw, you can finally start looking for ways to build on what you've got.'

William stood up again and beamed at his students as if he'd given them the secret of happiness, because that's exactly what he believed he had done. 'There we go then. Life isn't fair. Get over it.

'And if any of you still need convincing, then you are very fortunate. The fact that you're getting divorced means you have a whole set of professionals at your disposal to prove beyond all reasonable doubt that life is a bitch or a bastard, depending on your gender, and then you die.

'And what do we call these soothsayers? Yep, you guessed it. Lawyers.'

The unleashing of anger was going very nicely, so far. The timing of the session about the law seemed particularly good, from what William had gathered tonight. As well as Malcolm's wife's predictable legal move – and frankly any reasonable judge ought to conclude that fifty per cent was not nearly enough for putting up with him for so long – Carol-Ann was making a last-minute attempt to get her daughter to sort out a pre-nuptial agreement with her fiancé before the wedding this weekend. Tim was trying to bite his lip for the good of the children now that their mother was making escalating access demands, while Rani had written to her ex to explain why he ought to see his daughter as well as his sons. And poor Tess was trying to come to terms with the prospect of the roof over her head being sold to the highest bidder. Though at least she looked rather less peaky this week.

'So did the two firms of estate agents agree on a valuation?' William asked. Everyone was writing a letter to the person they were currently the most angry with, before a cathartic paper-burning session at the end of the lesson. Tess's was to the estate agents who'd visited her only yesterday

'More or less. They're talking about astonishing amounts of money; I suppose I should be grateful for that at least. I thought the first one was a bit deranged when she said it'd go for £195,000 but then the other guy reckoned if we were lucky we'd hit two hundred. For a terraced house!'

Natalie shook her head. 'That's nothing, for Harborne. Very desirable area. You could probably get more if you've got a big garden, now the summer's approaching.'

Natalie struck William as a woman who knew the value of money. 'That's true, Natalie. So what will you aim to do with your half, Tess? Will you try to stay in the area?'

'God knows! That's another thing for this bloody letter.' On the page there was already a list of complaints, written in red ink block capitals. William always brought along red pens, for their extra therapeutic value. 'The bitch who came round first was giving me all this fake sympathy, like, "Is it a sale due to divorce, dear? But no kiddies? Terribly sad at your age," and then she had the gall to say she could put me in contact with a very nice agent at their Bearwood branch, "because you need to be realistic now, dear; you're not going to be able to afford around here any more." I nearly hit her. The bloke was no better. He didn't make any kind of conversation, just moped about with his electronic tape measure. No social skills.'

'Yep, estate agents definitely give lawyers a run for their money when it comes to being the most loathed profession. Is it making you feel better writing it down?' William asked.

'A bit, I suppose . . .' Tess looked at her watch. 'I think I've gone on too long. It should be your turn now, Natalie.'

'I don't feel very angry,' she said, but William didn't believe that for a moment. More like, she was too scared of how angry she was even to begin to talk about it, in case she could never stop.

'So there's never been a moment in the period since you knew you were getting divorced' – William fought the instinct to cast a meaningful look at her ring – 'when you've thought, "Life is so bloody unfair, I could scream."'

'Maybe.' She mustered a thin smile. 'Then again, maybe there've been more of those when I've seen no way out of being married.'

'Why don't you try the exercise? It might be useful. And I'll fail you if you don't do all the exercises.'

'Really?'

'No, that's a joke. There's no graduation certificate. But they are tried and tested methods. If you do this letter now, you'll find it much easier to do the exercise after the break, the action plan. So have a think. You can write the letter to your estate agent ... your husband, his lawyer. Anyone. And you don't have to send it.'

'It'd make a change to be able to get a word in edgewise with my husband,' she said. 'I can never quite win any argument with him, mainly because he always talks over me.'

'He can't talk over you if you write him a letter.'

'All right. OK.' She took the pad and pen, ripped off Tess's letter and began her own. 'Dear Tony ... now what?'

Tess smiled encouragingly. 'I started with the most recent thing that happened.'

'Right. God, this is tough. I don't know. Dear Tony. You'll never see this letter so I suppose it doesn't matter what I say.' She stopped talking while her red handwriting caught up. 'Do I have to write everything down?'

'I did bullet points,' Tess said.

'I'll try that ... I can't work out if I am angry with you or not, Tony.' She drew a dash in the margin and wrote the words ANGRY OR NOT? alongside it. 'I know I should be. It's the way you talk to me, like I'm stupid, even when I am not and

286

never have been.' A new bullet point, NOT STUPID, joined the first. In block capitals; Natalie's handwriting had no girly loops.

'Good, good. When was the last time he behaved that way?' William asked.

Natalie flinched. 'Honestly?'

'Honestly. I don't know if this is reassuring or not, but an awful lot of people who come here are in situations that are ... unresolved. I noticed earlier that you were wearing your ring. It doesn't matter to me. Sometimes it takes coming to a group like this to realise that divorce is the last thing you want.'

'I didn't say that.'

'No, I know you didn't. You were about to tell us when was the last time Tony treated you as though you were stupid. Which you're not.'

'Last night. And the time before that was the previous night, though I had Saturday night off because he went out with his golf buddies from the bank. Friday wasn't great, though we both took the day off to spend with Zach, to try to be a family again, but ...' She tailed off.

'Natalie, I hope you'll forgive me for saying this,' William paused, trying to choose the least loaded words, 'but is it possible that you're perhaps very sensitive to the comments your husband makes, even when he doesn't mean to upset you?'

A flash of anger showed up in Natalie's eyes, before she brought it under control. William wasn't trying to goad her, but if that's what it took to get to the real feelings, then so be it. 'You think I'm being oversensitive?'

'Not *over*sensitive, because I am not judging you. But it is a fact that couples who've been together for some time may fall into patterns of behaviour that are very difficult to break, however hard they try. Part of the way forward is to recognise those patterns, because then you can break them.'

'Patterns?' She spoke quietly but defiantly. 'You want to see patterns? You asked for it.'

And she rolled up the sleeves of her baby-blue soft-velour jacket, to reveal patterns: bruises in regal purple and cerise, in antique lemon and soft mauve, leading all the way up her arms, the shapes of fingers and thumbs and fists still showing, layer upon layer. 'I've got more if you want to see them,' she said.

William gawped. 'No. Those are more than enough.'

Chapter Twenty-seven

When I joined William's group, I suppose I expected a bit of preachy advice, a weekly moan with other divorcing depressives and maybe some practical tips on screwing over my soon-to-be ex.

I didn't expect the worst sex of my life.

I didn't expect an invitation to a wedding.

And I didn't expect two house guests on the run from an abusive man.

'I know it's not very big, but it'll look much better when I've cleared some of my clobber into the loft,' I shout, above the sound of baby Zach's crying.

'We probably won't be here long enough to make it worthwhile,' Natalie says. I don't know who is more surprised about her being here. William swung into action as soon as she told us what her husband had been doing and we were carried along by his energy, without questioning what would happen once this immediate drama was over.

I mentioned my spare room and the next minute we were racing into her enormous posh house in Edgbaston, paying off the babysitter and doing a kind of supermarket sweep to try to pack up her stuff before her husband got in from the Rotarians' night out. Apparently he takes his charity work very seriously.

I sat in my car, cooing hopelessly at a bawling baby, while William and Natalie ran from room to room like deranged burglars, working out what was essential to tide her over until . . .

And that's the problem. Until when? It's all very well turning 107 Victoria Terrace into a refuge for one battered woman and her noisy son. I am more than happy to help someone out in a crisis, especially when it takes my mind off obsessing about an adventure sports leader from Gloucestershire. But now St William has dropped off the baby bath and the baby gates and the bumper baby toiletries, not to mention a large percentage of Natalie's not inconsiderable wardrobe, we're left here clueless about what to do next, like a couple of amateur actors without a script.

'Do you want to try to settle him for a bit and then we could have a drink? You probably need one; I know I do.'

'It might take a while. I'll see,' she says. She's an odd woman. If it was me, I think at least I'd be trying to show my gratitude. Not everyone would take in a stranger and her baby, but she seems to see it as her right.

'Well, as you wish. I go to work at quarter to eight, so I'll be up an hour or so before that. Will you be going to the gym tomorrow?'

'I don't know. I haven't quite taken it in yet.'

Join the club, love. 'Well, I'll find my spare keys and leave them on the kitchen table for you, then you can come and go as you like.'

'Hmm . . . thanks.' She's already unpacking, moving furniture and cases around swiftly and ignoring Zach's continued wailing.

'Will he be OK?'

'Zach? Yes, he's always been a noisy baby.'

'Well . . . don't forget the offer of a drink. Otherwise see you tomorrow.' I leave the room as she hauls a pair of dumb-bells across the room. Her idea of essential supplies is obviously rather different from mine.

I negotiate my way round the baby clutter in the hallway. Thank God Mel got that cleaner in: Tip Top Tess is still absent without leave, but at least I didn't die of shame when Natalie came through the door. I pour myself a whisky. To hell with my new friends – they're too much bloody trouble for words. I need to talk to an old friend.

As I dial her number, I wonder what I'm going to say.

'Hello?'

'Mel, it's me. God, I am so sorry I haven't been in touch for so long.'

'Tess!' She sounds surprised, and maybe not as thrilled as I'd hoped. That's the trouble with mates as laid back as Mel. They can make you feel insecure. If she doesn't mind when you don't get in touch for a few weeks, maybe she doesn't care at all. 'How's it going, honey? Hang on, let me take the phone into the other room.'

'Am I interrupting something?' I say, slightly huffy.

'No, it's no problem. So . . . how have you been?'

I tell her, in reverse order. My new housemates, the missing kids at the adventure centre, snogging a man in Bobby Brown's, my dad's infidelity. She hums and hahs at all the appropriate points, though whatever it is I've distracted her from, I get the impression she wishes she was still doing it. Maybe a spot of snatched sex with James. Well, tough. Friendship comes first.

The only thing I don't mention is Robin's moonlight confession, even though it's the thing I've been thinking about most.

'Bloody hell, Tess. You pack a lot in compared to us boring couples . . .'

I'm about to say that I would rather be a boring couple again, but then I think about it. Would I really? Smug nights out and smugger nights in with people you feel obliged to see, though you've long since forgotten why you became friends in the first place. 'Oh, I forgot, I also talked to Sara. Called her to ask why she hadn't been in touch and the silly cow said she thought it was partly my fault . . . no, mainly my fault, that Barney left. Can you believe it?'

She hesitates. 'He was the one who was out of order, Tess, no doubt about that. It doesn't really matter what anyone else thinks.'

'Have you seen her, then, Sara?'

'Um . . . yeah, you know. Once or twice.'

Something about the tone of her voice gives the game away. 'She's there now, isn't she, with Ed?'

A long pause. 'Yes.'

'Right. OK. I see.' I don't see. I take a swig of whisky just to stop me starting to rant about disloyalty and whose side is she on and whose best friend is she meant to be anyway . . .

'It's difficult when people break up, Tess. Awkward.'

'Tell me about it.'

'I don't agree with Sara's verdict on what happened between you and Barney, but I don't think you can really expect me and James to give up our entire social life because of your divorce.'

Another thought, far worse, occurs to me. 'Barney isn't there too, is he, with that bitch?'

'No, don't be ridiculous. I'm really surprised you think that little of me. Though . . . well, I don't know whether to tell you this or not, but it might help. I bumped into them in Boots the other day. The big one in town. I was downstairs buying a present for a girl from my toddlers' group who's having another one, and there they were. Mid-argument. She was really going at him hammer and tongs. But he'd already seen me so I had to stop and talk.'

'They were buying baby things?' I feel like choking.

'Browsing, I think.'

'What did she look like? Is she very pregnant?'

'Pretty huge. What has she got, I dunno, six weeks to go? She's given up work; she said that much. She looked grim: fatter all over, not just her belly, and no make-up. I mean, on one hand I sympathise; I can remember when everything felt like so much effort that I could hardly make a cup of tea. But then again, with what she's done, she deserves a crap time.'

'Did he say anything?'

'Not much. They both looked pretty miserable.'

I'd always imagined the times we'd spend in Mothercare and Boots and that cute French place, Petit Bateau, as being some of the happiest we'd have as a couple. Planning for the life we'd created, bickering companionably about the colour of the nursery. 'He'll come round, when the baby arrives.'

'Maybe he will, maybe he won't. The first months aren't a picnic, you know. You have to have a strong relationship to survive a baby – and you don't know what a nightmare they are until you're saddled with one.'

'I guess I'll never know now.'

'That's not true. You do have time.' She sounds impatient

with me. I suppose she's right technically, but even if I have the time, do I have the energy to find someone I'd want to father a child?

'No, I think I can be pretty sure that the secret society of motherhood won't be admitting me as a member.'

'OK. I think you're wrong, but so what if you never do have a child? You and Barney had long enough to get round to it, so if it was such a big deal, why didn't you? And anyway, we're meant to be feminists, in case you've forgotten. Since when did having a baby become the only measure of your success as a woman?'

'Since it ceased to be an option. I don't know. Listen, I'm keeping you from your *guests*.' I spit the last word.

'I . . . All right. If that's what you want. But let's sort something out soon. You can come round here or we can go to the pictures or . . . ?'

'I'll let you know. Bye, Mel.'

I put the phone down and pour myself another whisky to take to bed, but before I get there, I see all the baby stuff in the hall. Feeling like a spy in that secret world, I trail my hands across a massive plush green frog, a plastic tractor, one of those activity panels that goes in the bath. I press the centre of the telephone dial and a tinkly noise echoes through the hall.

Zach is a noisy variety of baby. I manage two hours' sleep maximum, grabbed in tiny, unsatisfying moments and interrupted each time by terrifying howls. I try to make excuses for him. The poor child must be traumatised by being somewhere strange. Imagine how disturbed he must be after being born into a violent household. Perhaps he's teething? But by six a.m, I've decided he's a guerrilla baby, sent to disrupt households with his underhand terror tactics.

I pad down to the kitchen in my dressing gown and make a huge pot of tea. Unfortunately, Natalie must hear me moving around because just as I am settling back with my toast, she skips downstairs with Guerrilla, who pauses in his screaming to give me a quizzical look, then resumes.

'Doesn't he get a sore throat?'

'He doesn't seem to. Would you hold him for a second?'

I don't seem to have much of a choice. Guerrilla stops crying again as he's placed on my lap. Close up he's much *bigger* and heavier than I expected. His father must be built like Pavarotti. To express his displeasure at being dumped on a stranger, he starts whimpering, but still very, very loudly, until his mother arrives back in the kitchen with a huge bag of cups and beakers and bibs and jars. Once she's stacked them up across every spare inch of work surface, she spoons some organic gloop into a plastic dish and microwaves it for a few seconds, then fetches a high-chair contraption, which she erects in no time next to the kitchen table. It looks incongruous: Natalie in her designer gear, surrounded by these ugly plastic bits and pieces in primary colours. So much for a baby being the perfect accessory.

'Right, I'll take him back now. Come here, soldier.'

Even she thinks he's a squaddie-in-waiting. 'How did you sleep?' I ask her.

'Surprisingly well, considering. That duvet in the spare room is very hot, though. Do you have a summer-weight one? I forgot to bring mine. But then I guess Tony would really have hit the roof if I'd taken the bedding as well as everything else.'

'How do you think he'll react?'

'I already know. I've had about twenty text messages, threatening to do God knows what when he finds me. He's very organised, though. He's got this pay-as-you-go mobile that no one can trace back to him, which he uses to send the abusive stuff. He did it before, too, when I went to stay with my sister.'

Her calmness worries me more than if she was sobbing in the corner. 'What ... what happened when you went to your sister's?'

'Don't worry. He didn't burn her house down or anything.' Guerrilla spits out a huge dollop of gloop, which lands on the floor. She doesn't make any attempt to clear it up. 'Once he'd realised that the threats were counterproductive, he just kept on and on about changing, and like an idiot I believed him. Plus the gym was going to rack and ruin while I was living down in Essex and there was no way I was going to let that happen after all the work I've done.'

'So, now you've slept on it, do you have an idea about what you'll do next?' I say, trying not to sound as desperate as I feel.

'I'm going to call my PA at the gym and get her to organise a few viewings of rental places. But I don't want to rush it; we need the right place, me and Zach.'

'Right. And what about the threats?'

'Oh, he won't do anything that could damage his career in the bank. It's all bluster. I suppose I'll have to go back to the solicitor about pushing on with the divorce again. I really did want it to work this time, if only because I know the bastard will stitch me up if I don't have my wits about me. He always warned me not to leave him. The risk of him coming after me is the least of my worries; it's the danger of him coming after my assets that's the real threat.' She wipes Guerrilla's face with the bib, then pulls it off and throws it into the washing machine. My washing machine. Which I was intending to put washing into before I go to work. Dear God, now I am turning possessive about my white goods. So this is what happens when you live alone.

'I'd better get ready for school,' I say, before my irritation gets the better of me.

'Oh, yes. Listen, I was wondering . . . I suppose, being a teacher, you tend to get home quite early?'

'Ye-es . . . by about four thirty usually. Why?'

'Perfect! It's just that I do think I ought to drop in on the gym if I can and I thought maybe I could go when you're back from work and . . . leave Zach here. It would only be for an hour, maximum, and then you could do your marking and keep an eye on him.'

'But . . .'

'It would be a massive help.' And she adopts a pathetic look that convinces me it would be churlish to refuse.

'OK. But please, no more than an hour. I am no use at all with babies.'

I forget about my rash promise until I arrive home, tired,

fed up and ready for a long, hot bath. It's been a tough week so far; my lot were quite shaken by what happened with Craig, but now they're really milking it and I don't have the energy to put them back on track. Plus all the staff are waiting for the lawsuit we're convinced his mother's going to have hand-delivered before the week is out.

It's touch and go whether Craig'll come back this term. Or at all, I suppose. I'm not even convinced it would be the right thing, because it's only in the movies that a crisis like that will help a scapegoat like him be accepted into the group. I overheard Sanjay this morning saying, 'Bloody Craig wrecked it – we could have had another day at the centre. We should 'ave him.'

I thought about telling him that Craig's disappearance actually provided them with a far more memorable trip than anyone could have hoped for, but thought they probably wouldn't understand.

And I can't stop thinking about Robin. I never really got teenage crushes, but I guess this is what it would have felt like. He's there at the back – no, the front – of my mind all the time. So while realistically I know the most likely stranger through the school gates is indeed the despatch rider with the writ for negligence, I can't stop myself imagining Robin rushing into reception, casting aside Mrs Timkins' demands to fill in a visitor's badge and carrying me from my classroom to his waiting Land Rover. Any similarity between this fantasy and *An Officer and a Gentleman* is, of course, purely coincidental.

So my plans for the evening revolve around soaking in the bath, indulging in daydreams so unrealistic Mills and Boon wouldn't entertain them.

'Oh, there you are!' Natalie must have been watching from the living room window because she opens the front door just as I am getting my keys out. 'You're later than you said you'd be. Zach's in his travel cot, I've made up bottles with instructions and I will definitely be back by six thirty.'

'Um . . . hang on . . .' She's already rushing past me. 'You said it'd be an hour at the most.'

'Are you planning on going out?'

'No, but—'

'Well, then. He's very little trouble,' she says, though we both know that's a massive fib. 'And I've left you my mobile number on the note, if there's a real emergency.'

With that, she flounces out of my house, leaving my bathing plans in tatters and my heart rate increasing with the prospect of taking sole responsibility for Guerrilla for nearly two hours.

I walk into the front room, where Zach is staring at me, his cheeks bright red, his eyes brighter blue. No wonder he's so grumpy; he never seems to get any sleep. Isn't sleep supposed to be when babies do all their growing? Not that it seems to have held him back. He's monster-sized at nine months old, broad and powerful like a prop in an under-twos rugby team.

The trick with animals and older children is to show no fear. The only strategy I can think of is to try the same tactic with him. I take a deep breath.

'Right then, Zach. Let's get a few things straight. I have no intention of waiting on you. If you cry I will pick you up, try you with food and check your nappy, but that's it. OK? Do we have a deal?'

He stares back at me for a good minute but I am not deterred by some kid trying to spook me. Then his bottom lip trembles and he lets out a howl that would wake the dead.

Maybe I haven't quite got the hang of this baby-taming stuff.

When Natalie finally gets back at quarter to eight, I am beside myself.

'You were meant to be no more than two hours!' I say, like a Seventies housewife berating her straying other half.

'Sorry,' she says, but she doesn't sound nearly apologetic enough for my liking. 'I had some things to do . . . security stuff.'

'What kind of security stuff? This wouldn't be to do with your husband? The one you said was harmless, really?'

She blushes slightly. 'He is . . . I think. Look, I don't know. But once . . . well, he did threaten to torch the gym if I left.'

Zach is still crying. He hasn't stopped for three hours. But at least now I think I might be beginning to understand why the kid's so disturbed. 'Oh. Well, that sounds like a reasonable response to a relationship hitch.' A car drives slowly past the house. 'He wouldn't have followed you here, would he?'

She starts, crabs towards the window to peer through the edge of the net curtains. 'No, that's not his car.' She sits down on the sofa.

Zach senses a lull in proceedings and adds his own comment, in the form of an even louder scream.

'Have you fed him?' she asks me.

'Yes.' Though it did involve two changes of clothes on my part.

'Changed him?'

'I ... tried.' Before I bottled out when his massive legs threatened to kick me into next year.

She sighs. 'No, fair enough. Why should you, really? Why should you even be putting me up, with a husband on the warpath and a baby from hell.'

'No, he's not that bad.'

She looks at me sadly. 'He is. Don't argue, I know. I mean, I do love him to bits. But the crying ... it's taken the shine off motherhood, I can tell you. I hope it'll get better, but right now ...'

'It must be tough. Especially with what's been happening.'

'I'll survive,' she says, sounding less certain than the words. 'After all, what's the alternative?'

Natalie looks embarrassed by this expression of weakness and I'm not quite sure what else to say. 'I think I might go for that bath now.'

'Yes, you do that,' she says and I hover as she seems about to say something else. 'Um ... Tess, I know Zach and I aren't the easiest of house guests. I don't find it very comfortable being a burden. But thank you.' She blushes.

'Hey. It's nothing.' I wrestle around for something else to say. 'Are you coming to Carol-Ann's daughter's wedding on Saturday?' As I say it, I realise that inviting the snottiest woman on the divorce course might not go down that well with poor Georgie.

'No. I didn't know it was happening,' she says and looks even more depressed at this clear evidence that she's the black sheep of the Survivors' Course.

'Oh, it's only me and Jo that are going, but I'm sure ... I mean, I don't like to leave you here alone. And I think a good wedding could be just what you need. They're a great spectator sport. It's only marriages that don't have much entertainment value. I'll ask Carol-Ann. Unless you've got other plans, of course?'

She avoids my eye. 'Not really. I haven't had a social life in ...' she looks at the Guerrilla, '... about nine months.'

Chapter Twenty-eight

By Saturday I am forced to admit that my knight in shining armour is not going to whisk me away. Not altogether surprising, I suppose. I'm no great catch. In any case, he'll always associate me with the moment he thought he'd lost his only child. Hardly a great start to a romance. Now all I have to do is put that down to experience, along with everything else.

I'm beginning to wonder whether Aaron's wife had the right idea and I should consider women for a change. The lesbians I know seem pretty happy and I can see the advantages – emotional connection, affection on tap, plus with two females sharing a house, you'd never run out of toiletries. It's just a shame I only fancy men.

When I get downstairs, the sunlight is pouring through the kitchen window. It's a lovely day for a wedding. 'Morning, Natalie. I was going to make some coffee, if you fancy some?'

'Yes, but only if you use my fresh stuff out of the fridge, the Java blend. Your instant is revolting.'

She's already sitting at the table, immaculately made up, though I bumped into her outside the bathroom yesterday without her concealer and her eyes have such heavy shadows that I asked her when he'd punched her.

'Oh, those aren't from Tony. They're from Zach. That's what nine months without proper sleep does for you,' she said. Then she pulled out a golden tube from her make-up bag. 'Thank God for Touche Éclat and Calpol. Without them, I'd have gone totally ga-ga.'

We're getting on surprisingly well now we've settled into a routine. I could be kidding myself but even Zach seems a little less disturbed than when he first arrived. His cries are more like a normal baby's, lacking the banshee quality that alarmed me so much. Or maybe I am just getting used to it.

'So what are you going to wear this afternoon? And more important, what's Guerr . . . um, Zach, going to wear?' I spoon out six tablespoons of Natalie's frighteningly posh coffee. She does have very good taste and I am reaping the benefits. I never thought I'd say this, but I almost enjoy her company.

'Well, it's a registry office do, so I thought I'd keep it fairly understated. I wouldn't want to upstage the bride,' she says, though I have a hunch that that's exactly what she'd like to do. Natalie might be witty and well-read and beautifully coiffed but sisterhood is not high on her list of priorities. 'So Zach and I will both be wearing chocolate brown.'

'Very practical, if he should have any kind of nappy-filling accident!'

She glares at me. 'It's nothing to do with that. It's just a colour that suits us both. I have this rather sweet Chanel pants suit I bought to wear on my honeymoon – I checked and it fits me better than it did then – and Zach's got a new jumpsuit.'

'Where from?'

'I wish you hadn't asked. Baby Gap of all places. Promise you won't tell anyone. But the designer offerings really aren't his colour this season. Chocolate-brown really does contrast so gorgeously with his eyes. It's the same combination I was going to use once we'd bought our cottage in the Peak District. Baby-blue suede sofas with huge brown cushions.' Natalie's own eyes fill with tears. And there was I thinking she was a bit of a cold fish.

'It must be hard to give up aspects of that life,' I say, pushing the plunger down on the cafetière, 'but you have to remember that at least you're safe now. You and . . . um, Zach.'

'I know. I'm not complaining. I can make it work for the two of us, I know I can, but it's an adjustment. Well, you know.'

'Yes.' I do know and I'm not convinced that I am any closer than Natalie to accepting the changes ahead, despite the fact that she's only had four days to get used to it and I've had six months. 'Like getting married in reverse.'

Natalie gives me a massive grin. 'Does that mean I can buy a new outfit?'

The wedding is at two, at the register office. Natalie's driving because her car, an Audi TT convertible as sleek and stylish as its owner, was deemed more appropriate than mine for a summer wedding. The only trouble is that her baby-seat has to go in the front, so I am hunched in the impossibly tiny back seat.

'Were you there when William was talking about starter marriages?'

'Hmm?' Natalie is one woman who loves to be at the wheel. Her eyes are only half-open and her cheeks are flushed, as if there's some lithe young man crouched in the footwell doing unmentionable things to her as we progress towards Broad Street.

'Starter marriage? William mentioned it during one of the lessons. It means a first marriage where you're kind of sussing out what it is to be married, rather than actually committing to someone for life.'

'Like a training bra?'

I giggle. 'Yeah, I suppose it is kind of like a training bra. It supports you for a while and then you outgrow it. So . . . was yours a starter marriage, Natalie? I can't work out if mine was or not.'

She opens her eyes wide, while she considers my question. 'I don't think so. I mean, Zach wasn't a starter *baby* and our house certainly wasn't a starter home. We were deadly serious, weighed it up like a business arrangement. Or maybe that was just me.'

We cut down the road to the car park. A banner outside proudly proclaims it 'National car park of the year 1999'. Birmingham never ceases to amaze me.

'A business arrangement?'

'Not in a bad way,' she says. 'I mean, that's how I met him, anyway. Went to the bank for a loan and he was the business manager. But he was looking for a wife and as soon as he realised I fitted the bill, he decided it was the romance of the century. I sensed it was up to me to be the practical one – work out our likely long-term compatibility, what both parties had to offer and then decide on the terms of the merger.'

My jaw drops. 'Really?'

'No. Made the last bit up. But it makes more sense than the usual way our species decides we're in love.' She climbs out of the seat in that flowing way that movie stars have and begins the long process of unstrapping Guerrilla's car seat.

'Didn't work for you, though, did it?'

She looks up from unbuckling. 'No. You can't really allow for a man who says he thinks you're the most beautiful thing on the planet and then decides to beat your face to a pulp. To give him his due he only did it the once because it made him feel so guilty looking at the mess he'd made.'

I clamber out of the back, feeling pins and needles in my feet where they've been squashed in at an odd angle. 'Which is presumably why he started to hit you in places where no one could see.'

'Yes.' She shivers, although as we leave the car park and walk past the fountains, it's hot and sunny. 'I know I shouldn't feel guilty myself but somehow I can't help wondering if he would have been different with someone else. Someone less business-like, someone softer. After he hit me, I'd carry on as normal. Maybe he was just looking for a reaction and because I never gave him one, he kept going.'

'You mustn't feel that way. You're a survivor, that's all. The trouble with being a survivor is that keeping up appearances doesn't always do you much good. Sometimes you have to ask for help.'

She laughs. 'You know why that's so hard for me, don't you? It's because I never *ask* anyone for anything. I always tell people what to do. Believe it or not, I even used to do it to Tony and he usually obliged. I think that's why none of our friends ever had the first idea what was going on.'

I think of Sara and how she knew that my marriage was over before it began. 'You certainly learn who your friends are when you get divorced. Or who they're not.'

We walk into Broad Street, and when we get to the registry office Carol-Ann and Jo are smoking outside like a couple of teenagers. Carol-Ann looks more like a pantomime dame than the mother of the bride, with her purple and white outfit which is completely co-ordinated from her feathery headdress down to her winkle-picker shoes. Her tights are spectacular in themselves, decorated with lacy lilac flowers that resemble a very bad case of varicose veins. I suspect she's also celebrated her only daughter's impending nuptials with a dawn raid on the Rackhams beauty counter, to pick up glossy, glittery and shiny lipgloss, eye-shadow or blusher in every shade from regal purple to mousy librarian mauve. Somehow she manages to carry it off. Jo is wearing a very ordinary floaty floral dress but sparkles like a wartime starlet.

'Hey!' I run over and embrace Carol-Ann, feeling a greasy slick of make-up rub off on my face as I kiss her cheek. In contrast, Natalie's air kiss is a model of restraint. Even with the bawling Guerrilla in her arms, she has the grace of an American First Lady.

'So how's Georgie doing?' I ask, trying to rub away the make-up without being too obvious.

'The condemned woman ate a hearty breakfast.'

Natalie adopts a sympathetic expression. I've explained the background to Georgie's wedding and she's obviously decided to make an effort, though it definitely shows. 'Oh dear. Tess did say you disapproved, but it's good of you to come. Is he a real waster?' She speaks the last word like she's having to use simplified language to make herself understood.

Carol-Ann takes a puff of her cigarette, then stubs it out under her winkle-picker. 'It's not her fiancé. It's the whole bloody institution. But it's like talking to a brick wall. An especially thick one. And at the end of the day I never turn down an invitation to a party.'

'I guess none of us are exactly believers in this institution,' Jo says, pointedly stubbing her own cigarette out on the metal grid on the wall and throwing it into the bin underneath. 'But I guess it's a triumph of hope over wisdom. Anyway, how are you getting on at Tess's place? And how's the little chap?' She reaches out a tentative finger, which Guerrilla regards with an expression somewhere between contempt and suspicion. No prizes for guessing where he learned that.

'We're settling in fine, thank you.'

'Such a shame you don't have all your clothes with you, though. You must be terribly hot in that business suit,' Carol-Ann says, raising her eyebrows at me. She'd been happy enough to invite Natalie along to the wedding, not bothering to ask Georgie – 'She's only got a few friends coming, after all; she's barely been alive long enough to make any real ones.' But I don't think there'll ever be much of a bond. Carol-Ann's got a highly tuned snob detector and Natalie probably goes off the scale.

I look around for the other guests. It's hard to tell who is coming and who is just strolling along Broad Street on their way to the shops on a sunny Saturday afternoon. Dressing up for a ceremony here seems as inappropriate as putting on the ritz for a trip to the council tax payment office. But maybe I've got it wrong – maybe the fact that Georgie is happy to make this massive commitment in a gloomy municipal building is sweet and charming rather than unpromising. And maybe my snobbery quotient is off the scale, too.

Eventually I spot some other girls from Georgie's hen night clustered together. They haven't exactly made a massive effort, but at least they look more excited than Carol-Ann.

'Hey – there she is!' Jo points over my shoulder and I turn to see a tatty white Rolls Royce lumbering down the street.

Somehow it makes the last couple of hundred metres without the exhaust falling off and Georgie steps out. She's wearing an off-white shift dress that ends just above the knee and carrying a small bunch of daisies. She looks too bulky for the dress, her legs are the same width from thigh to ankle and her make-up is more clumsily applied than her mother's. But something about the overall look – her naivety, perhaps – makes my eyes water.

The girls rush forward, buzzing around her like honey bees, while Carol-Ann holds back. 'It must be pretty emotional to see your daughter getting married, whatever your reservations,' Natalie says. We all look at Carol-Ann, waiting for her to snap back.

Instead, she nods her head. 'I just don't want her to be hurt the way I was. A man will break your bloody heart in the end, even an ugly bastard like Paul. Especially an ugly man, because he'll have that much more to prove.'

I look over at Georgie, who is talking to a scruffy guy who is probably my age but looks much older. 'That's her fiancé?' He wears a pale-grey suit, which matches his greasy grey streaked hair and an equally greasy moustache. He walks with a stoop, as if life has already taken its toll. Perhaps Georgie is his way of feeling young again.

'Yeah. Not exactly Brad Pitt, is he? The thing is, I don't think he's an especially bad person, but he will hurt her; she's too young to know how to play the game.'

I shake my head. 'I know it's hard but she's an adult, Carol-Ann; you have to trust her to know what she's doing.'

'I've spent my whole life trying to protect her. It's so bloody difficult to let go.'

'But if you don't, you'll lose her anyway.' I know I am in danger of sounding like an amateur agony aunt, but it seems to me that Carol-Ann has no one else in her life who will stand up to her and point out how much damage she might be doing.

'Maybe you're right. But I'm here, aren't I? And I went to the bloody divorce course for Georgie; that's as far as I can go. I am not about to start ringing church bells or dancing a jig in the middle of Broad Street. And now I haven't got time for another bloody cigarette before we have to go through with the charade.'

'Mum.' Georgie is hovering, her husband-to-be standing well back, looking nervous. Not altogether surprising, given the fact that Carol-Ann is about to become his mother-in-law. 'Mum, are you coming in now?'

Carol-Ann manages a weak smile, flicks a strand of auburn hair out of her eyes and looks at the rest of us. 'Yeah, why not? No time like the present.'

As we follow mother and daughter into the registry office, Natalie nudges me. 'Poor thing. I give it six months.'

The ceremony is held in a beige room that reminds me of an Eastern bloc airport lounge. The whole thing lasts no more than fifteen minutes, enough time for Guerrilla to be evicted for breaking the sound barrier and for me to feel the tears that were already welling up at the sight of poor, sweet Georgie trickle down my cheeks. I really am no fun to be around at the moment. It's the way she sounds utterly sincere, as I am sure I did and Barney did and every married couple does, with the possible exception of people marrying for Green Cards. Or maybe they sound even more sincere, just to throw the authorities off the scent.

When we step back outside into the bright sunlight, a photographer is already waiting to snap the bride and groom and guests.

'That was a nice thought, Carol-Ann. Did you arrange that? He looked very professional,' Natalie says.

'You think I'd want a lasting memory of today? Maybe he hangs around the registry office on the off-chance of finding people who want to buy his snaps. Like the pictures you get at amusement parks when you're going down a log flume and your hair is all over the place and your mouth is wide open in a scream.'

'Or maybe he's hoping some celebrity will decide to get married in Birmingham registry office and he will be able to retire to the Bahamas as the only photographer on the spot,' Jo says.

'You're the nearest we've got to a celebrity around here.'

'I don't think I exactly make the grade any more,' says Jo. 'That's one aspect of my old life that I don't miss.'

We walk in convoy across the road, and round the back of the canal system towards Carol-Ann's brewery. 'So will you ever go back there, back to London, back to your old job?'

'I suppose I'll have to. Mum does seem to be on the mend, touch wood, though I won't feel ready to leave her for at least another couple of months. I don't exactly relish the prospect of having to work alongside my ex in the newsroom. Or having to go back on the road, maybe having to work with the cameraman I left my marriage for.'

'Surely they wouldn't make you do that? Can you ask for a transfer?'

'It doesn't really work like that. In fact some of the bitches in that newsroom would deliberately assign me to stories so that I'd have to work with him – post me to the Gaza Strip or Afghanistan, just for the comedy value.'

'What about working around here? It's not like there are only TV companies in London.'

'That would either mean going back to regional news, where their top story would be the opening of the jumble sale, or if I was really lucky, I might get to work on a daytime DIY show. But I never have been any good at rag rolling or stippling.'

'They haven't done any of that since the Eighties, so I don't think you'll be putting Handy Andy out of a job.' We pass a kissing couple blocking a narrow bridge across the canal. 'So there's definitely no hope of a reconciliation with your husband?' I've forgotten his name.

'Even if he would have me back, which he won't, there'd be no point. No point at all. I thought I loved him, but it was more a case of loving the idea of loving someone, thinking it would somehow make up for what was wrong with my life. The fact was, there was an awful lot more wrong with my life once I'd dragged him into it, poor sod.'

'What about the other guy?'

'I didn't love him either, though I definitely lusted after him. He was more of a distraction, or maybe a Get Out Of Jail Free card. I thought I loved him, for a little while. It seemed more justified somehow to break up my marriage if I'd found my soulmate. We've seen each other off and on since I left Laurie. Not often, but whenever he came home from his latest stints in dangerous places. But it wasn't love and if anything I felt jealous, because he was still doing the job I loved, once, and I knew there was no going back. No going back to my husband and no going back to that belief that we might make a difference by pointing our cameras at so much human suffering.'

I can see the brewery ahead; the bride and groom have already disappeared through the wooden gable doors. 'When was the last time you saw him?'

Jo blushes. 'Two weeks ago. I would have said something but, you know, there we are at St Gabriel's pouring out our hearts and yet we don't really know each other, do we? I sneaked away from my mother while she had her afternoon sleep, told him that was that, in some seedy hotel room he'd booked in the hope of ... well, you know. I considered going along with it, for old times' sake. Then I thought of Laurie and I couldn't. I don't know if I ever will again.'

I try to reassure her. 'You will in the end. I mean, I felt exactly the same, and then Aaron popped up, my knight in a shining condom, and that was that.' It suddenly occurs to me that my experience with Aaron is more of a cautionary tale than an uplifting example of someone getting over their husband. I try to think of something else to distract us. 'I was talking to Natalie earlier on about William's starter marriage idea – do you remember it?'

Jo mulls it over. 'Oh yes, he reckoned I'd had one with Laurie, didn't he? He was probably right, I suppose. Well, you don't think about the fact it's "till death us do part" until it's too late and you realise that's a hell of a long time in a crap marriage.'

We walk into the brewery, the sweet sickly smell of yeast overpowering us momentarily. We snake our way around huge metal vats which seem to tremble as we pass, before we reach a room with a tiny bar. There's no DJ, just one of those portable stereos playing some simpering romantic ballads collection. Even with fewer than twenty people in the room, it feels packed, which I suppose is what you want at a wedding. Paul only seems to have a couple of friends as guests, and I wonder where his family are. It's hardly a great start to married life if one side of the family is only there under duress and the other can't be bothered to turn up at all. But then again, maybe Georgie's sincerity and her fear of repeating her parents' mistakes will somehow carry them through.

Carol-Ann is clapping her hands. 'Welcome to the party, ladies and gentlemen, and thank you for coming. It's been a few years since I last catered for a wedding, so I may not be totally up to date on what's served. But I've made some snacks and nibbles – help yourselves. And as for the drinks, well . . . for my present to the happy couple' – somehow she manages to say this without sounding bitter – 'I've made a special brew, Georgie's Gorgeous Pint. Flavoured with chocolate malt, in honour of

Georgie's favourite food. So all the beer is on the house. Bottoms up!'

She pulls the cloth off the buffet table tucked in the corner of the bar. Every inch of space is packed with food: tiny savoury tarts, sausage rolls, deep green salads, freshly baked rolls, vol-au-vents, chicken drumsticks and tiny little meringues studded with raspberries. And at the centre, a small but intricately decorated three-tier wedding cake, with the cheesiest of bride-and-groom figures holding hands at the top. After the applause has died down, she joins us. 'Hey, that was a sweet gesture,' I say, feeling close to tears. I must have PMT or something; my hormones are all over the place.

'It's not as though they've got many friends to cater for, and a buffet is cheaper than your average bone-china dinner service.'

'Oh Carol-Ann, you're all heart, you are!' Jo says.

'I'll drink to that,' she replies. 'Cheers, girls. To marriage, and all who suffer in her.'

Chapter Twenty-nine

Free beer has very few benefits, at least not the morning after. I wake up feeling fuzzy, Guerrilla's cries echoing through my hungover head.

'Tess, come down here. You'll never believe what's in the paper.'

I drag my body down the stairs, which are littered with all manner of child-friendly paraphernalia, and then into the kitchen, which smells of freshly brewed coffee and freshly filled nappy.

'You sit yourself down. I'll get you a cup of finest Costa Rican blend, and then you can take a look at this.' Natalie seems excited by her discovery. I wonder if it's a new law giving more money to battered wives. Or maybe it's an advert for her gym.

I go to snatch the paper away from her, but she hangs on to it fiercely. 'No, no, you'll have to wait.' Only when she has poured the coffee, stirred in organically grown Demerara sugar and topped it up with fresh milk from spiritually aware cows does she place it in front of me, open at page nineteen.

TV blonde uses sick mum to mask love triangle

Under the headline is a picture of Jo, her floaty floral dress clinging to her body in the light summer wind, the outline of her thighs clearly defined, like that 1980s shot of Princess Diana. Then there are more pictures: a fuzzy shot showing her getting out of the car to embrace a blurry man, and a photo of her holding hands with her mother as they walk outside the Pavilions shopping centre in town. The accompanying article runs over four columns and describes how 'blonde bombshell' Jo, aged thirty-three, ditched her handsome husband Laurie for caddish cameraman Mike during an assignment in the Middle East. It details how 'loyal Laurie' discovered their affair thanks to a producer colleague, who was 'sickened by Jo's shameless carrying on in a war-zone full of human tragedy'.

'Shit. So that's what the photographer was doing there. How the hell did he know that she was going to be there?' I wonder if poor Jo has seen it yet. I look at the clock on the oven – only eight o'clock, so unless someone else has rung her, she's probably sleeping off her hangover in blissful ignorance.

'Never mind that, what about the rest of it? I mean, I knew she'd been up to no good, but that's one lousy trick, isn't it? He looks so sweet.'

There is a tiny photograph of Laurie. Looking closely, I wonder if it was taken on his wedding day. He's smiling broadly and there's a hint of a stiff collar and morning suit in the picture. He's a good-looking guy, and he definitely comes out the best in the article, though he's not quoted. All the information seems to come from 'close friends of the couple'. Close friends with one hell of an agenda.

'We don't know that these are the real facts,' I say. 'I think I should ring her, warn her in case they come round looking for her again. Think of the damage this could do to her mum; it's not even as though she's that famous. And it's on bloody page nineteen for God's sake! Couldn't they have found some other trash to fill the newspaper?'

Natalie gives me a superior smile. 'So you've never bought the *News of the World*, then? And it's not as though she avoided having a public profile. I vaguely remember seeing her in *Hello!* magazine when she got married; you know what they say – if you live by the sword, you'll die by the sword, and she's a journalist herself. She knows the business.'

'I don't think anyone deserves that,' I say, getting up from the table and leaving my coffee untouched. There is something horribly sanctimonious about Natalie and I resent having to mind my Ps and Qs in my own home. But it's easier to walk away than to argue.

My mobile is upstairs so I make the call from my bedroom.

Jo answers straight away. 'Hi, Tess. I take it you've seen it then?'

I sigh. 'Yes, the delightful Natalie made sure of that. I can't believe they've done this to you, especially with your mother so ill. Don't they have a conscience?'

'No. They have it surgically removed the day they start on the tabloids. The sleazeball reporter called me last night on my way home to ask for a quote, believe it or not.'

'What did you say?'

'Nothing printable. Which wasn't all that sensible in the circumstances, but I was a bit pissed at the time, if you remember.'

I do, vaguely. Carol-Ann was so far gone that she was even claiming to really like her new son-in-law. 'Has your mum seen it yet?'

'No, but my bosses have. I've already had a phone call. It seems it's one thing half the newsroom knowing, another thing for the rest of the world. Or, I suppose, the *News of the World*.'

'They wouldn't sack you though, would they? I mean, they couldn't.'

'No, no. No danger of that. If they sacked every reporter who'd had a bit on the side, there'd be no news programmes left. But let's just say they're not encouraging me to return to work in a hurry. The person I feel worst about is Laurie. This kind of humiliation is the last thing he needs. I think it's kind of better to look like a scarlet woman than to look like a cuckold.'

'Would you like me to come round? I've got nothing else planned, apart from recovering from a hangover, that is.'

She pauses. 'Well – if you're sure. I mean, if it isn't too much trouble.' She sounds so grateful.

'No trouble at all, I promise. Give me your address and I'll be there in the time it takes me to swallow a couple of sachets of Resolve.'

As soon as I put the phone down, it rings again. 'Shit, Jo, that made me jump. And you're not going to talk me out of coming round.'

'Mrs Leonard?' The man on the other end of the line sounds uncertain. 'Mrs Leonard, it's Colin here from Marchant's estate agents. We were trying to get hold of you yesterday as well.' His tone changes to scolding and I look at the screen of my mobile. Six missed calls.

'Sorry about that, had a wedding to go to.'

'Oh,' he says, as if this is an extremely poor excuse for not answering. 'Well, we have a couple who are very interested in your property, but they're only up from London this weekend and they'd like a viewing today if possible. I know you haven't instructed us properly yet, but they're so keen, and I think your house is exactly what they're looking for.'

I sit down on the carpet. My carpet. Or our carpet, to be divided down the middle. Or perhaps Barney could take the underlay. 'Well, I don't know if . . .'

'It wouldn't take a moment. They really are terribly keen.'

'I'm going out.'

'We could pop round right now and pick up keys. I'd be very happy to show them around personally.'

My stomach heaves. I need to get him off the phone before I'm sick. 'I'll see what I can do and call you straight back.'

I make it into the en-suite and vomit three times before I feel able to stand up. Even the thought of Resolve makes me want to throw up again. I walk downstairs, one step at a time, wincing in anticipation of Guerrilla's screaming as I enter the kitchen. But for once his mouth is otherwise occupied, while Natalie forces purée into him.

'Natalie, do you have any plans today?'

She looks at me, caught out and irritated. 'Well, not exactly. I thought maybe I could go to the reservoir for a walk. I'm not in the mood for shopping. I must be coming down with some-thing.'

'Would you mind letting an estate agent in to do a viewing if I get a time? I wanted to go out, and I don't really fancy being here while they do it.'

I think she's about to refuse – why should she fit in with me, after all? – but then she relents. 'Yeah, fine. Would you like me to do stuff to put them off? Tell them you have a rehab centre next door or a divorce lawyer for a neighbour or something equally offputting?'

I shake my head, which makes it hurt still more. 'It's tempting . . . but I guess there's no point fighting the inevitable.'

Jo's mother's place is the smallest detached house in a modern cul-de-sac; Jo's car is parked alongside a bright yellow 2CV, which has the compulsory 'Nuclear Power, No Thanks' sticker on the back windscreen. It's a museum piece.

I check the street for cars or bushes that might conceal a tabloid photographer but the coast seems clear. Jo sees me walking up the path and opens the door. For a hungover woman under siege from the gutter press, she looks surprisingly chirpy.

'Hi, Tess. It's good of you to come over.'

'Does your mum know yet?'

'Yes. She's had a bit of a laugh about it, actually. Come through.'

Jo's mother is sitting on the sofa, wearing a grey-white hooded kaftan which manages to look brighter than her complexion. 'Hello, love. It's Tess, isn't it? Nice to meet you.' She reaches out to me; her handshake is firm, though the skin feels papery and I worry that if I grip back, her hand might disintegrate in mine.

'Nice to meet you too.' I look around the lounge: it's calm and cool, with no shade brighter than oatmeal or perhaps eau-de-nil. I can't see a TV set. I wonder if she's ever watched her daughter on the news.

Steamy, smoky patterns swirl from a stone humidifier in the shape of a Chinese temple on the coffee table and an aromatherapy burner is sending an uplifting citrus fragrance into the room. 'Your house is lovely and soothing, Mrs Kemp.'

'Call me Louisa, please. Thank you. I've always liked my home to be a sanctuary. You wouldn't believe what a relief it was to get back here from hospital. I know those places are meant to be healing, but they're seriously toxic.'

'Yes, Jo told me about your . . . illness. How are you feeling?'

'Oh, don't be nervous about calling it cancer, love. That's part of the problem; people spend so long pussyfooting around me, it drives me quite to distraction. And how are you? I know divorce can be a horrible business too, another one of those unmentionables, even now. Though it was worse when I did it, what, twenty years ago now? Jo? Would it be twenty?'

'Yes, Mum. Maybe you'd like an anniversary party? What do you get for a twentieth wedding anniversary – copper or something?'

'Maybe not. Don't you want to get our guest some green tea? Just the thing for a hangover, I think you'll find, Tess. I do think this group of yours sounds marvellous. It was me who suggested it to Jo in the first place. I saw an ad in the local freesheet, and although she was reluctant at first, I thought it was the perfect place to meet kindred spirits. Though it's a shame there are no eligible men.'

'No,' I say, pleased that Jo has given her the censored version of events. 'But at the same time, maybe none of us are ready for men at the moment.'

'Well if you aren't, then I'm certainly not,' she says, pointing towards her chest. 'It'll be a while before I feel ready to strip off in front of anyone except my doctor!'

I don't quite know what to say, so I look around the room for inspiration. On the wall there's a photograph of a tea plantation viewed through the mist, all the vivid greens toned down by the morning. 'That's lovely; it really reminds me of Sri Lanka.'

'Oh, yes! It is! Wonderful. I went there a couple of years ago on a yoga retreat. Beautiful place, so spiritual, don't you think?'

'Yes,' I say, thinking of the five-star hotel where we stayed during our honeymoon and the lovely but tourist-heavy attractions we were driven around in our air-conditioned car. 'The people were very friendly.'

We sit in silence again. If I didn't feel quite so ill, I'd probably manage to keep the conversation going, but it's an effort staying upright. Then I look at Louisa again and realise she's not uncomfortable at all. She's asleep. The kaftan hood has slipped off and I catch sight of her bald head, the veins showing through the skin.

The clinking of the tea pot and mugs on the tray breaks the spell. 'Green tea's up,' Jo says. 'I've made some coffee too . . .'

Louisa half-opens her eyes. 'Terrible toxin, coffee, you know.'

Jo sighs. 'Well, if it's so upsetting, I think we should go in the garden so you don't have to watch us drink it. And you're getting tired. Come on, Tess. Let's leave Mum to her meditation.'

By the time I stand up to follow her, Louisa is asleep again.

'Is that normal?' I ask, as we sit down on the tiny patio. The garden is flat and featureless; Mrs Kemp must have had better things to do than tend plants.

'Yes, she's sleepy a lot. No amount of herbal tea is going to give her the energy she needs. I was really worried to begin with, but now I think it's just her body catching up after all the intrusions and horrors of the last few months.' Jo reaches into her pocket. 'I've got some chocolate here as well. Mum regards it as the devil's work and eats carob instead but we can get away with it while she's out for the count.' She cracks off each row of the Fruit and Nut. 'It's the best hangover cure in the world. And at least it's organic.'

'So, do you have any idea which of your "close friends" thought it would be a good idea to leak the story?'

'It's not a big deal, really. There's a lot of jealousy in my industry. And there are no secrets. It might not even have been deliberate; they might let something slip at a party when a journalist says, "Haven't seen that Jo Kemp on screen much lately," and the next thing they're skulking round my house with a telephoto lens.' She hands me a piece of chocolate. 'I suppose I am more angry at myself that I didn't spot the bastard photographer. And that I didn't look a bit nicer in the photos.'

'Don't be daft. You looked lovely in the one from yesterday. Didn't you suspect anything was up at all, though?'

'Maybe. Maybe it did feel a bit like we've been . . . watched, if you like, me and Mum. But I dismissed it. I thought I was going mildly stir-crazy, the two of us rattling round the house like a couple of maiden aunts.' She takes a bite of the chocolate. 'I suppose it's a lesson in following your instincts.'

'What next?'

'Nothing, I'd guess. What's a story on page nineteen to the rest of the world? It does make me wonder even more about work and going back, though I don't have a clue what I'd do instead. You know how it is. You get to this point when you're so used to the life that the money buys you, and you're not sure you enjoy it any more, but you still can't face giving up the luxuries. The Fruit and Nut!'

'Has he . . . your lover? Has he been in touch?'

'Called my mobile a couple of times. I let it go to voicemail. I don't owe him anything.'

I find myself sympathising with poor Laurie, which I know isn't sisterly. But maybe the guy really does love her, and maybe she's incapable of loving anyone back, because her father left. Or maybe my amateur psychology is barking up the wrong tree. God alone knows what someone would make of *me*.

'I had an ominous phone call this morning,' I say, to change the subject. 'The estate agent. They've got a couple champing at the bit to see the house.'

'Oh, God. Poor you.'

'I've left Natalie in charge of letting them in.'

'Clever girl; she's enough to put anyone off.'

'She's not that bad . . .' I think back to Natalie's comments about Jo this morning. 'I just don't think she relates to other women all that well. Or to men that beat her up, of course. Maybe that's why she's so spiky – because she's scared of getting close.'

'That's no excuse. Scratch the surface of anyone over the age of eighteen and they're in the same boat. If you're not afraid of getting hurt, then you ought to be. Anyone who isn't is a girly virgin.' And she laughs. I suppose that's what I was, really, an innocent when it came to getting hurt. I was academically advanced but emotionally remedial. A seriously late starter.

'I suppose she knows all about getting hurt.'

Jo nods, serious again. 'However much of a snotty cow she is, God knows she doesn't deserve that. Hope she stays away from him for good now.' She chews thoughtfully on another piece of chocolate. 'So what will you do if they make an offer?'

'Don't have a clue, to be honest.' I look at my watch. 'They've probably been and gone by now.' I rummage around in my bag for my phone. 'Maybe she's tried to call. Oh, two texts.'

I press the button to access my inbox. The sender appears as 'Shitface don't answer', thanks to Mel. 'It's from Barney. Oh, God. They must have made an offer already and he's probably telling me to get a move on and . . .'

Jo places her hand on my arm. 'Calm down, Tess. What does it say?'

'It says . . .' I take a deep breath as I open it, 'It says, "Tess. Sorry to text but it's difficult. I need to see you. Can you make Tuesday? Barney."' As if I wouldn't recognise his number straight away. 'What do you make of that?'

She shrugs. 'God only knows. Does he make a habit of texting you?'

'No, the last time was . . . when he needed to see me to tell me she was pregnant. Nearly two months ago.' It feels much, much longer, a scene from someone else's drama.

'What will you do? You could just tell him to go through your solicitor.'

'Maybe. I just don't know if I want to see him.' It's true and totally surprising. I wouldn't say I no longer care, but I don't know if I care enough to risk reawakening the feelings that are finally fading away like scars from a childhood accident.

'I think that's a good sign,' Jo says. 'Who's the other one from?'

I scroll back through the message and find the other unread one. 'I don't know the number; let me have a look . . . "Tess. This is Robin from River Cross." Shit, it's the man from the adventure centre.'

'The guy whose daughter went missing?' Jo says. I've told no one what Robin said. It seemed as irrelevant as repeating the contents of a teenage love note.

'Yep.' I read the rest silently. *I hope u don't mind but Juliet gave me yr number. I seem to remember we were interrupted at a crucial point. I wd love to take up where we left off. What about u?*

'So why is he texting you?' She looks at me closely and I feel myself blush. 'I do hope you haven't been keeping anything from me.'

Lesson Seven
Rebound Revolution

William was looking good. He always looked good, of course, but tonight he'd made a special effort. Chinos, polo shirt, and a special 'hair thickening balm' that the woman in Boots had recommended. He wasn't totally sure why he'd gone to so much trouble, but he could already sense that when the current course was over, he'd miss this batch of students.

Jo was the person who popped up in his mind the most often. He did feel slightly conscious of the dirty-old-man potential of this . . . crush, but being with her – being with all of them, in fact – made him feel so much like the William he used to be.

'Good evening,' he said, taking the time to beam a truly dazzling smile across the gathering. 'You're on the home straight now, let's face it. I feel like a parent, watching you grow, and next week you'll be heading off to university with your new jug kettles and your pot plants and your stereos in the back of my estate car.

'But before you go, I need to have words with you.' He paused. 'About the Opposite Sex.'

Most of them smiled back. What a difference from six weeks ago. Any mention of the opposite sex then was much more likely to elicit a scowl or a lump in the throat. William was most surprised to see how well Natalie looked; he'd been expecting her to be edgy and strung out after leaving her husband, but she grinned more than the others. He felt good about his performance last week: the way he'd stepped into action, sensitive yet purposeful, making her see how much danger she was in and then, with a little help from Tess, finding a solution.

He was the fourth emergency service.

'Now, I bet you're wondering what the heck I'd have to tell

you about the Opposite Sex. After all, you know the worst: what total bitches and bastards they can be. How they manipulate, how they complain, how they shag about indiscriminately.

'What I want to tell you is that it's not about the gender, it's about the person. If there's one thing I'd like you to remember when you walk away from St Gabriel's after the final session, it's that.'

William left another long pause while they took it in. 'Right. There endeth the first lesson. Now we're going to have some fun. Who's brought their homework?'

They all raised their hands. It was hardly the most arduous of tasks. They'd each found two photos or cuttings from magazines: one of a celebrity they fancied and one of someone famous they didn't necessarily lust after but felt was a better match personality-wise.

'Let's have a look, then. Tim? Who are your pin-ups?'

'Definitely Marilyn Monroe for the most fanciable.'

'A classic choice. Good stuff.' Though Marilyn would have made mincemeat of mild-mannered Tim. 'And your perfect match?'

'Um . . . well, I thought maybe . . . Meg Ryan in *Sleepless in Seattle*. Or in *When Harry Met Sally*. Or any of them, really.' Tim's cheeks glowed pink.

'Right, right. I can definitely see that one working out. Very nice. Let's have another one. Jo?'

'You can't go wrong with Brad Pitt,' she said, to William's disappointment. He'd been hoping she might go for something that little bit more . . . mature. 'As my pin-up. But I don't know for sure that he'd offer me the intellectual stimulation I'd need, so for my soulmate, I've chosen' – she unfolded the page – 'Jeremy Paxman. What a mind!' She licked her lips to reinforce the point.

At least Jeremy Paxman was heading in the right direction, age-wise. 'So a man's mind is more important than his looks, to you?'

She raised her eyebrows, and when she spoke, her tone was

half-mocking, half-smiling and very, very familiar. 'If I didn't know better, I'd think you were flirting with me, William.'

It was the way she said his name that did it. As soon as he realised, he couldn't think why he hadn't seen it before. Her hair, her eyes, her dry sense of humour, and her disillusion with the world. He didn't *fancy* Jo. She reminded him of his wife.

'Uh . . .' For a moment, he couldn't find the words to respond. 'No, no. I'm old enough to be your father, after all.' He stared around the room, trying to work out what to do. 'Right, who's next? Malcolm?'

'Simple. Felicity Kendal. For both.'

He was so bloody predictable, but at least it gave William something to latch onto, to distract himself. 'Ah . . . but do you mean Felicity Kendal or do you mean Barbara Good? I mean, I know Felicity won that Rear of the Year competition, but apart from that, I don't think she bears anything more than an uncanny physical resemblance to her gardening alter ego and it makes a big difference if you're trying to match your character traits.'

'Barbara, I suppose,' Malcolm said, looking put out. 'A feminine woman. But willing to muck in when required. Like my wife was, before—'

'Thanks, Malcolm. What about you, Rani?'

'Oh, I would have to say the most beautiful man in the world for me would be Arnold Schwarzenegger. I do not like the man at all. Not in any way. But he has a body to launch a thousand ships.' Rani smiled her twinkly smile and everyone laughed, unsure whether she was being deliberately funny. William guessed she was.

'And your soulmate?'

'Tony Blair. There is a man who absolutely knows his own mind, is not afraid of women but would not dream of being unfaithful. A family man. Hard-working. Committed to his religion.'

'Right. Well, not to everybody's taste, I suppose, Rani, but your reasons seem extremely well thought out. Aaron?'

'Um . . .' He looked awkward, reluctant to divulge the details. Perhaps he still had his eye on someone here, William thought.

He'd have to move fast. 'I do think that Halle Berry is a bit of a babe, all round.'

'Who's Halle Berry?' Malcolm asked.

Aaron passed over the picture. 'Cute, isn't she? Not girly, but sparky.'

'Does nothing for me,' Malcolm said. 'So unfeminine.'

William held up his hands. So long as he didn't look at Jo, he would be OK. 'Luckily we don't all like the same things in a woman. Or a man. So what about the woman with the right personality, Aaron? Who would that be?'

'She'd have to be incredibly patient to put up with me. And very faithful. And preferably worship the ground I walk on. So I think maybe a sheepdog is what I really want.'

William led the laughter this time. But he was curious. It was a strange, guarded reply from a man like Aaron who clearly had more than a passing interest in women of all kinds. 'I've heard women called bitches before in this room, but I've never had anyone actually consider the real thing as a life partner. Who's left, then? Tess?'

'I think that guy from *ER* is cute. Goran. The one who was in the Madonna video. More than cute, actually. Probably the most attractive guy in the world. Clean-cut, chisel-jawed.' She glanced at Aaron, who looked away. William tried to interpret that look, but Tess was already revealing her choice of soulmate. 'As for the man to complement me best, I think it'd have to be ... John Cleese. Funny and witty and at least as screwed up as I am.'

'Good stuff. So that leaves Carol-Ann and Natalie. Let's hear it, girls.'

Natalie spoke first. 'Mine is definitely Nicolas Cage. A big, Latin-looking man. Does it for me every time. And personality-wise? Bill Gates. A go-getter with more money than just about anyone else in the world.'

'Bill Gates?' Carol-Ann frowned. 'If you're going after money, can't you at least find someone *interesting*? A gambler or a gangster or something. Mine would have to be Sean Connery for looks and ... well, Sean Connery for personality too. You can't improve on perfection.'

It was only when William found himself straightening up, trying to convey the manner of a suave secret agent in his posture, that he realised: it wasn't Jo he fancied.

It was Carol-Ann.

His mind went into freefall as the revelation slotted into place. Of course. She was the feistiest, cheekiest, sexiest, most resilient woman he'd ever come across. And she was sitting only eight feet away.

Waiting for him to speak.

'I ... er ... well, that's very interesting, Carol-Ann. And everyone else, too. Of course. Thank you. Um. Right. The next thing I'm going to be asking you to do is to lay out a little gallery for me. Yes, pin up your pin-ups. Not with pins, obviously, but with Blu Tack. On the wall, over there. Have a look at yours and at the others, then, working in pairs, I want you to draw up a list of qualities you want in your next partner.

'After the break, we'll work out where you can find this specimen, and what on earth you do with them once you've found them.'

As the students dispersed to post their photographs, William wondered if he was the right person to be advising anyone on looking for love when he'd had such trouble realising his own soulmate was right under his nose.

William was about to begin a rundown of the twenty-first-century matchmaking scene – taking in internet dating, textual intercourse, speed-dating and lonely hearts ads, before moving onto safer sex, a subject that he suddenly found far more embarrassing than he ever had before with Carol-Ann in the front row – when the door to St Gabriel's swung open.

'NAT! NAT!' An anguished voice echoed around the church hall.

'Oh, shit.' Natalie sounded irritated but her face told a different story. It had drained of colour and her whole body had gone tense, like a wild animal sensing the proximity of a predator.

William moved briskly towards the interloper. The man had a rugby-playing physique but an unbroken nose. He had blond highlights in his hair and wore a linen suit: both looked expensive. 'Can I help you?'

The man scanned the hall and spotted Natalie cowering next to Aaron. 'Oh, so that's it, is it? This is the real sodding reason you've left?'

'Tony, he's got nothing to do with me going. You know why I left.'

The interloper started towards Natalie but William stepped in front of him, blocking his path. 'This is a private session. Please leave.'

'I'm not going anywhere without HER!'

The other men had stood up now, moving forward to form a barrier protecting Natalie. William felt surprisingly calm, despite Tony's aggressive tone. It defied the laws of probability that there'd never been an incident like this before and at least on *this* course there was a good sprinkling of men, even if the line-up was more *Dad's Army* than *S.W.A.T.*

'Well, I would have to advise you that the tone you're using is not normally an effective one when it comes to relationships. I'll give you ten seconds to leave the premises or I will call the police.'

William stared at Tony, trying not to be perturbed by the definite craziness in his blue eyes. It was like trying to tame a rabid dog. For a fraction of a second, William thought he'd won, as Tony took a tiny step back. But it was the preparatory move for the desperate lunge that followed, like a man throwing himself at the finishing tape after an Olympic sprint. Tony was launching himself through the line of men, towards his prize on the other side.

'Nat-aaaa-leee . . .' His scream was perfectly timed for shock value, so by the time William and the others realised what was happening, Tony had already reached his wife and flung his large arms around her. She whimpered as, with one meaty forearm gripping her throat, he rummaged in his trouser pocket for something.

A Stanley knife. He looked triumphant as he rested it carefully on the side of Natalie's neck.

'Now then,' William said, feeling less calm. It appeared that some sort of siege situation was developing in his own church hall. One of the photos in the 'fantasy partner' gallery fluttered to the floor, caught in the draught Tony had created in his dash towards Natalie. Nicolas Cage. William tried to remember the rules of hostage negotiation, gained not through the Californian training course (they'd somehow omitted this essential part of the curriculum) but from watching *The Bill*. Create a rapport and find out their demands. That seemed a good place to begin. 'Anthony, isn't it? What is it you want, Anthony?'

Tony didn't seem to know. 'I want . . . we want, that is . . . to be left alone.' His forearm was now wrapped around Natalie's neck, like a hairy stole. He wasn't strangling her but she'd gone as limp as a ragdoll, a gesture of defeat that made William want to cry.

'I'm not sure we can let that happen right now, Anthony. Nothing personal. But we're in the middle of a session. I'm sure your wife would be happy to see you afterwards, though. We finish at nine. You could wait in the office, and I can make you a cup of tea to help pass the time.' *While I call the police*, William thought.

'I'm not bloody stupid.'

'No, of *course not*,' William said, trying to work out what on earth to do next. 'I suppose . . . well, perhaps if the other members of the group don't mind, we could carry on with the session while you're here. You'd have to respect everyone's confidentiality, but if you could agree to that . . .' It was a risky strategy but he didn't have any other ideas for now. If he could make everything seem normal, perhaps Tony would forget to keep such a tight grip on Natalie and she might be able to get away. At least it would buy time until a better idea occurred to him.

Tony looked confused. 'I don't know.'

'You see, it's against insurance regulations to leave the two of you here alone.' God, he really was clutching at straws now. 'So if no one objects to your presence . . .'

William looked around at the others, hoping no one would. They nodded, trying to replace their shocked expressions with masks of calm, as if knife-wielding new recruits turned up most weeks. 'Excellent, excellent. Well, welcome, Anthony. Apologies if we don't do the introductions now; there's no time to waste. So what we've been doing so far this session is . . .' He paused, realising that a discussion of tactics for rebound romance would probably not go down too well with a jealous, violent spouse. 'Um, yes, today's topic is . . . forgiveness. That's right. Forgiveness.'

Anthony still looked sceptical.

'Yes, forgiveness of the people who have hurt you – even if they didn't mean to – is a *very important* part of what we're doing here.' William was bluffing: after years of following the same script every session, improvising was risky but he couldn't think of any other options. 'Recognising that sometimes a relationship reaches a critical stage that needn't end in divorce is actually something we are *very keen* to stress here.'

He paused. Carol-Ann raised her hand and he breathed deeply. She was obviously going to try to help, but she didn't have his advanced conflict resolution skills. 'Yes?'

'Well, William . . .' she began, and despite the circumstances, he sensed a little frisson of excitement as she said his name for the first time since he'd realised how he felt. 'I wanted to tell the group a little more about my reconciliation. Brought about, as you all know, by the words of wisdom I have been privileged to receive from everyone here. But especially Natalie.'

'Go ahead, my dear.' Reconciliation? With her dead ex-husband? She obviously had a plan, but it was anyone's guess what it was.

'Yes. You know how long my . . . situation with Alan had stayed unresolved until I came here and saw the light.' She smiled beatifically, as though some kind of spiritual event was unfolding before their eyes.

'Right . . . go on.'

'I can't explain. After listening last week to the things everyone said – especially Natalie – I had to take it on myself to tell Alan how I felt.'

Tony was frowning, his eyes darting between Carol-Ann and William. He had extremely shiny shoes: indeed, apart from his undoubtedly scary expression, he was very good-looking, in a clean-cut, corporate way.

'And what was it you told him?' William felt wary. Mentioning Natalie seemed risky, but he didn't have a clue what else to do.

'I took on board what Natalie had said, about having needed space to work out her . . . intense feelings for her husband. And how she felt sure that with a bit of distance between them, she would be able to rekindle those feelings . . .' Carol-Ann paused to allow her words to sink in. Natalie had, of course, said nothing of the sort. 'I too went to my husband and I told him that despite all that had gone on between us, I wanted to say sorry and to hear him say the same.'

William looked over at Tony again. He seemed to have relaxed his arm around Natalie's neck. Ah well, in for a penny. 'Anthony, it's a little unusual to ask this of a newcomer, but as we are in the fortunate position of actually having the other half here for a session, I wondered if you and Natalie might like to share with each other how you're feeling right now.'

Tony looked even more disorientated, control of the situation slipping away. 'I . . . don't know.'

Natalie stared across the room at William as if she hoped he could somehow transmit the most soothing words she should use, telepathically. She gulped, then began. 'What I've been wanting to say is . . . I do miss you, Tony. God, this is so hard.'

William took a tentative step towards them. 'It might help if you were able to say things face to face?'

Tony's mouth hung open as he considered the dilemma: let go now and trust her to come back, or never let go again.

Slowly, as though he was testing out a limb that had just been freed from a plaster cast, he released his arm from Natalie's neck. There was a red mark across the white of her skin where he'd applied a little too much pressure.

She turned towards him, took his hand in hers. His other hand still held the knife. It was such a tender move after the force of his desperate hold that William felt like a voyeur, watching this private goodbye. Except, of course, Tony probably didn't realise it was goodbye.

'I do miss you, Tony. I do. I just don't miss the other side to you. All I want is for Zach and me to feel safe. And we don't.' She was stroking his hand, with a gentleness that seemed at odds with her coiffed, cool demeanour. Tony looked down at her, then grasped her to him, burying his head in her cashmere-covered shoulder and letting the knife fall onto the parquet floor.

'Go,' William mouthed to the others. Aaron, Tim and Malcolm joined him in a last surge forward, pulling Tony away. He howled in protest, but he knew when he was defeated.

By the time the police had left – the older sergeant muttering under his breath about 'bloody new-age therapy, more trouble than it's worth; in my day we put up or shut up' – it was nine thirty, but no one seemed in any hurry to leave. They hung around uncertainly, like witnesses to a shocking road accident, unable to face the normality of the people they lived with, or the emptiness of their post-divorce homes.

'We'll have a bit of catching up to do next week,' William said. 'But I don't think I can promise a session as dramatic.'

A few people laughed half-heartedly. It was not meant to be like this at the end of session seven. There should have been banter, a little teasing, a sense of optimism about the future before next week's finale.

He tried again. 'I know this might not seem the right time, but I will leave it up to you all to decide. Usually on the last session we bring in some wine, Twiglets, that kind of thing. Have a bit of a party. Now, I realise we're not exactly feeling in a party mood at the moment, but it would be a shame not to celebrate what you've all achieved.'

There were nods and murmurs but William couldn't tell if they were up for it or not. As they drifted towards the door, he took a deep breath and walked up to Carol-Ann; he knew he had to say something to thank her for her quick thinking.

'Well done, by the way,' he said, feeling like a nervous debutant. 'I did wonder what you were driving at there for a minute, but it was the right thing to do for sure.'

She tossed her head and smiled at him. 'I think we both stayed pretty bloody calm, considering what a nutter he was. I hope they lock the bugger up. Poor Natalie.'

'She's quite a tough cookie, I think. I'm sure she'll be OK. Not sure Tony will, though. The police looked fairly determined to make an example of him.' William searched for more to say, to keep her talking. 'But, I mean, you really did make all the difference there.'

'What is this, the bloody St Gabriel's mutual admiration society?'

William felt his face heat up and his mind go blank. 'Something like that.'

'I don't know how I'm going to sleep tonight, after all the excitement.' She looked around her. 'Hey, you lot. Who fancies a drink now? Just a quick one. We definitely deserve it.'

A murmur of approval went round the group, pleased to have a reason not to go just yet. Only Tim mumbled a reluctant no, because his mum was babysitting. But William was speechless at the sudden image of Carol-Ann tossing and turning in her bed.

Carol-Ann clapped her hands together. 'Great! And I know you don't usually fraternise with the troops, William, but why don't you come with us? Just this once . . .'

He focused on her plump lips. The opportunity to spend more time with her was falling into his lap. He could chit-chat rather than do deep relationship analysis, amuse and charm and flirt . . . He'd always been good at that, before. It was ideal.

So William couldn't understand why he opened his mouth and said: 'I don't think so, my dear. I wouldn't want to cramp your style. But make sure you all have one for me.'

Chapter Thirty

I don't think Barney's very happy at being postponed by text twice but I don't really care, which is a revelation in itself. I have to make a big effort to drag myself away from the pub, where I sense the inquest on the night's dramatic events will carry on beyond closing time.

He's so lacking originality that he's suggested meeting in the Pitcher and Piano, just as we did back in May. Last time, I dressed to the nines and spent hours planning what I should say. This time, I don't even bother to reapply my lipstick.

I spot him sitting at the bar, slumped on a tall stool. I shiver. For all my bravado, seeing Barney isn't quite the emotion-free experience I'd hoped for. But once I've caught my breath, I realise what I am experiencing is not regret. It's something between contempt and pity.

'Hey.' My voice makes him jump. His face looks older, wearier, or maybe I am just seeing him as he's looked for years to everyone else – without the affection that blurs the wrinkles, reduces the eye-bags and airbrushes away the dark shadows of the one you love.

'Hey, Tess.' He looks irritated, glances towards the clock on the wall of the bar, waiting for me to apologise. After a few moments, he realises he's going to be waiting a long time. 'You look well. What would you like to drink?'

'Mineral water, please.'

He frowns. 'Can't tempt you to a wine?'

'No, I've already had one.'

'Oh right. So that's why you've kept me waiting? Dutch courage?'

Cheeky bastard. 'No. We just had a bit of a dramatic time

tonight at the group.' I wonder how Natalie's getting on at the police station. She's more than a match for them.

'Group?'

I would never have admitted it six weeks ago, but what the hell? 'Yes, I've been going to a divorce recovery course.'

'Blimey.' He seems to be fighting the urge to sneer. 'Wouldn't have seen you as the type. So have you "recovered"?' He makes quotation marks with his fingers in the air.

'Yes.' I stare back. 'The patient has made a surprisingly rapid recovery.'

'Right.' He turns away to order the drinks, and when he turns back, he's also turned on the full Barney charm, which makes me more convinced that he wants me to accept some terrible offer on the house. 'Shall we go onto the balcony bit?'

It's quiet outside. I guess that 10.35 p.m on a Tuesday night is a time when bars are only really frequented by the desperate: mistresses and alcoholics and soon-to-be ex-wives.

'Not long now, then?' I say, when the gap in conversation becomes too gaping.

He stares at me.

'Till the baby's born?' I am determined to seem mature. Even as the words come out of my mouth, I realise they no longer have the power to hurt me. I have seen a baby close up now and the desire for a Guerrilla of my own has diminished somewhat.

He flinches. There's no smile. 'No. I haven't really come here to talk about *that*. Not directly.'

'So what is this about? The house?'

'That's part of it.' He gives me a long, lingering look that I suspect is meant to look sad and regretful, but actually looks rather clueless. 'This is hard.'

'What, harder than telling me you were leaving? Harder than explaining that the Curved . . . Dawn was having your baby?' It surprises me how easy it is now to say her name. Less than a month ago, just to think it made me catch my breath in pain.

'Yes.' He is still staring at me. 'Because I realise what a terrible mistake I have made.'

For a moment, the world stops. There is only me and Barney. He is waiting for my response and I am doing the same, waiting for a surge of something: happiness, anger, satisfaction. After a few seconds, when nothing happens to me, I say: 'Meaning what, exactly?'

'Meaning . . . what do you think it means? It means I don't want to be with her. I want to be with you. I always have. I got distracted, dazzled by headlights.'

'Oh, so that's what you call them.' I can't resist a little dig.

'This isn't a joke.' He sounds irritated, but then he adds, more softly: 'It doesn't have to be the end, Tess. I really want to try again.'

'Right.' I am still waiting for the emotions to kick in. The euphoria that would have accompanied his announcement only six weeks ago is nowhere to be found. The best I can conjure up is a very slight sense of irritation. What makes him think he can press the reset button on our lives, after all that's happened?

'So what do you think?'

'Well, I don't know what to think, Barney. I don't quite understand what you're suggesting. A *ménage à trois*? I suppose, actually, it'd have to be four of us, wouldn't it: you, me, her and the baby? I'm not sure there's room.'

'I'm not suggesting that at all and I'd rather you didn't take the piss out of me. I am talking about getting back to how it was – or, better than it was. Sorting out the things we weren't sorting out and getting our lives back in order.' He smiles at me. 'Isn't that what you want too?'

I don't know. Whoever said 'be careful what you wish for' knew what they were talking about. Because by the time your dreams come true, you may not want them any more. But I can't bring myself to say so. 'You seem to have forgotten that things can't ever be the same. How could they? You're about to become a dad.'

'I told you before, this isn't about the baby. It's about us. Of course, I will provide for him financially—'

'It's a boy?'

'Yes.' He looks a little ashamed. 'We asked. We've been going to private ante-natal sessions. That's the thing: I will provide for him, make sure he's fine. I'll want to see him, too, but that doesn't have to affect us. The bottom line is there's no point in carrying on with Dawn. I don't love her. It's easier to end it now, when she can find her own ways of doing things, than a week or a month or even a year after Oliver ... the baby arrives.'

I don't like this one bit. The child has a name, yet his father's already planning to abandon him. Was my husband always this selfish? 'And does Dawn know all this?'

'No ... I thought I would talk to you first.'

'Hedge your bets, you mean?'

He shrugs. 'It's about honesty. About following your heart. And my heart says I want to be with you. That we belong together.'

He's going to start singing the *Home and Away* theme tune in a minute. 'I don't know what to say, Barney.'

'How about ... let's try again?' His voice is playful, but confident that he's in the right. 'Listen. I know I've done the wrong thing. I know I've hurt you and I am so sorry. I wish I could put back the clock. I am a stupid, stupid man and I couldn't see what was obvious: how good our life was.

'But we shouldn't cut off our noses to spite our faces, should we? We should be together and we both know that. I'm just a bit slow on the uptake. Don't punish me – punish *us* – for that.'

Barney's words seem carefully thought out, painstakingly rehearsed to hit the right balance of remorse and certainty. Like a speech in court. He never had the ambition – or maybe the quick wit – to use his law degree to become a barrister. So this is the performance of his life, with our marriage, not a criminal, in the dock and him pleading for clemency.

It leaves me cold.

'You can't undo what's happened,' I say.

'No, I know that. But I can make it up to you.'

'You can't undo ... Oliver, either. That's much more important.'

He looks a little less certain, surprised at my resistance. 'I know that, but I can have a relationship with him. I just don't want one with Dawn any more. I want one with you.'

'And what if I don't want to share you with a baby? What if I wanted us to have a baby of our own, not some kind of messy step-family?'

'You shouldn't be jealous of a baby,' he says. His piety makes me want to hit him.

'It's not jealousy, Barney. It's much more complicated than that.'

A look of panic crosses his face. 'But . . . we can still have a family of our own. The family we planned.'

'The one we never loved each other enough to get round to having?' He opens his mouth to disagree. 'I'm not going to argue, Barney; it's too late. That's all you need to know.'

'I didn't think you were a vindictive person, Tess.'

'You want vindictive? Try this. You are not the person I thought you were. You are weak and short-sighted. And though I love you, I don't like you any more. I can go on.'

'I . . . Tess . . .' I hope he doesn't cry. I don't think I can handle that. It's not in my nature to be harsh, but I feel so angry at the terrible waste: of my love, of Dawn's love and a baby's life. 'We could bring up Oliver ourselves. Dawn's too young to be tied down. It could work.'

Now it's my turn to struggle to speak. 'You *are* kidding?' He shakes his head. 'You really don't understand anything about people, do you? You are so different from the person I thought you were, Barney. A disappointment. A bloody great big disappointment.'

I stand up. 'I think we should accept the first offer we get on the house. You'll be wanting to get yourself sorted. And I just want this over with.'

I leave the pub without looking back. I only wish that turning my back on him felt like a decision rather than a fait accompli.

Natalie and Guerrilla are still up when I arrive home. I'm not looking forward to seeing them. My 'all men are bastards' radar is on overdrive at the moment and I don't really need any extra evidence to prove the theory, but I force myself to ask the question.

'So what happened with the police?'

Natalie's cheeks are flushed and there's an empty wine glass next to her on the coffee table. At least these days you can see the coffee table in my living room, so I must be improving.

'It went well. They were falling over themselves to be nice. There's some kind of initiative going on about domestic violence at the moment so they couldn't have been more politically correct about it. The WPC seemed really pissed off that I didn't burst into tears; she was obviously dying to practise her tea and sympathy routine.'

I laugh, though I find Natalie's lack of emotion chilling. I'm never sure whether it's just a self-protection mechanism or she's really as tough as she makes out. 'So what about Tony?'

'In court tomorrow. They don't quite know what they're going to charge him with – he made up some story that he hadn't intended to attack me and that he was only carrying the Stanley knife so he'd remember to buy replacement blades, but after his performance at the session, he'll probably end up remanded in custody. I almost feel sorry for him. He's only crazy five per cent of the time. But he's done me a favour by going off on one. The police records are going to help so much when we sort out what happens with the divorce.' She strokes the top of Guerrilla's head. 'So now you've seen Zach's daddy, don't you reckon he's a bit of a chip off the old block to look at? I just hope that's the only way he takes after him.'

'I'm sure it will be,' I say, even though I am not sure at all. In my experience, the nastiest, most brutal kids at school all have dads exactly the same, as surely as a Pit Bull breeds another Pit Bull. I wonder if baby Oliver will be a lying, cheating, weak-willed little bastard like his father. Well, he's a man. These qualities are also handed down from father to son.

She nods, then remembers where I've been. 'Ooooh, how did it go with Barney?'

'Fine.' I don't really want to talk about it and I know that Natalie's self-obsessed enough only to be feigning interest.

'So does he want the house to be sold straight away?'

Even that question is about her: she needs to know where she's going to be living, after all. 'He just wants things over with.'

'Don't we all?' She kisses Guerrilla's forehead. 'It's been an evening of reunions one way or another. Which is why I think we deserve another little drink.' She stands up, walks through to the kitchen and opens the fridge with her one free arm. She waves a bottle of Cristal champagne at me. 'I thought we could toast our futures, if you wouldn't mind doing the honours.'

I choose two fine-stemmed glasses – is it only eight weeks ago that I couldn't find two clean glasses in the whole house to share a drink with Mel? Then I wrap the neck of the bottle in a tea towel and gently prise the cork out with a quiet release of pressure rather than the exhibitionist Grand Prix-style explosion that Barney always preferred. The foam tumbles out of the bottle into the glasses. I pass one over, then hold the other to my nose, savouring the biscuity smell. 'Cheers.'

'To new beginnings,' Natalie says, clinking glasses with me.

'New beginnings,' I agree. Though if I'm honest, I'd rather be toasting to independence and a life without men.

Which presents an immediate problem, given that I'm meant to be meeting Robin for drinks in less than twenty-four hours' time. The way I feel as the bubbles go up my nose, twenty-four years would be too soon.

Chapter Thirty-one

I wake up sweating. It's seventeen years since I last went on a date and I didn't enjoy them back then. Now that I have enough baggage to sink the QE2, I relish it about as much as a cervical smear. And at least you only have to have a smear once every three years. Whereas I shudder to think how many dates I might have to go on before the likes of Mel will say, that's enough, you are a lost cause, you no longer have to try . . .

I start looking for excuses to cancel my date with Robin as soon as I step out of bed. I study myself in the mirror, searching for the slightest sign of a bug – a cold, conjunctivitis, tuberculosis – that might let me off the hook. But, despite the half-bottle of champagne last night, I look healthier than I have in months.

'You could do with a night out, Natalie,' I say as I sip my coffee and she shovels organic Wild Mushroom Pasta baby food into Guerrilla's mouth. 'I could babysit . . . tonight, even? Strike while the iron's hot.'

'Normally I'd say yes like a shot. But I know what you're up to. Jo told me you'd got a date and she warned me you might try to chicken out. So no way, Jose! I will help you with your make-up later, though, if that helps. I've got some great new stuff to even out the skin tone, just what you need.'

Maybe I don't look healthier after all. The evenness of my skin tone had never occurred to me as something to check. Another aspect of my appearance to be paranoid about.

At school, it's no better. The sun is shining so everyone's in the perkiest of moods. In the staffroom, people are talking about summer holidays and then Roz comes in to announce that the weather's far too good for the weekly staff meeting so we are all obliged to go home on time. And if we don't she'll consider disciplinary action.

It's a conspiracy. There's even a text there from Robin when I switch my phone on, saying how much he's 'looking 4ward 2 seeing u'. Which seems to offer further ammunition to cancel the date, until I remember he has a teenage daughter so she's probably taught him all he knows about the Joy of Text.

The message on my voicemail does finally offer me an excuse.

'Mrs Leonard, hello, it's Diane from Marchant's estate agent's here. I know it's been a while since we had the viewing on Sunday but I am very pleased to say we have had an offer at the asking price. Very good news, I'm sure you'll agree. Please give me a call back as soon as possible.'

I suppose to her it is very good news. Maybe it'll seem like good news to me one of these days. But it doesn't right now. Right now it feels like the beginning of the end. I can cope with losing Barney, but the house . . .

I really want to cancel seeing Robin but I don't think I have the energy to explain. I've got no real need to worry, though. Five minutes with me in this mood will be enough to persuade him that I am the girl of his nightmares.

When we finally spoke on Sunday – after an hour's pep talk from Jo – he'd insisted on coming to see me in Harborne, rather than meeting at some kind of godforsaken halfway point like a service station just off the M5. He had some business to deal with in Birmingham anyway, he said, so he might as well kill two birds with one stone.

I liked that willingness to use the sorts of clichés Barney would have avoided like the plague for fear of seeming naïve or suburban. Robin, it seemed, was his own man, the kind to call a spade a spade without worrying about what other people thought.

But as I wait for the doorbell to ring, I wonder if I have misjudged him. Perhaps he isn't the confident rough diamond, happy in his own skin.

Maybe he's plain stupid.

He's late. I don't think much of a man who doesn't have the courtesy to turn up on time for a first date. We couldn't be much less compatible. It's rude not to be punctual.

I have the TV on, but I can't concentrate on the latest developments in *Coronation Street*. I think of my mother. Her voice, her face, her life sneaks up on me and once she's there, I find it very hard to get rid of her. How have Dad's revelations affected the finely balanced deceits on which their marriage is based? She probably finds the knowledge that we know everything at least as painful as the original affairs. She likes everything to be controlled and hidden and outwardly perfect.

Maybe we're not nearly as different as I like to think.

Finally, a full eighteen minutes after he should have been here, the doorbell co-operates and rings, loud and clear. I head wearily for my hall.

I see the flowers first, a huge bunch of white supermarket chrysanthemums and carnations with an excessive helping of fern. He peeks from behind the bouquet but the contrast between the gloom of my hallway and the bright white outside means he's hard to see. 'Hello, Tess. I hope you like flowers.'

I don't have the heart to say what I really think, to repeat the jokes Barney and I used to make about 'petrol station posies' and how they were only fit for people with no imagination. Because all the hand-tied arrangements of freesia and tea roses and unusual succulents Barney sent me over the years can't make up for infidelity.

'Lovely, thanks. Come in while I put them in a vase.' I can already picture them in a week's time, all their colour and life drained away into the browny-green water. 'Did you find me all right?'

'Yes. Sorry I'm a bit late. I had it all planned out but then the person I was meeting persuaded me to give them a lift and it was miles out of my way.'

'Right.' Now he's inside the house I can see him properly and I feel a tightening in my stomach. He is better-looking than I remembered, in that slightly SAS way. But there's an awkward- ness about having a man in the house again. In *our* house. With Aaron it was different because he never intruded into my space, or really into my consciousness. Allowing Robin to see how we lived as a couple seems far more intimate than the things I did at the crummy bedsit in Kings Heath.

'Shall we go?' I say, after I have tried and failed to create some sort of balance in the flower arrangement. With the piece of elastic band around the stems they cling together like an old-fashioned twig broom. Without it, they splay out to the sides of the vase as though each flower is ashamed of its neighbour.

I've suggested a new, trendy pub that's opened at the very end of the High Street. It used to be an old bloke's boozer, a glorified front room with a lager pump and a bitter pump and a few optics. Now it's a riot of textures: leather, suede, fake-fur, wood, bamboo. The colours are as subdued as my living room, all beige and brown, and stepping into the pub from the warmth outside, they feel wrong for summer, as if someone has decided that sunlight is just plain unsophisticated.

'Very hip,' he says. 'We don't get too many bars like this where I live.'

'We can go somewhere else,' I say, hovering by the door.

'No. Don't worry. It makes a nice change for a yokel like me to see how city folk live.' He's smiling that smile again, the one that makes me feel unsettled. 'What will you have to drink?'

We order: a gin and tonic for me, a non-alcoholic cocktail for Robin, chosen from a huge menu. The drink he ends up with is bluey-green; it clashes with the décor and looks incongruous grasped in his massive hand. But he laughs at it, sticking out his little finger – which is far from little – to mimic the kind of person he imagines would normally order a drink like that.

We sit down, and now that the ritual of choosing drinks is over, we're wondering what to say next. 'How's your daughter?'

'Oh, God. Impossible. She was a bit subdued for a day or two after doing her bunk, volunteering to do the washing up, that kind of stuff, but it wore off so quickly. She's moping around like a sick dog, sighing a lot. I've tried talking to her but I can't get through.'

'You won't be able to. But then she'll wake up aged nineteen and turn into a human again.'

He grins. 'That's the thing. I've never been a teenage girl, never had that much to do with them because I went to a boys' school. I feel like I'm navigating unfamiliar territory without a map or a compass. Though even that would be better than this. I'm trained to read the signs, work things out through the position of the sun or the moon. So this is like trying to find the way with a blindfold on.'

'She can probably find her own way, if you let her,' I say, cursing how pretentious I sound the moment I've finished the sentence.

'I've always missed Eleanor, but this is the hardest it's ever been. If she was here . . . well, she'd just know what to do.' He is miles away for a moment, then looks up at me, smiles. Again. I really wish he'd stop doing that. 'God, this is not exactly the done thing, is it? Talking about your dead wife on a first date.'

'Dead?'

He winces. 'Shit. You didn't know? Sorry, I just assumed . . . Eleanor died four years ago. She was in a car crash.' His voice tails away . . .

'Poor you. Poor Charlotte.' My mind is struggling to digest this new information, to dump my old mental image of Robin as a divorcee in favour of a new one featuring him as a tragic widower.

'I am quite used to the . . . absence now, but I wish there was some way of her communicating what I should do. I wish I believed in messages from the grave. Crystal balls.' He takes a sip of his blue drink and pulls a face. 'The thing is, a teenage boy I could handle. We could bond over a game of table football or something. But there's been nothing in my life to prepare me for the hormonal imbalances of a girl, and I feel like I'm short-changing her, because she's got nowhere to go to reassure her about life.'

'She knows you love her.'

'Does she? Do you really think so? Thank you for saying so, Tess.' He sighs. 'God, I've really cocked things up now, haven't I? It's like I've got emotional diarrhoea. Your turn.'

Is this how dates are at our age? Mutual unburdenings of tortured souls, trying to find out if your traumas are compatible with the other person's? It seems the strangest thing to do when you've just met someone, yet I feel more comfortable than I would have expected talking about this stuff. Perhaps William's group is partly responsible – but then I'm sure if Tony and his Stanley knife hadn't interrupted our session yesterday, the advice for first dates would have been small talk, not soul-baring. 'I feel OK. Well, not OK exactly. There's been an offer on the house, so I suppose things will start to happen very soon. It might take me a little longer to move on.'

'And your ex?'

'I think he's getting cold feet, even though it's what he wanted. It's like that song, 'A Little Time', where the guy wants to try freedom again and the woman agrees but by the time he realises the grass isn't greener, she's moved on and doesn't want him back anyway.'

'That sounds like sweet revenge.'

I think about it. 'You know, I would have thought exactly the same, if I could have predicted the future. But there's nothing satisfying about it. I feel ... disappointed, more than anything. And bemused. Barney is not the man I thought he was for all those years.'

We sit silently for a while, each lost in our own loss. Then Robin holds up his glass. 'Shall we have a toast to the future and then begin again, like this is a date between kids who're not old enough to know better?'

He smiles and I feel unable to refuse. 'Cheers.' I try to think of something light-hearted or adolescent to say, but my mind is empty of wit or trivia or playground gossip.

After an agonising wait, he laughs. 'Well, that's worked well. I'm as tongue-tied as any teenager in the company of a beautiful girl.'

I blush violently. 'Shut up!'

'And you're as bad at taking a compliment as every beautiful woman who doesn't know it. You are lovely, though, Tess. As soon as you walked into the centre, I was bowled over and it was agony trying to work out whether I dared to chat you up or not. When Juliet told me you were getting divorced, I felt all excited but nervous too. And then I found out about your fear of water and I really wanted to help. I mean, I knew you could do it, but my heart was in my mouth. I didn't want you to think I was taking advantage.'

I attempt a girlish giggle. 'No, of course not. But didn't you prefer Juliet? She usually attracts lots of attention.'

'No. I was brought up with girls like that. Always trying to out-bloke you. I liked your . . . femininity. Your vulnerability.' He stops. 'God, that sounds a bit odd, doesn't it? I just mean that I can't imagine having a conversation like the one we've just had with Juliet or most of the Action Women I've worked with.'

'But don't we always look for people who are like us? Share the same interests, even look like each other?'

He shrugs. 'I was very happy with Eleanor and she couldn't have been more different from me. In fact, I—'

'Go on?'

'This sounds weirder still. But, well . . . You don't *look* anything like each other, but there's something about you. Your gentleness, maybe, the way you're calm and seem to be very ordered with the world. Well, it reminds me of Eleanor. Does that give you the creeps?'

I think about it for a moment. 'It depends.'

'On what?'

'On whether every woman reminds you of her. In which case, you probably haven't quite moved on.'

He thinks it over. 'How many women do you think I've been out with, since . . . well, since Eleanor?'

'I don't know.' He is, I now have to admit, a good-looking man. And women school teachers rarely have access to a hunk like Robin, so I'd guess he could pull every trip. 'A dozen.'

He drains the cocktail. 'You're the third.'

'In four years?'

'I guess I haven't felt ready.'

I can't help but feel excited at the tense he's using. Once a school teacher . . . 'Haven't?'

'No.' He doesn't smile this time, just looks into my eyes for so long that everything around us seems to stop. 'Perhaps I do now, though.'

The room spins, the way it does when you're drunk and you

close your eyes. Except mine are wide open. I feel excited and then panicky in the space of a second. 'Right.'

'I don't mean to come on strong,' he says, scoring another point for sensitivity. 'It's just that I don't want you to think I'm playing you along, either. You're lovely but you're also worth waiting for.'

I feel myself blushing again. 'Don't be daft.'

'Your husband's crazy. He'll work out what he's missing but it'll be too late.'

He already has. Then I remember what he was prepared to do – abandon his baby before it's even born – and I wonder about my own judgement. Is this man really any different? It's easy to play sensitive for an evening, but what about a lifetime? I bite my lip.

'Tess?'

'Sorry. I was just thinking.'

'Dangerous occupation. What about another drink to stop that?'

I'm scared. Another drink. Then another. Before I know it I could be falling in love. Tip Top is trying so hard to intervene but I shake her off to murmur, 'OK. Same again, please.'

Somehow it's last orders. Then chucking-out time.

'Shall I walk you home?' Robin says. When I hesitate, he adds, 'My car's there, after all.'

'Yes. Fine.'

Harborne is hot tonight, smelling of sweet peas and traffic fumes. We walk at a distance from each other. He seems to respect that but I find myself slowing down the closer we get to my place. I'm scared of what comes next.

'Thank you for getting me back safely,' I say, standing at my door like a sentry, determined he won't come in.

'My pleasure,' he says, but he sounds hesitant. 'Tess . . . if you're not ready for seeing someone, I do understand.'

Will I ever be ready? 'I think you're a great guy, Robin—'

'There feels like there's going to be a but somewhere in that sentence.'

His smile confuses me again. Confusion is the wrong word,

actually. There's a gulf opening up in front of me and I daren't look down. Standing still is far the safest option. 'I don't know. I don't know anything much any more.'

'I don't know either, but . . .'

In the gloom of my dim security light, his cheekbones are steeper than all the rockfaces he must have climbed. Even as he moves towards me, I am entranced by these sharp edges. Too much in my life is soft, safe.

His lips touch mine, then pull back so quickly I am not convinced they ever landed, except for the volcanic eruption of my nerve endings where he made contact. Oh, and the earth-quake from those nerve endings through my body, via the place where hiccups begin to the place where orgasms end. That's how I know he's kissed me: I could measure my body's reaction on the Richter scale.

The gulf opens up again, like a crevasse between two pieces of land. Road Runner's got nothing on me. It's too wide to bridge and my courage is slipping away from me. The moment when I thought everything could be OK has gone. How long did it last? An evening? Maybe I should count my blessings. Back in May, when I was as low as I could go, an evening of optimism would have seemed impossible. But when reality hits now, it's almost harder. It's like life is offering me a tiny glimpse of what it could be, should be, just to taunt me. And then it reminds me that I had my chance and from now on I have to be a spectator, to protect myself from anything that might cause damage.

Like kisses.

We stand a hand's width apart. Eventually he says, 'I don't suppose that makes things any clearer, does it?'

I shake my head. Speech is beyond me.

'I'll go, Tess. I want you to know that I will come right back if you want me here. But I won't pester you.'

He turns, and rather than watch him walk away, I turn too, back into my house. Natalie must have gone to bed, but she's left a light on in the living room, silhouetting the flowers. The carnations are drooping already. Supermarket flowers age so badly.

Lesson Eight

Do It Yourself

'Let's start as we mean to go on,' William said, as soon as his disciples were gathered before him. He wished he'd taken a photograph of them eight weeks ago, so they could see how much better they looked. Thanks to him.

POP!

The first bottle of champagne exploded with just the right level of enthusiasm. Well, it wasn't actually champagne. William couldn't quite run to that. But three courses ago, a flash student had brought in some fizz for the last session to supplement the usual tea and custard creams and it had been such a life-affirming moment, raising plastic cups to a better future, that William had bought a case of Spanish cava from a wine warehouse. He rationed them at two per course, and found that the bonhomie it generated tended to be reflected in donations. Not that running the course was ever going to make him rich.

He dribbled a couple of inches of wine into each cup, then passed them round. 'So first, let's toast you all. For staying the course' – he shot a look at Aaron, who smiled ruefully – 'by and large, and for taking that important step towards a better life. Cheers.'

They tapped together the sides of the plastic cups. It lacked the satisfying ring of glass on glass, but William had to keep half an eye on health and safety, what with the mum and toddler group using the hall tomorrow morning.

He most wanted to clink plastic cups with Carol-Ann but the instinct to ignore her was stronger. All week he'd been thinking about her, imagining situations in which a braver, less vulnerable version of himself presented her with flowers, or a note, or simply asked her if she'd like to go out for a drink, now that the course was over.

But the thought of doing that in reality made him cringe or want to hide behind a cushion in embarrassment. He could also hide behind the ethical complication of a facilitator getting involved with one of his students, but William knew that it was an excuse. He was chicken. For all of his urging the students to boldly go back out there and pursue happiness with the determination of Neil Armstrong, he was too set in his bachelor ways to do it himself.

'Right. Just because we're in celebratory mood does not mean you won't be expected to do some work.' He forced himself to look at the other students. Rani had the same patient expression as the first time she'd attended, but she seemed less isolated somehow, wedged between Aaron and Tim, who probably found her reassuring, motherly. Tim was making a little bit more effort: he looked less like a man who was sleeping rough, and he made eye contact with people. He wouldn't stay alone for long. That vulnerability, along with the heroic aura his single-dad status would give him, would appeal to a kindly woman looking for a man who would stay loyal and gentle and in her debt. It was a shame that single-motherhood did not have the same appeal for men, because women like Natalie would find it a hundred times harder to build a new relationship. It was a fact of life but it still disappointed William. Though Natalie would stand a better chance than most, with her iron will and steely post-baby muscles.

'Please feel free to tell us to mind our own business, Natalie, but I am sure we would all like to know how it worked out after the incident last week.'

'Oh, don't worry. In fact, I wanted to thank you all. I know a problem shared is meant to be a problem halved, but I think it's a bit different in the case of violent husbands. So thanks. I can't believe how supportive everyone's been. Tony's been charged with threatening behaviour and possessing an offensive weapon and, as a bonus, my solicitor thinks it's likely I'll be able to get back into the house. So Tess will get her own space back again.'

Tess shook her head. 'There's no hurry. I've quite enjoyed having you and Guerr— erm, Zach around.'

William thought Tess looked the least improved of all of them, which surprised him. She was, after all, bright, slim, moderately pretty, professional, self-supporting, childless, non-smoking: all the qualities that would make her score highly with men of a certain age looking for a date. OK, so her age might weigh against her with some particularly choosy guys, but so long as she moved fast, she probably had the best chance of all the women on this course to start over. Yet she still looked restless, resentful.

You can lead a horse to water . . .

'Right. Glad we could all help. So let me explain what we're going to do today. It's important that the last session should be fun, empowering, so we're going to make a poster advertising the movie of our lives. Not our past, but our future. So I've got lots of magazines and pens and a big sheet of paper for each of you. Use any images you want, but they've all got to be positive, things you aspire to. And the most important thing is to think of a fantastic title and an exciting strapline; the line on a movie poster that tells you why you should go and see your life story and not the latest Arnold Schwarzenegger blockbuster. This should be the motto you can remember after you leave here. Any questions?'

They gave him the usual blank looks that accompanied his more eccentric exercises, but he knew they'd enjoy it once they began. And he liked to send them away with a souvenir of the course. Some would throw their posters away in the litter bins outside St Gabriel's, but most would hang onto them and rediscover the poster in a few years' time, prompting a wistful moment as they recalled how much their lives hurt then and how much better they were now. Or so William hoped. Everyone deserved happiness.

Except perhaps Malcolm, whose gnarled hand was now raised. 'Yes?' William knew his voice betrayed his irritation, but he was beyond caring. Some people would never change.

'I'm really not sure there's much purpose in making a poster. We're not in kindergarten now, are we?'

William counted to five, then said: 'I know sometimes the purpose of the exercises isn't totally clear, but I'd have hoped that by now I might be able to ask you all to trust me, to trust my experience to provide tasks and tools that will help you. It would be much easier for me to just give you back your old questionnaires to look at while I make myself a cup of tea. But I'm not doing it for my own enjoyment.' Perhaps he'd gone too far, but he was fed up with being undermined.

Malcolm stood up. 'So what exactly are you doing this for? Do you get a kick out of other people's misery?'

William had lost count of the hours he'd spent asking himself exactly that question. He hadn't really come up with an answer he was satisfied with, though distraction from his own unhappiness had probably been as important in the early days as a vague desire to change people's lives. Then there was curiosity. And he knew deep down that the power fed his ego. He wasn't about to admit that to Malcolm. But before he could say anything, Carol-Ann was on her feet.

'Malcolm, what is your bloody problem? If you hate this course so much, why have you bothered to come and whinge every week?' And before he could answer her, she did it for him. 'It's because you're a friendless, grumpy old git. We can all tell why your wife left you, and the biggest surprise is that she put up with you for so long. If you'd listened to some of the stuff William's said over the last two months, you might have stood a chance of getting her back. As it is, you'd better bloody get used to being on your own.'

William was torn between applauding, which would have been unprofessional, and telling Carol-Ann off, which would have been hard to do convincingly, as he agreed with every word she'd said. Malcolm simply picked up his coat and walked towards the door. 'Thank you for confirming everything I thought about women. I would rather stay alone than have to deal with the self-obsessed, militant feminists who seem to have replaced the girls I grew up with. And the sluts.' He raised his hand towards Jo. 'I saw you in the paper. It's no wonder our society is rotten to the core.'

No one stopped him leaving. William's only gripe was that

it'd be one less donation towards the costs of the course, but then again, Malcolm didn't strike him as the generous kind. 'Does anyone else want to make an early exit?' They shook their heads, smiled encouragingly, especially Carol-Ann, which made him feel like the temperature in the hall had risen by ten degrees. 'Right, you've got an hour to do your poster before we open the other bottle of fizz.'

They took five minutes to enter into the spirit of it, but soon they were crouched on the parquet floor laughing and shouting and snatching each other's pens. William was feeling confused. He'd forgotten that love made you feel this way: there was the certainty that the object of your affections was the only one, but it was constantly competing with the fear of jumping without a safety net. You spent every moment in the presence of the loved one looking for signs from them and trying out all possible interpretations of the slightest glance, the shortest comment.

Right now, he was yo-yoing between being convinced that Carol-Ann's defence of his methods was tantamount to a declaration of love, and being convinced that she did it purely out of irritation with Malcolm. He watched her out of the corner of his eye, her presence dominating the whole group, from her red bouffant hair to her generous stomach encased in red Lycra to her pretty stiletto heels with bows at the ankles. She was more than a woman, she was a life force.

'Hey, William. Aren't you going to do a poster?' Her voice challenged him. 'It's about bloody time you showed us what you're made of.'

He hesitated. What could he put on his poster that wouldn't give away too much? But not to take part, after Malcolm's protest, would make it seem like he didn't believe in the exercise.

'OK then. I suppose there's a spare sheet going, now we've lost Malcolm.' He lowered himself to the floor, feeling his knees tighten and the brand new jeans, bought from the trendier part of the men's department at Rackhams, move downwards, revealing some of his back. He turned towards Carol-Ann so that she wouldn't see his moles.

The posters were as varied as the students. Tim's was exuberant and childish, crammed with cut-out pictures of couples walking towards tropical sunsets, smiling toothless babies and mud-coloured families lining up in front of a cosy earth mother, waiting to be washed whiter after a day in the park. 'What's your strapline going to be, Tim?'

'I think ... Home is Where the Heart Is. Yes. Because it will be. I am going to find someone who'll help us be a family again.'

'Fantastic. That's great, Tim, it really is.' William looked over at Aaron's. He'd found various dark skies from magazine adverts and had glued them next to each other, transforming the page from virgin white to brooding black and navy. He was about to add his strapline with Tipp-Ex. 'And what's yours?'

'Expect the Unexpected.' Aaron raised one eyebrow. He'd be picking women up again in no time, now he'd got his confidence back.

Rani's poster was a riot of flowers with glittery additions to represent pollen-covered stamens, and crepe paper foliage. It was surprisingly good; she'd created a vibrant jungle of colour in just half an hour, with a few old pens, a kids' craft compendium and some glue.

'We've discovered hidden talents here, folks. Rani, that's terrific. Where did you learn to do that?'

'At school. I haven't really done anything artistic since I married.' She looked embarrassed at the attention. 'It's silliness, really. I enjoy it, but what is the point?'

Carol-Ann frowned. 'Oh, spare us the false modesty. You're good at it, and you've got to promise us that you're going to do something with it – I dunno, classes or buying some paints. I wish I had a talent like that.'

Jo said: 'You're a brilliant cook, aren't you? That's a talent.'

'It's not very lasting, though, is it? I make some food, people eat it, then it's washing-up time. Not a great bloody contribution to the world, especially one where we prefer takeaways or microwave TV dinners.'

William knew what Carol-Ann's real gift was, but he couldn't tell her. It was to pull people together, to liven them up and make them see the funny side. He said: 'So, Rani, what are you going to write on yours?'

'I am going to write it in glitter, once Tim has finished with the glue! One word: Grow.'

'Ah, that's so nice,' Tess said, smiling. Her paper was still blank, a pile of collage images next to her. They were perfectly cut out, no missing noses or sharp edges. 'I wish I could think of something.'

William felt on surer ground here, as the attention switched from Carol-Ann. 'Well, a good way to think of it is to imagine what you'd like your life to be like in a couple of years. Still living in Birmingham, or on a desert island? Still teaching? Or taking a year out to travel to the places you've always wanted to see? With a baby, perhaps?'

But Tess stared back as blankly as her paper. 'I don't know. I had dreams and they didn't work out. I don't know how easy it is to invent a whole new set of fantasies.'

There were always one or two failures. William liked to think that they'd make their breakthroughs after leaving the sessions, that the process he began would continue, like fermentation, until one day Tess or the others who'd resisted his optimism would wake up and smell the coffee, to use that terrible American phrase.

'You know, Tess, you don't have to set out big objectives for yourself. A nice holiday or a new job or a new car ... they're all achievable dreams that can help you feel you're moving on.'

She didn't look at all convinced. 'What scares me is that I don't know how I will ever be able to trust anyone again. Or trust my own feelings.'

It was a dilemma, really, answering this kind of question. Should William pretend that trust would return automatically, given time? Or should he be honest, tell her it might not reappear of its own accord, but that it was possible to live a life without trust, albeit not one that felt as full as the one that had been left behind? He'd made his own choice – to live a limited life – but that made him feel even more strongly that he should try to save people from making the same mistake. Wasn't it a case of physician, heal thyself?

In that moment, William made a pact with himself. He would tell her the truth but he would also follow his own example by telling Carol-Ann how he felt.

Once he'd made the decision, it was easier.

'Tess. Trust is something that, until you lose it, you think is a natural part of being human. When it goes, you wonder how the hell you ever did it. Like suddenly developing a fear of something: flying or spiders or water, or in this case, loving someone. You look at the past, that fearlessness, and you can't believe you were like that. But if you want to regain the good things in life, you have to retrain yourself to love. It won't happen overnight; you just have to keep trying, being gentle on yourself when it scares you, but forcing yourself to keep doing it, until it becomes a habit.' They were all listening closely. 'Sorry, I don't mean to lecture, it's just something that is very important to me.'

It was Carol-Ann who spoke first. 'William, you shouldn't be apologising. I didn't think anyone could bloody well teach me anything when I first came here, no way. I knew it all. But I think we've all taken something away and it's not down to the course, it's down to you. So don't you dare go all modest on us.'

Her little speech ended. For a moment there was silence but then someone – maybe it was Aaron, maybe Tim – began to clap. Then everyone was applauding and Carol-Ann began singing 'For He's a Jolly Good Fellow' and despite his protests they sang it twice before applauding again. When eventually they stopped, it was because they wanted a response from him.

'Right . . . well, thank you. I have never had a reaction like that before. In fact, I have never had a course like this one before. I definitely learn something from every group, but somehow you have done more than any previous course. So I should be thanking you back.' He hesitated. 'Of course, that doesn't mean you get out of finishing your posters. Ten more minutes, then we'll crack open the other bottle and I'll give you my top tips on how you can keep the spirit of survival alive once you've left St Gabriel's tonight.'

Chapter Thirty-two

Tonight's session has to be the weirdest ever, and it's getting stranger by the minute. Carol-Ann and Rani have just frog-marched William into the pub and everyone else seems to have got a babysitter organised, so we're obviously all up for a bit of a final-night bender. They look so bloody happy that I feel rather embarrassed by my own gloominess. Like a would-be prime minister at a student party, refusing to inhale.

At least I can drink, because Natalie is driving. She's hoping to be gone from my place within a fortnight. And then I'll be alone again. I will miss her and Guerrilla, just as I'll miss the girls here. But I'm realistic; I know what it's like. We'll promise to keep in touch, but this is a time and a place in our lives that we won't want to be reminded of.

'God, you look like a wet weekend in Walsall,' Carol-Ann says, punching me on the arm. 'Make an effort, Tess. We're meant to be celebrating.'

'Yeah, I know. Sorry. I'm in one of those moods; shouldn't really be out at all. Not really in a socialising state of mind.'

She tuts. 'Don't be so self-indulgent – you'll spoil it for the rest of us. So your date didn't go that well, then?'

I hadn't even mentioned my date. Bloody Jo must have told her. 'He was nice enough, but not really my type.'

'Huh! Your type? You married your type, didn't you? Look where that got you! Like William's been saying, you need to speculate to accumulate. Try new things. And he can't be as bad as hairy old Aaron.'

He's over at the bar, trying to impress some random girl half his age. Good on him, really. It's not his fault he made me feel

suburban. 'Robin was nice enough, but there was no fire there.'
As I say the words, I know they're a lie. If anything I was
melting in the heat his kiss generated.

'All the better to practise on, then.'

'Oh, and he's a widower. I've already got plenty of baggage of
my own. I don't have room for someone else's.'

She sighs. 'You are hopeless. JO!'

Jo joins us with our drinks. 'What's happening? How was
hunky SAS man?'

'Oh, not you as well. Look, what I do or don't do in my
personal life is my business, isn't it?'

Carol-Ann says: 'I've told her, she's hopeless. You're not
getting away with it that easily. I want to hear every detail. It's
the least you can do for your soul sisters who haven't had a sniff
of a date in years.'

I fill them in, stopping short of the kiss and its Weapon of
Mass Distraction effect on my central nervous system.

'Aw, he sounds a sweetheart,' Jo says. 'Didn't he try to kiss
you? After all that build-up?'

'No,' I say, trying not to blush.

'You must have said something to put him off,' Carol-Ann
says. 'Or maybe you had the same bloody moping expression on
your face that you've got now. That'd put anyone off.'

'What are you girls gossiping about?' William edges his way
nervously into the circle. He seems far less confident away from
the safety of St Gabriel's. I'd love to know what secrets lurk
behind the mystery of his personal life, but I'd never dare ask.
It'd feel like overstepping the mark.

'You!' Carol-Ann has no such qualms. 'We were wondering
what our very own man of mystery gets up to when he's not
being Mother Theresa to the broken-hearted of Birmingham.'

'Ah . . .' His face drains of colour and he looks around for an
escape route. 'Well, there's not much to tell.'

'Come on, William,' Carol-Ann teases, putting her arm round
his waist. 'You know everything about us. It's only fair that we
should know a bit about you, especially now the course is over
and we're all equals. Or we could guess. Mine would be that . . .
well, there must be a divorce somewhere in the background,

otherwise you'd have chosen a more obvious way to help people, like collecting milk bottle tops for blind children or knitting blankets for Africa.'

Jo butts in: 'And if you're divorced, then maybe you're a man about town on the quiet. A male escort, paid to keep ladies of a certain age company with your sparkling repartee.'

Poor William looks desperate to get away. I try to rescue him. 'Leave him alone. God, these two are a nightmare, aren't they? They're just as bad nosing about my life. The trick is to ignore them.'

He gives me a thin, grateful smile, unsure whether he's been rescued or whether the predators are simply preparing to take another bite. 'So, have you found the course useful?' His voice is hesitant, as though he dreads a negative answer.

'Yes. I have. I guess I had hoped for a magic wand, but what you've done is show me that I have to do the work myself. And that it won't be easy all the time . . . but I can do it.' I hold up the carrier bag that contains my movie poster, with the strapline 'If at first you don't succeed . . .' 'And I've got a lovely picture for my new home, wherever that might be.'

He nods, as though he's thinking about something. 'Look, ladies. I suppose it's fair enough that you should know my credentials. I do have a divorce in my history. Long time ago now. Not as messy as some I've heard about since I began doing the courses, but it hurt at the time.'

We wait. It feels strange, the way the tables are turning like this. 'My wife left me for someone else. It felt sudden, brutal. But when I had the chance to think about it, I realised it wasn't sudden at all. I hadn't seen the signs.

'I was ashamed. Humiliated. It was so bad that I moved house, moved jobs. Cut off all contact with the people I knew.'

I feel so sad for him. 'William, that's awful.'

'It was. It's all a very long time ago, mind you. Moving didn't help, not really. All it meant was that I hated women for . . . years. I did bad things, in revenge, which achieved nothing. Played with their feelings. It didn't make me happier, and it didn't hurt my ex-wife, of course. Pointless in the extreme, I admit that now. If I'd had someone to talk to, I might have realised it that bit sooner. So when I read about this American group coming over here to start divorce survival courses, I knew it was a sign. Fate, if you like.' He stops, shrugs.

'And your life now?' Carol-Ann asks. 'Are you a good advert for the course?'

'Um ... well, I don't hurt people for no reason any more.' William seems embarrassed. 'As for finding the woman to spend the rest of my life with, well, I guess I'm not the best example. I am still looking, though.' He stares at his feet.

Jo says: 'God, you found that hard going, didn't you? I think you deserve a drink.'

'I think we all do,' Carol-Ann says, kissing William on the cheek. 'We deserve a medal for getting this far. But a pint of bitter will have to do for now.'

Half a dozen rounds later, even I have to admit that the world looks a little rosier. So rosy in fact that I am wondering whether I'm wrong about Robin. With my natural reserve temporarily disabled by alcohol, I find myself confiding in Natalie.

'You know Robin?'

'Not personally, but I hear he's the hottest ex-SAS man in a fifty-mile radius. Something everyone but you seems to have grasped.'

'Maybe I am wrong. He was nice, you know. *Really* nice.' I give her a meaningful wink.

'Oh. So there's something you haven't been telling me then?'

'Well, the thing is ... he kissed me.'

'And how was it?'

Just thinking about it makes me feel slightly light-headed. 'Nice.'

'Nice?' I think she's laughing at me, but then again, she is sober and I am not, so I probably am mildly amusing.

'Really nice, then. Nice enough to scare me.'

'So what are you going to do about it?'

Now she's got me. 'What can I do? I wasn't very encouraging. I don't think he needs someone like me.'

Natalie pulls a face. 'Don't be stupid. Come over here.' She drags me over towards the others. I haven't actually moved for at least half an hour and the wobbling in my legs suggests that I've had more to drink than is good for me.

'Tess has a confession to make!' Jo and Carol-Ann wait while I squirm.

'Um. Yes, you know how I said that Robin didn't kiss me? Well, I lied. He did. And it was nice. Well, more than nice.' I know I am pissed because my mouth is moving faster than my brain, and by the time I try to apply the brake, it's too late. 'It was *lovely*.'

'I hope for your sake that you lied about not having organised another date as well, then,' Carol-Ann says.

'Um . . . no. No, I don't have any plans to see him again.' The incongruity of my two statements hits me. 'That doesn't really make much sense, I suppose.'

'Right!' says Carol-Ann, and the determination in her tone worries me suddenly. 'Natalie, you've got your car, haven't you?'

'Ye-es?'

'We're off to Gloucestershire. To play Cupid!'

Natalie sighs. 'You do know it's quarter to eleven?'

'Yes, I know what bloody time it is. Perfect. There'll be no traffic on the roads. Come on, girls. Hasn't this course been all about seizing the moment, making a difference? This is our chance to put our money where our mouths are!'

I open my mouth to protest, but Jo gets in there first. 'Let's do it. It'll be a laugh.' God, she must be pissed as well.

Natalie still seems uncertain but it'd take supreme willpower to resist Carol-Ann in full flow and I think she knows when she's beaten. And secretly, I think she enjoys a bit of drama. 'OK, OK. I'll drive just to keep you all out of trouble as I seem to be the only person who is thinking straight.'

I hover in the background as Carol-Ann tells Rani, Tim, William and Aaron what we're about to do. William looks the most perturbed – I suppose he never thought he was encouraging a bunch of semi-hysterical females to go stalking their prey. Jo tells them she'll email them the news on this round-robin system we've all signed up to. I know it won't happen and I actually have to fight back tears as we leave them huddled together in the pub. It feels like the end of an era. But then after seven G and Ts you've either got to laugh or cry.

It only hits me what I'm letting myself in for when Natalie accelerates along the slip road onto the M5. The others are in the back, singing along to some kind of chick flick soundtrack, about love and kisses and hearts and all that nonsense.

'I feel sick.'

Natalie looks at me. 'Shit, really? You're worse than Zach. Do I need to pull over?'

'I think I'll be OK.' I don't think it's the booze that's making me queasy. It's the madness of what we're doing. 'This doesn't seem the best idea in the world. Robin'll be in bed.'

'All the better for you to join him,' Carol-Ann sniggers.

'I've got school in the morning.'

'Throw a sickie!' she shouts back.

'I couldn't do that.'

'Yes, you can,' says Jo. 'Sometimes you have to forget about being Tip Top Tess and think about being Tess the Tigress.'

I giggle, and instead of three lanes in the motorway I seem to see six. The next thing I know, Natalie is asking me if I think this is the right junction. It's past midnight and the navigators in the back have found the village on the map, but somehow Natalie still thinks I might have a better idea than they do.

'It might be,' I say, feebly. It's dawning on me that however much this seems like a group effort, it will be me who has to knock on the door of River Cross and me who has to explain what the hell possessed me to call on him in the wee small hours. Something I'd find hard enough sober . . .

My clutching-at-straws hope – that I can pretend I have no idea how to find the centre when we reach the village – fades away when we pass half a dozen handwritten signs to the Activity Centre.

'I don't know what I'm going to say.'

'It's a bit late for that,' Carol-Ann tells me, as we turn onto the narrow approach road. Natalie has turned off her headlights and a couple of rabbits jump out of the path of the car, their eyes momentarily reflecting half-moons before they disappear into the bushes. This feels like a horribly bad idea. 'You just need to tell him you like him and you'd like to kiss him again.'

This is not the way I run my life. I like odds-on certainties, carefully calculated probabilities, not the kind of mess that this situation has to end in. 'You'd better stop here, save waking up Wirewool.'

'Wirewool?' Natalie looks at me like I am barmy.

'The dog.'

She stops near the last turning circle before the end of the driveway. They all climb out of the car; Natalie fiddles with my hair and then pats me on the shoulder. 'We'll wait for half an hour. Come back and let us know what you're doing. But if you want to stay over, we won't tell on you . . .'

'Lots of bloody luck, girl!' Carol-Ann says, kissing me. 'Knock him dead.'

'Just think, Tess the Tigress is unbeatable,' Jo whispers in my ear as she gives me a hug. I walk towards the house, and when I look back, they're waving and grinning and pointing the way.

There's only a dim light in the hall as I approach the front porch. I shiver slightly, even though it's not cold at all.

The doorbell echoes around the countryside. I wait, holding my breath.

Season's Greetings

My arms ache as I drag four paper carrier bags from Harvey Nichols back towards the flat. That's what husbands are for, isn't it? Heavy work like carrying shopping or unblocking drains.

Then again, Barney never carried the bags of stuff for the annual Christmas party. That was down to me.

The underfloor heating in my flat is such an invitation to walk around barefoot that I dump the shopping – was that crack a bottle of Chipotle marinade breaking? – the moment I walk in the door and peel off the layers of footwear. I take off thick boots, thick socks, then tights before my mottled feet make contact with the boards. They're as warm as Caribbean sand and my toes curl in pleasure.

I empty the bags on the glass-topped dining table. I've got a couple of hours before people are due to arrive, and if I'm not ready, this time I'll only have myself to blame.

I'll miss the flat. It's been my declaration of independence. Basically one massive room divided by multicoloured partitions into kitchen, living room, bedroom, study. Oh, and a wet room. It's that trendy and it couldn't be more different from number 107 Victoria Terrace. But it's suited me pretty well. This kind of small space demands tidiness, or it'd descend into something resembling a store cupboard.

The mulled wine is already prepared in a Tupperware lidded bowl and the vol-au-vent cases are laid out on three baking sheets, waiting to be filled. This is my coming-out party, in a way. My decree absolute came through a month ago: a single piece of court letter-headed paper that finally set Barney free. Not that he looked terribly free a fortnight later when I bumped into him and the Curved One and their frighteningly red offspring. Our trolleys collided in the frozen food aisle of Marks and Spencer. It wouldn't have happened six months ago, because I kept my eyes open at all times to avoid awkward moments. But that habit had slipped, and in any case, I still pictured him and Dawn as a couple, not a family.

'Tess,' Barney had said, quietly. I tried to work out what that one word might be trying to convey: regret, sadness, guilt? The baby let out a howl: whatever it was that tiny Oliver wanted, he was making sure everyone in earshot knew things were not to his liking.

I did take some satisfaction from the exhaustion on both their faces. Only Oliver looked hale and hearty, as pink as glacé cherries. It could have been me steering the pushchair while Barney loaded the trolley with ice-cream and frozen chips and peas and all those convenience foods you need because there's no time to cook in a home full of nappies and washing.

I didn't talk to him; I didn't have anything to say. But I saw him cast a long, lingering look at my basket, with its Parma ham and raspberry-orange smoothie and pre-prepared Mediterranean salad. Irresponsible shopping. The kind we never bought when we were married, because I always insisted on buying in bulk, to cook from scratch. We were bad for each other. I can see that now.

The phone rings. It's my dad. 'Hello, Tess. Just wanted to wish you the best of British for tonight, really.'

'Thank you! So nice to hear from you.' I don't know if we'll ever regain that easy relationship we had before Mum's outburst. I saw them last weekend and it was obvious that we were all Trying Very Hard. In my more Pollyanna moments, I think that at least now I understand my mother better, can see why keeping up the appearance of a happy family meant so much to her.

'No sign of there being a white Christmas, though, Tip Top?'

I look out of the window at the night-time cityscape, multicoloured lights softened and magnified by rain. 'No, I don't think so, Dad. Just good old Brummie precipitation.'

'Ah well,' he says, drawing out the sound as if he wants to talk longer but has nothing to say. 'Ah well, I'm sure it'll be a lovely evening anyway. Better go, Tess. Your mum sends her best, too.'

Mum's still got the hump because I'm not going to be there for Christmas. 'Thank her for me, too. I'll ring you tomorrow, let you know how it's gone.'

I wonder about pulling down the chrome-effect Venetian blind, but it seems a shame to obliterate the view. If you screw your eyes up tight, it could almost be Manhattan. City living has been just what I needed, but only as a break from the routine. I like pretending to be spontaneous, but one of the things I am most looking forward to when I move to Gloucestershire is the larder in my new cottage: it has a dozen shelves of different depths and heights and I can't wait to squirrel away endless combinations of foods, so I can easily rustle up a post-ramble supper or a light lunch from my stores, like a domestic magician. Like Roz and her Marie Antoinette game of playing the country wife, except that I am going to live the rural role to the full. After all the money nightmares I heard about on the survivors' course, I know I'm so lucky that Barney didn't play dirty over the financial settlement – and I'm luckier still to find a place in my price range. I'm counting the days till I move in.

The buzzer sounds. 'It's meee,' Mel shouts, then sticks her tongue out, still excited at my video entryphone. I'm relieved she hasn't tried mooning yet. 'Come on up, you freak!' I say, pressing the access button.

'How's it looking, honey?' she asks, sashaying through the door with six bottles of fizz. We both know that she didn't exactly make herself a front-runner as Best Friend of the Year, but then again, I didn't make it easy for anyone to help me. Which I suppose is the point. I was the only one who could really do that.

'All under control.' The last bits and pieces – blue-corn tortilla chips, spiced dried pineapple, green-tea jelly – are indulgences, gastronomic proof that I have moved on from being Mrs Leonard. But all the traditional Robert Carrier recipes are there too because that's what everyone will expect. 'Shall I get the mulled wine on?'

'Does it feel weird, doing this on your own?' Mel asks,

helping herself to some crudités and destroying my carefully colour-coded arrangement.

'I suppose it felt like I was doing it on my own anyway for the last few years, if I'd stopped to think about it.' Until the last few days, I've done pretty well at looking forward, but there's something about this time of year that invites hindsight into your home along with tinsel and mince pies.

'And at least you don't have to cater for all those fussy lawyer types!'

'True.' Writing my Christmas cards was the strangest task: I ruined half a dozen by automatically starting to write 'Love Tess and Barney' at the bottom. And then there were the people like Sara, who were off my list and out of my life for good. But beyond a little wistfulness, swiftly remedied by a glass of port, what surprised me most was how detached I felt from my life twelve months ago. I replayed it in my head like a movie, with only a passing interest in the fates of the two main characters and not a little contempt for their silliness. 'Most of that lot I'm quite happy never to see again, though I kind of wish Sara was coming. Apart from you and Barney she's been the only person to come to every single one of our do's.'

'I had dinner with her the other day.' Mel studies me warily. 'She's pregnant.'

'Oh.' Every time I think I am immune to life, something gets through my defences to prove I can still be hurt. Jo told me once that the only time you stop hurting is when you die. 'Good luck to her.'

'Good luck to the brat, more like. Poor little bugger will need it, the expectations Sara will have. She'll be playing it language tapes through her belly in the hope it'll emerge trilingual.'

The mulled wine has reached simmering point, so I reach for two glasses and the ladle. I pour out two gloopy spoonfuls into each one, with not a hint of a splash on the floor. Poor Barney. He couldn't even get that right.

The buzzer sounds again and I see Robin's shaven head loom into view on the blurry screen. I invited Charlotte, but she preferred a sleepover with her friends to a night with a load of boring adults. And we'll see enough of each other over

Christmas in Tunisia. She's a sweet kid – she's even stayed in touch with Craig and keeps posting him diets cut from teenage magazines to encourage him to lose weight.

I can't pretend we have the closest relationship, but I don't think she regards me as the Wicked Stepmother either. We exist uneasily, like a cat and a dog from two broken homes, aware of the damage we could do to each other, but choosing not to exercise that power.

'Come on up.'

'Is that the Knight in Shining Armour?' Mel checks her lipstick in her handbag mirror. Robin has proved a bit of a hit with my friends, which has helped me to keep my nerve during the moments of doubt that came, to begin with, roughly three times a day. When he didn't text, or when he texted back too quickly. Before, during and after a date. In the days between dates and especially after our first long weekend together.

Gradually the blind-panic moments diminished to maybe one a day and that was only because I had nothing to think about during the summer holidays. By the start of the Autumn term it was every couple of days – and the last time I can remember feeling scared was probably Halloween.

He must have been climbing the stairs two at a time because he's knocking on the door within seconds. I open it.

'Hello, Tip Top!' However hard I try, I can't escape the nickname, but the way Robin says it, I can forgive him. And the fact that he follows it up with a kiss on the lips makes it harder to be cross. Even five months on, it creates the same electric current from my brain to my groin and back again that the first kiss did. Only now I have more information about what usually follows and that makes the anticipation even more intense.

Robin proved to be a bit of a tease after my midnight flit to River Cross made it impossible for me to pretend to play hard to get.

As I shivered in the dark, I'd decided to count to ten. After ten I was allowed to turn back to the car, tell the girls there was nobody in and go back to my own life.

TEN.

NINE.

As I stood there, I imagined my life taking two different paths, depending on the next few moments. If he didn't answer, there was nothing much to look forward to. Months of signing documents that I didn't want to sign: to sell my lovely house, to get rid of my inconvenient marriage, to make sure my unconstant ex had no chance of inheriting my share of our former life if I died.

EIGHT.

And if Robin did come to the door, I had all that *plus* the uncertainty of working out how someone else felt about me, which was high-risk, given how I felt about myself. I wouldn't go out with me in my current state.

SEVEN.

A rebound relationship was definitely *not* what I needed. It stood so much more chance of bringing me down than building me up and I wasn't sure how much further down I could afford to go.

SIX.

FIVE.

There was no clue from the house. Perhaps it was letting me off the hook.

FOUR.

But did I want to be let off the hook? Was it worse to have nothing in my future than to have something to scare me into doing more than existing?

THREE.

Was that a creak? Oh shit, what was I going to say to him?

TWO.

I guessed not.

ONE.

I was in the clear. So why was I hesitating?

ZERO.

I began to walk away, but heard noises behind me, the rustling and unbolting of a properly fortified country front door. I froze, like a child in a game of grandmother's footsteps.

'Hello, who's there?' Robin's voice sounded more confident than mine would if I was opening the door to a stranger's knock in the middle of the night, but I wondered if this was all a bluff –

that he'd been taught it in the Advanced Bluffing Skills module of SAS training. Breathe deeply, project your voice, above all . . . SHOW NO FEAR.

'Me,' I said. Or squeaked. After all, I hadn't done the bluffing module. I turned around to see Robin silhouetted against the hall light, his familiar jug-eared frame only interrupted by a strange glow around the area where I calculated his groin must be.

A torch.

'Tess?' He sounded less certain this time. 'It's one o'clock in the morning.'

'Quarter to,' I said. I could taste gin at the back of my throat and wondered if he'd be able to smell it if we had a repeat performance of *that kiss*. Though I suppose no one would be surprised that alcohol had played a part in getting me here. 'I wanted to see you.'

'Well, here I am,' he said. 'Was it anything in particular you wanted to see me about?'

As I moved towards the light, I could smell mint and malt; at a guess, it was toothpaste and whisky. *He's like me*, I remember thinking. *Lonely enough to need to drink to forget, but too sensible to forget to brush his teeth before he goes to bed*. I'd been careless enough to neglect my marriage, but had never neglected my dental hygiene. And I'd thought it was Barney who'd got his priorities wrong.

'Not as such. I suppose I realised I was quite rude to you last week, though you'd done nothing to deserve it.'

'I appreciate the sentiment. But sixty miles is a long way to travel to say sorry. You could have sent me a text.'

By now he was standing very close, the torch diffusing a mild light that bound us together in the black yard. He didn't kiss me that night: we talked till four a.m. (the girls had left, barely concealing their satisfaction at a job well done, after I nipped back to the car and told them that Robin and I wanted to talk) and then he drove me all the way to school, both of us knackered, yet more alive than we'd felt in years.

Even when he confessed he'd never been in the SAS it wasn't too much of a disappointment. I haven't told Mel, though. She'd be devastated.

We carried on like this for ten days, talking for hours, and struggling to stay awake through work, until school broke up for the holidays. I packed a suitcase and went to stay with him, knowing we had six weeks to explore each other's psyches. We slept together that night. After all the build-up, it was a gentle kind of sex, though that first time was over fast enough for Robin to feel the need to apologise. I was flattered rather than frustrated. It'd been so long since I'd felt someone desired me for *me*. And it simply meant we could do it all over again. We spent a lot of time over the holidays practising to make perfect. I think we got to perfect after about a fortnight, but we haven't stopped practising yet.

'Hello, gorgeous!' I say, reluctantly extracting myself from the kiss. Passion is all the more awesome when it doesn't just seem like a free gift that comes bundled in with being young.

'Hi, Robin,' says Mel, fluttering her eyelashes. 'You want my number one word of advice for surviving Tess's Christmas celebration?'

'Yes?'

'Steer clear of the vol-au-vents.'

And poor Robin smiles indulgently as Mel and I fall about laughing.

Roz and Gerald arrive a few minutes later, dressed in matching Burberry coats. I think it's their idea of a joke.

'So this is the new pad! Very modern!' It's clearly not Roz's style, but she tries to pretend she likes it.

'More the old pad, now,' I say. She'll like my new house much more, though I know she doesn't much like its location: forty miles down the M5, a ten-minute drive from my new school and a handy twenty minutes away from Robin. Even though it was she who encouraged me to think big, to apply for the headship despite my lack of confidence, she's not doing a particularly convincing job of pretending that she'll be pleased to see me go. But then if she couldn't wait to get me out of the door, I'd be even more insulted.

'More importantly, this is the new man,' I say. 'Robin, this is Roz, the biggest influence on my career ever.'

He kisses her on the cheek. 'Thank you.'

'Why?' She looks at him suspiciously.

'Because if it hadn't been for you and the school, I'd never have met Tess.'

When I first got to know Robin, I didn't trust these cheesy comments. They couldn't be sincere; they seemed as creepy as a compliment from a chat-show host. But after a while I realised that he has no side to him, no nasty edge. He is the genuine article.

Roz smiles uncertainly. She's going to take some convincing, too, but that's fine. I have this feeling he'll be sticking around long enough to do that. Eventually she says, 'And you're the reason we're losing her after all these years. I hope you appreciate her as much as we do.'

Gerald decides to take charge of the mulled wine, which must be the winter equivalent of a barbecue, the primal focus of the warrior male. And like every other warrior male, he splashes. Maybe I was unfair to Barney in thinking he spilled it because he was incompetent. Perhaps he was simply marking his territory.

Jo arrives next, with her mother.

'God, you two look fantastic. Especially you, Louisa.' Jo's mum's hair is growing back, a faint coating of white curls where apparently it was straight and dark before. She has the faded elegance of a Bohemian actress. And Jo has lost that pinched, edgy expression she wore throughout the course.

'We're off on holiday next week,' Jo says. 'A girls' holiday in Tenerife.'

'Five stars, but with alternative therapies and yoga at the spa,' her mum says. Jo pulls a face. I can't imagine that a woman whose idea of a good trip is going undercover in Afghanistan or Zimbabwe will enjoy a week of pampering, but I know why she's doing it. Guilt. A week after Christmas, Jo's heading for Africa, to her new job working for an aid charity. Disaster relief. You can take a girl out of a war zone, but you can't take the war zone out of the girl.

I leave Louisa, Roz and Gerald discussing the relative merits of the Canary Islands while Jo and I crash on the sofa. I won't miss the sofa, actually. It's as hard and unforgiving as it is fashionable.

'How's your mum feeling about your new job?'

'Fantastic, actually. You know what a bleeding heart she is. She's seriously excited about me heading off to save the developing world. I mean, it's one up from her neighbour who donates fifteen quid a month to feed a family in Bangladesh – Mum's effectively donating an entire daughter.'

'And how about you?'

'I'm excited. And scared. It's one thing criticising what the charities do when you're a reporter – it's another thing trying to make a difference.'

'Does your ex know?'

'Hmm. Yes, my friend told him. I think he's just relieved I won't be in the country too much.'

'And you're definitely off men?' Now I've fallen hook, line and sinker for Robin, I want everyone I care about to find true love too. It's hard to believe that just five months ago I was as cynical about the whole idea as she was.

'Yep. For now and for ever. Or at least until I've saved the world.'

The buzzer goes again and again, as a succession of people arrive: my sister and the ever-monosyllabic Patrick; Rani and her rather gorgeous nineteen-year-old son, Rav; half a dozen people from work, including Juliet; my old neighbours from Harborne; and finally, Aaron and Malcolm. They make an unlikely pairing, though they are united by a bloke-ish grumpiness with the world. And, as it turns out, they both share a passion for enforcing petty rules ...

I found out how far Aaron had travelled from the rock 'n' roll lifestyle a month or two after the course ended. I'd nipped into the city centre on Saturday to buy a birthday present for Mel, and for once in my life I overstayed my parking meter by a good ten minutes. As I skipped back to the car, congratulating myself on the fact that the old Tip Top Tess would never have taken such a gamble, I saw a dark figure hovering by my car.

A traffic warden.

I picked up pace and my irritation was growing with every

step. Not fair, not fair, not fair. By the time I reached the meter I was out of breath with exertion and righteous indignation.

'Please don't, I've never done anything like this bef—' I stopped, confused. Above the anonymous uniform, I saw a familiar face. Grey eyes, long hair pulled back more smartly than usual, and a mouth that was doing anything but smiling. 'Aaron!'

He blushed. 'Oh . . . er, hello, Tess.' God's gift to women was lost for words. If I hadn't been spitting blood, I might have savoured the moment a little more.

'Is this . . . I mean, have you always been . . . a traffic warden?' My brain was struggling to make sense of it, to recast the Lothario of the group as one of the most loathed public servants around. A fuzzy image of a uniform and peaked cap falling out of the wardrobe in his crummy little bedsit came back to me. To think that I'd assumed it was an outfit for some sort of sex game.

'Parking attendant,' he sniffed. 'I haven't always, but if you're a roadie who plays the guitar – badly – there's not a lot else you're qualified for.' He looked at me, and then the car. 'Oh, shit. This is yours, isn't it?'

'Yes.' I stared at him. 'And that had better not be a ticket.'

'Well, you see, once I've started to put one through the system,' he waved his portable computer in the vague direction of the car, 'I can't cancel it.'

'What about if I ran you over? Would that change things?' I concentrated on looking menacing.

He wouldn't meet my eye. 'Um . . . I can't . . . look, how about if *I* pay the fine? In return for . . . well, you not telling anyone?'

'You want to buy my silence?' Now I was starting to enjoy myself. 'I have a totally unblemished driving record, you know.'

'I can't . . .' He was panicking. 'The only way I can cancel it is if I put through an error. That I've made an error. And we're monitored on those and I haven't been doing too well lately; it's a bugger to keep your concentration, you know. But if there's no option . . .'

I held up my hand. Teasing was one thing. Out and out

sadism was another. 'No, I won't do that to you, Aaron. It's a fair cop, I suppose.'

The look of relief – and that moment of power – was almost worth the forty-pound parking fine. And as he skulks behind Malcolm now, carrying two bottles of unnecessarily expensive wine, I make a mental note to rub it in later on. Though the fact that he's reduced to hanging out with the world's most boring local government planner is probably punishment enough.

Natalie's managed to get a babysitter, and when she arrives, the men turn to admire her gym-toned body in her YSL designer dress. Without the stress of worrying about Tony – currently on probation and under threat of instant incarceration if he so much as drives past her front door, unless he's on one of his finely choreographed contact visits to Guerrilla – she is unstoppable. I think she's seeing someone but it doesn't stop her flirting to bust with Rav, who falls in love the instant she flutters her implausibly curly eyelashes.

Even Tim turns up, frazzled as ever, but hopeful that one of his internet dates will work out. His mum is helping him to vet every candidate for the job of the second Mrs Tim Ross.

I watch them from the sofa, the alcohol just starting to soften the scene and the people in it. I haven't been drinking nearly so much lately, thank God, so I feel distinctly emotional. Like a proud parent, watching them laugh and joke and flirt together. My friends.

Someone's missing.

The buzzer again. My heart leaps. Could it be . . . ?

The first thing I see in the intercom screen is a massive cleavage. 'Carol-Ann! That's one hell of a Wonderbra!'

I haven't seen her for months, because . . . well, I don't know why, exactly. I have called her, but she's always out. Now I'm back on track, I thought maybe she'd headed off to inject a bit of pizzazz into someone else's life, like a latter-day fairy god-mother.

I open the door and the reality of the cleavage hits me. 'Bloody hell, Carol-Ann. You've only gone and had a boob job.'

She beams. 'Well, that's not the only bloody surprise.' She

walks through the door and beckons behind her. 'Come on, lover-boy.'

'William!'

He blushes as he steps into my flat. 'Hello, Tess. I hope you don't mind me coming too.'

Behind him, Georgie and Paul appear, hand me a bottle of Piat D'Or and shuffle into the room, hand in hand.

'Aw, don't be embarrassed, pet,' Carol-Ann calls after them as she throws her arm around William's waist, sending her newly plumped bosoms thrusting further out and leaving me in no doubt about the nature of her relationship with our former tutor. 'I think my daughter's ashamed of me again. Isn't he adorable? But that bit too shy for his own good, let's face it. Get us a beer, Bill, while me and Tess have a catch up.'

He does as he's told. Most people do, after all, when confronted by Carol-Ann in full flow.

'So which do you want me to tell you about first? The tits or the boyfriend?' Her smile is so broad that I wonder whether she's had her lips surgically enhanced at the same time as the boobs.

'Well, the bustline speaks for itself. But the . . .' I can't quite bring myself to call William a boyfriend, 'love-life. That really is left of field.'

'I know. Can't quite believe it myself. He rang me, you know, Tess. Never heard anyone sound so scared. Kept apologising for using the confidential contacts list from the course for personal reasons, but I couldn't work out what he wanted. He went on about all sorts before finally coming clean and asking me out.'

'I never even realised you fancied him.'

'Nor did I,' she says. 'He suggested going to a real-ale pub I love, so it seemed bloody rude to refuse, when he was making the effort. And then when I got there . . . well, I wasn't bowled over. But I have let my heart rule my head all my bloody life, so I thought I'd give my head a chance for once.' She looks over to check he's still occupied rummaging in the fridge for a drink. 'You've got to be practical at my age. He's got a lot going for him. He loves his beer, he's a real livewire, even if he can go on a bit. And he's good with his hands, if you get my drift.'

I do, and it's an image I want to erase instantly. 'Is it love?'

'Put it this way,' she says, speeding up as he crosses the room with two bottles of Czech Budvar. 'We're planning to run the next survivors' course *as a double act.*'

She gives him a huge smacker when he nudges her with her pint and I exchange raised eyebrows with Jo. 'Bloody hell,' she mouths back. I feel all warm inside and it isn't just the mulled wine.

I suddenly think of Barney. The ghost of Christmas past. It seems a million years – not twelve months – since he left. I wonder what's happening in *his* house tonight. Wonder if baby Oliver is aware of the lights and the presents and the festive music.

I stop myself. The truth is that however intensely I'd have liked my own Yuletide baby under the tree, having one with Barney would have been a disaster. Maybe we knew that, somehow. Maybe even I knew at heart that ours was a Starter Marriage.

I feel a hand on the small of my back.

'Are you feeling tip-top, Tess?' Robin asks.

'Like a new woman,' I reply.

'Now that could be a problem.' He pulls a face. 'I rather liked the old one.'